DESIRE'S SONG . . .

Shy, she no longer felt the bravado of a modern woman. She no longer felt like the self-assured, educated scientist. She felt only the unique emotions of a woman in love, a woman filled with a yearning for the impassioned touch of her lover. She lowered her eyes and buried her face against his chest. "I believe it is time for this wife to know her husband."

"And it is time for this *husband* to know his wife," Wolf replied, his warm breath falling lightly upon her cheek, igniting her spirit with its touch, inflaming her soul with his words.

She closed her eyes. Nothing in her rational mind could stop the tide of desire rushing to every secret place within her body. She loved this Lakota warrior and she would joyfully give him that love with her words, her touch and her body.

Somewhere in another tipi in the encampment, the throbbing beat of the drum continued, its cadence now harmonizing with the meter of Ryan's heart . . .

A LOVE BEYOND TIME

Judie Aitken

JOVE BOOKS, NEW YORK

TIME PASSAGES is a registered trademark of Penguin Putnam Inc.

A LOVE BEYOND TIME

A Jove Book / published by arrangement with
the author

PRINTING HISTORY
Jove edition / January 2000

The Penguin Putnam Inc. World Wide Web site address is
http://www.penguinputnam.com

ISBN: 0-515-12744-2

A JOVE BOOK®
Jove Books are published by The Berkley Publishing Group,
a division of Penguin Putnam Inc.,
375 Hudson Street, New York, New York 10014.
JOVE and the "J" design
are trademarks belonging to Penguin Putnam Inc.

PRINTED IN THE UNITED STATES OF AMERICA

10 9 8 7 6 5 4 3 2 1

This book is dedicated to the memory of
my beloved parents who never built fences around
my dreams;
to my family, friends, and IRWA sisters who
encouraged and believed;
and to Tekonshila who made it all possible.

Author's Note

Dear Reader:

A Love Beyond Time is a work of fiction and as such, some creative license pertaining to the topography, geography, community, and citizens of the area surrounding the battleground at the Little Big Horn has been taken. Those of you who are very familiar with the site, please pretend along with me. The historical facts, the layout of the original encampment, the sequence of the battle, and the site of the first skirmish are all true.

A Love Beyond Time is a story about love and respect and the continuing struggles of the American Indian people. I hope you enjoy your journey to the other side of time.

Judie Aitken
10535 E. Washington St., PMB105
Indianapolis, IN 46229-2609

Chapter 1

*When the impossible has been eliminated, whatever
remains, no matter how improbable . . . is possible.*
—Sir Arthur Conan Doyle

A QUICK SCAN of the taxiway and paved aprons around the small airport told Ryan Burke one thing. She was alone.

Dr. Edwin Gaffney's letter had mentioned someone would meet her and take her to the project site at the battleground, but no one was waiting at the gate. Perhaps her two-hour delay out of Chicago had caused Gaffney's driver to lose patience and leave. A magnificent magenta and crimson sunset splashed across the mid-May Montana sky but Ryan didn't notice. She had to find the driver.

The squat terminal building seemed to be her best bet. A weathered sign hung over the door. "Welcome to Big Sky Airport." From what she could see through the dirty windows, the terminal was still open. Tucking her briefcase under her left arm, Ryan wrestled her other pieces of luggage through the double doors.

Bleak and sparsely furnished, the room smelled of neglect and rancid coffee. Dirt coated everything in sight. A quick look around gave her even more concern.

Behind the counter, a bleached blonde with one hand propped coyly on her hip flirted with a heavyset man in a grease-stained mechanic's uniform. On the far side of the room, an Indian dressed in jeans, a red shirt, black Garth Brooks-style cowboy hat and freshly polished boots slouched in a chair sound asleep. Gaffney's driver didn't seem to be here either.

Ryan dumped her luggage in a precarious heap on the floor and tried to catch her breath.

"Ya s'pecting someone to meetcha, honey?" the blonde's nasal voice carried across the room. "If ya need a ride, Carl here can give ya a lift." She affectionately rubbed the mechanic's arm. "It'll be quicker'n waiting for the taxi to come out from town."

Ryan approached the counter, ignoring Carl as he ogled her from head to toe with a couple of stops along the way. "Someone from Dr. Gaffney's project at the Little Big Horn Battleground is supposed to be meeting me." She looked at her watch. "But I'm over two hours late."

"You're probably lookin' for him," the blonde answered with a sharp jerk of her thumb toward the sleeping Indian.

Hiking up his low-slung pants, Carl swaggered over and gave the sole of the sleeping Indian's boot a hard kick. "Hey, Sittin' Bull! Your passenger's here."

Slowly rousing, the Indian stretched, offered a prolonged grunt and sleepily looked around. "Yeah? Where?"

"Right here. I'm Dr. Burke." Ryan stepped closer.

His dark eyes narrowed as he made a deliberately slow and silent appraisal of her. He tipped his hat to the back of his head. "Naw," he said, yawning. "No way." Lifting his arms over his head, he stretched again. "I'm lookin' for a man."

The blonde sighed and ran her fingers over Carl's arm. "Me too, honey. Me too."

"If Dr. Edwin Gaffney from the Little Big Horn project sent you to pick up someone—it's me," Ryan said, hoping to settle the matter quickly. "I have his letter in my briefcase and can show it to you if there's a problem."

"Humpf," Carl jeered. "Don't bother. Most of these redskins can't read."

Rising quickly, the Indian left his chair in a smooth, easy motion. The tightened muscle along his jaw relaxed enough to allow a sardonic lift at the corner of his mouth as Carl quickly stepped back. "Come on, Dr. Burke. You're late." Without glancing at Ryan, he headed out the door.

"Hey!" Ryan called after him. "What about my bags?"

"You want 'em?" his words floated back.

"Yes, of course I do."

"Well, I guess you'd better bring 'em."

The old Ford pickup reminded Ryan of the airport lounge—rundown and tired. The dust-coated dashboard rattled loudly and a rusted-out hole in the floorboards offered glimpses of the passing road beneath her feet. The truck smelled of too many miles of dirt roads and spilled oil. A pine tree-shaped air freshener hanging from the rearview mirror helped some—but not enough. The headlights flickered each time the truck jolted over a bump and the bent coat hanger antenna wasn't doing its job too well, either. A mournful Hank Williams song whined on the radio but old Hank was having a hard time singing the blues through the crackle of heavy static. A faded Pendleton blanket lay across the seat to tame the sharp ends of the springs that stuck up through the worn upholstery. After a few painful jabs, Ryan knew the blanket failed in its duty, too.

Twice she tried to start a conversation with her driver, but neither attempt worked. Resigned to silence, she gave him a sidelong glance as the truck bucked out onto the highway. He was much younger than she had first thought, perhaps no more than seventeen or eighteen. He wore the timeless features of his race, which reminded her of the copies of old photographs from the Smithsonian's archives in her briefcase. Like the men in the sepia-toned photos, his hair fell in long braids that nearly reached to his waist. Wrapped and tied white buckskin thongs encircled the end of each braid.

He was neatly dressed, his clothes clean and pressed. His boots, though veterans of hard wear, were polished to a rich shine. The cowboy hat was new and sat squarely on his head with very little Montana dust on its wide brim. A hatband, made with colorful beads and porcupine quills, encircled the crown and a single eagle feather, tucked under the band, lay across the right side of the brim. Ryan suspected he was aware of her scrutiny but he never took his eyes from the road ahead.

Turning away, she yawned. Her day had begun in Washington before dawn. A mix-up with her reservations and then the cancellation of her direct flight had soured her day. Neither the crowded commercial plane to Great Falls nor the small charter to the municipal airport outside of Billings had offered any chance to rest.

Yawning again, Ryan closed her eyes and soon dozed off, drifting away with ease. As sleep enveloped her, dream images began to take shape, becoming clearer and sharper until they completely filled her mind. From out of the billow and swirl of a dream fog, a large gray wolf trotted forward. Carrying its head low and moving with a loose easy gait, it ambled closer until Ryan thought she could reach out and touch its shaggy coat. Looking up into her eyes, the creature captured and held her prisoner in its amber gaze. A moment that seemed an eternity passed before the wolf turned away. The wolf took a hesitant step and after one last quick glance over its shoulder, it shook out its long fur and loped away into the mist until only the sound of its mournful howl stayed to echo and reecho in Ryan's head.

She awoke with a start. Her hand jerked forward, searching for something solid to hold onto while the truck bucked and plunged like a wild mustang. As the smoky fringes of sleep evaporated, the howl of the dream wolf quickly blended and dissolved into the wail of high-pitched voices. A tape player on the seat beside her was playing a cassette of powwow songs.

"Sorry," the boy said with a sheepish grin. "Didn't mean to wake ya. I thought takin' the back road would be quicker but I forgot about the potholes." He turned down the volume on the tape player. "These guys are the Red Thunder Singers." He grinned. "You've gotta play 'em loud to get that good powwow sound."

Ryan nodded and covered a wide yawn with her hand.

"Have I been sleeping long?" She tried to dismiss the odd sense of forewarning left by the yellow-eyed dream wolf, but failed.

He answered with a noncommittal shrug of his shoulders.

"I suppose we'll be there soon."

"N'other ten, fifteen minutes or so," he said, pumping the brakes and jerking the steering wheel to maneuver around another crater-sized hole. "Closer to an hour if I've got to keep driving from one side of the road to the other to keep from fallin' in these mine shafts. The roads are like this every spring after it thaws."

Ryan stifled another yawn, hoping the young Indian hadn't noticed. He had.

"They've got a nice tent ready for you so you can flop out on a cot when we get there."

"I'm hoping I can sink my teeth into a juicy burger before then." The grumble in her stomach concurred. She hadn't eaten since leaving her Washington, D.C. apartment and refused to count the two small packages of stale peanuts and the tiny plastic glass of cola she'd had on the plane as a three-course meal. Peering out the window, she watched hopefully for golden arches. It was dark.

"You'll just have to go back to sleep and dream about that burger, Dr. Burke. Ain't no place 'tween here and camp where you can get somethin' to eat." He stole another hasty look at her. "I suppose we could stop, fire up some wood and cook a roadkill 'coon—if we could find one." With a grin, he extended his hand. "I'm Buddy Crying Wolf."

"I'm glad to meet you, Buddy," Ryan answered, shaking his offered hand.

Buddy gave an apologetic smile. "Sorry I've been so unsociable and haven't talked much. That jerk at the airport really ticked me off." He steered the truck around another chuckhole. "But sometimes there ain't nothin' wrong with not talking, though. Sometimes not talking is a whole lot better than gabbing your jaws off." His smile grew into a grin. "You can learn a whole lot about people that way." The grin fell into a grimace as the old truck dipped and bounced in and out of a crater. "I found out lots about you."

"I've been asleep. What did you find out—that I snore?" Ryan straightened her aching spine, shifted on the seat and felt a different spring stab her backside.

Now that he had opened up, there was no stopping Buddy Crying Wolf. "Well, my grandpa says it's the best way to tell a good woman. He says the best ones are those who don't yackety-yak-yak-yak all the time. Grandpa says if a woman don't talk a lot that means they're hard workin'. He says a quiet woman doesn't gossip and it means they know their place, too."

Warming to Buddy's sudden burst of chatter, Ryan laughed. "It sounds as though your grandpa's a chauvinist."

"Naw," Buddy answered with an easy chuckle. "He's just an old Indian with too much time to sit around and remember the old days. Some folks might think he's two fries short of a Happy Meal, but among our people he's sorta like a . . . holy man. Know what I mean? Although he's Lakota and ain't from around here, the Cheyenne, and even some of the Crow people, come to him for advice—for prayers and ceremonies, too."

"You're not Crow? You don't live on the Crow reservation?" Ryan asked, surprised. The battleground was in the middle of the Crow reservation.

"Naw, I ain't no Crow," he quickly replied with a sharp edge of disdain to his words. "Like I said, the old man's Lakota. So was my dad." He slowed the truck and shifted gears. "After my dad's first wife died, he and Grandpa came here to visit some of her relatives on the Northern Cheyenne reserve. They liked it, so they stayed." He gave a shrug. "My dad ended up marrying another Cheyenne woman, my mom. I guess you could say that'd make my brother Dillon and me old George Armstrong Custer's worst nightmare." Buddy chuckled. "We're half Lakota, half Cheyenne, and a hundred percent FBI—full-blood Indian."

The old Ford groaned as Buddy eased it around a sharp curve in the road. "Our folks died about ten years back. A drunk tourist hit 'em head-on with a motor home. Ain't much left of a little old Indian car after something like that." His voice cracked and he gave the brim of his hat a self-conscious tug. "So, now there's just the old man, Dillon and me. Well, it's mostly the old man and me." He glanced at Ryan, then back at the road. "First Dillon went away to college and now he's always off somewhere workin' for the tribes. He's a big-shot lawyer with the Intertribal Legal Coalition. Maybe ya heard of him? Dillon Wolf?"

"Hmm, don't think so," Ryan replied, with a slight shake of her head. "Sorry."

"No matter." Buddy shrugged. "He fights for Indians' rights against the goddamn, thievin' whites and their jackass government." The moment the words had passed his lips, Buddy rolled his eyes and offered an embarrassed smile. "Sorry, Dr. Burke, those are Dillon's words, not mine. I meant no offense."

"None taken," Ryan responded with a slight smile. Buddy's brother sounded as though he carried quite a grudge. She had dealt with people like Dillon Wolf before and was happy to be riding with Buddy and not his biased brother. She quickly changed the subject. "So, tell me, do you speak Cheyenne or Lakota?"

"Both," Buddy replied. "They taught us Cheyenne in the rez school and Grandpa made sure I knew Lakota, too. There's more Sioux 'round here than some think. Grandpa says ya gotta speak the language of your people to be all you're supposed to be." He gave another indifferent shrug. "I suppose that's so."

Silence punctuated their conversation until Buddy spoke up again. "In the old days my grandpa would've been called a chief. Not a war chief like my brother Dillon, who's always hard up against something. Naw, the old man would've been a peace chief." He downshifted and the gears chattered in protest. "But now Grandpa just sits in his rockin' chair on the porch and talks about how things used to be a long time ago. Nothing much happened around here to excite him until Gaffney showed up." He shot a sidelong glance at Ryan. "Hey, what kinda name is Ryan for a girl, anyway?"

"It's an old family name." Ryan tried to shift away from the insistent prod of the loose spring and wished she had a dollar for every time she had needed to explain her mother and father's choice of Christian name for their only child.

"Mine's an old family name, too," Buddy added proudly.

"You mean there's been a whole long line of Buddys before you?" she teased.

"Naw, Crying Wolf, that's the old family name," he replied with a full-bodied laugh. "Good joke, Dr. Burke."

Ryan wrinkled her nose. "Call me Ryan," she urged. "Call me anything but *Dr.* Burke—it makes me feel so old."

"Anything?" Buddy replied, a dangerous twinkle in his eye.

"Anything," Ryan answered with a grin. "Anything . . . that's highly flattering and totally within reason."

"Okay, Doc, let's see . . . hmm . . . I think from now on you're Good-Woman-Who-Is-Late-But-Is-Big-Smart. How about that?" Buddy laughed and slapped the steering wheel with the flat of his hand, clearly approving of his own joke.

"That's quite a mouthful if you're calling me to dinner." She groaned and crossed her arms around her stomach, hoping to still its empty growling. "And speaking of food, can't we find a burger somewhere?"

Dr. Edwin Gaffney didn't seem to share Buddy's high regard for Good-Woman-Who-Is-Late-But-Is-Big-Smart. His displeasure began with his first glimpse of Ryan and continued for the next ten minutes at full speed and volume.

"I don't like being deceived," he charged. "Apparently you thought it insignificant to inform me of your gender."

Taken off guard by his complaint, Ryan failed to find a quick or fitting rebuttal.

Gaffney held up a sheaf of papers that Ryan recognized as her application.

"I hire only men." Gaffney swept his arm, indicating the

three men who stood nearby. "See, Miss Burke—no women."

"*Dr.* Burke," Ryan firmly interjected, her anger rising a notch or two.

"You, *Dr.* Burke," Gaffney continued, "have wasted my time and my money." He slapped her application onto the camp table, nearly tipping over the glowing kerosene lantern.

Edwin Gaffney wasn't anything like Ryan had expected. The dichotomy between the scientist's professional reputation and the man she had just met was baffling. Never one to make sudden judgments, she knew that in this instance her opinion of Edwin Gaffney would be difficult to change. She didn't like the man.

"I think you should leave," Gaffney continued. "It's the only solution."

"If you'd explain your rationale," Ryan rebutted, "perhaps we could reasonably settle the matter." She had dreamed about being part of an important project like this for too long to give up when her goal was within her grasp.

"What's not to understand?" Deep furrows creased his forehead. "From this application and vitae I thought I'd hired an anthropologist—a male anthropologist, not a . . . a *female*." He spat the word out as though it was a bite of spoiled food.

"My gender should *not* be an issue," Ryan countered, trying to keep her temper under tight rein. "I assumed from your letter that you were familiar with my work and knew exactly who I was, and *what* I was." She drew a deep breath. "Dr. Gaffney, you decided from reviewing my application that I was qualified to work with your team."

"Careful, old boy," one of the men standing behind Gaffney said with a muted voice. "I think she's got you cornered."

Gaffney shot a forbidding glare over his shoulder. "Stay out of it, Stockard! It's not your concern."

"Dr. Gaffney," Ryan offered in as peaceable a tone as she could muster, "in your letter you stated you believed my ability, experience and credentials to be 'impeccable.' "

How dare he dismiss her because of her sex. A light veneer of perspiration dotted her upper lip and she took a couple of calming deep breaths. She had worked too long and too hard to gain her independence from her overbearing parents, earn her doctorate and land a job with the Smithsonian to let Edwin Gaffney dismiss her simply because he was a chauvinist. His actions, aside from being sadly unprofessional, were leaving him wide open for a lawsuit.

"Dr. Gaffney, my work with Dr. Schueller at the Smithsonian on the societies and ceremonies of the Oglala has well prepared me for this job."

"Ah, Barton Schueller, of course, a brilliant fellow. I admire the gentleman a great deal." Gaffney's manner softened at the mention of the Director of the Smithsonian's Department of Native American Studies. "He wrote an excellent letter of reference for you."

"He sends his regards," Ryan said, surprised to see an expression of delight settle upon Gaffney's round face. Had she discovered his weakness? Did he revel in the notice of his peers? She decided to add more fuel to fire his ego. "Dr. Schueller is excited about this project. He's looking forward to hearing more about it as the work progresses."

"He is?"

The man Gaffney had identified as Stockard flashed a friendly thumbs-up signal from behind the project director's back, forcing Ryan to stifle a laugh.

"Your resume states you speak Lakota," Gaffney said, his manner appearing to soften.

"I have a good understanding of the language and adequate conversational skills."

"What about Cheyenne? Do you speak Cheyenne?"

"As my application states," Ryan answered, pointing to the folder on the table, "my knowledge of Cheyenne is limited."

Gaffney looked at Ryan for a long moment while tugging idly on his mustache. He gave a deep sigh, then shrugged. "I suppose now that you're here I could give you a try." He pointed to a tent at the edge of the camp. "That's yours and the privy and camp showers are over there."

He flipped his hand in one direction and then the other so quickly that Ryan realized she'd have to take her chances and find everything for herself.

"Nothing's been set up here with a woman in mind. You'll have to cope as best you can. Coed bathing facilities are not in my budget." He began to turn away but paused and then pivoted back to face Ryan. "By the way, what about snakes?"

"Pardon me?" she replied, surprised by his sudden segue.

"Snakes." Gaffney wiggled his hand through the air. "Snakes. Do you run screaming when you see one?" He seemed to watch closely for her response.

"I don't care for them but I suppose as long as they mind their own business . . ."

"There are rattlers here, Dr. Burke, and rattlesnakes when riled take care of their own business. I suggest you pay close attention to every step you take and never leave your tent open unless you intend to share your bed with one. Is that clear?"

"Yes, of course . . . perfectly."

"Good." Gaffney paused as if trying to think of anything else. "FYI, Dr. Burke—Buddy, the Indian kid who picked you up—he takes care of the camp, keeps it cleaned up, fetches water, runs errands, that sort of thing. If you need anything or want to go anywhere, he's available to drive you. Just make sure you clear it through me first. I don't want him neglecting his chores for forays into town for perfume, bonbons and romance novels.

"Buddy's old aunty, Edith Yellow Horse, is our cook. She lives on the Cheyenne reserve about ten miles or so up the road. Buddy picks up and delivers the meals the old woman fixes for us every day," Gaffney continued. "Buddy speaks Cheyenne and a little Lakota and can help you translate—when it's needed." Gaffney lifted the lantern from the table. "Welcome to the Little Big Horn and good night, Dr. Burke," Gaffney moved off across the compound to his tent, taking the lantern with him. Pushing aside the nylon door flap, he stepped inside. His silhouette danced on the walls as he moved about.

A collective sigh of relief resounded from the three men Gaffney had referred to as his project team.

"Now that's a welcome I suppose you won't forget in a long while! Don't worry, no matter what Gaffney says, we're glad to have you here." The blond-haired man extended his hand, grasping Ryan's in a firm shake. "I'm Dan Stockard. These two scoundrels are Pete Kovacs and John MacMillen."

"Anthropology, eh?" MacMillen remarked with an affable smile. "Welcome aboard. Don't worry about Gaffney, he gets a little tense once in a while and is a hard taskmaster, but for the most part he's a nice guy."

Pete Kovacs nodded. "He's been acting a little strange in the last few months and can be a tyrant at times but, let's face it—the man is brilliant. You'll do okay with him though; you didn't back down one bit."

Ryan took an instant liking to the three. All appeared to be in their late thirties and instinctively she knew their warm smiles were genuine. They had eased the sting of Gaffney's reception but it was only when Buddy Crying Wolf lightly nudged her arm that she really began to relax.

"Hey, Doc, your lantern's been lit, you've got fresh water, clean towels and a couple of blankets in your tent. I don't do bedtime stories, so you're on your own." Leaning closer, he whispered in her ear, "There's a ham 'n' cheese sandwich, a can of pop and a couple of Twinkies in there, too. Ya owe me, Doc. Ya owe me big time."

Restless, too excited about being on site at the Little Big Horn, Ryan lay awake on her cot for a long time. To realize the career she'd wanted, she had turned her back on a life of privilege and what she felt were the shallow amusements of her parents' Virginia high society set. Now everything she had dreamed of was within her reach and she couldn't wait until morning to see the valley. From pouring over old maps in the archives, she knew her tent sat on the same site that had once been the Hunkpapa camp. She plumped her pillow, tucked the blanket up under her chin and shifting frequently, searched for that perfect comfortable niche in the mattress. Finding it, she settled in and sighed. *I'm here. I'm really here.*

She breathed the cool Montana air deep into her lungs and tried to quiet the twinge of apprehension that continued to nag and demand her attention. All she had do was deal with Gaffney. Hadn't women like Margaret Mead or Frances Densmore already laid the groundwork for women in anthropology? There was only one course to follow. She would have to keep her objectivity and enthusiasm intact. She would do the best job she could. And, she would watch Dr. Edwin Gaffney like a hawk.

Somewhere in the hills to the west of the camp, a wolf howled. With sleepy thoughts of years past when warriors called to each other by imitating the sounds of animals and birds, Ryan Burke, Ph.D., anthropologist and newest member of the Little Big Horn Encampment Project, slid downward into the depths of sleep.

In the blurry halfway place where nighttime illusions begin, dream mists swirled and dream shapes began to form. Moaning, Ryan tugged at her blanket as once more the gray wolf trotted into her mind and caressed her with a glance from its amber eyes.

Chapter 2

THE RINGING METALLIC noise was god-awful. Wrenched from a deep sleep, Ryan reached out in search of the off button on her alarm clock. Her arm lifted and dropped in a blind swoop and encountered absolutely nothing. There was no clock, no bedside table, nothing until her knuckles grazed the floor of the tent.

Unrelenting, the noise continued, drilling into her head like a cruel auger. Groaning, Ryan buried her head beneath her pillow. The clamor came closer until it was outside the tent, mere feet from where she lay. She peered out from under the edge of the pillow and watched a man's silhouette move against the tent wall. A long-handled ladle rose and fell as the shadow earnestly beat reveille on a cooking pot. No. It couldn't be morning already.

"Dr. Burke," the silhouette barked with Edwin Gaffney's voice. "I insist my team rise early. Slackards are not ignored here, nor are they tolerated."

Clang. Clang. Clang.

"Dr. Burke, I refuse to be your alarm clock every morning."

Clang. Clang. Clang.

"If you plan to sway my view of women in a project camp, you're off to a very poor start."

Clang. Clang. Clang.

Gaffney's voice, coupled with the ringing pot, bore through the morning muzziness of Ryan's sleep-clogged brain. It touched the little button deep inside her head that triggered both headaches and poor humor.

"Does your silence indicate you've already fled this camp?"

Ryan rolled onto her back. *No such luck, you pompous jackass!* "Good morning, Dr. Gaffney," she answered pleasantly, trying her best to sound wide awake and praying she hadn't been snoring. *Let's see how a little boot licking works in the light of day.* "I'll be right out. I've been up for a while, reviewing some of the material I brought with me from Washington."

"Well, yes, how enterprising. Very good, Burke. Eagerness impresses me," Gaffney replied. "Join us at the table, your breakfast is ready and waiting."

Closing her eyes, Ryan sighed with relief. She had won temporary reprieve. There was little doubt; aside from time, it would take patience and hard work to appease Edwin Gaffney and earn his sanction. But, if that's what it took to stay with his project, then that's exactly what she would do.

It wasn't Gaffney who filled her in on the work at the site. Gaffney had assigned Daniel Stockard, the handsome archaeologist who had been so nice to her the night before, to be her tutor.

After the others had left for the dig and with a fresh pot of coffee on the table, Stockard and Ryan began delving through the pile of project notes and files.

"Gaffney suggested you take a day or two to look everything over and visit the digs. He wants you to have a clear understanding of the project," Stockard said, indicating one large pile of loose-leaf binders and placing a stack of colored file folders on the table. "The folders are for our daily reports. We've each been assigned our own color. Mine are blue, MacMillen has yellow, Kovacs's are orange. Beware the dreaded red ones, those are Gaffney's." He set a few folders on the table in front of Ryan. "You're green."

"I assume the color is just a coincidence and not because I'm the greenhorn on the project."

"Wow, the new kid on the block has a cynical sense of humor. I like that," Stockard laughed. "If you'd prefer, the other choices are a neon pink and mud brown. Want to change?" He picked up and wagged the green folders in front of her, grinning widely when she pulled them from his hand. "Look, don't worry about Gaffney, you'll do fine. He's prone to gripe and rage, but he hasn't fired any of us yet."

Ryan gave in to her curiosity. "Dan, what does he have against women working on his team?"

Stockard paused, nervously shuffled some papers on the table then raised his gaze to meet Ryan's. "Straight, hard fact?"

"Of course. Why would I want anything less?"

"Good girl." Stockard nodded appreciatively. "Do you handle everything so directly?"

"Yes, I suppose I do," Ryan answered. Her fight for independence had taught her well.

"Keep in mind that what I've heard have just been rumors," Stockard began, leaning forward and lowering his voice. "I heard the last woman who ever worked on any of Gaffney's projects, like you, was young and exceptionally pretty. She was a promising archaeologist with an excellent career ahead of her. Her only crime was rejecting Gaffney's romantic advances." Stockard took a sip of coffee, grimaced, added sugar to his mug and continued. "She fell in love with his chief assistant instead and they eloped. When Gaffney found out, he was insanely jealous and fired them both."

Ryan felt her dismay hit with a hard slam.

"Before Gaffney was even out of the field," Stockard continued, "they published an excellent article about the project using their own notes. Granted, professionally and ethically it was the wrong thing to do and Gaffney's retaliation was swift—and excessive. It was never proven that he was the cause, but neither worked on anything important again. They'd been blacklisted." Stockard idly stirred his coffee. "The assistant ended up teaching science in a junior high school and she got a job selling equipment for a laboratory supply company." Stockard continued in a hushed voice. "In two years' time he was a hopeless alcoholic and she was dead—suicide."

Ryan's stomach knotted with a sickening lurch. Why hadn't Schueller told her any of this? Surely he had known.

Stockard cleared his throat. "We'd better get on with your briefing."

His description of the project was exactly as Ryan had anticipated and she tried to concentrate on Stockard's words but found it difficult to forget the story he had just told her.

"We photograph the site before we set the measured grid over the top of the area. After documenting anything we find in the files, we'll restore the site until it's as close as possible to its original condition." Stockard paused, then continued with an apologetic shrug, "To be honest, I think your phase is the weak link of this project."

Ryan's job was very different but every bit as important as digging for artifacts. A little over a hundred of the people who lived in the area were descendants of those who had fought in the battle. She planned to interview as many of these old Sioux and Cheyenne as possible, hopefully putting together an accurate picture of the battle and Indian encampment once the two phases were joined. Perhaps the real Indian point of view could finally be documented.

"No offense," Stockard continued, "but I hope you've got some idea how to weed the genuine information out of the trumped-up stories you'll hear. The people you're interviewing weren't alive when it happened. Some can barely speak English and most are probably illiterate. Besides, none of them are less than sixty years of age." Stockard shook his head. "How do you plan to separate fact from overembellished campfire stories or senile dementia?"

"Dr. Stockard, I'm shocked," Ryan teased. "You must have been digging in the hot sun too long. You're forgetting your lessons in Native Americans 101. My work will succeed *because* of the culture. With every culture of strong oral tradition, the storyteller has always been the historian. Accounts of tribal history heard from them today are exactly as they were told over a hundred or two hundred years ago or just moments after the event occurred." She stacked the green folders neatly on the table in front of her. "It's unfortunate, but in projects such as this, a subject's illiteracy is to our advantage as well. Memories haven't been tainted by reading inaccurate history books." Ryan poured the cold dregs of her coffee out onto the ground. "As for the language, I can speak Lakota and have an elementary grasp of Cheyenne. Buddy will help me if I have any problems."

Stockard offered a salute with his cup. "Dr. Burke, I stand corrected." Setting his cup down, he soberly folded his hands on the table. The muscle along his jaw tensed. "There is something else I think I should tell you."

The tight knot in Ryan's stomach quickly returned.

"It's one of Gaffney's rules that might cause a problem in your work, especially if you want to use some of the artifacts when you're doing interviews." Stockard paused and seemed to gather his words carefully. "Once an artifact is found and all the photos and grid charts are done, Gaffney takes possession of it. Last summer there was a separate tent for the artifacts and we had free access to whatever the dig yielded, whenever we wanted. This year, he's keeping everything in a cabinet in his tent. They can only be studied with his permission."

She had already found Gaffney to be peculiar, but this was bizzare. Artifacts on a dig were always available to team members. "That doesn't make any—"

"I know," Stockard said, raising his hand to silence her. "It doesn't make any sense. If we want to see a piece, we've got to ask him to get it for us. The delay not only lengthens the workday, but how do I know that the artifact I found last week is the same one he's bringing out." He dropped his voice to a whisper. "How do I know if what I've found is even still . . . on the site?"

Ryan drew a quick breath. "What are you saying? Are you suggesting Dr. Gaffney is—"

"I am not suggesting anything," Stockard interrupted, refilling his mug. "Let's just say I'm uncomfortable with the current policy. Watch your step. We jump to Gaffney's rules and he changes them often to suit his own whim." Stockard took a sip and looked at Ryan. "He's not allowing any volunteers on the project this year. The site is closed to outsiders. He even turned down a *National Geographic* article. Doesn't this all sound a little strange to you? Funding is difficult enough to come by, but when you turn your back on possible sources . . . I don't know." Stockard shrugged his shoulders and sat back. "I'll be honest, if I hadn't signed off at my own university for the summer, I'd have been long gone. Kovacs and MacMillen feel the same."

He paused and glanced around as if checking on Gaffney's whereabouts. "Some of the local Indians, mostly the Cheyenne, have been here from time to time to see what's going on. They're upset with Gaffney. Although he's a full-blood Lakota, Buddy's grandfather has been one of the most outspoken. Gaffney's not happy with Buddy's older brother, Dillon, being involved, either."

"Buddy mentioned him last night," Ryan said. "He called his brother a war chief. I don't understand. The old warrior societies no longer exist."

"Dillon Wolf's a war chief, all right, make no mistake about it. He's the great red hope to all the Indian people out here. Even though they don't get along much with the Lakota in general, the Crow people like him, too. The two tribes are still fighting old wars." Stockard emptied his cup in one long draught. "Dillon Wolf is the local boy who's made good. They treat him like a hero. Some even call him the brand-new Crazy Horse."

"That's quite an accolade."

Stockard gave a concurring shrug. "Dillon Wolf is a long-haired, handsome red devil and the media love to photograph and hound him for interviews. When he went off to university, he dropped the 'Crying' from his name and now calls himself Wolf, Dillon Wolf. It's nothing more than marketing. He knew the new name makes a stronger, more threatening impression."

Again, the wolf. Apprehension scraped a disquieting finger down Ryan's spine.

"Dillon Wolf was a Phi Beta Kappa at Brown University," Stockard continued. "He won a Rhodes scholarship and went off to England. When he returned he passed his bar exam, cofounded the Intertribal Legal Coalition and is now their top cutthroat attorney. I'm surprised you haven't run into him in Washington. He's there a lot, hounding both Congress and the Senate over every Indian issue imaginable."

"I hadn't heard of him until Buddy talked about him last night," Ryan replied.

"Don't let all that white man's education fool you," Stockard said with a cynical laugh. "Dillon Wolf is still redskin through and through, and a damned belligerent one at that."

"Why are the Indians and Buddy's grandfather so upset? This is a legally approved dig, isn't it?" Ryan didn't like how her unease seemed to keep multiplying. If there was serious trouble on the project, could her career be in jeopardy? Should she think about leaving? No. That wouldn't serve any purpose. She should glean as much information as possible from Daniel Stockard and the others before making any final decision.

"Of course it's approved, but this is a special place for the Cheyenne and Lakota. Although the battleground and cemetery might be smack-dab in the middle of a Crow reservation and are hot tourist attractions, the Cheyenne and Lakota aren't about to let this stuff slip away without a fight.

"There are a couple of separate factions at work, too. The elders believe everything should be left alone. They say the earth has kept their ancestors' bones and belongings safe for all these years and shouldn't be disturbed. Most of the Crow people couldn't care less. After all, this isn't their history; these weren't their people. The only Crows here in

1876 were Custer's scouts, and records say they took off before the battle began."

Stockard shook the coffeepot to see if there was any brew left. Hearing nothing but the empty rattle of the lid, he set it back on the table. "The only advantage the park has for the Crow people is that some are making big bucks selling beadwork, dream catchers and other kitschy trinkets to the tourists. They hold a couple of powwows during the summer months to snag even more tourist dollars. The young people just want to get enough money to leave and head for the city."

Stockard's voice grew hushed. "Buddy's grandfather and his brother Dillon believe that Gaffney is stealing artifacts from the site and selling them to private collectors for big money."

"No," Ryan replied, shocked. "That can't be true." Surely Edwin Gaffney's reputation was too solid for him to be involved with anything so heinous? "They must be mistaken."

"Hear me out," Stockard said. "Three weeks ago I uncovered an oilcloth bundle buried in a stone cache. Inside was a glass bead necklace and a beautifully made hide doll. The doll was one of the best specimens I've ever seen. It was complete with a trade-cloth dress, human hair and tiny beaded moccasins. Amazingly enough, bugs and moisture hadn't touched anything; there wasn't even the slightest trace of rot. It looked like someone had just hidden it a day or two earlier." Stockard paused again and glanced over his shoulder. "When you read Gaffney's recovery list, see if the doll is listed. I bet you won't find it."

"You're saying Gaffney has stolen it, aren't you?" Ryan leaned forward to catch Stockard's answer.

Stockard shrugged. "I don't have any hard proof, but a week ago I heard through a friend in Denver that a doll, identical to the one I recovered, was offered to a *very* private collector. He was told the doll came from here. And who's the only person with free access to the artifacts?"

"You said Gaffney—but you must be mistaken," Ryan

countered. "His reputation—how can anyone believe that he's involved in anything so, so . . ."

"I know it's difficult. It's been hard for me, too, but other things have disappeared as well." Stockard lightly touched Ryan's arm. "I hope you understand the sensitive nature of this information. Don't talk about it with anyone but Kovacs, MacMillen or me. A scandal like this could ruin anyone involved with Gaffney."

Ryan gave a slight nod.

"I'm only bringing it up," Stockard continued, "because I'm familiar with the quality of your work from your publications and, well, the stigma a researcher gets from a bad association can kill a wonderful career."

Although she had good reason to believe the worst after Gaffney's treatment of her, Ryan still wasn't ready to accept *this* possibility. She didn't know either Gaffney or Stockard well enough to choose sides just yet. She wanted more facts. Gaffney might be an opinionated chauvinist, but his professional reputation was outstanding—unblemished. She couldn't ignore that.

"Ryan, believe me, you'll begin to see things, too. It won't take long for you to—"

"So, Dr. Burke," Edwin Gaffney said, interrupting their conversation as he approached from the south end of the camp, "if Stockard has finished filling you in on all of our procedures, we'll take you over to the digs after lunch. You'll see where Kovacs and MacMillen have been working. Tonight we'll go over your interview lists. There are a few Lakota who have already agreed to talk with you and we'll discuss how you can go about signing up others."

Stockard led Ryan along the southeastern edge of what, in 1876, had been the Lakota encampment. Custer's officers, Benteen and Reno, had made their foolhardy charge into the camp from across the Greasy Grass River at this point and their retreat from this area had been just as quick.

Away from the cluster of park administration buildings, the museum, gift shop and national cemetery, very little had changed in the years since the battle. Some bank erosion had occurred along the river edge and there was new growth of a few scrub bushes and small trees, but according to research it was much the same. The stout oaks and cottonwoods that had stood along the river on that June day in 1876 still hung their sturdy, leaf-covered branches over the water in the summertime. If someone were to look out across the valley and not know the history of the land, it would be merely another pretty panorama of the American plains.

Ryan spent the rest of the afternoon in camp under the canvas shade. Before delving into the papers Gaffney had placed at her disposal, she opened the tightly packed manila folders Dr. Schueller had given her before she left the Smithsonian. Smiling, she read the attached note written in Schueller's sprawling script.

> *Congratulations!*
>
> *Although I hate to lose your excellent services, I'm anticipating some good papers to be forthcoming. Gaffney's work is adding important material. Being chosen as a member of his team is quite a coup. Enjoy your summer and keep us posted. I look forward to your return in the fall.*
>
> *Regards, Schueller*

Dr. Schueller's written opinion about Gaffney eased her concern a little.

One of Schueller's packets held copies of some of the old photographs from the Smithsonian's archives. The photos were of many of the Lakota and Cheyenne warriors who had participated in the battle of the Little Big Horn. A second packet held photos of some of the women and children known to have been in the huge Indian encampment as well. Ryan studied them closely. Some she had seen many times before, some were duplicates of those she had personally selected to bring and others were new to her. The sepia-toned faces in the old photographs looked back at her through time with the familiarity of old friends. They all had an ageless beauty and dignity that touched her heart. She wished, as she had a hundred times before, that H. G. Wells's time machine was a reality. A ride back to meet and get to know these people who had been the last of the truly free Indians of the Northern Plains would have been an adventure beyond comparison.

After returning the reproductions to the envelope, she soon became engrossed in the project's field notes. She learned to recognize each man's handwriting: from Kovacs's tidy draftsmanlike print and MacMillen's tiny, cramped letters to Stockard's open and almost gregarious script. Gaffney's handwriting was fastidiously neat on some pages and sometimes an illegible scratching on others. His notes appeared as though two different people had written them and she uncomfortably thought of the word "dementia."

From the written and photographic records she could see an impressive number of artifacts had already been recovered in the few short weeks since the project had resumed this year. The list included cooking pots, knife blades, horn spoons, two Lincoln peace medals, shell casings and pieces of hairpipe bones that had once been a necklace or breastplate.

Two catlinite pipe bowls had also been found. One had been recovered the year before and the other the day before she had arrived. Ryan studied the photographs. The bowls were identical. Carved into the side of each were the paw prints of a wolf. "The wolf again," she breathed.

There was another oddity. Although the pipe bowls were identical, the one Dan Stockard found last year had been removed from the ground where her tent now stood. The other, recovered this year by Kovacs, had been found about three hundred yards away. Had they belonged to the same person? Were they related in some way to a warrior society or perhaps a clan?

From the number of items reclaimed, it was clear the historians were correct. The Indians had quickly dismantled the camp and left the valley soon after the battle with Custer ended. With their safety at stake, they had haphazardly packed their belongings, leaving a great deal behind.

Turning page after page, Stockard's words continued to bother her. She found the entry dated May 18 that listed his find that day. The doll wasn't on the inventory. She checked the record entries for the three previous days and for three days following. There was still no mention of the doll. Even the identification numbers tallied correctly. No gaps appeared in the series. It was as if the doll had never existed.

Despite the mid-May heat, Ryan felt cold. At this point she only had Stockard's word that the doll existed. Did anyone else besides Dan Stockard know about the missing doll? *Yes, Dan said both Kovacs and MacMillen knew about it.* Still, none of it made any sense. If Gaffney was stealing artifacts, he was being stupidly careless.

The drone and sputter of a badly tuned motor drew her attention away from the puzzle. A cloud of dust rose into the air to the west of the camp and the sound of the approaching vehicle became louder and louder. Like some cranky beast rising up out of the ground, Buddy Crying Wolf's truck bounced over the crest of the hill and careened down the grade straight toward the canvas shade where Ryan sat. The old blue Ford looked more decrepit in the light of day and Ryan shuddered, thinking of the miles she had traveled in it the night before.

If the camp had been a paved parking lot, the tires would have squealed in protest as Buddy jammed on the brakes. As it was, the balding tires slid with a spray of dirt and gravel before coming to a precarious stop beside Gaffney's jeep. Stones pinged off the Jeep's bright red paint. Through the settling dust that fell back to the parched ground, Ryan saw that Buddy wasn't alone.

Buddy jumped out from behind the steering wheel and waved. His cowboy hat had been replaced by a black ball-cap with the words "Eat Possum" emblazoned in a garish hot pink across the front. A clutch of yellow flicker feathers tied to the button on the crown of the cap fluttered in the summer breeze.

"Hey, Doc! I brought someone ta meet ya!"

Chapter 3

THE TRUCK DOOR opened slowly with a screeching, rusty protest. Reaching inside, Buddy helped his passenger get out.

The man was old. It was difficult to gauge, but Ryan guessed by his stance and the white fall of his long braids that he'd seen every bit of eighty-five or ninety years. His skin was the dark hue of finely polished red cherry wood and it had been carved and cut by age into deep creases and wrinkles. He had once been a tall man but the weight of his years had pulled him over until he walked with stooped shoulders and bowed legs.

An ancient and stained cowboy hat that might have once been a pearl gray sat on his head and shaded his face. The uneven brim drooped down in the back as though it was used to being pressed against the high backrest of a chair.

"Grandpa kept buggin' me until I brought him out here to meet you," Buddy said, loud enough so every old man in a ten-mile radius could hear each word. "He don't hear too well." Buddy helped the old man over a rough spot of ground. "When he wants me to do something for him, he don't stop naggin' 'til he gets his way. He don't give up easy . . . hell, he don't give up at all!"

Ryan found herself staring into eyes as dark as onyx. Their riveting gaze surprised her. At first glance she had expected the old man's eyes to be rheumy, but they were unusually young eyes—eyes that were carefully assessing her.

"This is my grandpa," Buddy offered. "His name is Calls to the Wolf, but he's on the government rolls as Charles Antone Crying Wolf. Take your pick." Buddy turned and spoke to his grandfather in fluent Lakota, glancing at Ryan from time to time.

Nodding at Buddy's words, the old man's eyes never left Ryan.

"This is Dr. Ryan Burke, Grandpa. Like I told ya, she's an okay lady." Buddy turned, looked at Ryan and winked.

Feeling more than a little uncomfortable under the old Lakota's scrutiny, Ryan settled herself in a chair across the table from her visitor. She smiled and gestured with her hand, inviting him to sit. "Does your grandfather speak English?"

"He can speak it fine, but he gets ornery sometimes and doesn't want to talk it at all." Buddy helped his grandfather into a chair and then plopped himself down in another. "I never know what kind of a mood he's in until he opens his mouth." Buddy glanced at his grandfather. "Ain't that right, Grandpa?"

The old man's gaze slid to his grandson, registered a hint of exasperation, then moved back to settle on Ryan. "Contrary to what my grandson says, Dr. Burke, I can hear very well and yes, I speak English." His voice was clear but strong with the lilting nasal accent typical of the older Lakota people. "For you, today, Dr. Burke, I will speak English, but someday I think you gonna speak Lakota for me." He extended a gnarled hand in greeting.

"I'd enjoy that," Ryan answered. Grasping his hand, she felt a surprising strength and vitality.

He sat quietly, a slight nod of his head the only movement he made. "Yup, someday maybe I think you gonna speak a *lot* of Lakota." He continued to nod. "You doubt my words but it will be so. You will see."

Charles Antone Crying Wolf was old and perhaps senile. Ryan responded with a slight, indulgent smile. "That would be nice."

"My grandson tells me it is proper for me to call you Dr. Burke, but you can call me Charley," he offered.

"I think I'd like it much better if you called me Ryan and I called you Mr. Crying Wolf."

He shrugged his stooped shoulders. "Whatever."

From the small smile that curved upon his mouth and the approving tilt of his head, Ryan knew Charley Crying Wolf recognized the respect she offered him as an elder.

He turned his attention from her and took his time looking about the camp. "The others, those archaeologist fellows, they are all away—over there?" He pointed toward the dig with pursed lips and a slight lift of his chin. "We are alone?"

"Yes, we are," Ryan responded, beginning to stand. "May I offer you a cold drink or perhaps some coffee?"

He gestured for her to sit. "My disrespectful grandson will get us something cold to drink. His legs are young and I like to make good use of them." A smile played across his weathered face, deepening the creases around his mouth and eyes.

Ryan realized she'd been wrong. The passing years hadn't touched his mind at all. It was agile and quick and steeped with a delightful humor.

Charley Crying Wolf set his elbows on the arms of the chair. Steepling his fingers, he rested his chin upon their tips and studied Ryan. "You are very pretty—for a *wasicu*, a white woman. I like your blue eyes. My people call them 'sky eyes.' Some Sioux are born with eyes like yours, but not many. Your hair is long and dark, too, like our Lakota women." He smiled warmly. "You look strong." He looked at her arms. "How many loads of wood do you think you can carry in a day? Maybe five?"

Flabbergasted by his question, Ryan didn't know what to say.

"Ah, it is such a shame," he added. "You are too old for my grandson Buddy and much too young for me." Pensively stroking his chin, his dark eyes twinkled. "Could be you're just right for my older grandson." He nodded. "Yup, might be." With a resigned sigh, Charley Crying Wolf shook his head. "It is a shame Dillon is away right now. Maybe sometime, maybe soon, you will meet him."

Remembering Stockard's uncomplimentary remarks about Dillon Wolf, Ryan was positive she didn't want to meet Charley Crying Wolf's older grandson.

Charley lifted his battered hat and scratched the side of his head, his gaze never leaving Ryan. "Hmm," he continued thoughtfully, "Yup, maybe, just maybe it'd work." He settled his hat back on his head. "You married?"

His blunt question took Ryan by surprise. "Uh—no!"

"Why not?"

She looked imploringly at Buddy but the teenager answered with the complacent shrug of his shoulders she was learning to know so well. Buddy ducked his head and studied the can of cola as though suddenly very curious about the listing of its ingredients. She was left to deal with Charley Crying Wolf on her own.

"To begin with, there's been no one I've wanted to marry, no one I've been in love with. Besides, I've been much too busy."

"And what has a pretty woman like you been so busy doing?" he asked, closely watching her.

"College, graduate school, my fellowship and now my work at the Smithsonian. I—"

"Slow down."

"Excuse me?"

"Slow down. You can't catch good fish if your bait's moving too fast."

"My what?" A blush burned her cheeks.

"I heard it on one of them TV fishing shows. It sounded like good advice to me at the time." The wide grin on Charley Crying Wolf's face proved how much he was enjoying her reaction to his teasing. His weathered face sobered but the twinkle in his eyes remained. "I understand you believe I'm a chauvinist."

Wishing she could disappear into thin air, Ryan imagined

her cheeks were now a bright tomato red. She silently promised herself to strangle Buddy later for repeating her remark to his grandfather. "I—uh . . ."

"It's true," Charley Crying Wolf confessed with a firm nod of his head. "Old habits are hard to break. It's like they say about an old dog, eh?" He chuckled and reached over the table and gently patted her hand. "Dr. Burke—Ryan, I am trying to learn these newfangled feminist ideas as fast as I can. I believe the old ways are still the best, but if you don't learn the new, you get run over by young turkeys like my grandson here." He pointed at Buddy with a slight lift of his thumb, paused and leaned forward. When he spoke again, his words were solemn. "I am what you scientific people call a traditional. I know the Great Spirit, the Creator Wakan Tanka, the one we call Tunkasila, grandfather. I honor the sacred pipe, the eagle and the buffalo. These things are important to my people, to our spiritual ways. One day, whether my two grandsons believe it now or not, they will get hungry for knowledge of the old ways, too. Someday they will seek it out and then they will know what the elders know—if it isn't too late."

"See?" Buddy said with a soft chuckle. "Didn't I tell ya he was the original Lakota Yoda?" The look he gave his grandfather didn't camouflage his love and true admiration one bit.

Ryan smiled and nodded. She liked Charles Antone Crying Wolf. She liked him very much. Having the opportunity to meet people like him made the years of hard study and dealing with eccentrics such as Edwin Gaffney worthwhile.

"So tell me, what will this science of yours tell you about this place, my people and about the Cheyenne?" With a wide sweep of his arm he gestured toward the valley and high bluffs of the Little Big Horn.

"Quite a lot, I hope."

"And your job with Dr. Gaffney, what is it you do? Do you study bones like some who have desecrated our burials? Indians have never had much good to say about anthropologists."

"Although some anthropologists work with bones, I

don't. In my work I prefer to speak with people face-to-face."

Charley Crying Wolf nodded but didn't say a word.

"I'll be interviewing many of the descendants of the people who were here in the 1876 encampment and who fought Custer and the Seventh Cavalry," Ryan continued.

Charley rubbed his chin. "It is good—no bones."

"The information these people are willing to share with me will be recorded and analyzed," Ryan continued. "I'll be asking about the time their ancestors spent in the encampment. I'd like to know the way they lived, the events leading up to the battle, the battle itself and then what happened after the fighting was over. The data will be totally from the perspective of the Sioux and Cheyenne." Ryan took a sip of cola. "There are stories that have never been told outside of the tribal circles. I'm hoping some of these will be shared with me so they may be recorded."

"And what will be done with this history you collect?" Charley Crying Wolf asked. "Will the truths be hidden if it is not what you want or will it become what scholarly men now call revisionist history? Already many books have been written about this place . . . most of them wrong . . . most of them rubbish."

"None of that will happen," Ryan replied with conviction. "The purpose of this whole project is to obtain *accurate* information. It will be published and used to educate people who want to know the truth about the Little Big Horn and the way the Lakota lived in those last years before reservation life began." She tried to read the expression on the old man's face. "Mr. Crying Wolf, my work is being done for your people, more so than anyone else. I know some of the young people aren't interested in listening to the old stories now. Maybe when they *are* ready to listen it will be too late; the old ones with the knowledge will be gone. Perhaps my work will help make it available . . . always."

Charley nodded thoughtfully and continued to stroke his chin. "So, you do not dig for Indian treasure with the others?" His voice was heavy with sarcasm.

"No. My specialty is people, the Indian people."

"Ah," he responded with another thoughtful nod. "*Wasté*. That is good." He tipped the condensation-coated can of cola to his lips, took a long swallow and lowered it, revealing a mischievous smile on his wet lips. His eyes sparkled brightly. "So, as my young grandson might say, you 'dig' people, not treasure."

"Grandpa!" Buddy breathed with teenaged dismay. "Please forgive him, Doc, I think he's getting . . . you know . . ." Buddy made a circular gesture with his finger beside his head. "You're not only crazy, Grandpa, but that was a lousy joke."

"So now he's a critic." Charley chuckled and then sobered.

No one spoke for a few moments. A somber pall seemed to fall over Charley Crying Wolf before he spoke again. "What has brought you to your career? What is it *you* seek with my people?"

His questions surprised Ryan. On the surface they seemed to be a simple inquiries, but the intensity of his dark gaze proved them to be much more. Not wanting Charley Crying Wolf to think she was another non-Indian dealing with historic angst, Ryan knew it was important to select the right words for her answer.

"When I was a child my parents took me on a vacation to Chicago. We went to the Field Museum. There was room after room filled with beautiful American Indian artifacts. I'd never seen anything so wonderful. There were things from almost every known tribe." Ryan took a small sip from her soda, then continued, keeping her eyes lowered. "There were a lot of people there that day, including an Indian family. They stood in front of one of the tall display cabinets—lances, shields and war trophies, I believe. The father's hands were pressed against the glass as he gazed at the items inside." Ryan's voice softened. "There were tears on his cheeks." She looked up at Charley. "I'd never seen an adult cry before. With a child's curiosity, I moved closer. He was saying something and I wanted to hear what it was. The anguished sound of his voice has never left me." Her own words faltered. "He . . . he said the old ways had been stolen and now the only proof they'd ever existed was in glass boxes, locked away from the people they belonged to. He said soon all Indians would be nothing but curious things for people to look at in a museum. Without someone to keep the knowledge alive, nothing would be left." Ryan felt the burn of unshed tears in her eyes. "Even as a child I felt his pain."

With a simple nod of his head, Charley urged her to continue.

"My mother then took me to another display, a wall completely covered with a collection of old photographs, the faces of the people, from the babies to the very old. I was fascinated." Ryan hesitated and glanced away, knowing the next words she'd say had elicited ridicule from her friends and family in the past. "I felt as though I knew each and every person in those photos. I felt as though they were in some way seeking my help." Fully expecting the usual scoffing response, she didn't look at Charley Crying Wolf. He didn't say a word. "Ever since that summer I knew I wanted to do everything I could do to ensure that the culture, the history and old ways of the Indian people weren't lost."

"And you chose this path?"

"Yes. I knew I wanted to be an anthropologist and work only with Native issues." Looking up, she offered a shy smile. "There is a hunger in my soul that's appeased only by the culture."

Charley Crying Wolf quietly nodded, his expression pensive. He looked away, his eyes not meeting Ryan's when he spoke again. "I have heard there is something bad going on here. Do you know what I am talking about? Is this so?"

The prodding finger of disquiet suddenly returned and gave Ryan a hard poke. She shifted uneasily in her chair. So, Stockard had been right. The Indians were suspicious of Gaffney, too. "Mr. Crying Wolf, this is my first day on Dr. Gaffney's project. I'm still acquainting myself with his work and haven't even begun my own study yet, so how could I know what you mean?"

"My people have many questions we would like your

Dr. Gaffney to answer, but he finds himself too busy to meet with us." He paused and idly turned the soda can on the tabletop. "He avoids us. The young people don't care. It is the old ones, like me, who worry about what happens when things are disturbed or taken away dishonorably. This place is holy, *wakan*."

"Please, let me assure you, from what I've seen and from what I know, this valley is being treated with the respect it deserves," Ryan responded. "I've seen where the men are digging and I've watched how the work is done. I'm impressed with the way Drs. Stockard, Kovacs and MacMillen work. They are careful and very respectful."

"And this man, Gaffney, he too is careful and respectful?"

"From what I've seen . . . yes."

"You hesitate. Something bothers you?"

Ah, those bright eyes catch everything. "Mr. Crying Wolf, I feel you're asking me to say something specific and I'm not sure what you want."

Charley Crying Wolf leaned forward, his dark, steady gaze holding her captive, commanding her undivided attention. "The history of my people and of the Cheyenne is being stolen from this place. A thief walks here." He made a circular gesture with his weather-beaten hand, encompassing the whole valley in his movement. "My older grandson, Dillon, is a lawyer. He plans to meet with the authorities in Washington and demand to have this project stopped. For now he makes demands in a respectful way. But my grandson is a true warrior, and if a warrior does not get what he wants, the way he asks doesn't remain gentle or respectful for very long. He will use the white man's laws as his weapons but he will make battle in his own way if the tribes' wishes are ignored."

Ryan froze. Stop the project! No! So much knowledge could be gained by the scholarly dig and interviews. If they closed the project, it would all be lost. "If you believe someone is stealing artifacts from the site, how do you know I'm not involved? How do you know you can trust me? You and I have just met. How do you know I'm not part of the problem?"

A slow smile lifted the corners of Charley Crying Wolf's broad lips, deepening the deep creases around his mouth and eyes. "I know about you. All I need to know about you is very clear to see—for someone like me." His eyes remained watchful. "We believe things are being taken from this place, things that should stay here. They aren't being put in museums and they aren't being returned to us. These objects are being stolen and sold for large sums of money to increase one man's personal wealth and to feed his greed." Charley Crying Wolf's gaze turned and followed the southern rush of the river.

"Mr. Crying Wolf, what proof do you have?"

"I have no solid proof yet. I just know it is true. I have heard many talk about it, I have heard about what is available from a man I have known for many years. He is a dealer—a curator, a collector in Colorado. And, I know it here." He raised his hand and with his index finger tapped first his head and then his heart. "I know it like I know you have been sent to help us. *Yahi acipe manké.* I have been waiting for you to come."

Ryan frowned. For the second time in their conversation his strange words left her feeling uneasy. *What could I possibly do to help?* She thought about the missing doll and the tight, sickening knot gripped her stomach again. How could she question the integrity of someone of Edwin Gaffney's stature?

For this Lakota elder and his people to be so adamant about their suspicions, there must be much more to question than just the absence of a single deerhide doll. And what did he mean when he'd said she had been sent to help? She looked at Buddy and realized he'd been paying close attention to the conversation.

"You ain't gonna let us down are you, Doc?" Buddy asked, leaning forward and putting his elbows on the table. He stared unwavering into Ryan's eyes. "This is important, not just to this old man, but to the tribes as well, the Cheyenne and Sioux people. My brother, Dillon, is hot and heavy on top of this fight, just like a pit bull—he's got a big bite on it and I know Dillon, he ain't gonna let go until—"

"Until this valley cries no more," Charley Crying Wolf interrupted, his voice soft.

The barking call of an eagle punctuated Charley Crying Wolf's words and they all looked up to watch the majestic bird float and soar on a wind current high over the bluffs across the river. The huge bird dipped its wings, turned in a wide arc and then caught a ride on a downward draft. It swooped to the ground then, lifting high into the air again, disappeared behind the rolling hills on the eastern side of the Little Big Horn River.

Ryan released the breath she had held throughout the eagle's aerial ballet. "Believe me, if what you say is actually happening, and I don't doubt your sincerity, I don't know what kind of help I can give . . . or if I can do anything."

"No one in Washington will believe this old Indian, *miye maLakota*, I am Lakota. They have never believed us. My hotheaded grandson, Dillon, is finding that out more and more each day. But if you should believe what I am telling you is really so, then would you help us? Your work gives you status. The authorities would believe you."

"Of course I'd help if it's true. I'd do anything I could to stop it and see the guilty person put in jail, but there has to be proof."

"Good, *wasté*, very good. That is what I wished to hear. For now, all I ask is that you be patient, be careful and be watchful, very watchful—like a little mouse." Charley nearly whispered his words. "When the time is right you will know what must be done, but first we must wait for that time." He slowly rose to his feet, fighting for balance on his old bowed legs. "Now it is time for my grandson to take me home for my afternoon nap." Charley placed his hand lightly on Ryan's arm. "*Kechuwa*, dear one, there is nothing here for you to fear."

His dark eyes scanned the valley once again, and in his

expression, Ryan saw the depth of the man's affection for the place.

Charley Crying Wolf smiled. "Ah, my delightful new friend, wouldn't it be wonderful if someone could go back to that time over a hundred and twenty years ago and set a trap, an old trap to catch a new thief? We could snare the one who is stealing from us today with something he believes came from many yesterdays. I'd love to go, wouldn't you?" Smiling, he paused, nodding his head slightly, and then gave his shoulders a short shrug. "But, that's impossible—isn't it?" He looked into Ryan's eyes.

Ryan realized with some dismay, *he's serious!*

"We will speak again soon," Charley added solemnly.

She stood and accepted his extended hand, feeling its calloused strength. His words had left her unsettled.

"I have enjoyed meeting you and I am very glad you have come. There is now sunshine in this old man's heart." He frowned slightly and leaned closer. "Those are very beautiful earrings you are wearing. They are little flowers, little golden daisies."

"Thank you. My grandmother gave them to me when I was younger. Daisies are my favorite flowers. They are engraved on the back with my initials and the date of my birth. I wear them all the time."

Charley nodded. "Very pretty, just like their owner." He reached up and gently touched one delicate earring with the tip of his finger. "It would be a shame to lose one. What is one without the other—except good proof that you once had two."

Again, Ryan frowned.

"I will leave now," Charley Crying Wolf said, quickly changing the subject and lightening his mood. "I don't want to overstay my welcome or prove the first time we meet that I *am* a chauvinist. I'll do that the next time," he teased. "One more thing," he added, facing her once again, "Now that we know each other so well, from now on you call me Charley."

The antiquated blue pickup coughed and sputtered as Buddy started the reluctant motor. The truck rumbled unwillingly up the hill, over the crest and out of sight, leaving a trailing cloud of red dust in its wake.

After he'd left, the sound of Charley Crying Wolf's voice continued to resound in Ryan's head, replaying his words about the stolen artifacts. Misgivings about the whole project weighed heavily on her mind and pushed a dull headache into place. *If I get involved in this, and everyone is wrong about Gaffney, it could ruin my professional reputation—hell, it could ruin my whole career! Help me, Dr. Schueller, what should I do?*

Charley's words returned and filled her mind. *Go back in time, over a hundred and twenty years ago.* "The very idea," she breathed.

"There's too much warrior in you," Charley said, scowling at his eldest grandson who was home for his first visit in months. "Ain't no use doing things in that hard, militant way anymore. You're gettin' a reputation for being too contentious."

"Yeah," Dillon Wolf replied. "So?"

"It gets you in a lot of hot water with people—you get a bad reputation and pretty soon they don't want to deal with you."

"No, it makes them stand up and realize I don't back down from a fight," Dillon rebutted. "Besides, that badass reputation gets my cases a lot of media coverage. It doesn't hurt to have the issues in the public eye."

"You gotta work *with* people, not pull against them or knock them over," Charley offered, knowing full well that his advice would be ignored.

"If I've got to kick butt to get all the facts I need for a case—too bad. And right now I need all the ammunition I can get against Gaffney and the project. How do you suggest I do that, Grandpa? You want me to be best friends with him?" Dillon shook his head then cast a glance at his grandfather. "Do you want Gaffney stopped or not?"

"Yeah, of course I do and so do a lot of the others; there's no question about that."

"Then let me do my job, my way," Dillon countered. He

moved to the edge of the porch. "What I need is a deposition from you and one from the tribal chairman stating your suspicions about the project and your demands to have it shut down. A petition with lots of signatures would help and if you've got any hard proof of the thefts, document that, too."

Dillon leaned back against the roof support on Charley's porch. A bare hint of old white paint still remained on the weathered wood. The paint had turned chalky long ago and now left a white mark down the sleeve of Dillon's navy blue shirt. Moving away from the upright, he wiped his sleeve with an annoyed brush of his hand. "Why don't you get this damn place painted?"

"Why don't you come home some time and help me paint it?" Charley challenged, watching Dillon closely. " 'Sides, when did you get so particular about how this place looks? It suited you just fine when you was growin' up."

Dillon crossed his arms over his chest and looked out over the weed-ridden front yard, squinting against the late-afternoon sun. "Yeah, well things looked a whole lot different then." He pulled the Washington Redskins ballcap down further on his forehead, shading his eyes.

"You hadn't been out there; that's the only difference," Charley replied, pursing his lips and lifting his chin as if pointing to anywhere else in the world. "You hadn't gone and gotten a college education and you weren't a big-shot, uptown lawyer in five-hundred-dollar boots, fancy suits and a fast, shiny new car."

Dillon turned. Looking at his grandfather, he raised his left brow in a cynical arch. "It's that education and your uptown lawyer who's going to help you get rid of Gaffney's project and stop the stealing, isn't it?" He moved to one of the old straight-backed kitchen chairs that now served as part of Charley's front porch furniture, and sat down. Extending his long legs out straight in front of himself, he crossed them at his ankles, boot over boot, and refolded his arms across his chest. "Just look at this place. You let Buddy play 'gofer' for Gaffney, but you don't put him to work around here." Dillon shook his head. "You and Momma and Pa always had me working from sunup to sunset and then some; fetching water, pulling weeds and sweeping this porch until it wore out the damned broom." He looked at Charley. "Grandpa, you've got to get him to do some work here instead of letting him goof off. Start making him pull his own weight."

"He's a good boy, Dillon," Charley said, nodding his head, the back brim of his battered cowboy hat bumping against the back of the rocking chair. "He ain't running wild. He ain't into booze or huffin' glue or spray paint like some of the kids on the rez. When he's home he works hard, just like he works hard for Gaffney. He's getting paid good money at the site and he's puttin' it all away for college."

"It's blood money," Dillon sneered.

"The university bill won't know that," Charley countered, determined to beat his grandson at the game of sarcasm they'd been playing from the time Dillon had arrived earlier that afternoon. "Maybe you should come back and raise him yourself if you don't think I'm doin' the job right."

Dillon shot an exasperated look at his grandfather. "Just because I work for tribal legal issues doesn't mean I want to live back here on the rez," Dillon retaliated. "I'll do all the helping I can from my office in Billings."

Charley silently appraised his grandson. Where had the happy boy he'd once been gone? There was anger and painful cynicism in the man he had become. Where was the Indian boy who had loved the rolling hills and grassy Montana plains? When had Dillon lost himself to the city? When had he become an urban Indian? He was a mixture of modern know-how and traditional ways, and the two clashed.

Dillon had grown into a handsome man, reminding Charley of his own son, Dillon and Buddy's father. Standing at least six feet three inches in height, well-muscled yet athletically lean, Dillon was long-legged and narrow-hipped like his father had been. Charley saw a lot of Dillon's Cheyenne mother in his features, too. His face held the elegantly structured proof of his heritage—the sculpted cheekbones; the straight, well-defined nose; and a full yet finely chiseled mouth. Dillon's hair, almost blue-black in color, hung well below mid-back and he wore it tied back at the nape of his neck, loose, or plaited in long braids as it was now. His eyes, a rich dark brown, were accented by black brows that arced like wings above them. Sometimes when Charley looked closely at Dillon he could see the proud warriors the Lakota people had once been.

A wry smile curved Charley's mouth. He figured there were probably more than five or six girls on the reservation who had lost their hearts, and possibly their virginity, to his good-looking grandson.

"I hope you've been keeping a sharp eye on what's going on down at the project," Dillon said.

"That's another reason why Buddy's down there—it gives me a good excuse to go visit and snoop around." Charley paused and scratched his chin. "You ought to go over there before you go to Washington to see that guy at the FBI. There's a nice new anthropologist working with the team . . . been here a couple of weeks. She's a good person, smart too, and she really cares about the work she's doin'." He grinned. "She's also real pretty."

Dillon smacked his hand against his thigh and quickly stood. "That's just what I mean," he said. "You talk as though everyone involved in that damned project, except the thief, is just wonderful. You act as though they're all doing great things for our people." Dillon pulled the ballcap from his head then roughly reset it. "They're stealing. They're robbing the history of our ancestors, old man, remember?"

"Just thought you might enjoy meeting this lady," Charley offered with a shrug. "She's kinda special. She even wanted me to ask you to reconsider closing the project."

Dillon shot an exasperated look at his grandfather. "I bet she did."

"But, if you won't," Charley continued, ignoring Dillon's cynicism, "she said she'd still help us all she can."

Dillon turned to face his grandfather, his anger boiling high. "Oh, she'll help, all right. She'll help herself to whatever she can get her hands on and then when this site's picked clean, she'll move on and start helping herself all over again somewhere else."

"She's not like that," Charley stated. "I bet if you'd meet her, you'd change your mind. Maybe you'd even like her and could take her out . . . for coffee . . . maybe."

"Yeah, sure," Dillon scoffed. "Not likely. She's white, isn't she?"

Charley shook his head. "You're missing knowing some good people all closed up like you are."

"Yeah, and we thought Christopher Columbus was only sight-seeing for an hour or two." Dillon raised his hands in resignation. "You amaze me, old man. In spite of everything that's been done to our people, you still trust the *wasicu*." He gave a scornful laugh. "No thanks. Keep your *wasicu* friends to yourself, Grandpa. I don't want anything to do with them." Dillon moved off the porch and headed for his car, his boots raising little puffs of dust from the dry ground with each step.

"Where you going now?"

"I've got a date."

"With Jennie Makes No Bow?"

Irritated, Dillon turned and with hands on his hips, faced his grandfather. "Yeah. Why?"

"She's a quarter *wasicu*," Charley said smugly. "You only taking out three-quarters of her?"

"Stop pushing, old man. I'm not going over to the project and that's final." Dillon opened the red Corvette's door and slid behind the steering wheel. "It would take Sitting Bull, the whole Hunkpapa Nation and a damn miracle to get me to meet your pretty little white anthro."

A chuckle rumbled deep in Charley's chest as he watched Dillon drive away. "Don't tempt me boy, 'cause that just might be arranged."

Chapter 4

THE AFTERNOON WAS warm and quiet and as usual when time permitted, Ryan settled herself into the comfortable elbow of the old oak at the river's edge. The tree had become her favorite place, her private office, a sanctuary.

With the small tape recorder resting against her leg, she listened to an interview tape and updated her notes. Twelve tribal elders had already shared their memories with her and within the short while she had been on the project, she'd garnered some exciting information that had never been published before. The old Sioux and Cheyenne had talked about the huge encampment of 1876, pointing out where each tribal circle had been and how their ancestors spent each day. A few even mentioned her favorite oak. They called it the white woman tree, but no one remembered why the tree had been given that name well over a hundred years before. They only remembered what their elders had told them.

The tape clicked and stopped and Ryan flipped the cassette over and the interview with Delbert Rides His Horse continued. The old Lakota's accent was strong, but using her earphones she could clearly make out each word. Closing her eyes, Ryan leaned her head back against the rough bark and listened. Delbert was a talented storyteller and she was soon engrossed in his words until a sharp and painful sting on her arm rudely demanded her attention.

"Ouch!" She grabbed her arm just as another sharp pain bit her left thigh. "Oww!" Startled, she jumped as a small rock struck her shoulder and landed in her lap. "What the . . ."

"Yo, Doc!"

Looking down, Ryan pulled the earphones off her head. "Buddy, what in the blazes do you think you're doing?"

"Sorry, Doc. I hollered but guess ya couldn't hear me with them headphones on." Buddy dropped the remaining pebbles from his hand. Shading his eyes against the afternoon sun, he squinted up at her. "Ya got company. There's some dweeb up in camp lookin' for ya."

"Who is it?"

Buddy shrugged his shoulders. "How'm I supposed to know. He's a jerk, though, a real snob. He looks like one of those preppy types." Buddy struck an exaggerated pose that was straight from the men's fashion pages of a catalog.

His antics made her laugh. "Must be someone from the parks office. One of the rangers offered to give me a guided tour of the battlefield sometime this week."

"Uh, I don't think so," Buddy snickered. "This guy wouldn't wear a pointed Smokey the Bear hat if his life depended on it."

"Did he give you his name?"

"Naw," Buddy answered, "just his snooty attitude." He impatiently jerked his head toward camp. "Come on, hurry up. Here, toss me your stuff—you can get down on your own."

"You're such a gentleman."

By the time she had walked halfway up the path to the camp, she could see her visitor. Bent over, he was rummaging through the ice chest, selecting a can of soda. His business suit looked incredibly out of place in the primitive camp.

Tentatively, Ryan approached the canvas shade. "I'm Dr. Burke. May I help you?"

Quickly straightening up, her visitor turned to face her.

"Richard!" she gasped. "My God, what are you doing here?"

"Surprised?" He offered a wide grin.

Surprise didn't describe what she was feeling. Shock was a lot closer. "Why didn't you let me know you were coming?"

"Well, if you had a telephone in this godforsaken place, maybe I would have," Richard Brockton replied, looking around the campsite with disdain.

"Why are you here?"

"Is that the best greeting you can give your fiancé?" His mouth moved with the hint of a pout.

"*Ex*-fiancé," Ryan quickly responded, accepting the can of cola he held out to her. Turning away from his attempt to kiss her on the lips, she offered her cheek instead. "Richard, if you've come to try to change my mind—I'm sorry, my decision holds." She dropped into one of the camp chairs and Richard settled himself across the table from her.

"Darling, I know you didn't mean what you said before you left Washington. Break our engagement, indeed." He laughed. "You were just all keyed up about coming here. Although I certainly don't know why." He offered a patronizing smile. "Both your parents and mine were heartbroken when I told them you were having cold feet. Your mother insisted I come and talk with you, and she told me not to take 'no' for an answer. So you see, everyone wants this engagement." Richard placed a small square black velvet box between them on the table.

Ryan was all too familiar with the box. It held the three-carat diamond engagement ring she had returned to Richard Brockton five weeks earlier. It had been a mistake to accept it in the first place. She had foolishly allowed pressure from both his parents and hers to sway her judgment. She and Richard had grown up together—they were friends, nothing more.

Richard tapped on the side of the ring box, pushing it

closer to her. "Put it back on your finger, darling. That's where it belongs." Taking another look around the camp he gave a cynical lift of his brow. "Although I hope you won't wear it while you're grubbing around this horrid, filthy place."

Clasping her hands tightly together on the tabletop, Ryan ignored the velvet box. "Richard, I don't want your ring. I should never have accepted it in the first place."

"My Lord, Ryan, what have you done to yourself?"

Richard either hadn't heard her words or was blatantly ignoring them. She believed it was the latter.

"Have you looked in a mirror lately? Darling, you look positively wrecked, and what kind of a getup are you wearing?" He screwed his face into a grimace. "That shirt and those khaki cargo shorts . . . my Lord, kneesocks? Please tell me that other people don't see you like this . . . well, at least not anyone who matters." A frown creased his brow as he continued to take inventory. "And what *have* you done to your hair? It used to be the most wonderful rich, sable shade of brunette. Now it's sun-bleached—and a ponytail? Really, darling, you look positively . . . agrarian."

Ryan took a long swallow of soda, hoping the icy liquid would cool the rising heat of her temper. It didn't. "Richard, this is what I wear in the field. I'm living in a tent. I'm outdoors at least eighty percent of the time." She took a deep breath. "I'm involved in what's called field research. There isn't a manicurist, a hair salon or a designer dress in miles. Just what did you expect?"

"Well, I certainly didn't expect you'd look like some migrant field hand." His mouth formed a little moue. "And, I expected a more ardent welcome."

Since following her back to camp, Buddy had been leaning against Gaffney's Jeep. Ryan shot him a quick look and with a flip of her hand, tried to shoo him away. Instead of moving off, he plastered a wide grin on his face and crossing one foot over the other, settled in for the rest of the show. Bristling, she turned her attention back to Richard. "Why are you here?"

"Being a part of this project might be fascinating for you,

but do you know how much you're needed at home? Your mother's health . . ." He placed his large, soft, well-manicured hand over her smaller tanned one. "Come home, sweetheart. We can be married by summer's end and . . ."

Ryan pulled her hand away. "Richard, I'm afraid you've wasted your time. I haven't changed my mind. I won't marry you. When this project is finished, I'm going back to Washington." Lifting her hand, she silenced Richard Brockton's imminent protest. "I'm sorry if it's not what you or my parents had in mind; it's what I want. And, as for Mother's health, she's as strong as an ox and you know it." She crossed her arms over her breasts and leaned back in the chair, holding her ground.

"You can't be serious. . . ."

"Richard, you're a dear friend and I'm fond of you . . . as a friend, but it isn't enough for me for a marriage." Ryan looked directly at Richard, her eyes meeting and holding his stunned gaze. "I'm not in love with you."

"In love?" Richard Brockton quickly stood and glared down at her. "Is that what this rebellion of yours is all about . . . being in love? My God, Ryan, grow up." He began to pace. "Our families have been close forever. Our marriage would be a wonderful merger." Richard patted her lightly on the head. "Believe me, darling, the kind of love you're talk-ing about will come after we've married, I promise. But in the meantime, our parents are getting on in years and don't you think we owe it to them to make them happy?"

Ducking out from under his touch, Ryan sighed. "I don't want our parents to be unhappy, but that has nothing to do with whether you and I get married or not. You might think I'm being naive, but I have special ideals about marriage and—"

"Well of course you do," Richard interrupted. "Every young girl does, but that doesn't mean they're realistic. But all this talk of yours about love . . . it's like gallant knights riding great chargers . . . immature drivel."

"Immature drivel?" Ryan shot back, standing and meet-ing him eye to eye. "If that's what you think, then you don't know me at all."

"Of course I do, darling," Richard chuckled as though humoring a child's dark mood. "I know you better than anyone else, I know everything about you."

"Really? What's my favorite color, my favorite food, music or movie?" She waited for a response but none came. "You don't know, do you? These are the easy questions, Richard."

"Ryan, aren't you being a little ridiculous? Do you know my favorite color, food or music or movie?"

"Blue, coquilles St. Jacques, Michael Bolton and *The Firm.*"

His eyes registered his surprise. Trying to parry, Richard Brockton stumbled on his words. "There darling, see, you've helped me prove my point. We're perfectly suited for one another. You know me so well, and as I said, the romance and passion will come after we're married."

"No, Richard, never. Those feelings won't ever exist between us." She wearily rubbed her forehead. "Maybe I'll never find what I'm looking for, but I want the chance to look. I want to marry a man because we're in love with each other, not because it would be a 'good business merger.' " She watched Richard's face, hoping to find some evidence that he understood. The derisive lift of his brow told her he didn't.

"So, until your Prince Charming comes along, you'd rather play at being some sort of female Indiana Jones?"

His words torched her anger. "Play? You think this is play? That's all the respect you have for my career?" She squared her shoulders. "I worked and studied hard, pulled down honors and got the position I wanted. No one gave me the job at the Smithsonian. I earned it. I have the career I want, and I plan to find the other things I'm looking for, too."

"Like romance, love and passion," Richard mocked with his hand dramatically placed over his heart.

"Yes," she answered. "Exactly."

"How can you even think of throwing away such a wonderful opportunity for us?"

Ryan sighed. Picking up the velvet ring box, she took

Richard's hand and folded his fingers around it. "Richard, there is no 'us,' there never was an 'us' and there never will be an 'us.' " She dropped into her chair.

"So you choose all this, this primitive existence, over a wonderfully comfortable life among your own kind of people?" The wide sweep of his arm encompassed the entire campsite and valley.

Ryan bit back the angry words that first wanted to tumble from her lips. Looking into Richard's face and taking a deep breath, she tempered her answer. "Look at this place, Richard. Tell me what you see."

"A river, some hills, a lot of dry grass, trees . . . nothing special. It's not even pretty."

"You are so wrong, so very wrong. This valley is steeped in history. It has an . . . an aura. The essence of an important event still lingers here. This beautiful land is alive with its past. But you could look at it for days and never see what I see. You'd never feel what I feel."

She glanced at Buddy. He still gave no indication of moving away and the maddening grin still creased his face. Resigned to having an audience, Ryan turned back to Richard. "This is what I want to do . . . where I want to be . . . who I want to be."

"Darling, look," Richard countered, using a patronizing tone once again, his hands held out in appeal. "I suppose this discovery of lost tribes, or whatever you're attempting to do, is all very noble. I commend your dedication." He paused to wipe his sweating brow with a pristine handkerchief. "Come home with me. I've got your plane ticket in my pocket."

"Is that a fact," she rebutted quickly. Standing, she met his eyes with a hard glare. She pushed the camp chair under the edge of the table and threw her empty cola can into the trash barrel with a forceful overhand pitch. "I think you should leave now. I've got a lot of work to do—playing Indian—and you've got a plane to catch back to civilization." She turned on her heel and began to walk away.

With a curt, how-did-you-like-that nod in Buddy's direction, she stalked from the camp and headed back the oak tree on the bank of the Little Big Horn River. Settling into the niche on the broad branch, she heard the grind of tires on gravel as Richard Brockton, his custom-tailored suit, marriage merger, his gaudy diamond ring and his rental car retreated up the dirt road to the highway.

At the age of ninety-two, Lucy One Star still cooked and kept house for six members of her family. Her memory was clear and she was having a good time talking about the old days, telling stories about the brave deeds of her ancestors.

"My father, *Aupahu Ma'za*, Iron Wing, was a strong man. He was old and almost blind when I was born, but young, maybe sixteen or eighteen, when he rode with Gall and fought Custer. His father died over there." Lucy pointed to a gully across the river with an up-tilted gesture of her chin. "I was born many years after. My mother was his fifth wife. I will tell you what I know, but I can tell you only about things I heard in the words of others."

Lucy's leathery hands began to unwrap a faded calico bundle that lay across her lap. "I brought these things."

She pulled the cloth back, uncovering a rawhide knife sheath. The decoration on the case that once had been colorful with paints made from berries and clays was now faded and dull. Lucy's package also held a bone hairpipe necklace, old and darkened by the oils and sweat from the skin of its owner. When Lucy unwrapped the last parcel on her lap, Ryan found herself staring at an antique army-issue Spencer rifle. Although the wooden butt of the gun was marred by deep scratches and the oiled finish had long since faded, it appeared as though the rifle would still shoot straight and true.

"My father counted coup on a soldier next to the river south of here when the bluecoats first attacked," Lucy said, lovingly caressing the wooden stock. "His war trophy." Her voice became a whisper. "It should have been buried with him when he died."

Ryan jotted a few lines in her notebook and hearing the click of the cassette in her recorder, opened the cover and turned the tape over to record the rest of Lucy's stories.

"Someone's coming," the old woman said, squinting her eyes and looking up the hill. "Never seen that car 'round here before," she added, her voice flat and unemotional. "Too fancy for any Indian car I know."

The car jolted down the grade toward the camp. A wall of sinister clouds, thunderheads, followed close behind, hanging in the western sky like the immense outstretched wings of a vulture. As the wind picked up, Ryan grabbed her scattering papers and jammed them into her briefcase. Moments later, rain broke from the clouds and began beating down in a torrent. The parched earth drank every drop until saturated, it refused to take in any more water and deep puddles began filling every hollow.

The white Lincoln barreled down the last small hill and pulled to a stop, sliding precariously on the mud. As the driver turned off the motor, a blinding slash of lightning carved across the sky. Startled, Ryan and Lucy One Star both flinched. The loud, rolling boom that followed shook the ground and a sharp metallic stench choked the air. Somewhere nearby the lightning had found a vulnerable target.

"Some old ones would say that was a sign," Lucy One Star said anxiously, looking first at the Lincoln and then the ominous sky. "It's gonna be a bad storm." She gripped the arms of her chair. "Sometimes when it rains hard like this, it makes a flood. I've heard them floods can carry off little kids who play too near the river." She nervously glanced over at Ryan. "Sometimes old women get floated away, too."

"I'll ask Buddy to take you home," Ryan offered, patting Lucy's arm reassuringly. "We can finish talking another time."

The rain increased from moment to moment but the man in the Lincoln stayed in the car, impatiently blowing the horn. Before the last bleat faded, the door on Edwin Gaffney's tent opened and the project director dashed through the downpour, trying to open his umbrella against the rising wind. Anxiously glancing around, he jiggled first on one foot and then the other as his guest quickly got out of the car.

The two men jostled for dry shelter under the small umbrella, the stranger trying to keep his expensive suit and black eel-skin cowboy boots dry. They quickly ran through the rain and disappeared into Gaffney's tent.

Bustling Lucy One Star to his truck, Buddy looked back over his shoulder at Ryan. He jerked his thumb toward Gaffney's tent with a quizzical look on his face and she answered his mute question with a shrug of her shoulders. When had Gaffney returned to camp from the dig site? She'd been surprised to see him, too.

She had barely seen the man's face before Gaffney hustled him into the tent, but he wasn't anyone she'd met from the battleground office. Who was he? What business did he have with Gaffney? Ryan didn't have the answers but she knew her misgivings were caused by more than just the sudden storm.

Less than ten minutes passed before Gaffney's tent flap lifted and the owner of the Lincoln came out carrying Gaffney's umbrella in one hand and a wrapped package in the other. Following close behind, oblivious to the drenching rain, Edwin Gaffney appeared to be upset. His eyes widened, registering his surprise to find Ryan still under the canvas canopy.

"Uh, this is Mr. uh . . . Herbert," Gaffney called out over the sound of the downpour. "He's the editor of the Billings evening paper. They want to do an article on the project."

Gaffney's Mr. Herbert shot a quick glance in Ryan's direction, then ducked out of the rain, sliding behind the steering wheel of the Lincoln. After placing the package on the seat beside him, he tossed the closed umbrella on the backseat. Without even a nod or a word of farewell to Gaffney, he drove out of camp. The Lincoln spewed mud from its tires all the way up the hill.

Gaffney glanced back in Ryan's direction and then quickly retreated into his tent, dodging puddles that stood in his way.

In an instant the deluge slackened to a faint drizzle, but

it was clear from the dark clouds that still hovered overhead it was only a brief lull before the storm unleashed its true fury. In that quiet moment Ryan heard the faint metallic click of the artifact cabinet door in Gaffney's tent being closed and locked.

She looked at the notebook in her hand where she'd jotted down the Lincoln's license number. Why would a newspaper editor from Billings, Montana be driving a car with a Nebraska plate? Why would the editor and not one of his reporters be covering the story? Why would Gaffney offer an interview to a newpaper and turn down *National Geographic*? And why would the editor be taking a wrapped package away from the site? Little doubt about Gaffney remained. Ryan believed she had just witnessed the disappearance of yet another artifact. But which one was now taking a ride to Nebraska? As soon as she could, she would check the ledger.

The wind picked up with a new, determined force and the trees on the riverbank swayed and groaned in protest. In dark, swirling clouds, the flocks of swallows that lived in the cottonwoods along the river darted for safety amongst the branches and huddled down into their nests. With another gust, the camp chairs toppled over and blew end over end until they became tangled in the guide ropes of the canvas shade.

"We're in for a real doozy this time."

Ryan turned to find Daniel Stockard standing behind her beneath the tarpaulin. His clothes were soaked and he was out of breath from running back to camp.

"The storms can get pretty nasty out here. I wouldn't be surprised if we get some hail, too." He peered at the dark sky.

"Do they always come up this fast?" Ryan asked, raising her voice against the building howl of the wind. She brushed her wet hair from her face only to have it blow back across her eyes.

"You bet," Stockard answered, pointing to the western sky. "Look how black it is."

Ryan looked up and shivered. Jags of lightning cut across

the sky and periodically stabbed like white-hot bayonets into the earth below. Soon the brilliant flashes and earth-shaking booms were so close together they seemed to fall one atop the other.

Kovacs and MacMillen rushed under the canopy moments before bean-sized hail joined the rain and began mercilessly to beat a frantic tattoo on the tarpaulin. Wind gusts lifted and released the canvas in quick succession, adding a snapping and popping chorus to the din.

"No telling how long this is going to last," Kovacs shouted over the renewed torrent of rain. He reached up and poked the canvas, raising it high enough to tip off a gallon or two of rainwater and melting hail. "We might as well take cover in our own tents. This canopy's not going to hold up much longer."

He had barely said the words before another burst of wind sent the canvas ballooning upward and the guide ropes twanging in protest. With the next blast, the stakes jerked upward, reluctantly releasing their hold in the ground. Whipping and flailing, the canvas canopy lifted once more before the poles and ropes crumpled and fell impotently to the ground.

"No sense trying to fix it now," Stockard yelled, flinching against the pelting hail. "We'll put it back up when this is over!"

Tightly clutching her briefcase with the recorder and laptop against her chest, Ryan dashed to her tent. The standing water and hail had created hazardous puddles and she almost fell twice. Drenched and shivering, she tried to get her chilled fingers to work at the tent zipper. Opening the flap as little as possible, she slipped inside, permitting only a little water to follow. She prayed the tent wouldn't spring any leaks throughout the storm—but more important, she hoped her notes and equipment were all right. Finding a plastic bag, she slipped her briefcase, the laptop and her notes inside it. Wrapping the bag tightly, she made it as waterproof as possible.

The sound of the pounding rain and hail was louder inside as it battered against the tent roof and walls. "Oh, no," she groaned, spotting puddles already forming in three of the corners. Overhead the nylon roofing bulged inward as a puddle of rainwater collected and began to seep through. Solitary drips soon became a steady trickle, and then a flow.

Gathering the rest of her books and clothes, Ryan stuffed them in her laundry bag and piled it with her other belongings on top of the cot. It was the only dry spot left in the tent. Outside, the wind continued its assault, alternately billowing and slackening the tent walls with loud pops. Once or twice it blew under the flooring, lifting it and spreading the water off in all directions.

The sound of ripping fabric spelled total disaster. Ryan glanced up just in time to see the roof separate from the wall in the southwest corner. Within seconds, the split widened and tore the whole length of the tent. Like a huge pennant, the shredded fabric flapped in the air until another gust tore it away completely. The walls wavered and fell. Inside had become out.

Soaked to the skin, Ryan stood shaking amid the tattered remnants of her tent. Helpless, she watched the wind lift her cot and flip it end over end, dumping everything she owned into the water. The cot continued to somersault across the compound until it crashed into the camp chairs and became entangled in the jumble of the fallen canopy.

Turning toward the camp, she frantically looked for shelter. The other tents seemed to be holding up under the onslaught, but no heroes rushed to her rescue. Stockard and the others probably weren't even aware of her predicament.

Hunched over, clutching the bag with her laptop and notes and protecting it with her body, she made a dash for Gaffney's Jeep. The rain and hail painfully beat down on her back and she felt the chill clear through to her bones.

The Jeep was locked.

Damn! Now what? She shook uncontrollably.

Crouching low, she discovered the Jeep worked as a windbreak. The rain still pummeled her with a vengeance, but at least she was shielded from the cold, driving wind. Closing her eyes, she waited for the storm to end.

She didn't know how long she'd been huddling in the

mud beside the Jeep before she felt the touch on her shoulder.

"Grandpa said we'd better come back and check on ya." Buddy's voice mirrored the concern that showed on his face. "Good thing . . . paleface woman looks like ugly drowned chicken."

She rewarded Buddy's joke with only a wan smile. The rain had slowed to a steady drizzle and the wind had blown itself out of the valley but she was cold—teeth chattering, freezing cold.

"My tent is ruined . . . everything's soaked," she croaked between shivers. "What am I going to do?"

The rain slowed to a mere sprinkling and then stopped completely. The canvas canopy was soon put back up and the tables and chairs were righted. Within an hour the camp was put back to normal, all except Ryan's accommodations. Nothing could be done to salvage her tent. Although the tent pegs still held the flooring to the ground, the roof couldn't be found.

"Looks like someone's going to have to double up," Stockard said.

"That won't be necessary. She don't need a tent," Charley Crying Wolf quietly offered.

Everyone turned to look at the old Lakota.

"Of course she does," Stockard argued. "What's she going to do, sleep under the stars for the rest of the summer?"

"She don't need a tent," Charley repeated with the same tone he'd used the first time. "She's gonna live in something better. I'm gonna bring her my tipi. Tipis don't blow down in a wind."

A little over an hour passed before Buddy's truck came rumbling back down over the hill with a bundle of long tipi poles lashed to the roof.

"There's no telling what kind of shape this thing's in," Kovacs muttered. "It'll probably fall apart in the first breeze and then we'll be right back where we started. Wouldn't a trip to town to pick up a new tent be a better idea?"

Despite everyone's doubts, Buddy efficiently wrapped and tied a long rope around three of the poles about four feet from their tops. With Kovacs and Stockard helping, the poles soon sat upright in a giant tripod. Before twenty minutes had passed more poles were added, the cover put in place and Charley's tipi stood tall in the sunshine. The smoke flaps were spread wide open at the top like the wings of a great white bird.

Ryan stood back and stared at the graceful, simple structure. The old lodge had been painted and although somewhat faded, the colors and figures still showed clearly. The smoke of many fires had discolored the flaps, but the design at the top of the tipi could still be seen—a field of blue broken by solid circles of white. The old people called the design hailstones and only men who showed themselves worthy painted their tipis with this *wakan* pattern.

A wide band of red encircled the bottom of the lodge. Years ago someone had painted a double row of paw prints, one set larger than the other. They appeared to be dog tracks but at close inspection Ryan noticed the pointed toes—wolf tracks, a male and a female. She unconsciously rubbed the goose bumps that immediately rose on her arms. More wolves.

Circling the perimeter of the lodge, Ryan lightly touched it with her fingertips. "Hide!" she said, surprised to find it wasn't made of waterproofed canvas, as modern-made tipis were.

"It's very old," Buddy offered, following close behind her. "Grandpa's had it forever. There's an old picture at home that was taken over seventy years ago. He's just a young buck and is standing in front of this tipi. He calls it his medicine lodge."

"But it's in perfect condition," Ryan said. The hides appeared to be newly tanned. The quillwork and dried deer-toe decorations on the door flap and the wooden pins above the door looked as though they had only recently been crafted.

"This tipi's just used for special times, very special ceremonies, stuff like that. Grandpa says it's his power." Buddy shrugged. "Whatever that means. The old man speaks real strange sometimes." Buddy tapped his fingers on the outer skin. "He's never used it for anything like this before, never let anyone camp in it. It's only been up two or three times that I can remember." He looked up at the long red ribbons tied onto the tips of the poles. They fluttered and waved in the refreshing breeze that had returned in the wake of the storm. "I bet there ain't been too many tipis put up on this land since old General 'Yellow Hair' Custer got his arrow shirt." He paused and ran his hand over the taut hide. "Once I heard Grandpa Charley tell my brother Dillon that this tipi was like a doorway to many places and many things beyond our understanding."

"And is it?" Ryan asked, a slight, teasing smile tugging at the corners of her lips.

"Who knows." Buddy gave another one of his infamous shrugs. "The old man gets kinda weird on us sometimes. Who knows."

"Dr. Burke . . . Ryan," Charley interrupted. "Would you come inside, please?" He held the door flap open, waiting for her.

As Ryan ducked inside, Charley Crying Wolf blocked anyone else from following. "Only Dr. Burke," he said before dropping the flap back down into place.

Too busy looking about the inside of the tipi, Ryan barely noticed she was Charley's only guest. The lodge was as lovely inside as out. The sun filtering through the thin hides created a soft golden glow. Beautiful geometric symbols and pictographs of a spotted horse and rider decorated the wall liner that stretched all the way around the lodge in a magnificent primitive mural. A carpet of thick buffalo robes covered the ground.

Charley stood beside the fire pit and when he turned to face her, his whole bearing had changed. He had suddenly become imposing and mystical. He seemed taller, straighter, younger and his dark eyes seemed to sear into Ryan's soul.

The fire in the pit had burned down to red-hot coals and tendrils of smoke drifted straight up through the open smoke hole. Charley had placed a bundle of sage, another of flat cedar and a braid of sweet grass on the ground beside the fire, leaving just the tips resting in the coals. The herbs smoldered, filling the tipi with a pleasant smoky perfume.

"I would purify this place and say prayers for you to ask the Great Spirit's, Tunkasila's blessings for you. Will you allow me to do these things?" In one hand Charley held a pouch made from the scrap pieces of a Pendleton blanket. He held a single, dark-tipped eagle tail feather in the other.

Ryan nodded. "Yes, I'd be very honored. Thank you."

In a voice soft with reverence, Charles Antone Crying Wolf began to speak the old sacred Lakota words. Holding the feather upright and high in front of himself, he slowly moved around the inside of the tipi until he had faced each of the sacred directions. Dipping his hand into the pouch, he withdrew a small pinch of tobacco. Holding it skyward between his thumb and index finger, he prayed and then scattered the tobacco on the floor. Next, he retrieved the smoldering bundle of flat cedar from the fire. As he slowly passed it near Ryan, a cloud of pungent smoke enveloped her. With flutters of the feather, he lifted the smoke over her body. As it enveloped her, he quietly said his prayers of cleansing and blessing.

"This tipi is very old," Charley began, his lilting Lakota accent strong. "It is older than I am, even older than anyone who still lives in my tribe. This is a special tipi. It is powerful, *wakan*, and filled with the voices of the ancient ones who are now gone a long, long time." The feather continued to move the smoke. "This tipi is filled with their crying. This tipi is filled their laughter and their love.

"This tipi is made from the skins of the sacred *tapté*, the white buffalo cows. It is good, *waste*, that it will now keep you warm at night and give you shelter from the wind and rain." He paused, and patted Ryan's arms and shoulders with the flat of the eagle feather. "This tipi will show you many things, tell you many secrets and give you many answers. The Creator, Wakan Tanka, will watch over you and send the spirit of *sunkmanitu*, the wolf, to walk with you and protect you. This tipi will give you wisdom. *Woiyokipi na wowiyuskin nica u ktelo*. It will bring you much joy and pleasure."

He lifted another cloud of pungent smoke with the blade of the black-and-white feather and moved it up and down her legs.

"You have been sent to help my people the Lakota, our Cheyenne brothers and the Crow people who live here now. This tipi has great power and will bring you the knowledge to do what must be done. It will bring a life to you such as you have never imagined in your time—or any other." He paused and moved the feather again. "Your days will be a great journey. You will see many sad things. There will be many dangers, but there will also be much happiness." Charley paused and continued to speak only after her eyes met his.

"Listen carefully to my words, granddaughter, and remember them well. This tipi is your sanctuary. It is a place of safety for you. In here nothing will harm you. Do you understand?"

Again he waited for her nod before continuing. "This tipi will shelter you and it will give you much strength—inside—here." He lightly thumped over her heart with the eagle feather. "In happiness come into this lodge, in danger come to this place. Do not forget these words I have spoken."

Once again he prayed in Lakota.

What did all his baffling words mean? What was the hidden mystery of his message? What was the power he believed this old tipi held? He had talked about a spirit wolf and the amber-eyed creature of her dream quickly came to mind. Again, the wolf. Why? A tremor, heavy with portent yet cloaked in tempting mystery, skittered through her body.

Chapter 5

DILLON WOLF STEPPED off the curb and strode across the bustling Washington, D.C. street, defying the oncoming traffic. He ignored the irate horn blasts of a city bus and paid little heed to the coarse insults of two taxi drivers. He faced everything in his life in much the same way—straight on and with a great measure of audacity. Most people with whom he came in contact found him abrasive, difficult to deal with and obstinate, but none had ever accused him of backing away from a fight, no matter who his opponent was. Women found him irresistible. It was a fact he was aware of, a fact he accepted and used for his own gain.

Holding his jaw clenched in a hard-edged, determined line, Dillon Wolf's eyes never wavered from the sprawling gray stone government building ahead of him. He stepped up onto the curb, his movements smooth and athletic, and began to climb the bank of stairs up to the entrance. He casually carried his briefcase in his left hand as though the information it held was not very important. But nothing could have been further from the truth.

Dillon had discovered early in his law career that just the right amount of expensive, perfectly tailored, white-establishment clothing set off by a few blatantly Indian touches kept his opponents completely off balance. He had carefully chosen his wardrobe for this meeting with Stanton Adams, in the National Parks Services office. His camel Armani sports jacket, dark brown slacks, silk shirt of the same dark color, custom-made boots and touch of expensive cologne were in complete contradiction to the colorful Indian-beaded bolo tie, buckle and belt he wore. He had tied his near-waist-length hair away from his face and it hung down his back.

When his parents had died, Dillon had followed the traditions of his Lakota and Cheyenne heritage. He had begun his year of mourning by cutting his hair off just below his ears. In the ten years since, it had grown untouched by scissors. Today, the breeze caught and lifted the long, ebony strands as he agilely scaled the broad steps to the building housing the Department of the Interior.

Another long-haired man, dressed in a tie-dyed T-shirt and torn, faded jeans sat sprawled on the steps. "Hey man, peace," he called out, holding his fingers up in the universal "v" sign as Dillon passed. "Custer had it comin', dude."

"Yeah, right," Dillon coolly replied, jostling past a group of camera-toting Japanese tourists and pushing his way through the heavy revolving doors.

The lobby was crowded and people were bunched into little herds waiting for the elevators. It looked like none had stopped on the ground floor in quite a while.

Dillon checked his watch. "Damn." His appointment was for nine. If he waited for an elevator, he'd be late. He didn't intend to keep Stanton Adams waiting for even one minute.

The National Parks office was on the third floor. Dillon took the stairs.

He hated the humid, musty smell of government buildings—they all reminded him of stagnant water or wet, rotting wood and the closed stairwell seemed to magnify the odor. He arrived on the third-floor landing not the least bit out of breath for his quick climb. Opening the fire door, he found the Department of the Interior office. The moldy scent was here, too.

Ignoring the stares of two elderly women and a Chinese man who sat in the waiting area, he approached the receptionist. She was filing her red nails and chatting on the phone with someone named Delores, and ignored him longer than he was willing to wait.

Sharply rapping his knuckles on the counter, Dillon interrupted. "If you wouldn't mind paying some attention to your job, tell Mr. Adams that Dillon Wolf is here to see him? I have a nine o'clock appointment."

The woman glanced up and did the most comic double take he'd ever seen. She clamped her hand over the telephone mouthpiece and from the expression that had frozen on her face, he realized he'd almost received a welcome as rude as the one he'd given her. He set a cold, challenging look upon his face and she backed down. His intimidating mien was well-practiced. Seasoned congressmen and state officials bowed and retreated from its dare. The receptionist didn't have a chance.

Within an instant her manner changed and her face slackened in surprise. She began to stutter and the telephone slid from her hand, clattering loudly as it struck the edge of the desk.

"Oh, my," she breathed, flustered. "You're an Indian, aren't you? Oh my, how silly of me, of course you are." A bright blush stained her cheeks. She lowered her lashes and giggled.

The sound grated like coarse-grit sandpaper on Dillon's nerves and he irritably shifted his briefcase from one hand to the other. *My God, I bet she's got one of those damned Indian warrior stud and breathless, captive white woman romance novels in her desk drawer!* he thought. "Mr. Adams is expecting me . . . today."

Stanton Adams's office was cluttered with files and books piled on his desk, the cabinets and the floor. The man had a comfortable cluttered look about him as well. Dillon brushed by the moon-eyed receptionist who sighed another deep "oh my" as he grazed her arm, and entered the office.

The musty government building smell had been masked by
the thin scent of cinnamon air freshener.

"Mr. Adams." Dillon greeted the man with cool disdain.
Dillon Wolf disliked whites, especially those who worked
for the government. They had done nothing but offer his
people hundreds of years of misery and in his opinion a
government official was lower than a snake's belly and less
trustworthy than the snake itself. He conceded his grandfather could be as benevolent as he wanted to be, but it
wasn't the road Dillon Wolf chose to travel.

"Mr. Wolf, it's a pleasure to finally meet you. I've heard
a great deal about you and the fine work you do with the
Intertribal Legal Coalition." Adams smiled, moving toward
Dillon and extending his hand in a friendly greeting.

Dillon gave the man's hand a perfunctory shake before
coldly dropping it and proceeding to the desk to open his
portfolio.

"We're finally having some good summer weather, aren't
we? I don't think there's a prettier place than Washington
in the spring and early summer. The tulips and cherry blossoms have been magnificent this year. How about some
coffee before we get down to business?" Adams offered.

Dillon ignored the man's attempt at hospitality and
friendly conversation. "How about we get right to it? I've
just gone through five days of moronic governmental red
tape, regulations and bureaucratic bull to get some of this
stuff together. I don't have time to sit and chitchat. When
I'm through giving you the rundown, I don't think you will,
either." Dillon turned to face Stanton Adams. "I want Edwin Gaffney's Little Big Horn project shut down and I want
it done today." He extracted a sheaf of papers from his
portfolio and passed them to Adams.

"All in good time, Mr. Wolf. But first, *I* want some coffee." Adams took the papers and placed them on his desk
without giving them a glance. "Are you sure you wouldn't
like some?"

"Damn it man, while you're sitting on your overstuffed . . . uh . . . chair here in Washington sipping your
damned caffeine, there's another overeducated, pompous

jackass in Montana robbing my people blind. Adams, if you think I'm going to settle for the same old governmental hospitality scam and tap dance, you're wrong. You can knock off your tea-party routine."

"Hmm," Adams responded with a slight smile. "I see the rumors I've heard weren't wrong. 'Opinionated' was the nicest thing I've heard anyone say about you." Adams pointed to an overstuffed chair. "Mr. Wolf, please, have a seat and relax. Since we made this appointment, a few things have come up, changes that might surprise you. We've got a—"

"Changes?" Dillon interrupted sarcastically. "Nothing's changed in a couple of hundred years, that's the surprise. All you *wasicu* still think you can stall me and my people, or promise us more shiny trinkets or a piece of useless radioactive land in Alamagordo. You think you can still get away with letting the white boys like Gaffney take everything that's ours." He pointed emphatically at the papers he'd given Adams that now lay ignored on the man's desk. He turned and glared at Adams. "Hell man, I've got clients whose great grandparents' graves were dug up and whose bones are now on display in some goddamn museum for Sunday sightseers. You ever been on a reservation?"

Stanton Adams shook his head.

"These people are poor. Every day they've gotta decide whether to feed the dog or eat the slop themselves. For many all they've got left are the special places, like the Greasy Grass, the Black Hills, Bear Butte, Wounded Knee, and the things their ancestors left behind. So, take all the coffee breaks you want but nothing is going to happen your way anymore. I don't care what it takes to get through to you people, but this time the only change is that the cowboys and the cavalry lose."

Dillon picked up his documents. Pulling selected pages out of the stack, he began putting them down on Adams's desk one at a time with a loud, deliberate pop.

"I have a signed petition from the Cheyenne tribal council in Montana stating they don't want the ground at the Little Big Horn site disturbed due to religious reasons. They believe there are Indian burials on the encampment side of the river. You'll find provisions for issues of this kind cited in the American Indian Religious Freedom Act."

Slap.

"I've got a petition signed by a majority vote of the tribal council of the Oglala Nation and a letter from the tribal chairman. They want Gaffney stopped for the same reason."

Slap.

"These are petitions signed by the Hunkpapa, the Miniconjou, the Brulé and Sans Arc councils. They want Gaffney out, too."

Slap.

"This is a signed deposition from Charles Crying Wolf, a respected Lakota elder now living on the Cheyenne reserve. He states that artifacts have disappeared from the site. There's evidence they've been removed and sold to private collectors."

Slap.

"I've got a letter and a couple of photographs of recovered items from the head curator of Indian artifacts at the Denver Museum of Art. Apparently someone identifying himself as a private agent for a 'well-known' scientist tried to sell the museum a couple of items from the dig."

Slap.

"I've got a copy of Gaffney's original grant application, where he clearly states the geographical boundaries of the dig, and this is a surveyor's report. Gaffney's digging over twenty feet out of boundary on the southern end."

Slap.

"And this little piece of paper should make you choke on your coffee. This is a stay of permit, signed, sealed and kissed on the backside by Federal Judge Theodore P. Mallory."

Slap.

Dillon turned and faced Stanton Adams. "I think that about covers it. Now, what are you going to do about it?"

Adams didn't appear to be the least bit intimidated by Dillon's hard delivery. "Looks like you've been real busy.

Now, do you take cream and sugar in your coffee or do you like it black?"

Dillon threw himself into the overstuffed chair beside Adams's desk. If it took him all day long, he'd break this man's indifference. This case bothered him a lot. Maybe it was because it hit closer to his own home and his own family more than anything else he'd ever handled through the coalition.

"Okay," Adams said, reentering the room with two steaming mugs and a friendly smile on his lips. "I think we're ready now to get to the bottom of this, don't you?" Adams placed the second cup on the desk in front of Dillon and settled himself into his chair. He began carefully to examine each of the documents Dillon had spread on his desk as if he was studying a serious game of chess. Periodically, he stopped for a sip from his mug or to jot down some notes. Without looking up, Stanton Adams flipped the intercom switch on his desk. "Gladys, when Herb Delveccio gets here, send him right in, would ya?"

Twenty minutes into Dillon's meeting with Adams, Delveccio arrived, sauntering into the office with a crumpled look about him.

"It's about time you found your way down here," Adams jousted. "Man, you look terrible."

"I just got off a plane, damn it. I haven't even had time to go home, kiss the wife and kids or change my underwear." Delveccio parried, grabbing Adam's hand in a hearty handshake.

"Pull up a chair, Herb, but not too close unless you were kidding about that underwear," Adams quipped. "Mr. Wolf here is the I.L.C. lawyer I told you about. He's a real sonofabitch . . . so you two should get along fine. Dillon's got some very fascinating information that's gonna make your day." Adams grinned as if he knew his easy manner irritated Dillon. "I'm sure you've picked up some good stuff since we last talked, too. Oh, sorry," Adams added with a point of his finger from one man to the other. "Dillon Wolf, Herb Delveccio. Herb here is one of the FBI's best. He grew up watching the *Untouchables* on TV and dreaming

of the day he could become Elliot Ness." Adams chuckled.
"Herb and a couple of his men have been assigned to find
out what's going on out there in Montana. They've already
started putting time in on the case."

Adams's news surprised Dillon. He had outlined his concerns when he first talked with Adams on the telephone but
certainly hadn't expected the government to be so quick to
get on the case or so willing to go forward with an inves-
tigation. Hoping to appear unaffected by Adams's disclo-
sure, he casually eased back in his chair. Every cell in his
body burned with hope but common sense and previous
experienced filled him with misgivings. Too many times
his people had heard empty promises and had suffered the
consequences of the government's whims. "I'm listening.
What's your plan?"

"I can certainly appreciate the views of your people and
everything that's gone into your request to have the dig
shut down, but we'd like to ask you to bear with us a little
longer. We don't want to shut Gaffney's project down, not
just yet." Stanton Adams held his hand up to stop Dillon's
impending protest. "Hear me out. Instead of shutting Gaffney down—bing-bang-boom—we've got something else in
mind. You might call it a little sting operation. We'd like
to send some of our boys in there and with your help, see
if we can catch ourselves a thief, 'red' handed, if you'll
pardon my bad pun." Adams looked at Dillon with a wry
smile and lifted his coffee mug in a mock toast before tipping it to his lips. "Are you willing to work with us on this
one, Wolf, or are ya going to be a pain in the ass?"

For the first time in a long time, Dillon felt very good about
something. Too many of his cases ended up with only small
victories or nothing gained at all. This case felt different.
Both Adams and Herb Delveccio seemed to understand the
problems at Gaffney's Little Big Horn project and were
sympathetic to the Indian people's concerns. Better yet,
they were willing to work with him, to do something about
it. For the sake of his people who put their trust and faith
in him, Dillon was willing to ease back on his personal

feelings for a while to see what Stanton Adams and his men could accomplish.

The meeting had lasted almost three and a half hours and in that time a good solid strategy had been put together. Dillon knew it would be difficult for him to stand back and let the government agents put their plan into motion, but they'd promised he would be a part of it all the way. He intended to make sure they kept their word.

Adams had given him photocopies of all of the additional information Delveccio had gathered and Dillon stacked the folders with his attaché on the passenger seat of his rental car. A copy of the "Smithsonian Runner," the newsletter for the institution's new North American Museum of the Indian, lay on top of the pile and he glanced at the headline on the front page. "Smithsonian Anthropologist Ryan Burke Joins Archaeological Dig at the Little Big Horn."

He'd read the article later, but first he wanted to get to the airport before the Washington rush-hour traffic kicked in. He wanted to be on the next available flight back to Montana and give Charley the good news.

Pulling out of the parking lot and into the street, Dillon eased the blue Hertz rental up to the intersection and stopped for the red light. Over the crystalline voice of Celine Dion on the radio singing about the power of love, and above the rattle and whir of the air conditioner, Dillon heard the distant wail and whoop of a siren. He glanced in the rearview mirror and saw the flashing lights on the oncoming police cruiser.

The cop car sped through the heavy traffic, weaving in and out. Its tires squealed with every turn, sending pedestrians scampering back to the sidewalk and forcing cars and trucks off to the side of the street.

The light changed to green. Dillon glanced to his right. If he moved one lane over to the curb, he'd be out of the way. Steering the rental to the right, he pulled to a stop and waited for the speeding police car to pass. As he looked over to the passenger door mirror, the newsletter on the seat beside him caught his attention again. The photograph of the young white woman smiled back at him from the buff-colored page. *So that's Grandpa's new little heroine.*

He had to admit, she was beautiful. She wore her long, dark hair pulled back from her face and a cascade of curls fell over her left shoulder. Her heavily lashed eyes had an intriguing tilt at the outer corners and there was a soft full-ness to her smiling mouth that he liked. If she was this attractive in the photograph, it was a safe bet that in person she'd be a real knockout. Too bad she was white.

Dillon Wolf never denied he was prejudiced. It had come naturally from growing up on the reservation and had left him with very definite preferences in women. Of all the ones he'd ever spent time with or shared his bed with, not all were Lakota, but every one of them had been Indian. A pale-skinned white woman had never turned his head, and yet there was something about the woman in the photo that curiously captured and held him, touched him somewhere deep within and stirred his interest. He picked up the news-letter from the stack of papers and began to scan the par-agraph beneath the picture.

The wail of the siren closed in and within thirty feet of the intersection the patrol car braked hard to avoid a city bus that had turned into its path. The rear tires of the cruiser shrieked in protest and began to slide, slithering left then right, pitching and skidding. Completely out of control, the police car smashed into the back end of Dillon's blue Hertz rental.

Dillon Wolf's last conscious thought was of a beautiful *wasicu* named Ryan Burke.

She was exhausted. Sitting at the table, Ryan fought to keep her eyes open while Stockard, Kovacs and MacMillen chat-ted about the most recent artifacts their dig sites had yielded. Although used to spending a great deal of time alone, Ryan found herself being easily drawn into a friend-ship with the three men. Gaffney had taken his supper alone in his tent and conversation was more animated and relaxed in his absence.

Taking a sip of tart lemonade and with the last crumbs of Aunt Edith's apple pie a delicious memory, Ryan sleepily watched as Buddy cleared and cleaned the supper dishes, lit the evening lanterns and left for home with a tired wave of his hand. The clank and rumble of his old truck disturbed the quiet evening for only a few minutes before it cleared the crest of the hill and dropped out of sight.

"I've got to admit," Daniel Stockard said, "this site is yielding a lot more artifacts than I first imagined it would. We've found some pretty impressive ones, too."

"Gaffney could put together an awesome museum tour, if he'd quit pilfering," Stockard murmured sarcastically.

"Come on, Dan," MacMillen rebutted. "We still don't have any positive proof he's stealing. Besides, at this point it could be any one of us."

"Really, Mac, sometimes I wonder about you. Look at the facts. Who has access? You? Me? Kovacs? I don't think so." Stockard tapped his spoon against his mug, emphasizing his point.

"Thanks Dan, I appreciate your vote of confidence," Kovacs chuckled. "What about Buddy? He's here alone in camp most of the day. Or what about his grandfather? That old man shows up regularly and not always when anyone's here, either."

"No. I think the old man's pretty much in the clear. Granted he's got a beef with the project, but I don't think he'd have the contacts to sell the stuff." Stockard pointed toward Ryan. "Ryan's in the clear." He leaned over and patted Ryan on the hand with feigned consolation, softening his teasing words. "Some things disappeared before she got here."

"Thanks," she grinned. "I guess I can cancel the retainer I had with Johnnie Cochran. Has anyone confronted Gaffney with—"

"With what?" Stockard interrupted. "He's very cleverly eliminated any proof the missing artifacts even existed. It wouldn't do any good to confront him and it might blow us all out of the water."

"Well, I'd like to know how he's getting the stuff out of here," Kovacs grumbled.

"Hell, he might be getting it out of camp by using trained gophers for all I know," Stockard offered.

MacMillen ignored Stockard's cynical humor. "You're right. There just isn't any proof and until there is I don't think we can convict anyone, not even Gaffney."

"I agree." Ryan offered a small nod but the image of the man in the Lincoln immediately came to mind and she glanced up at the men sitting at the table. Had any of them seen him, too? She hadn't said anything to them about Gaffney's visitor and was undecided whether she should now or not. *If I tell them, what good would it do? I don't know anything for sure. No, I'll wait. Without proof anything I'd say would just be gossip and speculation.*

"It appears that until the whole thing is cleared up, we've got a mystery on our hands," MacMillen mused.

"Why don't we call in the Feds and let them handle it? It's their jurisdiction anyway," Kovacs proposed. "That'll settle the whole thing once and for all and we won't have to worry about Gaffney ruining all of our careers, especially after it's known we blew the whistle on him."

"Are you crazy?" Stockard quickly challenged. "Bringing in the Feds would also bring this whole project to a screaming halt, along with our summer jobs, salaries and any possible publications. I don't know about you, but I've got a few creditors who'd be a little put out if my payments stopped. No, we'll have to bide our time and wait for Gaffney to make a slip."

Apologizing for a wide yawn and fending off MacMillen's offer to regale her with a bedtime story, Ryan headed for Charley Crying Wolf's old tipi. She hadn't been to bed this early in years but the golden glow from the lantern inside the lodge seemed too irresistible to ignore.

Stepping inside the lodge, Ryan felt warm and cozy. The feeling wrapped around her and eased her into a sheltered sense of lethargy. The storm had left her with a pile of wet and dirtied clothes and her favorite Mickey Mouse nightshirt felt damp against her skin. Her pillow and blankets did, too.

Settling down on the cot, she thought about Richard and

his recent visit. Yes, she'd made the right decision, even if it meant more discord with her parents. She snuggled in the folds of the damp blanket. *There's no turning back. This is what I want.* She glanced around the inside of the tipi and breathed the sweet, fresh Montana air. *My new life begins now, tonight—here in this valley.* "And, who knows what it will bring," she whispered.

Chapter 6

THE MACHINES BESIDE the patient's bed in the intensive care unit efficiently beeped and clicked. Digitalized information showed on each monitor, blood pressure, temperature, respirations. A luminous green line on the screen of another monitor peaked and dropped then peaked again, giving visual proof that the patient's heart was vigorous and regular. With a steady rhythm, a respirator fed an oxygen-rich mixture of air into the patient's lungs through the intubation tube in his throat.

Outside, night had fallen over Washington. Most of the vacationers had gone back their hotels but a few remained on the steps of the Lincoln Memorial gazing in awe at the large illuminated statue of America's great emancipator. Limousines glided along the streets, taking their bureaucratic passengers wherever politicians went after dark.

In the dim light of the hospital room, the evening-shift nurse carefully inspected the pump, double-checking the ratio of saline and mannitol intravenous in the patient's arm. Turning her attention to the tall column of high-tech monitors, she gave a slight satisfied nod and penned the information each was registering on the patient's chart. Closing the chart and placing it on the bedside tray, she moved back to the man on the bed and carefully lifted the gauze dressing from the wound on his forehead. The bruising extended beyond a cut that had required only a few stitches. There was very little swelling.

"Don't you know that heads don't go through windshields without breaking and causing you all sorts of trouble?" she chided as though Dillon Wolf were conscious and could understand. Her gloved fingers lifted the bandages covering the second wound, a long gash that ran the edge of his left jaw from his earlobe to his chin. The broken windshield had sliced mere inches away from his jugular vein, an inch or two away from certain death. Beth smiled. Whoever had sutured the wound had taken the care of a well-practiced plastic surgeon. She tenderly brushed a few long ebony strands of hair away from Dillon Wolf's cheek, gazed down at him—disheartened—and shook her head.

"Darlin', it's a damned shame," she whispered. "You're the most gorgeous hunk I've ever seen, and honey, I've seen a bunch. If you don't pull through this mess, how am I ever going to put my super-duper moves on you and show you off to the girls at my next Tupperware party? And where was your seat belt?"

"How's he doing, Beth?"

The nurse looked up at the young doctor who had pulled evening duty. Picking up Dillon Wolf's chart, he sank down in the bedside chair and flipped through the pages.

"Not too good, Dr. Sloan. He's slipping a little further away from us with each passing hour. His reflexes aren't as responsive as they were when he was brought in. I was just about to give you a call."

"Let's take a look at Mr. Wolf and see what we can find." Lowering the sheet from Dillon's chest, Ned Sloan pinched the aureole tissue of Dillon's left nipple. A slight shake of Sloan's head clearly reported Dillon Wolf's lack of reaction. Lifting the lid over Dillon's left eye and then his right, Sloan flicked his pocket flashlight on and passed the light back and forth, shining the beam first in one eye and then the other.

"Dilation and contraction are pretty sluggish."

"I'd take my clothes off and dance nude if I thought it'd help bring him back," Beth murmured, checking the connections on the respirator and monitoring the output of oxygen.

"We just might need to take you up on that if he slides any further into this blasted coma. I'd understand it more if there was more swelling. I just don't know. I've got Steve Douglas coming in from Neuro to take a look at him in the morning. Douglas is the best around and if anyone can turn Mr. Wolf around, he can." Ned Sloan moved away from the bed. "Call me if there's another change. I'm on 'til midnight."

Ned Sloan looked back over his shoulder at Dillon Wolf's tall frame lying impotently in the raised hospital bed, tubes and wires monitoring his tenuous thread to life. "Do you know who this guy is?"

Beth Thomas shook her head. "No, not really. I don't know anything more than what's on his chart."

"I've seen him on a couple of those network news-magazine shows," Sloan said. "He's some kind of heavy gun, militant attorney for Indian rights with that Intertribal Coalition group. He's got a reputation for really sticking it hard to just about everyone he's been up against. Take good care of him, Beth. Keep talking nice and don't piss him off." Sloan made a gesture as though he was drawing a knife across the top of his head. "No telling how bad you'd look without your pretty hair."

Alone once again with her patient, Beth Thomas settled into the chair beside his bed. "Dillon Wolf, great warrior lawyer, eh? You damned well better fight this thing harder than you've ever fought anything before in your life."

Chapter 7

FROM HER COT, Ryan listened to the soothing voices of the night critter lullaby. The scent of sage and cedar smoke still clung to the tipi walls offering the sweet essence of a perfumed drug. She breathed the pungent aroma deeply into her lungs and a delightful sensation of weightlessness washed over her body. She felt it gently lift and cradle her and the little voice of reason that resided in the sensible corner of her mind told her that floating over your bed was impossible. But another—the more beguiling voice of adventure and illusion—told her to believe anything she wanted to, and tonight if she wanted to float on air, she could. A languid smile lifted the corners of her mouth. Floating on air was exactly what she wanted to do.

Through eyelids heavy with impending sleep, her gaze wandered upward through the smoke hole to the night sky beyond. What she saw didn't make any sense but she couldn't get her brain to figure out the bewildering puzzle.

Twinkling brightly against the black velvet sky, the splash of stars appeared to be close enough to touch. She raised her hand upward lethargically, stretching and spreading her fingers wide, reaching as high as she could. Then slowly, almost undetectable at first, the sparkling pinpoints of light began to move. They stirred counterclockwise. She frowned—that didn't seem right. She followed the lazy spin of the stars with the tip of her index finger. Revolving and spinning, going faster and faster, they picked up speed with each rotation until they became a blurred eddy. One star blended into another, creating a misty whirlpool. Her finger could no longer follow the movement, and feeling light-headed, she closed her eyes against the dizzying spin. Her hand dropped back to her side.

Within moments everything fell back into balance and Ryan relaxed with a deep sigh. Surrendering willingly, she nestled into the sweet embrace of sleep. Somewhere in that special place between quiet sleep and beguiling dreams, she waited patiently for what was to come. Her wait wasn't long.

Shadows flitted and danced on tiptoe through the edge of her dream, filling her mind with furtive and unfamiliar visions and faces. Protesting, a light moan filled her throat and she stirred restlessly, tossing and turning on her cot until the blankets slid from the bed and fell in a heap on the ground.

A thick fog swirled and billowed, filling each corner of her dream. And then they were there.

Moving toward her, they slipped through the mist, their phantom arms extended, hands reaching out. With mouths open and eyes spilling tears, they cried and pleaded. They were the old ones—the Oglala, Hunkpapa, Minneconjou, Brulé and Sans Arcs; the Santee, Yanktonais and Cheyenne. Pain and distress etched their faces and she heard it in their plaintive wails. They beckoned to her. Without hesitation she went, crossing over the silver thread of reality, moving into the realm of her dream.

The cacophony of their pleas climbed higher and higher and then suddenly changed tone until once again the howl of a wolf filled her head and touched her soul. As if directed by some unheard command, the haunts floated away, dissolving into nothing more than vague shadows. Then, from deep within the mantle of mist, a lone figure stepped forward, a man, tall, mysterious, beautiful. He waited.

The disembodied voices joined together in a chorus that wound around and through her dream. *"Ei-yee tuwu u sunk-manitu e*, the wolf has come, *ei-yee tuwu u, sunkmanitu e."*

The fog swirled and surged in a maelstrom up and around the man's body as he moved forward. He held out his hand, reaching toward her, inviting her to join him on the misty path.

He was Lakota. He was magnificent. His tall body was lean and hard-muscled and creamed-colored buckskin leggings sheathed his long legs. A breechclout of navy blue trade cloth hung from his waist, with the bottom hem resting just above his knees. Elegantly decorated moccasins encased his feet and a finely made bone breastplate trimmed with glinting brass beads, abalone shells and red ribbons, hung from around his neck. The luxurious pelt of a gray wolf covered his head and shoulders. The furred skull of the animal, like a mask, nearly covered his face. Its fleeced ears stood upright, pricked forward as if listening for every sound and hearing all. The Lakota appeared to be half man, half beast, and Ryan feared both.

Dark eyes, glinting like polished obsidian, stared at her, captured her gaze and commanded her attention. In the shadows of her dream, she watched, spellbound, as a slight knowing smile curved his mouth. Again he beckoned to her, inviting her to move closer, coaxing her to deny reality entirely.

"Come to me now. Join me. Come quickly." His voice filled her head, her heart and echoed throughout her soul.

"No . . . please . . . I can't . . ." She shook her head and tried to turn away. She couldn't. He held her captive, ruling her heart and her spirit.

Blue flames leapt and danced behind him, outlining his body with a halo of shimmering light. He took a single step forward and then stopped. His dark gaze never wavered from hers as he slowly reached up and removed the wolf skin from his head. Holding the wolf skin out as though proving to her that it was only a furred hide, he gave it a slight shake. Then, with a "watch this" lift to his brow, he dropped the pelt to the ground where it gracefully settled

in a soft heap at his feet. He lifted his arms skyward as if
making an appeal and the blue halo around his body flared
high and the heat of it touched Ryan. It enveloped her. It
scorched her. It embraced her.

The Lakota slowly lowered his arms and his eyes sought
hers once again. A teasing smile lifted his beautifully
shaped mouth and he pointed to the pelt at his feet.

Following the command of his hand, Ryan looked down.

The hide stirred.

Her heart quickened.

Nearly undetectable at first, the fur began to shift. Gathering energy, it quivered, rippled and then moved more
openly, expanding, filling, swelling. Taking shape, it
molded itself until it was whole, until it was alive, until it
rose up and stood on four furred legs. Until it was once
again a wolf.

The beast yawned and lazily stretched low on its front
paws as if to remove the kinks and cramps that had touched
its muscles while it was becoming. As it moved, it continued to grow, increasing in length and height and bulk.
Slowly shaking its lush coat, the creature circled around the
Lakota, rubbing its body against the man's legs, moving its
bushy tail back and forth in a contented wag. Settling itself
complacently beside the Lakota, the wolf sat. Pressing its
broad, shaggy head against the man's knee, it looked up at
the warrior, adoration filling its amber gaze.

The Lakota's fingers grazed across the crest of wolf's
head, moving through the fur with a caress that told these
two were brothers. And then the beast turned and fixed its
beguiling yellow stare upon Ryan. Like its master's, its eyes
never wavered. Once again the mist thickened, enveloping
everything in a lazy vortex and then it waned. The Lakota
seemed to be closer now. Every detail about him was
clearer, sharper, and still Ryan couldn't take her gaze away
from him.

His hair was long, very long, and black as a raven's
shoulder. On the right side of his head it hung loose nearly
to his waist—thick, lustrous and free from ties or decoration. On the left it was plaited in a single braid and wrapped

with a strip of red cloth. Tied to the narrow scalp-lock braid at the crown of his head, two dark-tipped eagle feathers fluttered in a phantom breeze. A looped chain of tiny brass beads, hawk bells and polished shell disks hung from the knot and trailed down over his shoulder. His height was commanding, well over six feet, and his body was finely sculpted with muscles that lay carved and ridged with powerful definition across his shoulders, his arms and down the broad expanse of his chest to his narrow waist.

The bridge of his nose was straight, flaring slightly at the nostrils; and his lips were full, well-molded and curved in the slightest of smiles. There was a noble arch to his black brows and his dark eyes were temperate now but gave promise of a merciless nature when provoked. His face held the beauty of his race but there was also a refined, yet haughty, handsomeness that demanded admiration without conceit.

Once again he beckoned, his petition silent but very clear.

Hesitantly, she moved toward him and he rewarded her with a broadening of the smile. Her soul knew him, recognized the height and breadth of him, recognized the essence and spirit of him and all of her fears vanished.

"Wolf." She breathed his name, already knowing it in her heart.

"Come to me, it is our time. Come to me, be with me now."

Off somewhere on the grassy slopes of the Little Big Horn Valley and in a shadowed corner of her mind, she heard a lone wolf lift its voice and call out into the night air. The mournful notes echoed and reechoed, rose and fell and cruelly tugged at her, heartlessly coaxing her back to reality, pulling her further and further away from the extraordinary warrior in her dream.

Slowly his image slipped away, fading until he had completely vanished like the wisps of a morning ground fog along the banks of the Greasy Grass; fading away until nothing but the regret in her soul and the wild beating of her heart remained to prove his existence.

Ryan awoke with a start. Her heart was pounding a loud tattoo, loud enough to ring in her ears and her breath quavered in little shallow puffs. She squinted against the bright sunlight that shone through the tipi smoke hole and fell directly onto her cot. Her entire body was coated in a light film of sweat and her hair was damp and clung to her head and face. There was the lingering impression that she had fallen back onto her bed from a great height. She felt dizzy.

It was warm in the lodge and an odd tinge of electrical energy hung in the air. She could almost taste the tang of it in her mouth. It remained for only a moment and then quickly evaporated, defying anyone to prove it had ever been there.

"My God!" she panted. "What a dream!" She placed her hand over her heart and felt its rapid knocking beneath her breast.

Swinging her legs over the edge of her cot, she tried to stand but her knees trembled and threatened to fold beneath her. Her head swam with a giddy spin. She sat for a few moments longer, trying to collect her wits and calm the disquiet that still held her. If she closed her eyes, even for a moment, she was positive the image of the splendid Lakota would return, faithful in every detail. Then she discovered that even with her eyes open, she could clearly recall every facet of the dream, of the wolf, of the man.

It was late, well past eight-thirty when she stepped from the tipi and the sun had already begun to heat the day. It was going to be a scorcher, and with all the rain that had soaked into the ground the day before, it was going to be brutally humid as well. A quick glance around confirmed her suspicions. She and Buddy were the only two left in camp. The others had already eaten breakfast and gone off to the dig site.

"When you decide to sleep in, Doc, you don't kid around," Buddy said, handing her a tepid plate of scrambled eggs, boiled potatoes and a cold piece of fry bread. She sat down and stared at the unappetizing meal and allowed the lingering tendrils of the dream to wrap themselves around her mind again.

Buddy placed a mug of hot coffee on the table in front of her. "This is yesterday's, warmed up. Economics, Gaffney style."

Pulled from her thoughts, she looked into mug. The brew was the color of dirt and an iridescent oil slick floated on the surface. She closed her eyes, hoping to ignore its presence, and raised the cup to her lips. She grimaced with a hard shudder and wrinkled her nose against the bitter taste.

"I suppose you can make better?" Buddy sullenly questioned.

"Maybe."

"Maybe if you get up on time tomorrow and if our supplies don't get wet again, maybe you can show me how it's done."

Buddy's tone surprised Ryan. It was testy and so unlike him. She touched his arm. "Buddy, I'm sorry about the coffee, but it takes more than me screwing up my face to put you in this kind of mood. What's wrong?"

The complacent shrug of his shoulders returned.

"What's the matter? Something's bothering you."

He lifted his "Eat Possum" ballcap and wiped across his brow with the sleeve of his T-shirt, but his frown remained. "I'm sorry Doc, I shouldn't take it out on you." His eyes met hers and then as if he was unwilling or unable to allow her to see his emotions, he set his gaze across the river. "On top of Gaffney's usual ranting and raving, Grandpa got a phone call last night. My brother Dillon's in the hospital in Washington."

"Oh, Buddy, I'm so sorry." She took his hand in hers. "What's the matter? Is he—"

"From what the doctor told Grandpa, Dillon's car was hit pretty hard by a speeding cop car. I guess he's in bad shape. Charley says he's unconscious, like a coma or something." He slowly turned and looked at her.

Ryan could see the frightened, haunted look in the boy's teary eyes. He had lost his mother and father in an accident and now his brother had been seriously injured in another. "Is there anything I can do to help? I've got friends in Washington who could look in on him or if either you or

Charley are planning to go and need a place to stay, you're welcome to use my apartment." She lightly squeezed his hand, offering her support.

"Naw, that's okay. Thanks anyway, Doc." Buddy plopped the cap back on his head, passed his hand across his eyes and slouched down in the chair across the table from her. "Grandpa's home with his feathers and cedar, singing some old songs and doin' some heavy-duty old-time ceremony stuff." He straightened the cap with a tug on the bill. "Besides, rez Indians don't put much faith in big city hospitals. We'll wait here for news."

He lifted Ryan's coffee mug, took a sip and grimaced. "You're right. This stuff's shit." He pitched the coffee out on the ground, glanced up at Ryan and offered a wan smile. "When Grandpa talked to the doc at the hospital, he said he'd call from time to time and let us know how Dillon's doin'."

Ryan nodded, and swallowed an unappetizing mouthful of cold eggs. "Buddy, please keep me posted and let me know if there's anything I can do to help. Maybe my boss at the Smithsonian could keep an eye on things for you."

"Yeah, sure, maybe that'd be okay, but like I said, Charley's taking care of things in his own way. Aunt Edith's wailin' like Dillon's already dead. We ain't been that close, there's over twelve years between us, but he's still my brother, and well . . . you know?" Buddy's voice cracked with emotion and his eyes refilled with tears.

"Buddy, I'm sure he's going to be fine." She patted his hand. "Don't forget, let me know if there's anything I can do."

"Yeah, okay."

Looking down at her plate, Ryan pushed her cold eggs around with her fork and finally shoved the dish aside. "I don't have any interviews scheduled today but I do have a bag of wet, filthy clothes thanks to yesterday's storm. I need a Laundromat." She cast a quick look at Buddy. Maybe something to get his mind off his brother for a while, something to cheer him up a little, would be in order. "How about you and I take the day off? You can drive me to the nearest Laundromat and then we'll find a couple of thick, juicy hamburgers, two double orders of greasy fries, a couple of Mountain Dews and two huge triple hot fudge ice-cream sundaes with whipped cream and chopped nuts. That ought to cheer us both up. My treat."

"Sorry Doc, no can do." Buddy glanced at her, then quickly looked away and lowered his head, quickly hiding his reddened eyes behind a pair of wraparound sunglasses. "I've got orders to stick around here today and get this place back in shape." He forced a cheerful smile. "If you give me a rain check, I'll tell ya what . . . you can take my Ford pony and hit the Laundromat yourself. I'll give you directions to the Suds-Your-Duds in Hardin." Buddy cleared her dishes from the table and grimaced at the glob of eggs on the plate. "They've got a Laundromat down the road, but I think you're best to stay out of that Crow rez town. They ain't too excited about any of us down here at the park and you'd be a sittin' duck for some of them reservation romeos."

Ryan nodded. "Are you sure your truck can make the trip?"

"Hell, that old pickup can probably get there and back without a driver! Just be gentle, don't scare it, feed it some of that sweet 'uptown' gas and you'll get along fine." He dug in his jeans pocket for the keys and tossed them on the table. "By the way, how'd you sleep last night?"

Startled by his question, she answered too quickly, too sharply, as the exciting image of the splendid Lakota immediately filled her mind. "Fine. Why?"

"Hey, I just asked, just bein' polite—sorry." Buddy backed away from her, holding his hands up in self-defense. "I didn't know if that was the first time you'd ever slept in a tipi. I know some of you *wasicu* ain't never had that total Indian experience before and you get all excited and stay awake half the night imagining all sorts of heavy spiritual things." A mischievous grin lit up his face and he turned back to his chores, chuckling to himself. "Whew, ain't we touchy this morning?"

"Sorry." She laughed sheepishly. "You're right, I didn't

sleep too well." She rose from the table and headed for the tipi to get her dirty clothes.

"Hey Doc, you forget something?"

She deftly caught the truck keys Buddy tossed to her.

It was well after seven o'clock before Ryan had completed her laundry and shopping and was back on the shortcut road to camp. Six miles out of town, Buddy's pony decided to get ornery. Twice the motor died. It bucked and limped another four miles or so but the third time the engine sput-tered, it coughed and came to a dead stop. She turned the key in the ignition a few times. The resulting metallic click was very unpromising.

"Damn, this is great . . . just great!"

Ryan slid out from behind the steering wheel. Maybe a jiggle of a wire or a swat on something else black and greasy would get the motor running again. Her fingers worked at the hood latch. It was rusty, which didn't surprise her, but finally gave way with an agonizing screech. Hold-ing the hood up with one hand, she peered into the dark, oily maw of the engine compartment. A thin wisp of smoke trailed upwards from somewhere under an incredible tangle of wires and then dissipated into the dusk of evening.

"Wonderful," she groaned. "Couldn't you have just lived long enough to get me back to camp?"

Night was quickly settling onto the plain and she had no choice but to abandon the truck on the side of the road. Not wanting to tote the heavy bag of clean laundry five or six miles back to camp, she left it in the truck and set out on foot. Her sneakers kicked up wisps of dirt as she moved along the berm. Maybe someone would come along and give her a ride. No. Both Buddy and Stockard had warned her enough times to keep clear of the locals when she was alone. There probably wouldn't be much traffic on the road this time of night, anyway.

Overhead, the sky had taken on the dark shade of night and was clear except for one thin trailing cloud that had draped itself across the lower edge of the moon. It was bright enough to light her way. She kept to the road instead

of trying to cut across the wide grassy plain. With the go-
pher holes, rattlesnakes or whatever other wildlife might be
skulking around, she knew the road was the safest route.
Wolves. She'd forgotten about wolves. Were there really
any in Montana? She remembered the mournful howl she'd
heard the night before. Had it been real or just a part of
her dream? She shivered. "Get a grip on yourself," she
muttered.

The image of the Lakota flashed through her head. Had
he ever ridden these hills? She laughed. What a ridiculous
thing to wonder about. He *was* a dream, an illusion.

An eerie, uncanny pall blanketed the night and an uneasy
prickling niggled at the back of her neck. Her pulse began
to race and she felt the bitter sting of adrenaline as it surged
through her veins, heightening every sense. Her nerves felt
raw and sensitive enough to feel even the light brush of a
shadow.

She had experienced this feeling before. She had felt its
touch when she had toured the battlefield at Gettysburg and
again when she had stood at sunset on the ramparts at
Vicksburg in Mississippi. At both places she'd been filled
with an overwhelming sorrow. There had been the poignant
awareness that brave men had died on the ground where
she stood. The earth had been baptized with their blood and
because of that, the ground held some kind of special presence, an energy, a spiritual power. Ryan knew the Lakota
referred to something like this as *wakan*. The Little Big
Horn Valley was definitely *wakan*.

She walked purposefully, trying to keep her stride confident and sure, trying to keep her mind busy with daylight
thoughts, but the shadows and haunts stayed. Her footfalls
fell faster and faster and she soon found herself jogging. A
painful stitch bit into her side and she pulled to stop. She
couldn't run all the way back to camp. And if she didn't
get a tight rein on her imagination she would begin to en-
vision all sorts of spooky things.

Breathless, Ryan bent over. Resting her hands on her
knees, she drew a couple of slow, deep breaths. The cramp
eased and she moved off again toward camp, trying bravely

to whistle a jaunty tune, but the images of the ghosts of the Little Big Horn remained. They rode their war ponies along the road beside her and the women and children stood mute sentinel in the roadside grass.

Ryan had no idea how late it was when she finally walked into camp. Everything was dark and she'd almost missed the site entirely. It had been the old tipi, luminous in the moonlight, that had been her beacon. The lodge glowed with a soft golden light and when she lifted the flap she saw that Buddy had lit the small night fire. It burned a cheery welcome.

"Well, at least someone cares. Thank you, Buddy boy. You've earned a quadruple hot fudge sundae for this."

A clean towel and a couple of blankets lay on her cot. A note sat on top of the pile.

> *Doc...*
>
> *I should've given you a curfew! Why didn't you tell me you were going to keep my truck and run off with old Floyd from the Suds-Your-Duds? Gaffney's going to have to drive me home and he's real ticked off with you! I think you're going to get grounded!*
>
> *Aunty and Charley were here this afternoon. She brought you clean towels, soap, a couple of dry blankets and a pillow. I hope the fire lasts long enough so you won't stumble around in the dark trying to find your bed.*
>
> *Word's not too good about Dillon, he's still out of it. When you say your bedtime prayers, how about putting in a good word for him? I suppose white prayers are as good as Charley's red ones. Right?*
>
> *Buddy*

Smiling, Ryan folded the note and placed it on the small camp table. Gaffney would surely have a few choice words for her in the morning but she hoped she could postpone his grilling until after she'd borrowed his Jeep to go back to Buddy's truck.

Ryan was tired. Her legs were beginning to cramp and the muscles in her calves ached. A quick bath would feel wonderful. Taking the clean towel and the fresh bar of soap, she slipped out of camp and headed down the path to the Little Big Horn.

After rinsing her clothes, she stepped into the water. The river was still chilly from the slow melting snows in the Big Horn Mountains but she waded in until the water lapped at her waist. Before she could talk herself out it, she dunked and resurfaced in the next instant, shivering, and drawing a shuddering gasp. Ducking under again, she worked the bar of soap against her skin, suffering the cold water long enough to shampoo her hair and rinse the road dust from her body. Shaving her legs would have to wait.

With her teeth chattering and a renewed epidemic of goose bumps, she wrapped the towel around her body. Gathering her damp clothes, she dashed up the path to the tipi.

After adding another couple of pieces of wood to the fire, she dried herself as the logs crackled and popped and the hot flames licked at the bark. The dry wood was soon ablaze, giving off a wonderful heat that chased her chill away. Draping her wet clothing over the camp chair near the fire pit to dry, she drew the other chair close to the flames and sat. The delicious heat soon dried her long hair, warmed her naked body and made her drowsy. Yawning, she stood and stretched, then reached for her nightshirt. "Oh no," she muttered. "Damn, everything is in Buddy's truck."

With no other choice, she slipped naked under the pink blanket Aunt Edith had left for her. Pulling it up around her bare shoulders, she snuggled down, quickly finding her favorite sleeping niche.

Ryan closed her eyes and on the next breath, pungent and sweet, stronger than she remembered it had been the night before, the fragrance of cedar and sage filled her nostrils. She inhaled, taking the scent deeply into her lungs. She loved the smell of the old tipi.

Somewhere outside on the hillside—or was it inside her head—the lone wolf returned to howl a lullaby, its voice carrying clearly across the valley. Sleep came and so did the dream.

Chapter 8

"WHAT'S THE GOOD word tonight, Beth?" Dr. Sloan approached the patient's bed. "Looks like the joint's really jumping." He glanced around at the beds that held other ICU patients.

"Yeah, I guess you could say we're a little busy. We've got a full house," Beth Thomas answered, not taking her eyes from the monitors beside Dillon Wolf's bed. "You know, I just don't get it. This afternoon he was doing fine, his vitals were good, his pressure was up and according to the day shift's report, we were getting some good reflex responses. But tonight, we've got another story going . . . again."

Used to trusting her own skills and still not confident with all the newfangled equipment attached to Dillon Wolf, Beth counted the thready beats of Dillon Wolf's pulse, her fingertips riding lightly on his wrist. "Dammit, everything's down and it's still sliding. This one makes me nervous." The steady push and pull of the rich mix of air and oxygen through the respirator nearly covered her quiet voice.

"Well, if it makes you feel any better, Dr. Douglas from Neuro said he couldn't figure out why this was such a sour case, either," Ned Sloan answered. Picking up Dillon's chart, he scanned the entries made within the past twenty-four hours.

"His heart rate's all over the map and his O_2 saturations have dropped." She adjusted the bandage on Dillon's jaw and shook her head. "I keep telling him, he's not cooperating."

"CAT scan showed no brain swelling, his concussion is moderate, there's no fracture, no loose fragments of bone, and there's no damage to the cervical spine. I just don't get it. You're right, his response to treatment doesn't make any sense." Ned Sloan passed Dillon's chart back to Beth and watched as she added a few notations to the page. "He's got me stumped. It's like someone else is in control, pulling the strings and not letting us in on what's going on."

"You just might have that right," she whispered.

One day slid into the next. The evening shift left and the night shift signed on. In the nurses' station they gathered and chatted quietly among themselves, yet each was fully aware of the exacting rhythms of bleeps and blips on their patients' monitors. The only other sound on the unit throughout the night was the faint squeaking of their rubber-soled shoes as they moved about doing their bedside checks.

With the early light of dawn, the nurses began preparing for the day shift to arrive, making notes for staff report, thankful that the night had passed without an incident.

Ned Sloan ended his double shift and was ready to go home for some much-needed sleep. "Good-bye ladies, have a good day," he said, rising from the doctor's desk in the nurses' station. "I'm going to go home, climb into my jammies and hug my pillow for a couple of hours."

The hospital was waking up. Waiting for the elevator, Sloan impatiently punched the button and slouched against the wall, waiting for the car to climb to the third floor. Over the faint whir of the elevator cables he heard the subtle change of rhythm on an ICU monitor down the hall. In little more than a second or two, an alarm gave off a warning.

"Oh shit," he hissed.

"Code," one of the nurses called. "We've got Code Blue."

"Get some help up here!"

"Hurry, we're losing him!"

"We need a doc in here—STAT!"

Above the nurses' voices, Ned Sloan could hear the roll of the crash cart being wheeled to the patient's bedside and the Code Blue being called over the paging system. Turning, he ran.

"Who is it?" he asked, panting as he reached the nurses' station.

"Bed four," came the unit secretary's quick reply. "Dillon Wolf."

Chapter 9

HALFWAY BEYOND THE blissful curtain of sleep and close to that special place of dreams, Ryan felt the sharp ache of impatience. Would the Lakota return? Would he stay away?

A tendril of fog, wispy and spectral, uncoiled and swelled from the outer edge of her mind, filling her dream eyes until she could almost feel its cool touch.

Everything was as it had been the night before. The people, their faces young and old, Lakota and Cheyenne, swirling in a hazy cloud. Mournfully wailing, they called and reached out. Then they drifted away until only the mantle of mist remained.

She waited. Even in her sleep she felt anticipation, thick and tangible. And then she heard it, the sorrowful howl that echoed and reechoed, again and again, coiling around her soul.

She waited.

From within the dense miasma, the amber-eyed beast came to her, silently loping forward. In the cradle of the dream, she breathed a contented sigh, assured now that he would come.

The beast paused, turned its great head and glanced over

its shoulder. Its long, pink tongue lolled out of its mouth and its plumed tail swung back and forth with excited anticipation.

From the shadows, the voices rose in a mighty chorus, *"Ei-yee, ei-yee, Sunkmanitu tanka kin hi yelo! Ei-yee!* It is Wolf, he has returned, it is Wolf."

He walked toward her, the haze parting in his wake. In a wild surge, her pulse sped throughout her body as he moved closer. Lifting his hand, he slowly beckoned to her and without hesitation, she yielded. She reached out to him.

Her fingers uncurled as she stretched her arm forward until the blue fire that enveloped him sparked from the tips of his fingers and leapt to hers, licking up her hand, surrounding her arm, her shoulders, and then encircling her entire body, binding her to him. Ryan gasped at the magic his touch created. The wild rush of delicious sensations spread like wildfire through her body and touched her spirit with a lingering silken caress.

The breath of a dream wind blew all around, lifting the Lakota's long hair, blowing its strands in an ebony halo about his head. He grasped her hand firmly. Never taking the intense gaze of his black eyes from her, he drew her slowly across the crystal thread of reality. He drew her, through the gentle wind and mist of her dream and into the captivating circle of his arms.

She breathed his sweet scent—cedar and sage; sunshine and sweet, rain-washed meadows.

"Come with me . . . be with me," he said softly.

Her dream fingers reached up and touched his face, feeling his warmth.

"Be mine," he whispered close to her ear, the caress of his breath leaving her skin aflame wherever it touched. "Come now, be with me. Our time is now."

Morning sunlight filtered through the translucent skin of the tipi and boldly entered the smoke hole at the top. It heated the air inside and cast a shaft of glaring light onto Ryan's face. Roused, she stretched her arms over her head and wondered how she could feel so wonderful after barely getting any sleep. The incredible dream had come again and she had overslept . . . again, but somehow, she felt completely refreshed. Even if Gaffney grouched and grumbled when she asked to borrow his Jeep, absolutely nothing would ruin her good spirits today.

"Let him get angry. I don't care, I just don't care."

She stretched again, working the complacency of sleep from her muscles, and then reached to push the blanket away.

"What the . . . !" She had touched something oddly furred.

Lifting her head from her pillow, she looked down the length of her body. Where was the pink blanket? It was gone and in its place was a large fur robe. Puzzled, she tentatively wriggled her toes and felt the thick pelt against her skin, all the way down her legs to her feet. "A buffalo robe." Her hand tested the texture of the fur once again. "What's going on here?" She scrubbed her eyes with the heels of her hands and impatiently raked her fingers through her hair, pushing it away from her face. "Damn, I bet Buddy's pulling a fool practical joke to get back at me for being late last night. I bet he sneaked in and switched my blanket."

She shifted her naked body and felt the rough hairs of the pelt caress her skin from neck to toe. "Well I hope he enjoyed his eyeful!" Her good mood quickly evaporated.

Shoving the hide aside, she swung her feet over the edge of the bed. Her heels instantly hit the ground with a jarring thud.

"Ouch!" A sharp pain shot up each leg. What was going on?

She tried to scramble to her feet but her legs refused to cooperate and she fell back. Finally standing upright, she stared down at where she had been. She hadn't fallen off her camp cot—in fact, the cot wasn't even there. There were no fluffy pillows or pastel-colored blankets. The place where she had spent the night was a mat of soft grasses and reeds overlaid with trade blankets and animal skins; a traditional Indian bed.

"None of this was here when I came in last night . . . was it? No, of course not." She prodded at the bedding with her toe.

A quick look around the tipi caused her even more distress. There were other changes, too, drastic changes. A circle of round smooth rocks now rimmed the perimeter of the fire pit and overlapping hides carpeted the ground. Willow backrests had replaced her two folding chairs and the camp table had disappeared entirely. On the right side of the tipi, directly across from her own bed, painted rawhide boxes and large beaded bags were neatly cached. She whirled around, searching the tipi for the bucket of water Buddy usually left each night for her. It was gone. In its place, a water paunch made from a buffalo bladder hung on a tipi pole by her bed.

Everything modern had disappeared. What seemed to be perfect recreations of Sioux artifacts of the 1870s replaced everything.

Another bed, in the traditional man's place at the back of the lodge opposite the door, caught her eye. What was it doing there? Who did it belong to? She tried to remain calm but her breath became labored and ragged. If this was a joke, someone had gone to a great deal of trouble to set it up. She wasn't amused.

Where were her clothes? Ryan quickly scanned the inside of the tipi. "They were on the chair last night." She spun around, looking frantically for the only set of clothes she had. A glance at the willow backrests and then to the ground near the fire told her what she didn't want to recognize. Her clothes were gone. She wrapped her arms across her naked breasts.

"Buddy, if you did this, I'm going to skin you alive!"

A bundle, neatly folded and placed at the foot of her sleeping palette, caught her eye. Once opened, the pack revealed a hide dress. She held it up against her body. Fringe fluttered across the bottom of the hem, down each side and around the edges of the sleeves. Three rows of elk's teeth spanned the front of the garment from shoulder to shoulder. She knew it would fit her perfectly, as would the belt, the moccasins and leggings that were also in the bundle.

"I suppose this is another of Buddy's jokes," she muttered, rolling the dress and moccasins back in to the bundle. "What am I supposed to do now, role play?"

With an angry jerk, she grabbed the buffalo robe from the bed. Wrapping it around her shoulders, she lifted the door flap and stepped barefoot out of the tipi and into the sunlight.

"Okay Buddy, I don't think your joke is very funny! You'd better bring my cot and my clothes back . . . now . . . or I'll . . ."

Ryan's tirade came to a sputtering halt. The camp was a site of bustling activity and she squinted against the glare of the morning sun. "What the . . . it looks like the tourists have jumped the fence." She chuckled. "Gaffney's going to have a fit with all of these people invading the camp." Another look caused her even more concern. These people weren't visitors, they weren't tourists and they certainly were not colleagues of Gaffney's. What was going on? Maybe they were with one of those historical reenactment groups? No, of course not. Gaffney would never permit any such thing on his project.

The scene before her was nothing she could have ever expected, or believed.

Shaken, feeling as though she'd taken a battering ram's blow to the stomach, Ryan fell back against the taut hide of the tipi. Stumbling, she grasped at a lodge pole for support, painfully barking her ankles and toes against a ground pin. Shading her face against the morning sun, she gawked at the unbelievable spectacle.

"This isn't possible! I can't believe any of this!"

An Indian village, active with hundreds of people going about their everyday lives, stretched out around her in all directions. Through the stand of tipis she could see the river. It looked the same as she remembered, with its banks shaded by large oaks and cottonwoods. The high bluffs and hills across the river were the same as well, but everything else reminded her of a huge, finely detailed museum dio-

rama. She was standing in the middle of a living tableau
of life in an 1870s Indian encampment, complete with the
sights, the sounds and the smells. There was even the sweet
breath of a breeze and the warmth of a mid-June sun.

Ryan swallowed hard and fought to keep a tight hold on
her sanity. Was she still asleep? Was this a dream? It didn't
look like a dream and it certainly didn't feel like one. As
a scientist, her training had taught her to examine all she
encountered with objectivity and suspicion, but there was
no rhyme or reason to what she was seeing. She closed her
eyes, squeezing them shut. Maybe if she didn't look for a
moment, it would all disappear, everything would return to
normal or she would wake up. Slowly, hopefully, Ryan
looked again. The village and the people were still there.

A strong grip of fear wrenched her stomach. Grasping
for some semblance of logic and reality, the words of a
Bureau of Ethnography report she had recently read re-
played in her mind and she repeated the words slowly behind the shield of her hand.

*The village was large, larger than any encampment had
ever been in the history of the Lakota. It stretched three
miles along the west bank of the twisting Greasy Grass
River. No one knew for certain how many Indians were
there, but the number could not have been much smaller
than ten thousand. At the farthest south end were the Hunkpapa. They always camped at the head of the camp circle.
The Blackfoot Sioux were nearby and below them to the
north were the Oglalas and Minneconjous. Further north,
separate but still encamped with the Sioux, were the Cheyenne. It was June and it was known as the time of the
Chokecherry Moon.*

Trying to calm her nerves, Ryan took half a dozen deep
breaths. Her eyes darted about, catching every little scene
that continued to play out in the camp. Women, dark-
skinned and dressed in buckskin or tradecloth and calicos,
chatted with their neighbors. The cooking fires outside the
tipis blazed and paunches or kettles of what seemed to be
venison or buffalo stew cooked over many, sending pleasant aromas off on the breeze. Small children, naked and

happy, ran and played, their sun-bronzed sturdy bodies filled with energy and good health. Young boys of ten or twelve played games of war and hunting parties with small bows and arrows and the girls imitated their mothers' tasks by playing dutiful wives to the boy warriors.

There weren't many young men in camp, but a few old men had gathered in a small group and were enjoying each other's company.

Down by the river, a huge herd of horses, mares with foals, bays and sorrels, pintos and palouses, every color imaginable, were grazing on the tall grass that grew along the shady bank. A few of the horses stood belly-deep in the water, enjoying a drink.

"No!" she breathed. "I can't accept any of this. I won't accept it. It's some kind of a hallucination or delusion. I've been working too hard and I've been too worried about the disappearing artifacts."

From the edge of the encampment an excited ripple of voices rose, becoming louder and louder. Reluctant to discover another sight that she couldn't reasonably explain, Ryan turned slowly toward the commotion.

"Leciya ahitunwan yo, hipelo!"

She translated the Lakota words. "Look, there, they come!"

The people turned from their conversations and chores and rushed forward as a large group of riders approached the camp. They called out, greeting them. *"Hau Kola!* Welcome, friends."

A sense of wonderment slowly took hold, and bit by bit pushed back the terror that gripped her. Completely captivated by the scene that was unfolding before her eyes, Ryan stood on tiptoe, hoping for a better view.

As the riders neared, she heard the rhythmic chunk-chunk-chunk-chunk sounds of hawk bells and other decorative paraphernalia that shook and rattled on the horses' trappings and kept cadence with each hoofbeat. The warriors paraded into camp, wearing their finest clothes and holding their lances and coup sticks high. The war ponies excitedly sidestepped as some of the women surged forward to claim the trophy scalps hanging from the tips of the lances. And then it began, the beautiful eerie sound of the women's high-trilling honor yells. In a few moments, the loud whoops of the men answered the women's lulus and the din rose higher and higher and higher.

Ryan's eyes widened in disbelief.

As the first group of warriors passed, there were faces among them that she recognized. They were the faces she had seen many times in the old sepia photographs. Leading the Cheyenne were Two Moons and Old Bear. Fast Bull rode in front of his Minneconjous and Touch the Clouds, his awesome seven-foot height nearly dwarfing his sorrel war pony, rode behind. Leading the Sans Arcs was *Wanbli Gleske*, Spotted Tail. Next came the Hunkpapa and Ryan quickly spied Gall, broad shouldered, barrel-chested and handsome. Beside him rode Black Moon, Red Cloud and Crow King, their horses capering and jostling against one another. Behind these four was the Hunkpapa holy man who would become the best-known Indian throughout history. Her heart leapt and bound with excitement as she recognized the taciturn features of *Tatanka I'yotake*, Sitting Bull.

Among the many warriors who continued to ride into the camp, one rider caught and held her attention. He was a slightly built man, his skin coloring much lighter than any of the others. His hair was brown instead of jet black and an ugly scar reached from below his nose and traced a path across his face to the edge of his jaw. A smooth pebble with a single hole bored through the center hung on a thong from behind his left ear and bobbled with the trotting gait of his piebald pony. Although no photograph or likeness of this warrior existed, Ryan knew him.

"*Ta-shunka-Witco*," she whispered. "Crazy Horse."

Although the wild racing of her pulse and labored breath continued to plague her, she knew where she was. She knew the incredible, undeniable, unbelievable truth.

The month was June—it *was* the month of the Chokecherry Moon. The year was 1876 and Ryan Brenna Burke, Ph.D., Doctor of Anthropology, was standing with the gathering Lakota and Cheyenne on the banks of the Greasy Grass.

Chapter 10

RYAN COUNTED OFF the days since she'd left Washington. If she had really made an incredible slip through time and if the date had remained the same from one century to the next, it was June 18. Again she sifted through her mental files. If these were the warriors who had just defeated General Crook and his men at Rosebud Creek, then in eight days Custer and the Seventh Cavalry would be annihilated. She raised her eyes and looked across the river to the grassy hillside. "Over there."

She felt dizzy. She wasn't safe. She had to get back to her own time. But how? Panic, thick and suffocating, rose in her throat. If the Indians found her in camp, they would kill her. There were fresh scalps on these warriors' lances and some had just lost friends and relatives to Crook's bullets. There would be little or no mercy shown to a white intruder in their camp.

Staying close to the tipi, Ryan watched as a large party of travelers followed the warriors into the village. Horses' hooves and travois poles churned up waves of dirt that rose to join the dark clouds that already hung in the air from the war ponies. The procession came within thirty yards of her and she stared, her mouth agape. Over a hundred passed her, their possessions strapped to their backs, tied onto pack horses or slung onto travois. A herd of horses and yapping dogs accompanied them. The din rose to a deafening pitch as friends and relatives already in camp welcomed them.

Here it was, unfolding before her eyes. Here was everything she had ever learned about the formation of the Little Big Horn encampment. These were the people who had traded starvation and disease at the soldier forts for an unsure future as fugitives. Some had traveled from Fort Phil Kearny, others from Fort Smith or Pease. Defying the government's reservation laws, they chose to be renegades in their own land, traveling for days to reach the cool, sweet shade of the Greasy Grass. Soon close to ten thousand Sioux and Cheyenne would be settled on the three-mile plateau along the west bank of the river. Any anthropologist would gladly give a fortune for the chance to see this sight firsthand. Ryan didn't know whether to feel terrified or thrilled. She settled for seesawing doses of both.

A single horse and rider broke from the ranks of warriors and moved toward her. The horse was a pinto and its coat gleamed with large jagged splatters of black and white. Excited by all the commotion, it tossed its head, and the little brass hawk bells tied in its forelock gaily jingled. Three handprints painted in red, one for each coup counted in the battle, decorated the horse's neck and a clump of red-tailed hawk feathers tied to a hank of mane fluttered as the breeze ruffled them.

Each prancing step of the horse brought the warrior closer. Would he ride on to another lodge? His route never altered. Ryan knew she couldn't stay where she was. She'd be discovered. Her eyes darted from left to right, looking for an escape route, but her trembling legs threatened to defy the order. Huddling next to the tipi, she drew the buffalo robe up over her head. She heard the warrior answering greetings from friends and neighbors. His voice was strong and friendly . . . and familiar.

Her body felt numb with a wild concoction of wonder and fear and anticipation. Although the morning sun was hot, she shivered beneath the heavy robe. Her knees wobbled and she slipped to the ground. Crouching low, she closed the robe around her body and over her face. Holding the edges together beneath her chin, she left only a small gap to peer through. The Lakota rode closer and closer. The stifling robe was not a safe place to hide. If she could slip through time, why couldn't she make herself invisible?

The horse stopped a few feet away from where Ryan huddled. It snorted loudly. Her heart bolted but she didn't dare peek. The animal's hot breath blew through the gap in the hide and touched her face. She had never been so scared in all her life.

In a moment she heard the slight chunking sound of hair-pipe bone, the melodic tinkling of hawk bells and the subtle sound of the horse shifting its weight. The Lakota had dismounted.

Summoning the only fragment of courage she could find, Ryan peered through the gap in the robe, but all she could see were the warrior's moccasins. Curiosity outweighing fear, she slowly raised her eyes. Butter-colored buckskin leggings covered his legs and the navy blue tradecloth breechclout tied about his waist fell to just above his knees. Her gaze moved higher. A leather belt decorated with brass tacks encircled his waist and a sheathed knife hung from the left side. Except for the breastplate around his neck, his chest was naked and the bronze hue of his skin emphasized every muscle beneath. Two fresh wounds, red and not fully healed, lay high on either side of his chest—souvenirs from a recent sun dance piercing.

He was tall, at least two or three inches over six feet and when he stepped closer, his broad shoulders blocked out the sun.

A quiet, scheming little voice slid from its hiding place inside her head and spoke to her, whispering a secret that made her weak with fear. "This isn't a dream. You've left the dream world behind. He is here. You are here This is real." The voice whispered a caution. "Beware, beware. Don't look into this man's eyes. Do so and you will be lost—forever."

She had received fair warning but the enticement was

too great. Daring to look up at his face, she almost swooned. He was the Lakota from her dream.

Every feature was as she remembered—the noble arch of his brows, the angular plane of his cheekbones, the straight bridge of his nose and the appealing fullness of his mouth. His eyes, dark and fringed with ebony lashes, warily returned her scrutiny.

As he had done in her dreams, he held out his hand and motioned to her to stand. She couldn't move. Impatient, he gestured again. She was trapped. There was no place to run. There was no place to go . . . except to him.

Still clutching the robe with one hand, she reached up with the other. Only a second or two passed, but it felt like an eternity before their fingers lightly brushed and then fully touched.

When had she become so breathless?

His hand slid over hers and his fingers curled around her palm, engulfing her smaller hand in his strong, dark grip. The blended heat of their skin awakened and warmed every secret place in her body. Ryan tried to take a deep breath and failed.

He tugged, urging her to stand. Her body felt leaden and unwilling to move; but insistent, he pulled again. This time, still peering at him through the gap in the robe, she surrendered.

The Lakota's eyes narrowed and a frown suddenly creased his brow. Roughly pulling her closer, he raised her hand, yanking her arm out from under the robe. Turning it one way and then another, he examined her skin in the sunlight. The contrast between her fair skin and his darker shade was distinct. Bending his head, he tried to see her face, but only her nose poked out between the folds. Using just the tip of his index finger, he pushed the robe away from her cheek. His eyes immediately widened with surprise and he drew a sharp breath.

"*Wasicu!*" he spat, his hatred plain to hear.

Ryan frantically glanced around. Had anyone else heard him? Was anyone looking at them? How many Lakota would come running and demand their piece of white scalp? Terror gobbled up her meager cache of courage. There would be no help for a white woman in this place. She stepped away but he tightened his hold on her arm and pulled her back. His fingers gouged into her flesh but that didn't worry her half as much as the touch of the knife he now held against her ribs.

"Please," she begged, her voice croaking just above a whisper. "Let me go."

"Winyan!"

Her fear thickened. Her voice had given her away. He now knew she was a woman. Pushing her toward the tipi, he lifted the door flap and shoved her inside. Following behind, he dropped the flap and shut the world outside. It was as hot as an oven inside the tipi. A light film of sweat coated her skin but it wasn't all due to the heat or the heavy buffalo robe.

If being sent back in time to 1876 was possible, then no matter how magnificent this man was, she could only expect things to be as they were during this time—his time. His reactions to her would be predictable. She was white, he was Lakota, and to his mind they were sworn enemies.

She backed away from him so quickly that she stumbled, lost her balance, and careened against the tipi wall. He followed, his dark eyes never leaving her. Glancing quickly to the left then the right, Ryan tried to find a way to escape but he moved closer, blocking any route she might have found. She was trapped.

"Where would I go, anyway?" she muttered, glaring up into his dark eyes, a defiant set to her mouth. Above all else, she vowed she wouldn't let him see the fear that devoured her. She tried to reason with herself. Surely if he planned to kill her he wouldn't bloody the inside of the tipi. The sudden, renewed pressure of the knife against her ribs told her she might be wrong.

"Winyan, Nituwe hwo?" he demanded. *"Lel taku yacin hwo?"*

He wanted to know who she was and what she was doing in his tipi. What could she tell him? She took another step backwards. Her foot struck the side of the bed and she teetered on the brink of losing her balance until he grasped her shoulders and steadied her. The need to survive this implausible excursion overcame all good judgment. Ignoring the knife, she shrugged away, ducking to the left and out of his reach. It was futile. He caught her again.

"Don't touch me." She hissed, roughly shoving his hands away. "If this is your tipi, I'll just leave . . . though only God knows where I'd go . . . if He even knows where I am!"

The Lakota gripped her arm again.

"Let me go!"

He listened to her English words and with a contemptuous lift of his brow, poked her hard on the shoulder and repeated his question. *"Wasicun nituwe hwo?"*

"You want to know who I am? Fine. All right, I'll tell you," she replied with a defiant tilt to her head. The robe had fallen away from her face and her hair tumbled across her face and over her shoulders. She tossed her hair from her eyes and defiantly straightened her shoulders. "Just don't ask me where I'm from. Trust me, you don't want to hear *that* answer."

"Owotanla omakiyaka yo. Wicaka!"

"The truth, you want the truth? I couldn't top any of this with a lie if I tried!"

"Iya, iya."

"Okay, okay. I'll speak. My name is Ryan, Ryan Burke— Ryan." She pointed to herself and repeated her name. "Ryan."

A fleeting frown touched his brow and then he shrugged a "who cares, whatever" shrug. Without taking his eyes from her, he lifted the knife and drew the menacing point slowly across her neck as if giving a harsh warning. Then, with a slight nod of his head, he slid the blade back into the sheath on his belt.

Relieved, Ryan sighed. "That's better, maybe now we can try and talk this—"

With a speed she had not thought possible, he grabbed the front of the buffalo robe.

"Oh, no you don't!" She wrenched away.

He caught her again.

"Damn you!" She pushed hard against his arm, her fingernails leaving reddened trails along his skin. "I'd rather feel your knife instead of what I think you've got in mind!" She tightened the robe around her body. "Keep your hands off me, do you understand!" She felt the beginning of a hysterical giggle. What good were threats? She couldn't even call for help. Calling 9-1-1 in this time and place would only bring about ten thousand Indians and none of them would help her.

With a disdainful lift of his brow, the Lakota yanked the robe away from her body and tossed it across the tipi.

Naked and embarrassed, Ryan tried to reach for a fur from the bed, but he blocked her with his arm.

"*Inila yanka yo,* be still," he growled.

"Damn you," she hissed, boldly meeting his dark eyes. There would be no escape, it was useless to try. Where had the beautiful warrior of her dreams gone? She stared at him with a defiant lift to her head. "All right, fine, go ahead. Look all you want." Holding her arms down at her sides, she closed her hands into tight fists and stood proudly. "I'll be damned before I let you see me cower."

He stepped back and looked at her body, his eyes slowly following each line, each curve and hollow. Reaching out, he lifted a handful of her hair, testing the curl and texture before allowing its long strands to run slowly like water through his fingers and drop back over her shoulder. He touched her face. His fingers traced an arched eyebrow and suddenly stopped. Tilting her head upward until the ray of sunlight shining through the smoke hole touched her face, he leaned closer and peered at her eyes.

He's never seen blue eyes before.

His inspection continued, his fingers moving to touch her gold earrings lightly. Ryan immediately remembered Charley Crying Wolf's identical gesture. With this memory came another and in it she found the possible answers to the most improbable and pressing questions of all. *Charles Antone Crying Wolf, peace chief, holy man—what do you know of all this? What do you know of my fantastic journey?*

"Everything, everything," the small voice inside her head responded. "Everything."

And while we're at it, what am I doing here?

"You will see, you will see," the voice answered again.

For two, fitful nights in Charley Crying Wolf's tipi, this magnificent warrior had been a wonderful dream, a beautiful illusion, and now here he stood, flesh and blood, real— very real and very dangerous. How could any of this be possible?

The Lakota's fingers moved again, putting a stop to her thoughts. She held her breath as his caress outlined her lips, moved over the jut of her chin and down her neck to the hollow at the base of her throat. Her skin tingled and felt feverish wherever his fingers brushed. She trembled.

Long moments passed as they silently stared at each other.

The Lakota was the first to look away as he continued his downward exploration. He placed the palm of his hand at the base of her neck. Widely spreading his fingers, he trailed his touch across the ridge of her collarbone, then lower. His hand passed through the silken valley between her breasts and the tips of his fingers grazed the inside swell of their firm peaks. She drew a sharp breath, damning the treasonous response of her nipples as they tightened into firm, excited crowns. Looking away, she tried to command her body to ignore the disturbing, unbidden pleasure his touch had summoned. *I should be terrified, not tempted.*

"Takuwe ca yahi hwo?" he demanded, breaking the spell.

"I don't know why I'm here." Her nerves began to unravel and she almost laughed. *"Nituwe ki slolwaye kisto.* I know who you are." Without giving thought to the consequences, she had spoken in Lakota. *"Sunkmanitu!* You are Wolf!"

He jumped back as if she had punched him. Scowling, he stared at her and then cautiously layed his fingers across her lips. *"Lakotiya woglaka slolyaye he?"*

"Yes," Ryan answered. "I speak Lakota. *Lakotiyapi.*" She crossed her arms over her breasts. "I bet that's quite a shocker, isn't it?" she added in English.

"Inila, inila!" he fiercely commanded.

"So, you don't like the fact that I can speak your language. I suppose to you it's really strange to find a white woman in your tipi who can speak Lakota. Well, it's real strange to me, too."

Would it be foolish to let him know how much Lakota she did know? Maybe understanding everything she heard the Lakota say would make escaping the camp easier? It was difficult to decide. No, she finally concluded. Speaking Lakota might be the only thing that would save her life.

The wary expression remained firmly set on the Lakota's face as he pushed her folded arms aside and renewed his exploration. His eyes followed the downward path as his caress forged lower and lower, lingering at her waist a moment or two before moving on, then stopping again. He placed his hand flat against her belly. The heel of his hand rested just above the dark curls between her legs and she was bewildered by the deliciously disturbing weight of his touch. Every thought centered on his hand, the heat of his touch and what lay beneath.

She dared to look down. His skin was so dark against her pale shade and yet she savored the contrast. His hand moved ever so slightly, and the fragile moan that escaped her throat was only a mere hint of the chaos going on inside her.

He was gentle, too gentle, and it confused her. Where was the enemy, where was the angry warrior who had held the knife? Why hadn't he exposed her to the entire camp? Why hadn't he called the women in the camp and given her to them? She had expected anything, but not this, certainly not this.

The pressure of his hand increased and Ryan turned her head, not willing to watch what would follow.

"Cane wakansni yo."

Surprised, she quickly looked up at him. "Don't be afraid?" How ludicrous. "Should I fear *you* or what your

touch does to me?" Her heart pounded. "Maybe I'd understand this better if you acted more like a warrior than a . . .
lover." Once more she was imprisoned by his dark gaze.
Her breath caught in her throat as the enticing heat of
arousal spread throughout her body. The quickened puffs
of his breath brushed her cheek and Ryan knew he felt the
fire, too.

The Lakota quickly withdrew his hand and she suddenly
felt cold. A moment later, he roughly shoved something
against her breasts—the buckskin dress and the moccasins
she'd found earlier. Frowning, she silently questioned his
intent.

The tightened muscle along the edge of his jaw and the
brusque gesture of his hand gave his answer. He wanted
her to get dressed.

"Ena un wo, stay here." He stalked out of the tipi.

"Now what?" she whispered.

Chapter 11

WOLF HAD A headache. He had never had one like it before. The pounding in his head resounded like the hooves of a hundred war ponies, and when he squinted his eyes against the sunlight, the pain worsened.

He stood for a moment outside his lodge, his hand resting lightly on the closed door flap. He was confused. There was a white woman in his tipi. He hated whites. The whites were enemies of the Lakota. He had hated whites for as long as he could remember. Questions, one after another, besieged him. Who was she? How was it possible that a white woman could be in this camp? How could she speak Lakota? How did she know his name? What did the *wasicu* want? The pain in his head increased with each question.

Pressing his fingers against his temples, he shut his eyes, searching his mind for a fragment of a memory that might give him the answers. None came. Was it possible that she was his woman? He couldn't remember. Had he taken her in a raid, had he traded horses for her? There was no hint of her in his memory. He could not remember raiding any white settlements before going to *Wiwanyank Wacipi*, the sun dance. He could not remember seeing any whites for a long time before fighting the soldiers on Rosebud Creek a few days ago.

Wolf left the encampment and sought a quiet place to sit and think. The cool shaded bank of the Greasy Grass offered him the seclusion he wanted. He selected a place near the lip of the river where cottonwoods and willows cast cool shadows along the water's edge. Using the blade of his knife, he cut a couple of short, whip-thin willow twigs from a nearby tree and peeled off the bark. Sitting on the ground under a big cottonwood, he chewed the bark and patiently waited for its healing powers to begin to ease the ache that had plagued his head since the war party had left Rosebud Creek.

The whole incident puzzled him and with the mystery that had begun two days ago, the questions only seemed to increase as time passed. He remembered when his close friend *Tonca Wanbli*, Eagle Deer, had found him lying on the ground after the battle. Wolf could not remember being knocked from his horse. He remembered his own name and his horse and the names and faces of his friends, but everything that had happened before the battle was still unclear. If he had been badly wounded enough to make him lose some of his memory, surely some mark or injury would be plain to see and feel, but there was nothing.

Later they had made camp for the night, Wolf took off his leggings and breechclout and carefully studied his body, touching here and there, looking for the wound that had struck him down. None existed.

He felt humiliated. If no mark could be found on his body, had he been like a feeble old woman and fallen from his war pony?

Hoping to dispel everyone's uneasiness, Eagle Deer had made a joke. He told them *Sunkmanitu Ceye a Pelo*, Calls to the Wolf, had grown tired of all the fighting and had lain down and gone to sleep for a while. The warriors had laughed and politely pretended to forget the issue, but Wolf knew it was not finished. He knew by the furtive looks and the sudden silence that ended conversations when he approached. He knew by the uneasiness he sensed walking through camp that the story was being told over and over at each tipi. All these things confounded him. All of these and one more.

He had tried not to think about that one thing. He had tried to push it away but it was insistent and returned, again and again, making his heart pound, coating his skin with a slick coat of sweat and chilling him to the bone.

He rose and stood looking into the depths of the quickly running river. The Greasy Grass gurgled and tumbled, rushing off to the lowland. Its rippling surface refused to give back a clear reflection.

"Even here I cannot see who I am." He leaned against the tree. "Why do I not remember the things that should be in my head?" he asked, his voice echoing his desperation.

He vaguely remembered going with Crazy Horse to Rosebud Creek. He didn't remember pledging or dancing *Wiwanyank Wacipi* and yet the freshly torn and tender flesh high on either side of his chest told him he had done just that. He didn't remember all of the battle with the blue-coats, either. Only small visions of it darted in an out of his mind.

If he closed his eyes and concentrated, he could almost smell the sharp acrid stench of gunpowder, the sweating horses and the metallic scent of blood. But each time he tried to remember the battle, it was only that one disturbing image that returned to haunt him—over and over again. Its appearance made him shiver. It soaked his skin with sweat and made him breathe like a frightened dog. Of everything he remembered since going to Rosebud Creek, this memory was the most frightening.

There had been soldiers all around, some still fighting, others dead on the ground. The Lakota were strong that day and their war medicine had been powerful. The ground had trembled from the beat of the horses' hooves and the sky had darkened from the clouds of dust and smoking gunpowder. Very few Lakota had fallen, but Wolf was drawn to a place where three already lay dead on the ground. Nearing, he saw one rise up. Startled, he had stood and stared, his heart pounding wildly in his chest. The man had beckoned, calling him closer.

"He was familiar to me, his face was like my face, and I went to him," Wolf whispered out loud, fighting to keep the elusive memory clear. "He was made of mist and shadow, and yet when he touched me, his hand was solid and warm. He called me by name and when he smiled at me, I grew tired. He helped me lie down where he had been." Wolf pressed his forehead against the tree. "Who was this man who looked like me, and yet wasn't me? What am I to know of this?"

He threw himself back down under the tree and tried to shake the odd, cold feelings that washed over him. His headache persisted, and he sucked on the tart juice of the bark, but its healing continued to elude him.

He dug the heels of his hands into his eyes and the pain seemed to ease a little with the pressure. A fragrance, faint, unusual and unfamiliar filled his nostrils, and frowning, he sniffed at his hands. The scent reminded him of wildflowers. *Wasicu, the white one—this is her smell.* He leaned back against the tree and closed his eyes. Her blue-eyed image easily slid into his mind.

What was a white woman doing in a Lakota camp? Where had she come from? Why had she been waiting at his lodge as though she belonged there?

Had she been a man, Wolf knew he would have killed her. So why had his hatred changed when he discovered the white enemy was a woman? *Have I forgotten this loathing as well? No, my hatred still is there. I do not feel its strength for this one. Is it possible that a white woman is less an enemy than a man?* No, that wasn't possible. He had heard of women among the whites who could shoot a rifle and kill Lakota as well as any man.

He looked at his hand and smelled the fragrance once more. Who was she? Her sleeping palette on the woman's side of the tipi looked as though she had been living there for a while. Her clothes were in a bundle on her bed. Was she dressing when she heard the warriors return? He frowned. Why did the bundle hold Indian clothes and not the silly clothes of the whites that made a woman's hips too big to go through a tipi door? Was she his slave or captive? Had he traded many horses for her? He could not remember.

A baffling thought suddenly edged its way into his head. Was she his wife? He found her pretty, perhaps even beautiful, in a pale way, but her disposition was certainly not to his liking. "My woman would be gentle and agreeable, not like a snapping turtle." This one's skin was as soft as the fur on a rabbit and her hair was finer than the mane on his favorite war pony. "But, she is like the red berry bush with its delicious fruit hidden among the thorns." He studied the riddle a while longer. "I think she belongs to me. Her clothes and her bed are in my lodge and she speaks Lakota." But if this was so, why was she afraid when she saw him? Had she been disobedient while he was gone? Was she afraid he would beat her? "No, there is more I do not yet understand."

Not one single answer to his many questions came to mind. There were only more questions that made the ache in his head much worse.

"*Kola, nitoketu hwo?* How is it with you?"

Wolf hadn't heard Eagle Deer approach. Startled, he looked up to find his friend standing nearby.

"I have been thinking about . . ." Eagle Deer began.

Wolf gave a slight nod, letting Eagle Deer know he understood what he wished to talk about. It would have been impolite for Eagle Deer to speak the words that would remind him of his embarrassment at Rosebud Creek. It had been Eagle Deer who had found him and helped him after the battle. He was still concerned. Wolf decided that in the morning he would take three of his best horses to Eagle Deer's lodge to thank his friend.

"*Matanya yelo.* I am well, *mita kola,* my friend," Wolf said. "My head still hurts as though a big rock has fallen on it." He gestured for Eagle Deer to sit beside him among the tall grass.

Sitting together, neither spoke for a while, each respecting the other's thoughts, content to rest and share their friendship. The sound of the river and the choruses of the song birds could be heard over the low drone of voices in the village behind them. Wolf was glad he had a friend like Eagle Deer, it was just too bad he could not remember how long they had been friends. No matter—he felt comfortable in Eagle Deer's company.

"I have ridden there." Eagle Deer finally spoke, pointing northwest with a slight thrust of his lips. "The village grows, there are many circles and more people are still coming from the soldier forts. The Cheyenne are the farthest camp to the north and the Hunkpapas are the farthest in the other direction. Those who come from the *tiyotipi*, the soldier forts, all talk of many bluecoats on the trails. They say the one called Yellow Hair is among them."

"Yellow Hair! His name is bitter on my tongue!" Wolf fiercely exclaimed, spitting out the chewed bark. "Someday he will be nothing but shadow and still his name will be strong." He stood and paced in front of Eagle Deer. "In less winters than your oldest child is now, all of this will no longer be ours because of Yellow Hair." Wolf gestured widely with his arm, encompassing the broad valley in his action. "We will fight and many will die. The ground will drink up much blood and our people will claim victory, but still we will not win."

"How can you know of these things to come?" Eagle Deer asked warily.

A cold chill fell upon Wolf and he shuddered. He knew what he was saying was true, but how? He pushed his uneasiness aside and spoke with false bravado. "I know because it will be so. There will be nothing but scraps left for the Lakota."

"Can it be, my brother?" Eagle Deer whispered with awe.

"Can what be?" Wolf quickly looked at his friend, a whisper of apprehension pricking him. "Why do you look at me like that?"

"Maybe your illness at the battle was not an illness. Maybe it was a gift from *Wakan Tonka*. Maybe it was a vision, a powerful vision that came upon you, strong enough to make you look like you were dead."

Wolf turned and stared at his friend for a moment, the possibility unnerving. "The only one who has had a vision is *Tatanka I'yotake*, Sitting Bull."

"The only one who has *told* of his vision is Sitting Bull," Eagle Deer replied. "He speaks of many soldiers falling upside down into the village from the sky like dead grass-hoppers. He said they fall not as conquerors but as dead men. This was his vision that he has told to many, but you, what happened to you was different. Think upon it, my brother. You were as one who was dead and yet look, there is no mark of death on you. Are you sure there is no hole in your body from the soldiers' guns or from their long knives? Have you no wounds or scars?"

"*Takuni iyewaye sni*, I found none." Wolf hung his head, feeling all the more shamed. How could a warrior fall, lose his senses and have no wound? There was no wisdom to it.

Eagle Deer did not speak. He looked far away into the distance as though something of great interest was happen-ing in the mountains. Wolf knew his friend was looking for the right words to speak and he remained silent, waiting. The wait was short.

"*Maza Akicita*, Iron Soldier, said he saw you die. He says everyone should be afraid to speak your name. He said the soldiers' guns put holes in your body and that he saw you fall from your horse. He saw you bleed, here and here." Eagle Deer touched Wolf on the chest and the stomach. "Iron Soldier says you are dead and just do not know it yet. He says you are *wanagi*, a ghost, and because you are dead and still walk among your people, bad things will come."

"Bad things are already coming that have nothing to do with me." Wolf stood and gazed out at the hills across the river.

"How can you say that if you do not remember?"

Wolf looked down at his friend. Should he tell Eagle Deer of the strange things he did remember? Should he speak of the memory of the shadow warrior who frightened him? Should he tell him this man looked so much like himself that when he looked into the man's face it was like his own reflection in a pond? No. He would wait and think on it some more. "How can I put into words what I do not understand myself?"

Wolf sank back down onto the thickly grassed riverbank and toyed with a tall stalk of brightly colored wildflowers.

"I hope my words have not angered you, my brother," Eagle Deer said. "I only wished to tell you what Iron Soldier is telling others. He makes trouble for you."

"Iron Soldier is like an old dog. He makes trouble where none should be." Wolf paused again and tried to gauge his friend. "There are things I cannot remember, that is true, but there are other things that trouble me, things I see in my mind that I know do not exist anywhere where the Lakota live."

"Maybe you should speak of these things to Sitting Bull or some other holy man who can tell you what they mean," Eagle Deer said. "Maybe it is not wise for you to speak of them to me if they are *wakan*."

"Do you think *I* know what they are?" Wolf asked. "How can a man have memories of something he has never seen and yet cannot remember things that are of his own life?" He fell silent for a moment or two, as though waiting for Eagle Deer to answer. He tentatively touched the scars high on his chest. "I cannot remember my pledge to sun dance and I cannot remember being pierced and yet I remember wide trails, many trails, hard-packed and colored black with many villages near them. I cannot remember leaving here to go make battle with the bluecoats three suns ago, but I remember strange wagons, not like the ones we have seen near the fort or the white man's villages, but shiny wagons of many colors that move fast without horses pulling them.

"There are strange villages, too, stone lodges made higher than the trees, bigger than that hill across the river," Wolf continued. "There are many *wasicu*, more white men than the Lakota have ever imagined existed." Wolf rubbed his aching temples with his fingers. "What does any of this have to do with me?" He looked at his friend, hoping for an answer.

A deep worried furrow creased Eagle Deer's brow and Wolf suddenly wished he had not burdened his friend with his dilemma. Maybe Iron Soldier was right, maybe he was dead. He could not remember enough to make any sense of anything. He closed his eyes against the bright afternoon sun and the image of the white woman in his tipi filled his mind again. *What of her? Why is she here? What is she to me?*

"There is something else I must know," Wolf quietly continued, looking at Eagle Deer, hesitating as he searched for the right words. "Have I—do I—have I already taken a wife? Is she of this tribe?"

Eagle Deer stared at his friend with surprise. "How can you not remember this? No *kola*, you have no wife . . . yet."

"I remember giving many horses, many furs and blankets to *Mato Cante*, Bear Heart, for his daughter *Ptetawote*, Ground Plum. Is this not so?"

"Yes *mita kola*, my friend, I have spoken to him for you about Ground Plum, but you have not yet taken her to your tipi." Eagle Deer's face clearly showed his puzzlement. "Do you not remember this? Is that why you ask this thing?"

Wolf looked across the river again and answered quietly without meeting his friend's gaze. "When I returned to my lodge this morning I found a woman waiting for me there."

"Ah," Eagle Deer chuckled, heartily clapping his friend on the back. "Your reputation for strength in places other than the battlefield and the hunt have become well-known." He laughed again. "This woman who waited to warm your bed and test your skill, is she someone I know?"

"She is no one you can name unless you know a *wasicu*."

"*Wasicu!*" Eagle Deer repeated, stunned. His dark eyes widened in disbelief. "There is a *wasicu* in your lodge?" He turned and looked over his shoulder toward the encampment. "This woman, this *wasicu*, is still in your lodge?"

Wolf nodded, continuing to keep his gaze from his friend. He tore a leaf from the clump of flowers in his hand and wrapped and unwrapped it around his index finger.

"*Kola*, you must take her away from here, somewhere

far away from this camp and you must leave her there,"
Eagle Deer advised. "If you do not, many angry *wasicu*
will come here looking for her. They will make war on us
to take her back. They will kill our women and children
and our old people." Agitated, Eagle Deer began to rise.
"You must take her away from this village and leave her
somewhere where the bluecoats can find her. If you do not
do this then you must kill her."

"I do not think she is of these *wasicu*," Wolf answered
calmly, tossing the ragged remnants of the wildflower into
the breeze, his casual actions belying his misgivings. He
grasped Eagle Deer's wrist and drew him back down under
the tree, but was unable to ease his friend's distress.

"How is it you can say this?" Eagle Deer asked.

Wolf met Eagle Deer's questioning gaze. "Do you know
of any white woman who speaks Lakota?"

Eagle Deer stood again, pacing uneasily, back and forth.
"This cannot be so," he answered in disbelief. "It is true
some white men who have lived with the Lakota or who
take Lakota women for their own know our talk, but I have
heard of no white woman who speaks it." Eagle Deer
stopped in front of Wolf and looked down at his friend. "I
will talk of this to no one, not even my wife, but you must
speak with the holy man."

"I do not wish to have words with Sitting Bull about
this," Wolf replied.

"If you do not talk with Sitting Bull, there is another I
think you should seek out—*K'eya T'ucu'hu*, Turtle Rib. I
know him well. My father and he are as brothers." Eagle
Deer waited for a reply. Wolf was silent. "Turtle Rib is a
respected man. He will listen and give wise counsel." Eagle
Deer returned to his seat beside Wolf. "Do this soon, my
friend, before Iron Soldier makes trouble or your white
woman makes bad medicine. She may bring misery to the
Lakota. Maybe the whites are jealous of my brother's
strength and cunning. Maybe she has come to steal your
affections, your heart, and plans to give your strength to
the *wasicu*."

Wolf silently nodded, carefully considering what Eagle

Deer said. His friend's words were wise, but he sensed he was in for more trouble than Eagle Deer could imagine or Iron Soldier could cause. Somehow, in some way, Wolf knew the blue-eyed *wasicu* in his tipi would be the beginning and end of it all.

Wolf lifted the door flap and stepped inside. The tipi was sweltering and the air hard to breathe. A little scurrying noise drew his attention to the woman's side of the lodge. So, she was still here. She wore the hide dress, a film of sweat coated her face and her long, brown hair clung to her cheeks and forehead. He felt the light touch of compassion stroke his heart. It was too hot for anyone to stay inside a closed tipi, it was even too hot for a pitiful *wasicu*.

Why hadn't she raised the outer skin of the tipi to let air come in? He stepped forward but she quickly drew away, apprehension and distrust narrowing her eyes. He could see she was trying to judge his intent. Raising his hands, he showed he had no weapon and meant her no harm.

"It is too hot. Why have you not lifted the hides?" he demanded. Her response was a puzzled frown. He pointed to the bottom of the lodge wall. Her frown deepened. And then he understood. It was strange; she could speak his words but she did not know how to lift the wall of the lodge and capture the cooling breezes.

"*Unyin ktelo.* Come. I will show you." Wolf took her hand and although she tried to pull out of his grasp, he firmly held on until she submitted. It surprised him to discover that her touch was pleasing. Her hand was small and delicate and the skin was soft, not hardened or rough from skinning and fleshing hides or cutting tipi poles. He liked holding her hand. He knew she felt something, too. He knew because her eyes had grown wide and darkened until they were almost the blue of a late summer evening sky. "*Unyin ktelo,* please, come," he repeated softly. Pulling gently, he coaxed her to follow him outside where it was much cooler.

Inside the lodge she had been like a wilting wildflower; but now, outside, she seemed to revive, turning her face

into the light wind to catch its caress. Her skin looked much
paler in the sunlight and there were light yellow flashes of
sunlight in her hair. She glanced up and caught him staring
at her and he felt embarrassed.

Turning away, Wolf knelt beside the tipi and tugged on
her hand until she knelt beside him. He patiently showed
her how to untie the outer skin of the tipi from the ground
pegs and how to roll the hide until it was raised off the
ground. He pointed to the inner lining and using the same
rolling technique, lifted it, too. Taking her hand once again,
he held it under the opening. Her eyes widened with surprise as the rush of refreshing cool air breezed its way
across her skin and into the tipi. She nodded and smiled.
She understood.

"This is what you must do when it becomes hot," Wolf
said, the Lakota words falling quickly from his lips.

The white woman did not answer. Annoyed, Wolf
glanced up, ready to scold her for not paying attention. She
was staring across the camp and he followed her gaze to a
woman stirring the family's evening meal in a large cooking paunch over an open fire. The savory aroma of boiled
meat and wild onions was heavy on the air and he watched
as she lightly licked her lips with the tip of her tongue.

Wolf touched her arm and helped her to her feet. "*Loy-
acin hwo?* Are you hungry?" He pantomimed, pretending
to feed himself with his fingers. "Hungry?" He touched her
mouth and then her stomach with his finger.

The *wasicu* understood and lowered her eyes, responding
with an embarrassed nod. "*Han, lowacin ye*. Yes, I'm hungry."

"Wait inside, I will get you food." He watched, amused,
as she scrambled under the lifted side of the tipi instead of
entering through the door hole. *This wasicu has much to
learn.* A disquieting thought prodded him. *Could it be possible that I would enjoy being her teacher? Sni. It is not
so.* He dismissed the idea. *We are enemies?*

He strode off to get his evening meal from his mother's
sister. In the Lakota way of relations Wolf called her
mother. His own mother and father had been killed by the

bluecoats when he was a child and it had been his mother's sister who had raised him. She would be polite and not ask questions when he took double his usual portion and he would wait until later to talk with Turtle Rib. He would learn more of the white woman first.

They ate, neither talking, although the sound of the woman's busy fingers and lips as she devoured the deer stew was noise enough. She licked her fingers clean to get every drop of the meal and Wolf wondered when she had last eaten. He took the bowl from her hand and filled it with water from one of the bladders he kept tied to the lodge pole near the door. Returning the bowl to her, he watched as she drank down every drop, hardly taking a breath between gulps. Her eating and drinking customs were shameful and he looked at her with a stern, disapproving glare. *Do all wasicu lack manners or is it just this one?* he thought.

She began to speak. It unnerved him to hear the Lakota words from someone other than his own kind, someone whose skin was pale and whose eyes were so blue. But the soft quality of her voice was pleasing.

"Thank you. *Lila pilamaya*," she said.

When she made the words they sounded strange to his ears. Although the words were right, there was a curious sound to them and he almost laughed again, but checked the urge. It would be rude. "*Tanyan Lakota iyaye lo*. You talk good Lakota," he said instead.

She shyly nodded.

"I am *Sunkmanitu Ceye a Pelo*, Calls to the Wolf," he said, touching his chest with his fingers. "You called me *Sunkmanitu*. You knew me?"

She nodded again.

How was this possible? Had he known her before the battle with the bluecoats? No, he would definitely have remembered knowing a white woman.

"*Takeniciyap hwo?* What is your name?" he asked, reaching out and tapping her lightly on the breast.

She quickly pulled back. The fear in her eyes had returned.

"What is your name?" he repeated, this time raising his chin in her direction instead of touching her.

"Ryan Burke emaciyapi," she replied, "I am Ryan Burke," she added in the language of the *wasicu*.

"Iamryanbuk," he said, trying to make sense of the white words. "Iamryanbuk." He pointed to her.

"No," she answered, shaking her head, "Ryan." She pointed her finger at herself. "Wolf," she said, pointing her finger at him. "Oh," she gasped.

She looked down at her finger with embarrassment, then folded her hands together. Starting over, she lifted her chin in his direction and slightly pursed her lips. "You are Wolf." Placing her hand on her chest, she added, "Ryan."

So she did know something of the Lakota ways. She knew it was unmannerly to use a finger to point at someone. The realization made him feel good. "Ryan," he said, the word odd on his tongue. He was happy. Now he had a name for this beautiful creature. "Ryan, Ryan, Ryan," he repeated, nodded and smiled at her. *"Wasté,* good."

She lowered her head, but he had already seen the smile that had settled on her face.

The paleness of her skin suddenly didn't matter. To his eyes she was more beautiful than any woman he ever remembered seeing. Even more beautiful than Ground Plum.

He was pleased they could talk and find out what strange thing had brought them together, but an uneasy feeling still nagged at him. Why did it seem that she was as puzzled by her presence in the encampment as he was? There were other questions, too. If she could speak his people's language, and if she knew about not pointing with a finger, why did she not know about lifting the side of the tipi in the heat of the day? Why did she not know how to eat quietly? He shook his head. No. There was more.

Maybe she was part of the strange thing that had happened to him at the battle with the bluecoats. Maybe she was part of his vision. Yes, this made sense. *Tunkasila* had great power. *Tunkasila* could give the *wasicu* the gift of the Lakota language. She knew some of the ways of his people; had *Tunkasila* taught these as well? There was a reason for all the Great Spirit did. He must find out why *Tunkasila* had sent her to the Lakota, why *Tunkasila* had sent her to him.

He would talk about these things with the holy man.

Evening settled into the Greasy Grass valley before Wolf had time to think again of speaking with Turtle Rib. After placing some small pieces of wood beside the fire pit, he began sorting through his belongings, withdrawing a fringed tobacco pouch and a bright red trade blanket from his cache. The woman watched his every move.

When he moved to the door she tried to follow.

"*Ena un wo.* Stay here." He held his hand up, blocking her way. Confident she would be there when he returned, Wolf lifted the door flap, stepped outside and allowed the hide to fall back in place.

He walked slowly toward Turtle Rib's lodge. Although the disturbing occurrence at Rosebud Creek was truly something he should seek counsel about, he still felt reluctant about asking guidance from a holy man. His friend Eagle Deer was right. He had no choice. He had to seek the old man's wisdom. But what of the woman? What would Turtle Rib say of her?

He hoped Turtle Rib would like his gifts. He hoped he would like Turtle Rib's counsel.

Chapter 12

THE FLAP FELL down into place and Ryan felt curiously lonely. She moved to the door and reached out, allowing her fingers to graze the hide where Wolf's hand had last touched. As fantastic as this whole adventure might be, as unbelievable an opportunity as it was for an anthropologist to study the Lakota people firsthand, she was afraid. Her only link to life and safety was a warrior who had just ridden in a battle against Crook's soldiers. The bloodied scalps the men had carried back to camp were reminder enough of the danger she faced. This wasn't a Saturday movie matinee and Custer wasn't going to look like Errol Flynn when he came riding over the hill.

She rubbed her temples, trying to ease the dull ache that had settled in with a vengeance. "Where's all my well-trained, high-priced, scientific objectivity?" She raked her fingers through her hair. "My objectivity? Hell, that flew out the window the moment I saw Calls to the Wolf in the flesh."

The voice of common sense and unwelcome reason whispered in her head. "You're a prisoner in his time. You're at his mercy. Beware. Beware."

Just because Wolf looked like the warrior from her

dreams, that wasn't enough reason to trust him with her life. She feared him, but—why was there always a but—she couldn't deny she was drawn to him.

"It's much more than just his physical appeal," Ryan debated aloud, and oh my, he had appeal. He had been brusque, hard, arrogant, but he'd also surprised her with kindness. He had been patient and he had fed her. The sudden memory of his touch on her body ignited a puzzling disquiet and she quickly tried to shove the thought away, but it refused to budge. She stared at Wolf's bed. Where had he gone? Did she really want to know? The determined grip of fear made its presence known again.

There was no question, this was his lodge. His personal belongings were neatly stored in parfleches and beautifully decorated possible bags. Another, larger bundle wrapped in a thick-haired buffalo hide lay off to the side. He had carefully stowed his war shield and rifle in this bundle before he'd left. Ryan liked that. He took care of his possessions. It showed self-pride without vanity.

He also lived alone. Except for the hide dress she now wore and her bed, nothing else indicated that anyone lived with him. Ryan frowned. The many beautiful hides she had seen proved he was a good hunter and provider. The welcome he had received when he'd returned showed he was well-liked . . . so why didn't he share his home with a woman or a family?

With that question came another to poke and prod and demand her attention. "If he does live alone, why wasn't he more surprised when he saw my bed in his lodge? I'm certain he was puzzled, but . . ." As if searching for the elusive bean in a shell game, she turned over a few more clues in her mind. "Maybe another warrior had promised to bring him a white captive, a woman." She lightly pounded her forehead with the heel of her hand. "No, that's stupid."

Kneeling by his bed, the delicious fragrance of cedar, sage and sunlight teased her nostrils. It was his scent. She had been very aware of it when he had stood close to her. It was the same pleasing aroma from her dreams. Bent on ignoring the warm curl of pleasure that warmed her, Ryan set her mind to learning where Wolf might have gone.

"Well, my handsome warrior, you had two things in your hand when you left, a red trade blanket and a fringed quill-worked pouch." She glanced at the cache of Wolf's possessions. "You rode with the war party at Rosebud Creek. Many scalps were brought back, so there will be a scalp dance tonight and maybe the celebration will continue tomorrow night as well. But I don't think you went to dance. You might have taken the blanket to keep you warm, but I don't think you would have taken the pouch with you."

Unconsciously, her fingers stroked the luxurious fur that covered his bed. As she smoothed the pelt, she felt something hard under her fingers. Picking up the object, she turned it to the firelight and felt her heart leap into her throat. A beautiful catlinite pipe bowl lay in her palm, a pipe bowl decorated with carved paw prints, wolf paw prints. It was one of the pieces Stockard had found. She frowned. Two identical pipe bowls had been collected. Yes, she remembered Gaffney's files. One had been found where Charley told Buddy to put up the tipi. The other was recovered almost three hundred yards away. The same person had carved them both. If that were so, why were they found so far apart?

The answer came quickly and she laughed aloud. The pouch Wolf carried held *kinnikinick*. Tobacco. It was a tobacco pouch and the second pipe bowl was in the pouch. Wolf had a dilemma and needed counsel. He had gone to see if he could find answers about what a Lakota-speaking *wasicu* was doing in his tipi and he needed to take a gift.

She moved to her own bed. Stretching out on her back, she stared up through the smoke hole. "Now, who would you go to in this Hunkpapa camp?" Sifting through the facts as she remembered them from her years of study, two names came to mind. One man was *Tatanka I'yotake*, Sitting Bull. The other was a lesser-known elder, *K'eya T'ucu'hu*, Turtle Rib, a holy man who had sought or found little fame for himself in the history books.

She rolled onto her side and stared across the lodge at

Wolf's bed. "Well, you're not alone with your problem," she whispered. "I don't know what to do about me, either. Where's the holy man I can talk with? Charles Antone Crying Wolf is a little more than three hundred yards away."

A noise outside the lodge caught her attention. Had Wolf returned so soon? A blitz of adrenaline raced through her body. She heard the noise a second and a third time, closer and much louder. She held her breath and didn't move.

Scratch, scratch.

A black nose and then the head of a brown dog poked its way under the raised edge of the tipi. The animal's pink tongue lolled out of its mouth as it panted and looked expectantly at Ryan. She could tell from its wiggling that somewhere at the end of its body on the other side of the tipi wall, a tail wagged a friendly greeting. Relieved, she laughed. She'd expected an unfriendly Lakota, not an impudent camp dog.

The dog wriggled closer and soon nuzzled against her. She scratched behind its ears and a grateful pink tongue licked affectionately along the back of her hand. "Now shoo," she whispered as the dog rolled over onto its back for a belly rub. "Please, go away." She clapped her hands with a couple of loud pops and the dog answered with a brusque bark. With one last doleful glance, he scooted under the tipi wall and was gone.

Ryan left her bed and moved to the door. If her theory was right, Wolf would be gone for a while. She peered out the door. Except for the cook fires and the surrounding tipis that glowed from the small pit fires inside, the camp was dark.

Nearly undetectable at first, the sound soon became louder and louder. Echoing off the hills on the other side of the river, the beat of a drum pulsated throughout the camp and was soon joined by the high-pitched voices of the singers. The warriors had returned with a victory and the camp would honor them throughout the night with songs and dancing.

To her right, three men stood and talked. In a moment a couple of women stepped out of the fire-lit lodge and joined them. Throughout the camp she saw other Lakota moving about and chatting in friendly groups as they made their way toward the dance circle. Nearby, a pack of dogs led by the brown creature which had visited her earlier ran by growling and tumbling with each other, scrapping over a well-gnawed bone. Children played in the dusk of evening and Ryan stared, mesmerized by the scene, enchanted by its simplicity and the sense of reality fled once more.

Einstein's theory of relativity might have touched on the possibility of time warp or time travel or whatever he called this craziness, but Ryan knew his hair would really have frizzed if it had ever actually happened to him!

With an appreciative nod of his head, Turtle Rib accepted Wolf's gifts and gestured for him to sit. The two men settled themselves on the lodge floor, facing each other across the crackling fire in the pit.

"I am honored you have come to my lodge," Turtle Rib said. "You have brought generous gifts." His hand patted the thick woolen trade blanket. "*Wasté*, very good." He carefully folded the blanket and placed it behind him but kept the beautiful fringed and quilled pouch at his side. "I have heard you rode with Crazy Horse and Sitting Bull against the bluecoats two suns ago. I heard also you pledged again and danced the sun dance. It was good?" Turtle Rib glanced at the healing pierce wounds high on either side of Wolf's chest. "They say many received powerful visions." He closely watched Wolf, waiting for the warrior's answer.

"It was a good dance," Wolf answered quietly, feeling the old man's probing eyes on him. He offered nothing more.

"I have never seen our camp grow as strong as it does now. It is good that we are all together. Five big camp circles now fill the valley. It is a good time for our people. The weather has been kind, the river is filled with cool water and many fish and the hunting has been good. Our scouts have seen buffalo in the nearby hills and our people are happy. Our bellies are full again." Turtle Rib paused and stirred the embers in the fire pit with a stick. "Those that come from the soldier forts say there is no food as the White Father's treaties promised. There are just thin cows whose meat rots quickly. They say the grain the white man gives is old and filled with many worms. It is said the worms move faster than the old cows." He added another small piece of cottonwood to the fire and watched the flames lick up around it. "This treaty with the *wasicu* is not good. Their promises are empty and they have made our people's bellies empty. I do not believe our people will do well making peace with these *wasicu*, they do not have much honor."

Wolf nodded in agreement and shifted restlessly. How long would Turtle Rib insist they speak only of general matters? The question of the broken treaties was important but Wolf was anxious for the old man's counsel. He must be patient.

Turtle Rib picked up his pipe stem and taking the beautiful pipe bowl with the carved paw prints from the pouch, he fit it on the stem. He then took some of the *chanshasha*, the red willow-bark tobacco, from the pouch and began to tamp some of the pungent mixture deep into the carved bowl. "We are newly acquainted and should share a pipe together. *Cannunkunpapi*. For a while we will smoke some of this fine tobacco you have brought." Turtle Rib picked up a small faggot from the fire pit and lit the pipe. He puffed four or five times on the stem until clouds of redolent smoke encircled his head and almost obscured his weathered face. Adding more tobacco to the bowl, he sucked strongly one or two more times, drawing the smoke deeply into his lungs.

"I have come to—" Wolf began, only to be silenced by Turtle Rib's upraised hand.

"There will be time," Turtle Rib gently admonished. "There will be enough time for all we must speak of."

The pipe passed between them, back and forth three times before Turtle Rib cleared his throat, looked up and nodded. Now they would speak.

The holy man settled himself comfortably against a willow backrest, his head slightly bowed, his eyes gazing into the fire as he silently listened to Wolf's words. From time to time, as Wolf recounted the events of the past two days, Turtle Rib drew draughts of pungent smoke from the pipe and allowed the wispy tendrils to escape his lips and float up through the lodge poles and out into the night air. Occasionally he nodded, or squinted in reflection, but he offered no counsel until Wolf had finished speaking.

"I know of your bravery as a warrior. Others tell me you have earned many honors in battle. You have counted many coups and have returned to camp with many scalps and many horses." Turtle Rib paused, prodding the bowl of the pipe with the tamping stick. "Even as we speak, the women are scalp dancing in honor of the bravery of our warriors and yet you do not join the men to dance and tell of the battle. The counsel you seek must be very important for you to miss this celebration."

Turtle Rib drew on the pipe, then glanced at Wolf. "I have also heard the words Iron Soldier is speaking against you. Since returning he has talked with all who would listen. He is saying you are dead but do not know it. He calls you *wanagi*, a ghost. He tells these things to everyone."

Wolf looked up at Turtle Rib and their eyes met and held. The span of silence seemed long until Turtle Rib spoke again.

"I do not believe this is so. If you were dead you could not take up the pipe and smoke with me. You could not take the smoke into your body. Tunkasila has his reasons for what he does but I do not believe he would allow a dead warrior to smoke—even in friendship. I think Iron Soldier's words are false. I think they are the words of a jealous man."

Turtle Rib squinted his eyes against the pungent cloud of smoke that escaped from his mouth before he spoke again. "The *wasicu*, the white woman you speak of—no one else in the camp has seen her. Why is it that only you have seen her? Could it be because she is a vision and not true flesh?"

"No," Wolf quickly responded, remembering the warmth

of her body all too well. "She is not a vision, she is a woman. She stays in my tipi." Again there was silence and Wolf waited patiently for Turtle Rib to comment. His wait was short.

Turtle Rib nodded solemnly. "I believe the Creator has given you a powerful vision. He has made you *wakan*. You were already a great warrior, but now the enemy can knock you to the ground and think they have killed you. However, Tunkasila has given you strong medicine and you stand up without any wounds to fight, again and again. I think he has also shown you things that will be in times that are coming. You speak of wagons without horses. Does the iron horse of the *wasicu* not move without ponies pulling on it? The tipis, taller than you have ever imagined, I have heard of things like this from those who have gone to where the great White Father lives."

Wolf nodded in agreement.

"And the white person," Turtle Rib continued. "I believe she is also *lila wakan,* very sacred. The Creator once sent us another, *Ptsesan-Wi,* White Buffalo Calf Woman. She brought our sacred pipe. Perhaps he has also sent this one with a message for the people. Perhaps he has given her the gift of our language so that she may tell her message to you and to the Lakota people. I think it is important for you to listen to her words." Turtle Rib drew another breath through the pipe and then quietly added another thought. "Although you say you cannot remember if she was there before you fought the bluecoats, I think this, too, is Tunkasila's doing. When he placed the woman in your lodge, he wanted you not to be afraid when you returned. He took your memory so that she may tell you why she is here herself." Turtle Rib fell silent for a moment. His eyes, squinting against the smoke of the fire, never left Wolf's face. "I also think Tunkasila has sent her for another purpose." The old man shifted his folded legs as if ridding himself of a cramp, and then continued. "She has slept in your lodge, she has taken your protection and your food. I believe Tunkasila has sent her to be wife to *Sunkmanitu Ceye a Pelo*."

"No, that is not possible!" Wolf protested angrily, beginning to rise to his feet. "She is nothing but a pitiful *wasicu*, she is not Lakota." He was offended. "How can you say a Lakota warrior, this Lakota, must take a white woman as wife?" He struck his chest with a closed fist. "I do not think this is so."

Silently, with only a slight movement of his hand, Turtle Rib motioned for Wolf to remain seated. "I am not the one who says these things. Would you refuse Tunkasila?"

Wolf was mute. Dropping his gaze to the fire, he stared into the translucent red glow of the embers. Although he had challenged Turtle Rib's suggestion, although she was a white woman, there was a quickening in his veins and he felt the pleasant spread of heat throughout his body. The feeling surprised him, confused him, but it felt good.

He raised his eyes to meet Turtle Rib's scrutiny. Another obstacle also existed. "What you suggest cannot be," he quietly offered. "This white woman cannot be my wife. My friend Eagle Deer has already spoken to *Mato Cante*, Bear Heart, for me. I have already sent many horses, buffalo robes and blankets to his tipi, and my words and my gifts have been accepted. His daughter *Ptetawote*, Ground Plum, is to be my wife." He stared at his closed hand on his knee. "It has been agreed." Once more he looked up at Turtle Rib and then back down into the heart of the fire.

"It is acceptable that you have both," Turtle Rib said without hesitation. "You are a strong warrior. You are an honored member of the Kit Fox warrior society and a good hunter. A man such as the one who sits before me has need for more than one wife, maybe even more than two. The question is, who will be your first wife? Although your gifts for Ground Plum have already been given and accepted, I believe Tunkasila now tells you who is to be your first wife."

Wolf's brow creased into a deep scowl. Turtle Rib's counsel was more than he had expected, much more. True, there was something undeniably fascinating about the woman, but a *wasicu* as a wife? No. No, that was something he had never given a moment's consideration. How could he ever get used to her pale skin? He stiffly straightened his shoulders. "If this is to be," he declared with a scornful manner, "she must be quickly taught what is expected of a Lakota wife. She will yield to me at once. She will fill my bed and know that the ways of the whites are not welcome here."

Turtle Rib held up his hand, quieting *Sunkmanitu Ceye a Pelo's* hard words. "I do not think that is wise. You must be patient. You must allow this woman to come to you when Tunkasila tells her. Only she knows what Tunkasila wants of her, what is in his heart. To anger her, to take her to your bed when she is not willing may make her keep Tunkasila's message to herself. Remember White Buffalo Calf Woman. When one of the warriors who first met her tried to force her to his bed, her punishment was harsh. He died." Turtle Rib offered the pipe to Wolf once more. "If your *wasicu* is to learn the ways of the Lakota, perhaps the shy little wife of your friend Eagle Deer will help."

Turtle Rib pulled the pipe bowl from the wooden stem and tapped it against the heel of his hand, loosening the burnt tobacco. Leaning forward, his motion deliberate and slow, he emptied the ashes into the fire pit, signaling that Wolf's counsel was at an end. "Tunkasila has sent you a great gift. You cannot insult the Creator, *kola*, you cannot send his gift away and you cannot dishonor his gift." The old man closely watched for Wolf's response.

"Tunkasila asks much of this Lakota," Wolf answered quietly.

"Grandfather Creator has honored you with much. What may now seem to be a hardship to you in time will become a great blessing."

Wolf stood and nodded. "I will give much thought to Turtle Rib's counsel."

"That is good," the old man answered, carefully wrapping the pipe bowl and stem separately in two gray rabbit pelts. He looked up at Wolf. His eyes narrowed speculatively. "I would meet this gift woman. You will bring her to me in the morning that I might see what nature of woman the Great Spirit has honored you with." Turtle Rib placed the pipe bundle into a fringed buckskin bag. "If I see what I believe to be is so, I will have it known among our people that your white woman is to be respected and treated as a good Lakota woman and that no harm is to be done to your gift from Tunkasila." He offered a small nod and a warm smile. "Go now, your wife waits for her husband."

Stepping from Turtle Rib's lodge, the cool night air washed across Wolf's face, touched and refreshed his tired body, but he paid it no heed. There were too many baffling thoughts in his mind. Preoccupied, he slowly walked toward his own tipi. He didn't notice anyone who greeted him along the way.

The solid fall of a hand on his shoulder broke his deliberation. Two of the young men from Crazy Horse's camp had joined him on the path.

"You are going the wrong way, *kola*," Otter Skin said. "Can you not hear the drum and the singing? The women are scalp dancing and soon *we* will dance and tell of our brave deeds against the bluecoats. Come with us *kola*, come tell everyone of your vision."

"Feast with us." The shorter, heavier warrior, Yellow Hawk, tried to turn Wolf around and pull him in the direction of the sound of the drum. "There is much food, and the women," he grinned, "the women will be anxious to—"

"Not tonight," Wolf answered, detaching himself from Yellow Hawk's grip. "There will be dancing and feasting again tomorrow, maybe then."

"And the next night, and the next," laughed Otter Skin as the two warriors waved and walked away toward the celebration.

Wolf watched them disappear between the tipis. *Why does my heart lead me away from the voice of the drum and the dancing? It is more than Turtle Ribs's words.* He made his way in the opposite direction, back to his tipi, back to the woman Turtle Rib had called Calls to the Wolf's wife.

Chapter 13

"I'VE GOT A problem," Ryan muttered. Before Wolf had returned, she had already spent one night in his lodge. Now she faced a second and this time he would be sleeping in the tipi, too. The Lakota custom was clear. By sharing his lodge, she had declared that she was now his wife. Would he demand a husband's rights? And if he did, what would she do? What could she do?

As if her thoughts had summoned him, she heard him speaking to his horse picketed outside. Her heart began to race. *Sunkmanitu Ceye a Pelo* had returned.

Slipping beneath the covers on her bed, she pulled them up to her shoulders and turned her back to the tipi door. With any luck, maybe he would believe she was asleep.

A caress of cool air touched her cheek as Wolf entered the tipi. Feigning sleep, Ryan breathed deeply. With every nerve taut and every sense heightened, she fought to keep from shaking. The breeze stopped. The flap had been closed.

Ryan peered through the narrow framing of her lashes and could see Wolf's shadow on the tipi wall over her bed. The flickering fire caused his reflection to move, to shift and lengthen, but she knew exactly where he was. He was standing next to her bed. The piquant aroma of *kinnikinick* brushed her nostrils. He had shared a pipe with someone.

Time stretched into an eternity. How much longer could she lie quietly and endure the agony of her ruse? Why didn't he move away? What did he want? There was only one possible answer to her last question. According to tribal law she was his wife.

She heard him move. Peering through half-opened eyes, she could no longer see his shadow on the tipi wall. He was gone. Relieved, Ryan exhaled a long, slow sigh.

In an instant the covers were snatched from her body. Startled, Ryan cried aloud and tried to scoot away. So, he had made his decision.

"*Winyan*, woman, get up!" Bending over, Wolf lifted her as though she were a weightless rag doll and set her on her feet.

"Take your hands off me!" Not willing to give in without a fight, Ryan tried to push him away. "Leave me alone!" Wolf might believe he had the rights of a husband and he might have the strength to take her by force but she would make sure he knew he'd not found a willing partner.

Wolf's fingers bit into her shoulders and held her tight. Angry, she lifted her chin at a stubborn angle as his black eyes swept her from head to toe.

"If Tunkasila has sent me a white woman, why has he sent me one with such bad habits?"

"What?" she exclaimed. It was ridiculous, but she felt offended. "I don't have bad habits!"

"Do all white women live in hot tipis? Do all white women eat with much noise? Do all white women sleep in their dresses?" He tugged at the buckskin garment, ignoring Ryan's inept attempts to brush his hands away. "If this is so, it is not good. If Tunkasila has sent you to me and has given you Lakota words to speak, then you must be more like a Lakota woman." He disdainfully raised his left brow. "This one does not know why Tunkasila sent *Sunkmanitu Ceye a Pelo* a stupid woman." He tugged at her dress again. "Lakota women take off their clothes when they seek their blankets for the night."

She forgot all about being afraid. She forgot how vulnerable she was and she forgot about keeping a prudent rein on her temper. The Lakota words came fluently. "I am not Lakota, and if you expect me to get naked and spend the night alone with you—ha! Oh no, Tunkasila definitely did not send you a stupid woman!" She crossed her arms over her breasts and gave her head a haughty lift.

Wolf scornfully pinched his nostrils together. "This one understands *now* why all white men smell bad. Too much sleeping in their clothes."

He turned away. It was obvious that as far as he was concerned, their discussion was over. Ryan couldn't muster anything more than a frustrated, indignant splutter. She didn't smell bad. Besides, just what did he mean about her being some sort of gift from Tunkasila? Had she not been so unsure of Wolf's intentions, she might have laughed at his audacity.

Wolf bent to stoke the fire, then moved to his own side of the lodge. Relief soothed Ryan's nerves. Maybe he wasn't going to touch her after all. She stood ramrod straight, guarding her side of the tipi, but in the next moment her mouth formed a surprised "o."

Standing beside his bed, Wolf began to take off his clothes.

Ryan stared at his back. *I'll be damned if I'll let him think he scares me, that I need to guard myself against him.* In truth, she couldn't drag her gaze away.

He set his moccasins neatly at the foot of his sleeping pallet and turning away from her, placed the eagle feathers from his hair atop a rawhide parfleche case. Lifting the bone breastplate over his head, his muscles moved and stretched over his back and the washboard plane of his ribs. A small, unbidden sigh escaped Ryan's throat and she quickly clamped her hand over her mouth, deterring any other traitorous noises that might escape.

With shallowed breath, she watched the fire chase shadow and light across his copper skin. His broad shoulders and arms were cut with deep muscle, not the deliberate bulk of someone who willfully exerts himself for effect, but hard muscle that comes from natural male strength. Her eyes followed the straight, indented line of his spine, down the ladder of his ribs and further.

Wolf removed the brass-studded belt and Ryan knew she should turn away. If he caught her watching, he might take her curiosity for acceptance. Too entranced by the beauty of the man, she foolishly dismissed the danger and continued to stare.

With a quick tug on the knot of the leather thong around his waist, Wolf removed his breechclout. The last barrier was gone. Ryan's mouth suddenly felt parched. She had never seen such a wondrous sight. He reminded her of an exquisite piece of bronze sculpture that had magically become exciting living flesh.

His narrow hips flared into taut, hard-muscled buttocks and then descended, curving into well-defined thighs and long, strong calves. He wasn't modest about his nakedness and made no attempt to cover himself. He stood tall, not egotistically, but with the ease of someone completely comfortable with himself. Releasing his single braid, he raked his fingers through his hair. Firelight touched the lustrous strands as they cascaded over his shoulders and down his back.

She felt warm, much too warm, and tried to ignore the delicious tingling that spread and saturated her body until it finally centered itself in the pit of her stomach and demanded an easement she couldn't give herself. Breathless and a little dizzy, she attempted to calm her rampant pulse. Her fingertips ached to reach out and stroke his smooth skin, to feel the silken touch of his hair. *This is ridiculous.* She abruptly turned away from the captivating view. *No, damn it. This isn't ridiculous—this is dangerous.*

Wolf settled himself under his blankets and turned his back to the woman. Walking away from her had been one of the most difficult things he had done in a long while. Like many things that eluded him, he couldn't remember how many nights it had been since he had last lain with a woman. His hunger was strong.

Turtle Rib's words had been wise, but Wolf's desire fought to overshadow reason. It was his right to take this *wasicu* into his bed as a wife and ride her body for his pleasure. He regretted his promise to Turtle Rib. The discomfort would be worse than a deep wound, but he would follow the old man's advice and bide his time. If she was *wakan*, he didn't want to anger Tunkasila. He would wait until he knew why she was here. He would wait until the *wasicu* told him she was ready to be his wife. Although the craving in his body would goad him, he would wait. But he hoped Tunkasila wouldn't make him wait for too long.

His lips curved into a slight smile. The woman reminded him of a golden puma he had once hunted when the tribe had been north near the snow-capped mountains. She was graceful, wide-eyed and wary, but wild and all claws and screech when angry. His smile broadened. He knew of many ways to tame wild things.

He mouthed the word she had said was her name. "Ryan." It made no sense and was odd to his ears, but he liked the sound.

A slight rustling noise interrupted his thoughts. Without turning to look over his shoulder, Wolf's smile returned. *So, she follows my teaching. She removes her dress to sleep.*

With that knowledge, his decision suddenly vexed him all the more. He groaned, remembering how beautiful she'd been without her clothing, how soft her pale skin had felt when he'd touched her. Knowing she now lay naked beneath her furs, his smile disappeared. Restlessly settling deeper into his bed, he tried to turn his thoughts from the woman. He forced himself to think of his favorite horse staked outside the tipi. He pushed images of his friend Eagle Deer into his mind and he gave thought to the foggy memory of the last time he had gone hunting with Otter Skin and Makes No Bow. He drove his mind away from thoughts of the woman, but his body resisted, telling him in its own way how foolish he was to try. Wolf shut his eyes, determined to ignore the fevered need that grew hard and heavy between his legs.

Ryan lifted the furs up under her chin and moaned

lightly. With each slight movement, with each breath, the
soft pelts that protected her nakedness proved to be her
enemies. They stroked her skin like the sensuous touch of
a lover. Her nipples tingled and tightened. Turning over on
her stomach, she tried to dispel the disturbing sensation,
but the featherlike touches caressed her back and buttocks.

She gazed at Wolf where he lay on the other side of the
tipi. Firelight illuminated and outlined the long shape of his
body. His shoulders rhythmically rose and fell but she
didn't believe for one moment that he had fallen asleep so
quickly.

The pop of a dry log in the fire pit startled her and drew
her eyes to the flames. Focusing on the saffron glow, Ryan
tried to ignore the man who lay on the other side of the
hot embers by watching the slow rise of the smoke as it
wound its way upward through the smoke hole. Had it been
only twenty-four hours since the dizzying vortex had sent
her through the boundary of time? Time . . . it was such an
elusive thing. You couldn't hold onto it. It flew by too
quickly when you were enjoying something, it dragged and
took forever to pass when you hated what you were doing.
And now . . . now time had become a thrilling adventure, a
frightening escapade, a flip-flop of reasoning, a fantastic
gift.

I have the ability to change history. The thought had
come quickly and its import startled her. But, it was true
and very tempting. With a simple warning to either side,
she could make the Battle of the Little Big Horn disappear.
She could change the outcome and rewrite the history
books.

*If I escaped tonight, I could meet Custer and warn him.
He could keep his men together, attack and win the battle.*
As quickly as that thought faded, another tiptoed into her
head and settled in with a tenacity of its own. *But what if
my alliance is with the Indians? If I warned them, they
could escape and leave the valley, and the battle would
never take place.* She felt the bitter burn of tears as they
welled up in her eyes and she balled her hands into tight

fists until her fingers ached. *No, I can't think of this. If I do, I'll go crazy—if I am not already there.*

If she couldn't help either side, what was the purpose for her magic carpet ride through time? It had to be more than a sight-seeing excursion. There had to be an objective, a mission, something important enough to defy the boundaries of reality.

The battle isn't the reason I'm here, is it, Charley? There's something else. She searched her memory for some clue, some hint to Charley's plan. And then she knew. It was so simple, so wonderfully simple.

When they had first met, she'd given only a moment's thought to the old man's words but now they returned to her in a rush, tumbling quickly into place. Now they made sense and she understood it all.

Things are being taken from this place, things that have lain quiet in the ground for many, many years, things that belong here—sacred objects are being stolen and sold for large sums of money to increase one man's personal wealth, to feed his greed. I have been waiting for you to come—if only someone could go back to that time a hundred and twenty years ago and set a trap to catch the thief who is stealing from us today. But that's impossible . . . isn't it?

So that was Charley's fantastic scheme. Set a trap. But what kind of a trap? Her mind grasped the concept and ideas began to bombard her until one single notion sifted its way through all the others and made its way to the top of the pile. *What if I were to put together some sort of phony artifact. It would look authentic on the outside, but what if something on the inside was wrong. It would be something that could easily be recognized as wrong when the artifact was opened and studied. It's a good idea. It could work. But what could be put inside?*

Pushing her hair away from her face, Ryan accidentally pulled off one of her earrings. Carefully feeling around in the bed, she found the earring and the backing. Picking up both pieces, she stared at them. Her breath quickened. *Yes. It would be perfect. Just like Charley said, one earring*

proves the existence of the other. Immediately she saw the
genius to Charley's plan. A false artifact could have been
buried in her own time, that part would have been easy,
but the thief would have known it wasn't real. The ground
would have been freshly disturbed and too soft. But if she
buried something now, in this time, the dirt will settle for
over 120 years and although the artifact would look authentic when it would be dug up, the earring would prove
it isn't. *Charley, my God, this is so crazy it just might work.*
"You sly old fox," she breathed.

With fanciful images of the FBI hauling Edwin Gaffney
off to jail floating through her mind, Ryan drifted off and
found restful sleep.

No dreams filled her mind, no magnificent warrior with
his wolf companion came to her or called her to join him.
She had already answered his call and they peacefully slept
together in a tipi on the banks of the Greasy Grass.

Chapter 14

WORD HAD TRAVELED like a grass fire throughout the camp. From the southern Sioux lodges to the Cheyenne camp to the north, they had all heard about *Sunkmanitu Ceye a Pelo's* white woman and had come to see her for themselves.

Turtle Rib stood outside his tipi, waiting to welcome his guests. So this was the man from whom Wolf had sought counsel, but what did the holy man want from her? His eyes studied her and she gave back in kind until a slight, almost imperceptible nod of his head showed his approval. With one test passed, she steeled herself for the rest of the meeting ahead.

She remembered seeing an old photo of Turtle Rib. He had been in his eighties, and she guessed fifteen years would pass in this time before he would sit in front of the camera. It felt odd to know the future and the past at the same time.

"Welcome to my lodge." Turtle Rib's whole presence was steeped with dignity.

"Thank you," she replied. "I'm honored to meet with a man of your wisdom." Without thinking, she extended her right hand.

Turtle Rib frowned and quickly glanced at Wolf, silently questioning her gesture. Finding no explanation, his gaze dropped back down to Ryan's offered hand. "What is this?"

Ryan Burke, how can you be such a fool? Pay attention to where you are and what you're doing. This isn't a Washington parlor and he has no idea what a handshake is. Let's see you get out of this one. It didn't take long.

"*Le wasincu ogna, nape wicayuapi.* This is how my people greet each other. The open hand shows friendship. It shows I have no weapons or bad feelings." Ryan continued to hold out her hand. "If you'd take my hand, I'd be very pleased."

Turtle Rib looked back at Wolf. It was obvious he took Wolf's slight shrug to mean the gesture was harmless. The holy man slowly raised his hand to meet Ryan's.

Not waiting for Turtle Rib's fingers to reach her own, she closed the distance and firmly gripped his hand. "Thank you," she said, "I'm very honored."

Turtle Rib smiled. Nodding, he grasped Ryan's hand harder. "This is good, this *wasicu* greeting." Still nodding, he withdrew his hand and offered it to Wolf, grinning when it was accepted. "Come, we will eat food my wives have prepared and then talk."

Their talk lasted for two hours. Stepping out of Turtle Rib's lodge, Ryan was surprised by the number of people who were still waiting for a glimpse of her. Most were women and children, but some of the men had come also. They stood back, more suspicious of the *wasicu* than the women.

Curious glances and shy, polite nods greeted her and she replied in kind. These were not the modern Lakota. These were the people she had learned about through her studies, ethnographic treatises, books and lectures. These were the old traditionals. In a rush, the women crushed around her, pulling her away from Wolf. Ryan tried to escape but they completely surrounded her. Some reached out to touch her hair, some tentatively stroked her skin and one even pried open her mouth to look at her teeth. Each new discovery led to another flurry of discussion. Many had never seen a white human this close; some had never seen a white woman at all. The color of her eyes intrigued them the most and they pulled and pushed her face, to the left and to the right, exclaiming about their deep blue shade.

"Look, the white one's hair is not dark like our own. It is the same as the *Oglala*, Crazy Horse," one woman exclaimed.

"Ah," another uttered, moving closer to touch and tug at Ryan's hair.

They compared the color of Ryan's skin to their own darker hue and they studied her soft hands. One woman loudly judged that because her hands weren't rough and hard, she must be lazy.

Ryan stoically endured their inspection. If Charley couldn't arrange for a return ticket to her own time, living among these people might be a lot easier because of her knowledge, but it was friendships that would make it bearable. All she had to do is keep everything in its proper time. No more slipups like handshakes.

The people quickly filled her arms with gifts. Bundles of food, pemmican, dried meat, wild onions, camas and edible roots were shoved into her hands. Someone gave her a bone awl and another gave her a soft brain-tanned hide. A blanket, a ball of sewing sinew and some brass buttons were also added to the pile. She offered a polite thanks for each gift. *"Pilamaya."*

With childlike curiosity, one woman approached, and catching Ryan unawares, reached under the broad sleeves of her dress and fondled her breasts and hips. The gifts tumbled to the ground.

"Le wasté heca, this is good," the nodding gray-haired woman giggled. "Good for many strong boy babies."

"Ah," another old crone snickered with a near toothless grin, taking a peek for herself. "Better for many strong warriors."

Stunned, Ryan stood motionless while the women laughed at their ribald remarks behind politely covered mouths. Feeling the heat of a scarlet blush build in her cheeks, she crossed her arms over her breasts, putting an end to any further inspections. Finding an opening in the crowd, she quickly moved to Wolf's side, seeking safety in his company.

"*Winuhcala, inajin yo!* Old woman, stop! *Akiyopo. Le winyan ki ayustanpo!*" Wolf scolded the crone with a smile that proved he was hard-pressed to hide his own laughter. He moved through the crowd and waved everyone away. Taking hold of Ryan's wrist, he pulled her closer to his side. "*Cane wakansni yo,* do not be afraid," he whispered. "They mean you no harm." He sent another young girl away. "No one will harm you. To greet you is a great honor for these women. They know you are *wakan*. They know Tunkasila has sent you to live among us."

Astounded, Ryan looked up at Wolf, then back at the smiling people. "*Wakan*? They believe I have power? They believe Tunkasila—"

"It is known," Wolf replied.

Of course. It made perfect sense. How else could these people explain her sudden appearance among them. How else could she speak their language? Reservation life, the coercion of the missionaries and the enforced confinement in the Indian schools had not yet touched most of these people. They still held on to the mystic simplicity of their old beliefs. Yes, of course they'd believe she was *wakan*.

She looked around the camp. If there was absolutely no way she could get back to her own time, she could survive. These people would treat her well. She could ask them to take her to a white settlement or to one of the forts, Fort Phil Kearny or perhaps Fort Pease. *With my knowledge of history, I could fit into the 1870s well enough to live out the rest of my life safely. It's not what I want, but, if push came to shove, I could do it. But wait—what about Charley's plan? If we're going to dupe Gaffney, I'll have to take care of that before I go, and I'll need help.* She glanced up at the tall Lakota beside her. Was that why he had been in her dreams? Was *Sunkmanitu Ceye a Pelo* the one who was to help her?

Wolf returned her gaze. The warm excitement returned. Not ready to face the feelings he already stirred in her,

Ryan quickly kneeled to retrieve the fallen parcels only to find a young boy had already begun to collect them. The child shyly smiled at her but when he looked at Wolf, the boy's grin widened and his eyes filled with unabashed adoration. Glancing over her shoulder, Ryan silently questioned the tall Lakota.

"This is Little Hawk, the son of my friend Eagle Deer," Wolf explained, affectionately tugging at one of the child's braids. "He will carry these things to the tipi for you."

"*Lila pilamaya*, thank you very much," she said, before Wolf helped her to her feet.

With a bashful backward look, the boy trundled off, staggering under his heavy load.

"Everyone wishes to know the special woman. Even our children come to see you," Wolf said.

He placed his hand reassuringly on the small of her back, guiding her away from the crowd. It wasn't an intimate touch, they barely knew one another. It was the touch of a courteous gentleman, but yes, it was more. What an odd dichotomy. She had traveled many years into the past, into what the ethnographers called the "camps of the savages," to find someone who had the qualities she sought in a man of her own time. There it was again. There was the realization that there were things here that made her happier than in her own world.

Stay. Stay. You would be happy here. The niggling voice inside her mind had returned.

The heat of Wolf's touch warmed her. She tried to smile at the people who still surrounded them but she couldn't focus on anything else but the pressure of his hand. His hand had fought battles against the whites, but his hand felt gentle and pleasing against her back—it felt right.

Stay, the voice cajoled. *Stay.*

She looked up at Wolf and found his gaze already upon her. He looked away first but Ryan's new knowledge left her breathless. *You feel it, too.*

Wolf suddenly grabbed her arm. Pulling her closer. The muscle along the edge of his jaw tensed and his eyes narrowed, hardening his expression. Ryan followed the route of his stony glare.

Beyond the edge of the gathering, a man pushed his way through the crowd. Stepping in front of Wolf, the man blocked the path, his face rigid with hatred.

"Look people, does Iron Soldier lie?" Striking his own chest with his fist, he then pointed at Wolf with a scornful upward jab of his chin. "This *wanagi*, this ghost man, dares to walk among us."

Not as tall as Wolf, four or five inches shorter, the man was also heavier. A churlish twist curved his mouth and his black eyes were menacing. Cruelty and loathing lay heavy in their depths. Ryan could see he'd once been attractive, but a vivid scar marred his face. It coursed from his forehead through his left eyebrow, across his eyelid and then continued to his chin. He wore a fanning of coup feathers in his long hair but they didn't seem to reflect the same sense of honor as those Wolf wore.

"Look at him, my people. Did I not speak the truth when I told you *Sunkmanitu Ceye a Pelo* walks as though his heart still beats, as though he still has blood in his body? He lies. He is *wanagi*." Iron Soldier pointed to his own face. "With my eyes saw this liar killed. I saw the holes and the blood from the bluecoat's bullets." He then rudely pointed his finger, shaking it in Wolf's face, bringing a loud gasp from the people. "See, how he flaunts all of his lies? He wants the Lakota to believe this *wasicu* is *wakan*, a gift from Tunkasila." Iron Soldier spat on the ground at Ryan's feet. "Bah—I think she is nothing but a white whore this walking dead man has stolen from the soldier fort. I think this whore spreads her legs for any Lakota to keep her scalp."

With unexpected speed, Iron Soldier grabbed Ryan's hair and brutally yanked her head to one side. Laughing at her sharp cry, he pulled her away from Wolf's protective embrace.

Ryan stumbled, tripping over her own feet, and fell back against Iron Soldier. His body shook as he laughed and wrapped his free arm around her. His grip on her hair tightened and Ryan knew she couldn't escape without leaving half of her hair in his hand. His breath was foul and the rancid odor of his body assailed her nostrils. Ryan tried not to breathe. She looked at Wolf. Why didn't he help her? Wasn't he going to challenge Iron Soldier?

Wolf didn't move. He stood his ground and appeared undisturbed by Iron Soldier's assault. His face remained impassive, but the flint-hard look in his eyes soon answered all her questions. He was watching Iron Soldier, coldly gauging the man's intent and contemplating his move. For an instant Wolf's eyes met Ryan's, just long enough to offer reassurance, and then his gaze slid back to Iron Soldier.

She felt a slight loosening in Iron Soldier's grip and took a step away.

"No. You stay," he growled, jerking her back against him.

With a sickening wrench in the pit of her stomach, she felt Iron Soldier's hand travel downward over her breasts. He cupped one, and then the other in his blunt-fingered hand and cruelly squeezed and pinched her tender flesh. She tensed, sucking in a ragged breath as his hand wandered lower and lewdly rubbed her belly in a circular motion. He laughed in her ear, then clamped his hand between her legs, pulling her back against his body. Although the soft, thin hide of her dress separated his hand from her naked flesh, it felt as though nothing divided them at all.

"See how she easily comes to me?" he taunted Wolf. "Even as you look, she comes to me." He laughed. "I will take this woman and prove she is nothing but white man's dung."

"*Maza Akicita*, Iron Soldier, will take nothing that does not belong to him," Wolf coldly responded. Looking at Ryan, his eyes charged her to block out everything and everyone but him.

She obeyed.

The people silently watched and waited for the challenge they knew would come.

Iron Soldier couldn't wait. "Look, see how this fearless

dead one uses nothing but words to protect his white—"

"Choose your words very carefully," Wolf interrupted, his rage barely visible beneath an icy veneer. "It may be said you are jealous of my woman and seek to claim her for yourself."

"What would I want with a filthy white woman?" Iron Soldier sneered, suddenly letting go of Ryan's hair and shoving her away with a hard blow to her back as though her touch defiled him.

Reeling, Ryan fell against Wolf. He quickly drew her back into his protective embrace. She laid her head on his chest, seeking his comfort.

"Does Iron Soldier see where this woman goes?" Wolf challenged. "She goes with me."

"For now that may be so," Iron Soldier answered, his lips curling into a sneer, "but soon your lodge will be welcoming another woman. How will the one who is to be your *wife* accept this whore? Do you think she will stay once you have ridden this woman of our enemies?"

Wife? The word burned into Ryan's mind and then her heart. She no longer felt the pain in her head or her back, nor did she see any of the people around her. *Wife?* She tilted her head and looked up, searching Wolf's face for an answer. He didn't meet her gaze. His only response was a slight tightening of his arm around her shoulders.

"Do you make this quarrel because our friendship died a long time ago? Do you still claim ownership of a spotted war pony you lost to me in a race? Do you still blame me for the mark on your face? Or, do you make this quarrel because Bear Heart did not accept your horses and gifts for Ground Plum?" Wolf asked.

"I have no use for one thin pitiful horse. I own many fast horses." Iron Soldier paused for a moment and ran his finger lightly along the jagged scar on his face. "This means nothing to me. I cannot see it, but you can and it will shame you each time you look at me." Iron Soldier stepped closer. "No, my friend, you have not yet named the reason I face you now. Perhaps you are too afraid to put the truth into words."

Iron Soldier turned to look at the people and then met Wolf's eyes once again. "I make this quarrel with you because your lies will bring bad things to the Lakota." Iron Soldier's face twisted with rage as he raised his voice so everyone who had gathered could hear. "He cannot be trusted. How can anyone trust a *wanagi*—"

"Enough!" Turtle Rib silenced Iron Soldier's words. Every head in the crowd turned as the holy man moved forward and stopped by Wolf's side, silently stating his alliance. "Iron Soldier acts no better than a wild dog. You are Lakota, be Lakota. This woman is of no concern to you, but I warn you, she receives not only the protection of Calls to the Wolf, but mine as well. I have smoked the pipe with him and we have shared words." Turtle Rib looked away from Iron Soldier and his gaze met many in the crowd. "I tell this to all who hear my words," he said loudly. "Calls to the Wolf is not *wanagi*, he is not dead. Blood still fills his body like the waters fill the Greasy Grass."

"There is but one way to prove these words!" Iron Soldier lunged forward, his knife glinting cruelly in his hand. His scarred face twisted as his voice rose in a blood-chilling yell. "Eeeyaaaa!"

The crowd gave up a gasp, then fell silent as Iron Soldier's knife arced and carved through the air, its deadly intent clear.

Refusing to relinquish his hold on Ryan, Wolf tried to step out of the range of Iron Soldier's blade but the crowd had moved in too close and there was no place for him to go. Tightening his hold, he turned, shielding her from Iron Soldier, but the tip of the knife found its target and sliced cruelly into Wolf's flesh, carving a swath half the length of his forearm.

Only the thick, uneven spill of blood on his arm proved that Iron Soldier's knife had met its mark. Wolf hadn't flinched.

Ryan felt light-headed. Afraid she might faint, she bit down hard on her bottom lip, hoping the pain would keep her alert. She touched his arm but moving her aside, he stepped around her.

Wolf's angry gaze fell on Iron Soldier and without looking away, he raised his arm, causing the blood to flow in bright rivulets down his arm. "Lakota, what is this? Is this water? Look closely. Is this not blood?" He angrily pointed his finger at Iron Soldier, punctuating his insult. "Iron Soldier lies to you—again."

"Do I lie about the woman? She is *wasicu*. Why would Tunkasila waste Lakota words on a *wasicu* tongue?" Iron Soldier shouted, his face misshapen with rage. "Do I lie about the bad things that *Sunkmanitu Ceye a Pelo* will bring to this camp? Wait and see, and then you will remember my words and know who speaks the truth and who lies!" Iron Soldier raised his bloodied knife into the air and shook it in Wolf's direction. "This woman will bring you death, warrior! She will bring death to us all!"

From somewhere within the crowd, a softer voice spoke, its quiet tone an unsettling contrast to Iron Soldier's shouts. "Perhaps it will be the *wasicu* who dies."

There was a coldness in the voice that set Ryan on guard.

"Stand away, I would see the one who claims my husband."

"Ha," Iron Soldier scoffed. "It seems I am not the only one who questions the great warrior and his white whore. It seems your bride *Ptetawote*, Ground Plum, seeks answers as well."

Ryan watched the young woman approach and her heart sank. She was exquisite. She walked with graceful pride, carrying her slender, high-breasted body straight. The fringes on her dress swayed gently, accenting the feminine rhythm of her movement. The girl's brown eyes were large, slightly almond-shaped beneath arched brows. There was a fullness to the girl's mouth, the kind that usually drew men to crave its intimate touch, and the teeth that gleamed as she spoke were straight and white. Ground Plum's black hair fell down her back in two weighty and lustrous braids, both reaching her waist. No man in his right mind would take another to his heart when it had already been touched by someone so lovely.

Ground Plum stopped in front of Ryan and only then did she see the girl's flaw. Her eyes were cold. They didn't soften, not even when she glanced up at Wolf.

Ground Plum slowly walked around Ryan, appraising her with great deliberation. First she poked Ryan's ribs, then lifted her hair and finally tested the muscles in her arms. The inspection complete, she glared at Ryan, silently setting a challenge.

Although it took every ounce of restraint that she possessed, Ryan curbed her anger. Her safety depended on it. Tunkasila would not send a woman who was easily provoked.

"This one was not sent by Tunkasila," Ground Plum loudly declared. "She is too ugly. If she speaks Lakota, it is as Iron Soldier says. She is a whore from the soldier forts. Perhaps even Pawnees and Crows have been on her." She looked at Wolf, daring his rebuttal. "You would bring this ugly, unclean woman to our marriage as a second wife when you have yet to fulfill your promise of marriage to your first? She is enemy to the Lakota." She poked at Ryan's arms one more time. "She does not have enough strength to carry wood and water to be a good second wife. I will not accept her in my tipi." Ground Plum gave Ryan another sharp jab in the ribs and haughtily turned away.

Wolf didn't answer immediately. He seemed to wait and carefully weigh his words. When he did speak his voice was quiet and firm. "I will come to your lodge later and speak with your father. Now is not a good time for what must be spoken."

"This time is the only time you will have to speak your words," Ground Plum bitterly replied, turning back to face him. "I, not my father, would hear your words now."

"I will say no more," Wolf answered, attempting to keep his voice low and for Ground Plum's ears only. "I do not wish to speak in the ears of those who need not hear of our agreement."

Ground Plum plucked at the side fringes on the skirt of

Ryan's dress, pulling the hide away from her body. "How many times have you crawled between these pale *wasicu* legs and spilled yourself into her? You have disgraced me and my family."

"How can that be so? There is no marriage between us. I have disgraced no one. Be quiet, hold your tongue, or the disgrace will be your own."

"So, you admit you have ridden this—"

"I have admitted nothing."

"Your gifts were accepted by my father—"

"And that is why I will speak only to your father." With a simple upward gesture of his hand, Wolf silenced any further argument from Ground Plum, but her bitterness still blazed in her eyes.

Ryan felt sorry for the girl. Learning that your future husband was living with another woman had to be heartbreaking, but to have it known by everyone had to be humiliating. She stepped forward and gently placed her hand on Ground Plum's arm. "We are not—he hasn't—nothing has happened. . . ."

Ground Plum's hatred robbed her of every trace of beauty. She pulled away as though she had been touched by a hot brand and without hesitation struck out, her hand hitting the left side of Ryan's face in a resounding blow. The slap burned Ryan's cheek and filled her ear with a loud ringing.

"I did not speak to you, cow!" Ground Plum spat, pushing Ryan away. Flashing an angry glance at Wolf, she renewed her scornful attack. "I speak only to you, my *great* warrior."

"Then you have nothing to say," Wolf replied, his voice tight. "This matter is between your father and me. I will speak to no other." His eyes softened and a slight frown furrowed his brow as he looked down at Ryan and gently touched the reddened mark Ground Plum's hand had caused. He turned, meeting Ground Plum's arrogant stare. "This woman is to be given honor. It has been said to be so by the holy man, and it is said to be so by me."

"This cow will get nothing but spittle from me." Ground

Plum turned away to leave but stopped and angled to face Wolf again. She curved her mouth into a sly smile and volleyed one last salvo loud enough for all who listened to hear. "I see now that Iron Soldier's words are true. Calls to the Wolf is the one who lies, making promises he does not keep. Soon everyone will know, and Calls to the Wolf will no longer be greeted with honor. Then I will be happy."

Ryan didn't understand. Why was Wolf doing this? He had cared enough to ask for the girl. Why had he changed his mind? The gentle touch of his fingers on her face a second time gave her the inkling of an answer and Ryan Burke knew that destiny had much more in store for her than just Charley's scheme.

Chapter 15

WOLF KNELT BY the river's edge and washed the blood from his arm. He flexed his forearm and closed and opened his hand a few times. He was lucky. Iron Soldier's knife hadn't cut too deeply.

Ryan lightly touched his shoulder. "Do you have anything, a medicine, that you can put on it?"

"Nothing is needed. It will soon heal. Look, the blood has stopped." Wolf glanced up and his reassuring smile promptly faded from his lips. "Your face . . ."

Ryan placed her hand over her cheek where Ground Plum had hit her. She could feel the hot welt.

Leading her to the shade of a cottonwood at the river's edge, Wolf pointed to the ground where the thick grass offered a comfortable cushion. "Sit here." Hunkering down, he dipped his hand into the river and held it under water. After a few moments, he gently pressed his palm against her face. His cool, wet skin felt wonderful on her fevered cheek.

"You must agree with Iron Soldier and think I am one who speaks false," he offered quietly, his dark eyes closely watching her.

"Why would you say that?" Ryan flinched as he moved

his hand, refitting her cheek into the curve of his fingers. Ground Plum had hit her harder than she wanted to admit. "I don't think you're a liar."

"I told you no one in our village would harm you, but Iron Soldier and Ground Plum have both—"

"That wasn't your fault," Ryan interrupted. "I'm an intruder. It must be difficult for them to understand why I'm here." *God knows it's difficult enough for me!*

He sank his hand back into the cold water, then placed it on Ryan's face once more. For a moment the fierce warrior disappeared as he winced a silent apology when she recoiled again. He began to pull away but Ryan placed her hand over his and pressed her cheek into his palm. Closing her eyes, she was quiet for a time, absorbing the sensation of his touch. She was enveloped by the clean male and cedar scent of him. His skin felt so good against her own.

Slowly opening her eyes, she memorized the shape of his lips and the regal plane of his nose before losing herself completely in the velvet black of his eyes. She felt a delightful quickening spark that ignited deep within her and coursed throughout her body, leaving an exciting warmth in its wake.

My God, what's happening to me? Had her usually reliable common sense taken flight? In less than twenty-four hours after an unbelievable twist and slide through time and reality, she was sitting beside the Little Big Horn River with a warrior from Sitting Bull's Hunkpapa camp and she was quickly losing her heart.

But what about the girl? Before she allowed herself one more moment of this wonderful insanity, she had to know. "Is Ground Plum to be your . . . wife?"

Wolf didn't answer right away. He moved his fingers on her cheek in a light caress. "I have given many ponies and blankets to her father. My gifts were accepted." He turned and stared into the depths of the running water of the Greasy Grass. "Yes, she was to become my wife."

Ryan's heart pitched, then sank.

"Much has happened and much has changed since that

time," Wolf continued. "Now, it is not what I want," he added softly before turning back to Ryan.

"I understand now why she was so upset," Ryan said, her heart pounding with hope. "She must think that I—"

"Her anger is misplaced," Wolf said, unable to mask the angry flash in his eyes. "Her insults and attacks belong to me, not to you. I will speak with her father and she will be free to marry another." He looked away again. "I have known *Ptetawote*, Ground Plum, since childhood. We are friends. I do not want her to be unhappy and alone." His fingers brushed Ryan's cheek once again. "But she is not the wife I seek."

So, we have something in common. With you it's Ground Plum and with me it's Richard. Is there such little difference between your time and mine?

For the next half hour, Wolf tended her face. Each time he touched her, it became more difficult for Ryan to temper her feelings. She savored the sweet pang that filled her breast. There was a gentleness to this man. There was a sense of honor and a kindness that belied the image of the fierce warrior with the bloodied scalps tied to his lance. The man *Sunkmanitu Ceye a Pelo* wasn't softened by this image. If anything, it made him stronger, more noble. It was these traits that made the others in camp respect him and follow his lead. It was these qualities that drew her to him. It was why she was beginning to lose her heart.

"Why . . . why does Iron Soldier say you are dead?"

A haunted look shuttered Wolf's eyes. The time between question and answer lengthened and he finally spoke. "It is something I cannot easily explain. Perhaps it is also something you would not understand. You are *wasicu* and do not have the beliefs of the Lakota."

"Tell me, please."

He looked across the river and watched a pair of hawks soaring in a large, lazy spiral over the hills. "Iron Soldier tells everyone that I was killed in battle three suns ago."

A shiver slithered down Ryan's spine. "That's foolish."

"Iron Soldier says I was killed by many bluecoat bullets."

"That's a lie," Ryan quickly stated. "There aren't any bullet wounds on your body."

A knowing smile curved his mouth, and once again he placed his hand lightly on her bruised face. "*I* know that is so, but how is it that you know it is so?"

Her heart bounced. *He knows I watched him last night!* Ryan felt a blush heat her cheeks and she lowered her head, hoping he hadn't noticed. "I know," she whispered, embarrassed to meet his eyes, "I just know."

He drew his fingers over her cheek and paused at the corner of her mouth. His expression sobered and he dropped his hand to his knee. "Some things happened to me when we fought the bluecoats." Wolf paused and watched the hawks ride an updraft. "I had a vision, a powerful vision. I saw things that are not of this place. Some of these visions still come to me in my sleep."

He stood and moved toward the river, as if distancing himself from her would make the telling of his story easier. "I also do not remember some things that should be strong in my mind." He turned and looked at her for a moment, then sat down on the grass a few feet away, stretching his long, buckskin-clad legs out in front of him and leaning back on his elbows. "My vision revealed many things that are a mystery to me. I saw shiny birds, each one bigger than a hundred eagles. These birds fly high in the clouds without moving their wings. I saw—"

"A plane?" Astonished, Ryan whispered the words in English.

He showed no recognition of her word, and continued, "I cannot tell you all, but you also are a part of it."

"Me? I d-d-don't understand," she stuttered. The more he told her, the more astounded she became.

He rolled to his side and propped himself on his elbow. Picking a stalk of bright yellow-eyed daisies from a nearby clump, he idly spun the flowers between his fingers. He watched them spin for a moment or two, then looked up. "I believe I have seen your face before. The shape of your eyes and your mouth are familiar to me." The flower dropped from his fingers and he leaned over and touched the soft curl of her hair around her face. "This too is familiar." He drew a deep breath, and retrieving the sprig of daisies, sent them spinning again. "I believe as Turtle Rib says—you have been sent here for a special reason. I do not know how this has happened. Turtle Rib said only you know and only you can say." The flowers were suddenly still. "I agree with Turtle Rib."

Wolf held out his hand, offering the delicate blossoms to her. When she reached out to accept them, he allowed his fingers to linger against hers.

Ryan stared at their hands and held her breath. Light and dark. Night and day. She might not know how she had flipped in time and she might not know if she would ever see her own time again, but one thing she did know—Calls to the Wolf aroused feelings in her that had never been awakened before. How could she ignore these wonderful new sensations? But more important, what was she going to do about them?

"Tell me, *mitawicu*, tell me why Tunkasila has sent you to me."

Her eyes widened with surprise. He had called her *mitawicu*, wife. Daring a glance, she saw the teasing light in his eyes had returned and a smile now broadened his lips. *Damn him, he knows the havoc he's creating.* "Uh . . . what . . ." she stammered.

"I wish to know where you have come from and why you have been sent to me and to this place." He watched her carefully. "Turtle Rib asked these same things and I believe what you told was not all that you could tell. There is more and it would please me if you would tell these things to me."

Ryan tipped her head back against the tree before looking up through the leaves at the blue sky beyond the branches. How could she even begin to explain her mission? Would he understand what she needed to do, and if he did, could she count on his help? "I've come from a very long distance."

Wolf nodded.

"Where I'm from there are evil men, evil white men,

who would rob the Lakota of things . . . more things than they take from your people now. They will take not just the land or buffalo, but other things that are . . ." She hesitated, unsure how to put the words together so he could completely understand. "These things they would steal are things the Lakota have made, things that . . ." *Damn it, I'm not doing this well at all!*

To tell him about beads and moccasins and children's dolls would have no great meaning. They were nothing more than everyday objects, no more important to him than a pair of socks or a ballpoint pen would be to her. How could she possibly make him understand? She fumbled through her mind, searching for the simple answer that sadistically eluded her. Finally she knew. It had to be something sacred, something powerful with great spiritual meaning. She began again to explain. "These white men would rob the Lakota of their medicine bundles and use them to make themselves important."

Wolf's eyes widened. "That cannot be! The spirits of the bundles will become angry. Bad things will happen. They are to be used only in the way the makers of the bundles tell us to use them. They must be used with the proper ceremonies and songs."

"That's true," she replied, "but these men don't know how to use the bundles in a good way. They don't know the songs and the ceremonies and they have no respect for them." She paused again and carefully chose each word before she continued. "I've been sent here to help capture these men who steal from the Lakota and make bad things happen."

She waited. Did he understand? Her wait was short.

"Who are these men? Where are they?" Wolf began to rise. "There are no other whites here but you. I will take many warriors and go find these men. We will make war and I will kill them for you. We will stop them from stealing these things from my people."

Ryan anxiously tugged at his buckskin leggings. "Please wait, sit down. These men are not here now, Wolf—they will come after . . ." *Damn! How can I explain about the future? How can I tell him they'll come after a great battle, after more than 120 years have passed.* Once again, the words were there for her. "They'll come after this camp is no more, after the Lakota have gone from this place. The white men will search for things that are left behind and they will steal them away. Others will want to trade with them for these things and they will offer many horses."

Wolf's eyes narrowed as he digested what he'd heard. He bent his left knee and rested his arm upon it. "Your people are the worst enemies the Lakota have known." He spoke with hatred. "Not even the Crow and Pawnee are so bad. I would kill all of the *wasicu* my weapons would find and then I would ride many days to seek out more. I would cover the land, like the flooding of a river, with the blood of the *wasicu.*"

Ryan shifted uncomfortably and tried to hide her uneasiness, instinctively clasping her arms across her chest.

"Tunkasila asks much of you." His voice had softened and the direction of his thoughts had changed. "He asks you to go against your own people. He has put a great hardship on you. How can one small woman see that this task is done?"

His words surprised her. In the midst of his own outrage and hatred for her people, he understood the difficulties she faced.

Will the destiny we share be much more than Charley's plan to catch a thief? Ryan trembled and her breath became ragged. *Is our destiny to be . . . each other?* "Would you help me stop these men?"

Giving thought to her request, Wolf combed his fingers back and forth through the long, lush grass. A tiny ladybug, dressed in her finest red-and-black polka-dot gown, landed on his knuckle. He raised his hand and appeared to inspect the small insect meticulously. "Do you ask anyone else for help?"

"No," there is no one else," she answered, her voice barely louder than a whisper. "There is just you."

He looked up from inspecting the bug, his dark eyes carefully studying her. "I will help you." He punctuated his statement with a quick flick of his wrist that sent the little beetle flying away.

"Thank you." She touched his hand lightly, and tried to ignore her hastening pulse and the delicious warmth that followed in its wake. The feeling had nothing to do with a counterfeit medicine bundle, but it did have everything to do with her being a woman, a woman losing her heart to a man from a dream.

"Come, your face is still red, I will put more water on it."

Wolf rose to his feet, his movement agile and smooth. He held his hand out and gently pulled Ryan to her feet. They stood face to face, hand in hand, neither aware of the world around them. Time in his world and in hers stood still.

His hand slowly slid up Ryan's arm. As his touch lingered somewhere between her wrist and elbow, her breath quickened and she leaned closer to him.

"Ah, here you are, my friend."

Startled, Ryan quickly pulled away from Wolf and turning, found a man and a woman standing on the pathway. The woman stood slightly behind the man and shyly peered at Ryan. The top of her head came only to the man's shoulder and her ebony braids hung down over her breasts in the fashion of the married women of the Lakota.

"Hau, kola." Wolf placed his hand reassuringly on Ryan's arm. "I am glad you have found us."

"We are not intruding?" the man asked with a teasing grin.

Wolf laughed. "Perhaps a little, *kola.*" He motioned for the couple to move closer.

The man confidently stepped forward but the woman held back until introductions were made.

"I am called Eagle Deer," the man said, striking himself lightly on the chest. "This woman is *mitawicu,* my wife. She is called *Wiyaka Wasté Win,* Pretty Feather. We would be friends with Calls to the Wolf's white woman."

A smile broke wide on Ryan's mouth and she readily

stepped closer to the couple. "And I would be friends with his friends."

The afternoon was pleasant in the shade along the Greasy Grass. Across the river, four young boys rode their ponies along the brink of the hill. To the south of the encampment, a herd of horses contentedly grazed on the abundant grass along the bank and a few dipped their muzzles in the water for a drink. The spring had brought many foals and the mares fretted as their young bolted and charged about, kicking up their heels under the warm June sun.

The two men sat alone, resting among the shady trees along the river's edge.

"Things are better for you today, my brother?" Eagle Deer asked.

"They go well. The visions I do not understand have not returned but twice since we last spoke." Wolf paused, his eyes seeking out the white woman and Pretty Feather. Satisfied they were safe, he continued. "I followed my brother's advice and spoke with Turtle Rib."

Eagle Deer nodded. "*Wasté*. That is good."

Wolf watched the two women as they walked together along the bank of the river. He found he could not stop looking at the *wasicu*. It pleased him to see she was making friends with Eagle Deer's shy wife. They were a good match for friendship. He reluctantly dragged his gaze away and looked at his friend. "Turtle Rib's words were wise. We spoke of my vision and what it could mean." He swatted at a horsefly that had landed on his arm. "There is trouble coming for the Lakota but it is this special woman who will help us."

Eagle Deer nodded. "I have heard Iron Soldier and Ground Plum have already brought trouble for you and the woman."

"Iron Soldier, bah! That foolish one challenges me."

"And what of Ground Plum, my friend? She was to become your wife when you returned from sun dance."

"Neither Iron Soldier nor Ground Plum want to see and

accept what is so," Wolf declared. "The decision for these things have been taken from me."

Eagle Deer looked thoughtfully at his friend. "I think it is more than that for you. You do not appear to be troubled with this new decision. I think my brother makes up his own mind."

Wolf didn't answer.

"Iron Soldier is dangerous. His words are dangerous," Eagle Deer continued.

"Iron Soldier is *all* words. It is only bullets and arrows that can hurt me."

"Has he not already given you a wound with his knife? Has he not brought pain to the woman?" Eagle Deer lifted his chin, pointing at Ryan. "Has not Iron Soldier always wanted what was not rightfully his to possess? Does he not still blame you for the scar that—"

Wolf raised his hand to silence his friend.

Undaunted, Eagle Deer continued. "Since we were children together, has he not always been jealous of Calls to the Wolf? I would caution you, brother. Be careful. Iron Soldier's skill with bullets and arrows is well-known."

"I will watch, but I do not believe even in his anger that he would break tribal law and kill another Lakota. He hungers too much for power within the tribe. He wishes to be a war chief. Killing one of his own would bring dishonor. He would be turned out of camp and be the one they call *wanagi*." Wolf rested his hand lightly on Eagle Deer's forearm. "But I will heed your words and be watchful."

Eagle Deer nodded.

"Now, my brother, enough of this talk of trouble." Wolf watched the women and a smile played across his mouth. "I am pleased. Our women talk together well. I think they will be good friends to each other."

Eagle Deer's eyes followed the direction of Wolf's gaze. "I, too, am pleased," he said, meeting his friend's good humor with his own, settling his long legs out in front of him. But he pressed his concern again. "My brother, you cannot ignore Iron Soldier. Did he not challenge you when your ponies and blankets were accepted by Ground Plum's father instead of his? Be careful, *kola*, I fear you have an enemy among your own people."

"Enough of this talk of Iron Soldier. He angers me."

"Please, you must hear my words. Do not act a fool. Iron Soldier is not honorable and you will not know when he will strike. Protect what is yours, or what you wish to be yours," Eagle Deer gestured toward Ryan with a short nod. "Protect it very carefully."

Wolf looked thoughtfully at his friend and nodded. His attention drifted back to the river and he felt the anger leave his body. His eyes only saw the pale-skinned woman and he drank in the sight of her as a thirsty man would take in water. The sunlight filtering through the trees cast a shimmering golden light on her long, brown hair. She tipped her head back and laughed as Pretty Feather tucked a few flowers behind her ear. His gaze traveled down the fair column of her throat and unconsciously, he leaned forward. When he spoke again, his voice had softened. "We have been friends for many years. I have talked with the holy man as you suggested, but now I would seek *your* counsel, if you would give it."

"I will give what I can. Are we not as brothers?"

"This woman," Wolf glanced toward the river, "has touched my heart. It has happened quickly, but Turtle Rib said she has been chosen by Tunkasila to be wife to me. I feel his words are so and I no longer wish to take Ground Plum to my tipi. I do not seek a second wife."

"You have known Ground Plum since you were both children and this *wasicu*, you have known her little more than one day. Are you not too quick with your feelings?"

Wolf measured his words carefully. "It seems as though I have known this woman all the time I have been alive. It is as if she has lived within me, here." He raised his hand to his heart and looked up at his friend and then his gaze traveled back to Ryan. "Somehow I have seen her face before she came here, but it is a memory that still hides from me." He paused, then quietly added, "I think there is a feeling like this within her as well."

"What counsel do you seek of me?" Eagle Deer gave a

troubled sigh. "It seems you counsel yourself very well." Eagle Deer rested his hand compassionately on his friend's shoulder and then patted him lightly on the back.

"She stays with me in my lodge. There are no others with us. Is she not mine to take as wife."

Eagle Deer looked thoughtfully at his friend. "This is true. It is the way."

"Then I will go to Ground Plum's father. I will tell Bear Heart I have taken another as first wife and it is no longer possible for his daughter take this place in my lodge. I will tell him he may seek another husband for Ground Plum, that she deserves to be a warrior's first wife and there are others who would make good husbands for her. I will tell him he may keep my gifts and I will give him many new ponies as well. This would not bring shame to Ground Plum."

"Tell me, *kola*, do you have no feelings for Bear Heart's daughter?"

Wolf bowed his head. "My feelings are like a brother for his sister, nothing more. I believe her feeling for me is greater, but mine is not so. I chose her to be my wife because we have been good friends and no other woman pleased my eye until—"

"What of your people?" Eagle Deer interrupted. "You are Lakota. This woman you would have is *wasicu,* our enemy. You believe she is a gift from Tunkasila, and she may have the Lakota language inside of her, but she is still *wasicu*, and will always be *wasicu*. Will not your children carry this enemy blood? Will it not weaken their hearts?"

Wolf stood and restlessly paced back and forth. He knew Eagle Deer's words were true but there had to be an answer, some words that could free him of this dilemma.

"What if she were to leave quickly, as she came? Has she said she would stay? Would you keep her prisoner if she wanted to go to the soldier fort and leave the Lakota?"

"No," Wolf responded firmly, although his heart suddenly hurt with the possibility that Eagle Deer's words could be true. "That will not happen. She will stay."

• • •

Ryan trailed her fingers through the water, enjoying its cool balm. Venturing a sidelong look at Pretty Feather, she watched Eagle Deer's wife gently rubbing her stomach, and smiled. "How soon until your baby comes?"

Pretty Feather blushed. "Only a short time. Perhaps no longer than until the next full moon."

"Is this your first?"

"Oh no," Pretty Feather laughed, shyly covering her mouth. "My husband is a strong warrior. This is my third. I have two sons who will grow up to be powerful and brave like their father and Calls to the Wolf." Pretty Feather ducked her head and continued softly, "I would wish this baby to be a daughter."

"That's right," Ryan smiled, raising her hand roughly to the height of the little boy she had met earlier. "I met one of your sons today."

"Ah yes, my youngest, *Cetan Cik'ala*, Little Hawk."

The women fell silent, content to sit quietly and enjoy the warm afternoon.

Ryan scanned the riverbank. Everything looked much the same as did in her time. The big cottonwoods, her favorite large oak and the outbreak of boulders by the river's edge were all much the same. She stood and approached the big gnarled oak tree.

"Where are you going?" Pretty Feather asked.

"Up there," Ryan answered sprightly, pointing into the higher limbs. She grabbed onto the first branch and found it much lower than she remembered. The tree would grow another twenty inches or so before Gaffney's project would be in the valley. She easily swung up on the bough.

"No, you must not," Pretty Feather cried. "What if you should fall? Calls to the Wolf would not be pleased."

Ryan reached the second, third and fourth branches and continued upward. "If I fall, we just won't tell him."

"Stop teasing me," Pretty Feather pleaded, resting her hand on her swollen belly as she laughed. "Please, come down. Are you not afraid up there so high? I am frightened watching you."

"It's wonderful up here," Ryan exclaimed. "I can see all

the way up and down the village." She balanced herself on the broad limb. "I can see up the river, I can see down the river and I can see right into this little bird's nest." Ryan laughed. She could not remember ever feeling so free, so happy.

"Do you think you can fly like that little bird?" Wolf asked, stepping close to the oak and leaning against the rough trunk. "I think you should fly down to the ground, little white bird, before a big wind shakes the tree and you fall out."

Ryan giggled. "I see only one big wind and even as strong a warrior as he is, I don't think he can shake this big tree." It felt so good, so right, to tease and be happy with this man.

Laughing loudly, Eagle Deer clapped Wolf on the back. "Your words to me earlier must be so. This woman sounds like a wife."

Chapter 16

NED SLOAN FLIPPED through the pages of the chart scanning the handwritten notes entered by each nurse who had cared for the patient in ICU bed number four for the past twenty-four hours.

"I still don't get it," he muttered, turning page after page, browsing each report and then double-checking pages he'd already read. "There's absolutely no reason for him to go sour on us like that."

"Sounds like I missed quite an event," Beth replied, changing the bag of IV fluids being fed into Dillon Wolf through the subclavian line. "I take a day off and you guys can't even keep my favorite patient stable." She shook her head with a sad yet teasing smile. "He's leveled off nicely, though, and hasn't budged a bleep since."

Sloan looked up at the older nurse. In his opinion she was the best on the floor and he was especially glad she'd been assigned to this patient. "Good," Sloan mumbled. "It's about time." He closed the chart with a soft snap. "We almost lost him, Beth, and I don't know why. Besides, I don't like getting codes when I'm heading home for some well-earned R and R." He set the chart down on the night-stand. "I especially don't like getting 'em when there's nothing in the patient's etiology to make you expect 'em.''

He moved closer to the side of the bed. Slipping a pair of surgical gloves onto his hands, he lifted the gauze bandages from the wound on Dillon's forehead and the larger one on his jaw. "Hmm, these are coming along nicely." With proficient ease, he changed the dressing on Dillon's forehead and then inspected the longer cut on the edge of his jaw. "I'm afraid this one's going to leave a scar. It's a nice piece of repair work but Mr. Wolf is going to have himself a little souvenir from his crash."

Beth tore open the sterile dressing pack, offered its contents to Dr. Sloan and glanced at the wound. "I think it'll add a rakish look to our handsome patient. And you know what? It's not going to hurt his chances with the ladies one little bit."

"Speaking with a hopeful heart, are we, my darlin' Beth?" Sloan teased.

"Dr. Sloan," she flagrantly sighed. "At my old age, a hopeful heart is all that's left."

With the bandages changed, Ned Sloan stood back. "You know, I really think he's gonna make it through this okay." He stuffed his stethoscope back into his pocket. "Something tells me we're through the worst of it. I think from here on we're just going to have to coast until one day we walk in and he'll be sitting up wide awake, fit as a fiddle and demanding to be released."

"I won't bet against you, Dr. Sloan," Beth replied. "In thirty years of nursing I'm not surprised by too many things anymore."

Chapter 17

FACING THE TIPI wall, Ryan pulled the buckskin dress up over her head. She had dallied, waiting until Wolf was in his bed before she began to undress. In the faint glow of the fire she watched him lying on his pallet, his back to her. Placing her folded clothing at the foot of her bed, she slipped under the trade blanket and prayed sleep would come soon.

Slowly her eyelids drooped and the sweet caress of sleep drifted along her body, leaving a slight smile on her lips as she surrendered to its embrace.

Wolf listened and hearing the silence, knew she was asleep. "Ryan." He whispered her name. What special power did she have? What gift had Tunkasila given her that had made it so easy for her to capture his every thought?

He slept fitfully through the night, not finding any rest as the disturbing images returned and filled his dreams. He finally surrendered. Lying awake in the early morning light, he watched as Ryan uncurled from her night's sleep and stretched, raising her arms above her head. The blanket slid from her shoulders and bared her pale pink-tipped breasts. His body instantly stirred and filled. How could a *wasicu* woman give him so much hunger?

He glanced up to her face and drew a sharp breath. She was fully awake and watching him. Slowly pulling the blanket up around her neck, she covered herself, but her gaze never left his.

"It is morning," he said quietly, speaking the obvious and feeling like a young boy who had been caught peeking at things he should not see.

"I know," she replied, her voice soft and husky with the remnants of sleep.

Her hand remained at her breast, holding the blanket as if it were a shield that would protect her from danger. It offered weak protection at best, but he would honor her shield—for now.

Reluctantly, Wolf forced his thoughts away from her soft body. Rolling onto his back, he stared up through the smoke hole at the top of the tipi, trying to ignore the longing that had settled hard between his legs. He watched the red strips of cloth on the ends of the poles fluttering in the early morning breeze. They reminded him of the soft sweep of the white woman's hair and he tightly shut his eyes against the sight. Must everything make him think of her? If he intended to honor Tunkasila and keep himself from giving in to the enticement of the white woman, he must put his mind to other things.

"I have asked Pretty Feather to help you find your way in this village," he said authoritatively. "She will show you the things you must know about the ways of a Lakota woman, how she cares for her husband and her lodge."

The *wasicu* made no answer.

Wolf moved onto his side and looked at her. She sat on the edge of her bed, trying to slip the buckskin dress over her head while still holding the blanket protectively against her breasts. He checked the urge to smile.

"You may put the blanket aside, it will be easier to dress." He saw her reluctance. "I have seen a woman's body before." Her sky eyes lifted to meet his. They were filled with apprehension, and he offered a small smile. "I have seen *your* body before." Obviously embarrassed, she turned away, leaving him filled with disappointment. "You are made no different than Lakota women, you are only white." Her blue eyes shyly sought him again and he gave a dispassionate, nonchalant shrug that lied about how he really felt.

"If you like, I will help," Wolf offered, standing up, unfazed by his own nakedness.

"*Sni!* No!" Ryan quickly turned away. "Stay where you are. I can manage."

Pretty wasicu Ryan, you are like a child-woman. Your face becomes the color of red spring berries. "I will bring us food."

He quickly dressed and moved to the door. "Pretty Feather will be here soon." Before stepping outside, he ventured another look over his shoulder. Ryan had finally succeeded in dropping the dress down over her body and now stood barefoot by her bed. Her sun-touched hair fell in disarray about her shoulders, tangled and mussed from her sleep. He liked the way she looked—soft and pleasing—and he knew her breath would come in short little gasps if he were to pull her tightly against him. She would feel warm, very warm in his arms. Wolf took that thought with him as he left the tipi. He needed a pleasing thought in his mind this morning. He couldn't shake the disquiet his dreams had left behind.

Wolf's mother's sister generously gave him some berries and roasted rabbit, but not before she teased him about his new wife. He took her heckling with good humor and added another shank piece of rabbit and a third handful of the juicy berries for his trouble. Swatting his hand, she continued to laugh but dropped a fourth handful of berries into the bowl before sending him away.

Ryan was sitting outside the tipi and Wolf joined her on the buffalo robe, placing the wooden bowl between them.

"Eat," he offered, holding a joint of the meat out to her. "It is very good. My mother's sister is a good cook."

Ryan hesitated. Although the food smelled delicious, she didn't know what he was offering her. She hoped it was prairie chicken or rabbit but it could be opossum or raccoon, or . . . she quickly glanced around the encampment and found the small brown dog sleeping by Eagle Deer's lodge. At least it wasn't dog—well, it wasn't *that* dog. Her fingers grazed Wolf's as she accepted the meat and quickly looked up, meeting his gaze in reward.

"Thank you," she whispered.

He nodded. Watching her closely, he motioned with his hand. "Eat, it is good."

She took a bite and a trickle of fat ran from her lips and down her chin. She reached up to wipe it off, but Wolf's hand was there first. His fingers cleaned the grease away, then lingered near her mouth, tracing the fullness of her bottom lip.

"Your mouth is different in shape than a Lakota woman's," he said huskily. "The color is much lighter and the shape is softer, more rounded." His fingers continued to follow the outline of her lips, the slick coating of grease allowing his touch to slide smoothly over her skin.

A delightful ache tightened in the pit of Ryan's stomach and breathing became next to impossible. Unable to permit the disturbingly delicious caress to continue, she grasped his wrist and stilled his inspection. "How can I eat my food? I might bite your fingers instead."

Wolf grinned. "It is wise, then, that I move my hand away from your sharp teeth. I would have much trouble shooting my gun or my bow without these fingers and we would become very hungry."

Ryan took another bite of the roasted meat, then popped a small handful of berries into her mouth. Wolf still watched her. Her mouth full, she glanced up at him.

"I can see I will have to hunt many times a day to keep your stomach filled," he teased.

After finishing their meal down to the last berry, Ryan was content to sit on the buffalo robe and watch the morning activities in the encampment. Even in silence, his company delighted her.

Everywhere she looked, there were families beginning their busy days. Children eagerly bound away from their campsites to join their friends in play. Across the river, the

horses had made their way down to the water and with a
little jostling and shoving, were tasting their first cool drink
of the day. Here and there men gathered in small groups,
laughing and sharing stories. This was as close to paradise
as she had ever seen, but it was a paradise that was in its
last days, a paradise that would soon be destroyed. It wasn't
fair. With all the knowledge she had, she couldn't help
these people. There wasn't a thing she could do.

"Tell me about your people."

Drawn from her disturbing thoughts, she glanced up at
Wolf.

"You must miss them very much." He lifted his hand
and gently pushed back a wayward strand of hair from her
cheek.

*What can I tell you that would make you understand
about my people? What could I possibly say that could
sound reasonable in the face of what history has in store
for the Lakota?*

At that moment Pretty Feather arrived, saving Ryan from
having to find an answer.

The muscles of the horse beneath Wolf pumped in a steady
rhythm as it galloped across the flat land. Wolf's long hair
whipped in the wind and streamed out behind him as he
rode crouched low on the animal's back. He rode hard,
trying to elude the disturbing dreams and memories that
continued to follow and plague him. He needed to find a
quiet place to sort through all that had happened since the
battle at the Rosebud.

The pinto labored through the belly-deep water at a gallop and then scrambled up the bank on the opposite side
of the river. Shale and clumps of dirt broke off the embankment and splashed back into the water, but Wolf drove
the animal onward.

He rode north of the encampment and soon the village
disappeared from view. On top of a hill he brought the
sweating horse to a halt. The animal's lathered sides heaved
and its nostrils flared as it gulped in huge breaths of air.

Wolf had never been up this far from the camp on this

side of the river. The land rolled in hills, mounds and long gullies. Very few trees dotted the area but the buffalo grass was high, thick and rich, enough to feed a large herd of horses for many, many days.

It looked like a good place but although the late morning sun shone brightly, Wolf felt chilled to the bone. He slid from the pinto's back, his moccasined feet landing silently. What was this place? What was there on top of this hill that made him think of death?

The ground sloped away on all sides, and turning slowly, he scanned the land all around. It was very beautiful but the icy feeling never left him. It relentlessly touched him with a wintry chill and in the heat of the summer day, he shivered.

"What is this place?" His voice sounded so loud on the quiet hill. It startled him.

The pinto dutifully followed Wolf as he walked around the top of the hill and looked out in each direction. To the southwest Wolf could see the smoke of the village camp-fires and the cloud of dust that rose as some of the men moved the horses to graze on new grass. Overhead, the clear sky offered a blue ceiling free of any clouds, remind-ing him of the blue-eyed woman who had come to fill his heart. And still the cold remained.

The land here was familiar and yet he knew he had never ridden up this hill before. He felt as though a thousand eyes were watching him and he turned and glanced around un-easily again. There was no one.

The pinto quickly lifted its head and gave a sharp whinny. It pricked its ears forward and looked off into the distance. Wolf's gaze followed. There was nothing.

Lightly placing the palm of his hand over the animal's nostrils, both man and horse stood still, diligently watching. Still nothing. Beneath his hand, he felt the horse relax and then suddenly tense again. The pinto turned its head. Gaz-ing out over the opposite side of the hill, the horse began to tremble. Nervously dancing and sidestepping, the pinto jerked at the rein and then, wide-eyed, tried to bolt. Wolf firmly held the rein and the horse wheeled around, snorting puffs of hot air from its nostrils. With its quivering muscles bunched, the horse anxiously pawed at the ground.

And then Wolf heard the sound. He had heard the sound before but this time it was different. It was like the muffled sounds in a thick fog—not here, not there, but everywhere. It was all around him, hollow and flat, gunfire and galloping horses, the clinking sounds of the bluecoat's long knives, the metal clink of horse trappings, flying arrows and war whoops . . . and screams. Wolf's vision blurred. Dizzy, he stumbled and leaned against the horse. Was he becoming as one who had no mind? The sounds faded as if carried off by the breeze and then it was quiet once again. The hilltop and the gullies were empty. He was alone. There were no soldiers, no warriors, no guns, no horses but his own. But he knew—somehow he knew there would soon be many soldiers and many warriors, many guns and many horses. Death would soon be in this place. The dead would be all over this hill and the ground would run wet and red with their blood.

Vaulting onto the pinto's back, Wolf kicked the horse into a wild gallop. He drove the animal down the hill as though the flames of a thousand fires were licking at its heels. He rode toward the only comfort he had found. He rode back to the *wasicu* who had come with Tunkasila's blessing.

The anguish that had been with him since the battle at Rosebud Creek cruelly harassed him. Why did everyone call his vision a wonderful thing when it only brought him torment?

Sunkmanitu Ceye a Pelo yelled against the wind that pummeled his face and tore his voice from his throat. "Ryan! Ryyaaaann!"

She was the only good that had come of it all. She was the only joy to this gift of trickery from Tunkasila.

The spotted horse laid its ears flat against its head, bared its teeth, and plummeted down the side of the hill. It didn't hesitate at the edge of the bank, but leapt into the cold water of the Greasy Grass, plowing through the tall stand of bull rushes on the opposite side before scrambling up the steep embankment and onto the flat trail.

There was only one comfort Wolf sought—the white woman.

He wanted to lie with her, touch her pale skin, press his face in her brown hair, breathe in the sweet scent of her body and bury himself deep within the hot, moist core of her. He knew he could forget all the bad dreams and the strange visions in her arms, in her body. But Turtle Rib was right. Until she chose him he would have to wait, and his need would goad him like a thorn in his flesh.

He knew he could not keep himself from her if he stayed in the tipi with her another night. Somehow, some way, he must keep his promise to Tunkasila. But whatever he did, he needed to be close to her. She was like the sun and the cool breezes; she was alive, she brought him joy and only she could take away the stench of death that filled his nostrils.

Chapter 18

RYAN COULDN'T SLEEP. Giving up, she rolled onto her side and allowed the buzz of thoughts in her head to run rampant. She counted off the days in her head. It was the early morning of June 22. Both she and the Lakota were running out of time.

The bundle! How could she have forgotten? Or had it conveniently slipped her mind? Could she really be sure Charley wouldn't zap her back until the bundle had been made and buried? How would he know when, or even if, it had been done?

"He'll know." The damn little voice had returned.

She gazed across the tipi to Wolf's bed. Empty, for the third night in a row. She glanced at the closed tipi flap. Why did he leave her at night? If he was worried about more trouble from Iron Soldier or Ground Plum, wouldn't it make more sense for him to stay with her?

He had spent two nights in the tipi but just when they had begun to feel comfortable with each other, he'd chosen to sleep elsewhere. Why? Where was he? Intuition told her he hadn't gone far.

She kicked the trade blanket from her body and impatiently waited for a cool breeze to touch her skin. Closing her eyes, she tried to find sleep again, but it was impossible. "Enough," she muttered. Leaving her bed, she slipped into the buckskin dress, and stepped outside, barefoot.

From the slight rise of ground where he sat under the cottonwood, Wolf had a clear view of his lodge. Ryan was safe inside. The only danger she faced was from him.

The camp slept. Even the dogs had stopped their forays around the encampment for scraps of food and had curled up and gone to sleep. He would try to do the same. Leaning back against the trunk of the tree, Wolf closed his eyes. Immediately and unbidden, her image filled his head. "*Kechuwa*, Ryan," he whispered, liking the sounds and the feel of the words on his tongue.

He couldn't remember when he had begun calling her Kechuwa—Dear One—but it suited her well. Once or twice he had called her that name when he spoke to Eagle Deer or Pretty Feather and they had obliged him with indulgent smiles.

As a child he had learned to hate all whites. The *wasicu* had come into the Lakota lands, making roads and stealing and killing. The soldiers had come and killed his mother and father; they had killed many mothers and fathers. They had brought *wicaranran*, the fever sickness that left scars on the faces of his people; and they had killed the buffalo until there was barely enough to feed all the people. The *wasicu* had run off the game, they had brought long months of hunger and it was the *wasicu's* laws that now told the Lakota they must give up their ways and live only where the white men told them they must live. The *wasicu* had done all these things, and yet Wolf could not put any blame on *Kechuwa*.

He had seen the pitiful tipi villages outside of the forts. Staying just out of reach of the soldiers' bullets, he had watched the once-proud people of his tribe become no better than camp dogs waiting for scraps of food to be thrown their way. He had smelled the stench of sickness and death and he had fled back to the tall-grassed prairies and the cool waters. He had promised himself he would never live worse than a dog at the heels of the white man. He would kill all whites who tried to make him go to the forts. He would kill all whites who tried to make him forget he was the Hunkpapa *Sunkmanitu Ceye a Pelo*, warrior of the mighty Lakota.

He had nurtured and tended his hatred, and as he had grown tall and strong, it, too, had grown. So how was it that this small *wasicu* could take it all away when he looked at her . . . when he was with her . . . when he had thoughts of her? How did this woman make him so willing to leave the comfort of his soft bed and endure the discomfort of the hard ground to follow Turtle Rib's counsel?

"She is one of great strength from within," he whispered to the night. "Tunkasila has favored her and she has proven herself to be kind and honorable. My people forget the paleness of her skin and see only the good woman that lives within her heart." No longer could *Sunkmanitu Ceye a Pelo* say he hated all whites.

Dear One, Kechuwa—yes, the name suited her well. He smiled and knew that thoughts of her would always bring a smile to his lips, to his heart. He was glad his friends found her pleasing as well. Eagle Deer's wife had spent hours patiently showing her many of the things a Lakota woman should know; where the sweet early berries and the best wild onions grew and how to clean and prepare them for the cooking pot. He chuckled, remembering when they had returned to camp. The telltale berry stains around Kechuwa's pretty mouth proved that more berries had been eaten than had found their way to the *wojapi*, the fruit stew, cooking over the fire.

Pretty Feather had shown her how to start the cooking fire. She had shown her how to take the small bones from the river fish and how to slice meat thinly and place it on the racks to dry. Pretty Feather had also shown Kechuwa how to soften the dried meat in water before cooking it. Wolf grimaced. The first meal Kechuwa had cooked had not been good. How could anything taste so bad and be so hard to chew?

Each morning Pretty Feather took Kechuwa to the river

to bathe with the other women in camp. He had followed the first day, hiding behind a thick stand of willows. He had excused his improper actions by telling himself it was to protect Dear One from Iron Soldier or Ground Plum. If his head believed this lie, his heart knew the truth.

Crouched behind the willows, his gaze had traveled from her long hair to the high fullness of her breasts, down her ribs to the slim span of her waist and the soft swell of her hips. He had marveled at the gentle curves of her legs and the dark brown hair at the juncture of her thighs. The shape of her woman hair had puzzled him. It was very different from the shape of the female hair on the Lakota women. Kechuwa's woman hair was rounded at the top with a small gap in the middle and it narrowed as it disappeared between her thighs. Was this the way with all *wasicu*?

It was these memories that plagued him now and kindled his desire. He passed his hand over his hardened sex beneath his breechclout. Quickly drawing his hand away, he closed it into a tight fist and struck the ground beside him, hoping the hard blow would cause enough pain to make him forget the misery of keeping himself from Dear One. It wasn't possible. It would take a killing wound to do that.

"Ha," he grunted. "Even here it is the same as in the tipi with her. It is not possible to find sleep."

He drew his knees up, and leaning forward, rested his arms across them. Had he stayed with her at night, she would no longer be sleeping alone. Had he stayed with her in the tipi, he would have taken his husband's due without regard for Tunkasila's wishes. He glanced up, his gaze seeking out his lodge again. Turtle Rib's words were right—he must wait for her to say the words. Only Kechuwa could tell him when she was ready to be his wife.

A ragged sigh left him and he dragged his fingers through his long hair, combing it back from his face. There were other women in camp he could go to who would happily lie with him and ease his hunger. He tried to select one. It was useless. No, it was impossible. His appetite was for only one. Earlier, he had plunged his body into the cold water of the Greasy Grass but it had done little to alleviate his misery. The chill had stayed with him for only a few minutes after he had pulled himself back up on the riverbank and then the hot hunger had returned.

Wolf pulled his blanket up over his shoulders. Leaning back against the tree, he closed his eyes. He had spent many nights sleeping under the stars. He wasn't bothered by the dampness, the sounds of the night creatures or the lumpy hardness of the ground. None of these had ever kept him awake before—the blame lay elsewhere.

Suddenly every sense was alert. Over the muted sounds of the night there had been a noise, soft and nearly undetectable. There . . . there it was again.

He raised his head with the slow practiced patience of a good hunter. In the pale light cast by the moon, Wolf saw the woman walking down the pathway toward the river.

The village was still. Wispy tendrils of smoke floated upward from the near-dead embers of the campfires and a comical chorus of snores blended together from tipi to tipi. Stepping away from the lodge, Ryan looked up at the sky. She guessed the time to be well past three. The little brown dog that had befriended her crawled out from its sleeping hole near Eagle Deer's tipi and sniffed at her legs.

"Hello, my little nosy friend," she whispered, bending to give the dog an affectionate light scratching behind its ears. The dog wriggled, and offering a friendly lick to her hand, trotted back to his bed.

A light breeze rustled through the stand of oaks and cottonwoods, twirling the leaves on the ends of their stems and filling the night with soft sighs. Blending with the gurgle of the river and the songs of the frogs and crickets, it all became a gentle symphony of nature.

Ryan paused, listened and smiled. She loved the peaceful contentment she had found in the beautiful valley of the Little Big Horn. But heartache wasn't far away. She knew in a few days the valley would be changed forever.

Her footfalls were silent as she sought her favorite oak. Nimbly climbing up into the branches, she settled herself on the broad limb. It was the one place that had remained constant in her slip through time. Relaxed and content, she leaned back. The air smelled sweet and fresh, and closing her eyes, she finally dozed.

"You spend too much time up in the tree, *mitawicu*. I am afraid you will become a bird and fly away from this place."

Startled by the sudden intrusion and sound of the deep voice that always set her heart racing, Ryan's eyes flew open. She peered down through the branches and her heart cadenced a rapid beat. *Sunkmanitu Ceye a Pelo* . . . Wolf. She couldn't keep the smile from her lips. "And you," she replied, "you walk too quietly. Why do you sneak up on me like a little mole?" The Lakota language came fluently now, the words rolling smooth and natural off her tongue. She no longer had to translate the words mentally before speaking.

Wolf chuckled. "I was afraid you would sleep and fall to the ground." He moved to the base of the tree and held his arms up to her. "Come down, my little bird. Come down here and be with me where it is safe."

She considered his suggestion for a moment. "No, I think I should stay in the tree, friend mole," she teased. "I don't think it's safe on the ground with you. But you can come up here and share my nest. You would be able to see everything in this beautiful valley."

"Ah, my little bird," Wolf answered, laughing. "Have you forgotten? If I am a mole, I cannot see." He raised his arms once again. "Fly down, I will catch you, and then everything beautiful in this valley will be here under this tree with me."

His words delighted her. She was happy he had followed her, happy that his mood was lighthearted, and happy he wished her company. Swinging her legs over the wide limb, Ryan leaned over and placed her hands on his shoulders. She carefully began to lower herself. Wolf grasped her around the waist and she placed her hands on his shoulders, savoring the feel of his smooth skin and the play of his solid muscles beneath her fingers.

He slowly lowered her, inch by inch, her body sliding

against his. The buckskin dress rode up over her knees and thighs and Ryan grew keenly aware of every place their bare skin touched. The hard power of his body pressed against her, filling her with a maelstrom of pleasure and desire. She looked down into his face, their eyes met and she gave up her heart.

She felt dizzy. How long had she been holding her breath? She didn't know. She didn't care. The world around them had disappeared and time stood still.

Wolf held her tightly against him, not allowing her feet to touch the ground. Her skin felt hot as embers where it touched his and a hungry sound—a deep, needful groan— filled his throat. He wasn't willing to let her go—not now, not ever. His craving for her tightened in his belly and sent its message of wanting to the part of him that would join him with Kechuwa and make them as one.

He buried his head against her neck and breathed her sweet wildflower fragrance. Her response was silent and almost immediate. Cupping the side of his face with her small hand, she leaned forward in his arms and placed her cheek against his. Her soft sigh caressed his ear and Wolf closed his eyes, reveling in her sweet touch. The arrival of this woman had changed his life forever. Eagerly, he held her closer than he had ever held any woman in his life. He was tired of wanting what he could not have. He wanted her now. He wanted her forever.

"Kechuwa." His breath came in unsteady bursts as he felt her fingers delve into his long hair, sending a wild thrill coursing throughout his body, igniting a wildfire that made him tremble.

Within moments he became aware of another curious sensation. Strangely delightful, it began to cause even more enjoyable pleasures. She had placed her mouth on his face and moved it with a light sucking touch. She did this on his cheek, his forehead, his neck, and along the sensitive edge of his ear. Her lips slid down the side of his jaw and then moved higher until they lightly touched his own mouth. Her tongue slipped softly across his lips and she began pressing her mouth against his, moving slightly to capture his lips beneath hers.

What is this? Startled by her odd intimate touch, Wolf pulled back and then, wanting to feel the delightful sensation again, slowly lowered his mouth within her reach and sighed as she pressed her lips to his once again.

Loosening his hold, he eased her down until her feet touched the ground. Her dress had ridden up and was caught at her waist. Seeking the soft flesh that lay beneath, he slid his hands under the fringed hem and moved them up over her ribs until his fingers rested gently against the swells of her breasts. Her skin was as soft as the feathers on a dove's belly.

"What is this strange thing you do with your mouth, little bird?" he whispered against her cheek.

Ryan gaped at him wide-eyed and then giggled aloud. She had made another blunder, but it was a wonderful one. She had forgotten that kissing was not readily known among all the Siouan people, and now she had a dilemma. How could she explain to Wolf what a kiss was? In the old Lakota language there was no word for a kiss. She shrugged. No problem; she would teach him the English word.

"It is something my people do when they care for someone. It's called a 'kiss.' " She repeated the word more slowly and clearly: "kiss." Then shyly asked, "Did you like it?"

"Ki-iss," Wolf repeated, the English word sounding odd.

"Do you like how it feels . . . the kiss?"

A slight frown creased Wolf's brow. "And this is done by whites when they have a caring for someone?"

"Yes."

He continued to caress the smooth sides of her breasts with his thumbs. "I care very much for my brother Eagle Deer. Would this 'ki-iss' be something I would do with him?"

Ryan almost choked. "No! I—uh—I think I should explain this to you a little better." Suddenly, she became aware of Wolf's intimate touch and her eyes widened. Tendrils of delicious heat began to unwind in the pit of her belly. It tightened her nipples and started a delightful tingle that spread like melting butter, becoming a feathering sensation between her legs. She yearned to feel his hands completely cover her breasts, hold them and caress them.

"Before you tell me more about this 'ki-iss,' perhaps you should show me again what it is like."

"Of course," she murmured. Standing on tiptoe, she drew Wolf's head down to hers. Placing her hands lightly on each side of his face, she set a row of teasing kisses along his lower lip. Setting her partially opened mouth on his, she moved against him and her arms slid up around his neck. Slowly, she increased the pressure of her mouth.

Wolf's lips were soft and tasted wonderful. Her longing for his response grew. Her tongue licked and teased along the edges of his mouth, then dipped inside to caress and coax an identical reply from him.

Surprised, Wolf pulled back. "Ah," he breathed. "That also is part of a 'ki-iss'?"

"Yes," Ryan answered, her word a husky whisper. She tried to slow her quickening breath. "A kiss is something very special to be shared between a man and a woman—a man and a woman who care deeply for each other."

"Hmm, I think now I understand," Wolf said. "I could greet Eagle Deer's wife, Pretty Feather, or my mother's sister with this 'ki-iss'?"

"No—well, not one like this kind—no. . . ." Flustered, Ryan dragged the back of her hand in exasperation across her brow. Couldn't he understand this was something intimate, something between lovers—or at least, possible lovers? Couldn't he feel the same burst of emotions that she did each time his lips touched hers? Exasperated, she looked up, ready to explain once more, but the puzzled expression that had been on Wolf's face was gone. In its place, a teasing grin played across his mouth and a devilish twinkling filled his eyes.

"You know already, don't you?"

"I know," he whispered against her mouth, his voice a throaty growl. "I know."

Ryan tilted her head and accepted the delightful deep pressure and the delicious impact of Wolf's kiss. His lips rubbed hers apart, his tongue probed and explored, dipping into her mouth in a caress she joyfully returned. Closing her eyes, she clutched handfuls of his hair and pressed her mouth up into his kiss.

When he drew away, she kept her eyes closed but she could feel the heat of his gaze upon her face. Moving her hands down over his hard chest, her palms rode across the taut ridges of his ribs.

"You're a good student. You learn very quickly," she whispered, laying her head against him, listening to the rapid beat of his heart.

"I think I like this ki-iss. I must do this more until I do it well," he answered, tipping her head up with his fingers. "Why do you not watch me when we do this ki-iss? Why does Kechuwa close her eyes?"

"If I tried to watch you when we kissed, my eyes would cross," she giggled.

"I do not understand."

"If I tried to look into your eyes when our faces came close together, I'd look like this." She deliberately crossed her eyes and stifled another laugh.

Wolf grinned. "You are right, *mitawicu*. We will close our eyes. We must try again."

He gathered her more tightly into his arms and practiced his kissing lesson with newfound expertise. He crushed his mouth over hers and sighed when her lips parted and her tongue sought and caressed his. It pleased her to know that this was a special joining he had never shared with another woman. It was only with her.

He slid his hands from her sides and captured her breasts again, cradling each gently in his palms, stroking back and forth across her nipples with the pads of his thumbs. His touch sent electric tremors racing from the tips of her breasts throughout her body and settled with delight in the cleft between her legs. Ryan gasped, and pressing her body closer to Wolf's, settled against the hard ridge of his arousal and slowly moved against him.

"*Mitawicu*, my wife," he breathed raggedly, dragging his mouth from hers and sampling the taste of her skin down the edge of her chin and into the crook of her throat.

Twining her arms around Wolf's neck, Ryan offered her breasts up to his touch, to his lips.

Wolf pulled the buckskin aside and bent lower, drawing first one taut nipple and then the other into his mouth, sucking them, stroking across them with his tongue, gently grazing the edge of his teeth across their sensitive tips. A soft, hungry moan escaped from his throat and his breath felt hot as it fanned in rapid traces against her skin. Ryan was sure she would burn to ashes from the heat.

Suddenly she was cold. The chilly night air washed over her body and put out the fire as well as a bucket of ice water would douse any blaze.

"Wolf?" She was disoriented, and her voice was husky with unslaked passion.

She reached out to touch him but he took her hands and held them away from him with his left hand. With his right hand he tugged at her dress until it fell down over her body, covering her, shielding her from his eyes and from his touch.

"Go to your bed," he ordered, his voice an embittered growl. Turning, he left her.

"Wolf?" Her voice was half sob, half plea.

He didn't look back. "I have told you, go to your bed."

"Please. Why are you so angry? Tell me. What is it? Was it something I've done? The kiss? Was it the kiss?" Tears blurred the sight of him and spilled over onto her cheeks. "Please, tell me."

He turned and faced her. His hair had fallen over his eyes and he tossed it back over his shoulder with a quick, angry lift of his chin. He stared at her for what seemed an eternity, but his eyes held no hint of his emotions and the expression on his face remained closed. The tightening of the muscle along his jaw gave the only hint to his forbidding humor. Without a gesture, without a word, he turned and walked away.

Ryan bit down hard on her lip, mindless of the sharp

pain. The other pain, the pain in her heart, was worse. It pierced through to her soul and she stumbled back to camp, despondent, roughly scrubbing the tears from her face.

Pausing outside Wolf's lodge, she woefully glanced around at the camp. She wished Charley would take her back that instant. Bundle or no bundle, she wanted to be gone from this place and leave behind the ache she felt in her heart. Lifting the door flap, she stepped inside, feeling so much more alone than she had ever felt in her life.

She dropped the flap behind her and she leaned her forehead against the tipi wall. "I want to go home," she sobbed, lapsing into English for the first time in many days. "Please, Charley, stop all of this. Stop it now and just take me out of here, take me home." She beat her fist against the tipi wall.

As though an icy finger had grazed the back of her neck, Ryan shivered and adrenaline shot in a wild rush through her veins.

Someone else was in the tipi.

Chapter 19

AN ARM GRIPPED Ryan about the waist and a roughened hand clamped over her mouth, shutting off her words and stifling her breath. Terrified, she began to choke. Striking out with her elbows, she gouged her assailant in the ribs, trying to gain her freedom. A couple of deep grunts told her at least two blows had connected well, but not well enough. She was still imprisoned.

It was a man. The mere breadth and strength of the grasp that held her and the deep sound of the groans were proof enough.

Twisting one way and then the next, she fought against the attacker's suffocating grip. Turning her head, she bit down hard on his fingers as they strayed into her mouth. He yelped and the cruel hand slipped from her face. Gulping air into her starved lungs, Ryan tried to pull further away but his grip tightened around her ribs and he lifted her off her feet. Kicking wildly, her heels struck the man's shins and waves of pain shot through her feet and legs. Without shoes, this tactic was useless. In desperation, she raked her nails along his arm and received another small victory as he sucked in his breath with a pain-filled hiss.

"Be still, white whore. I will not toss you away as quickly as your great warrior did."

An icy chill constricted in tight bands around her heart and filled her with terror. His grip loosened only a fraction but Ryan took advantage of the slight relief and dragged in another much-needed breath. "Iron Soldier!"

"Are you disappointed it is not *Sunkmanitu Ceye a Pelo* who waits for you in the dark?" Iron Soldier sneered, crushing Ryan's breast beneath his fingers. "You will learn to like me much better. You can feel I am a strong warrior." He squeezed her breast and gave her nipple a hard pinch. "I have counted many coups in battle and I am the best hunter in our camp circle. Many buffalo and *wapiti* have been killed by my arrows and bullets. Many women have cried with pleasure beneath me."

"With my man weapon I will give you many strong babies to suck at your tits." His lewd laughter came from deep within his throat. "Your brave warrior is a *wanagi*. Do you still not believe me? Has he taken you to his bed?" He rubbed his engorged penis against her. "Has he put himself inside of you? Has he filled you with his seed?"

"Wolf isn't like you," she gasped. "He's a warrior with honor. He hasn't forced himself upon me."

"Only a dead man would keep himself from laying with you." He took his hand from Ryan's breast and drew it down across her stomach until he reached the juncture of her legs. His hand closed over her and he tightly gripped and kneaded her flesh through the hide dress. "I am not dead. I will show you how a warrior who lives feels."

"You will be the one who is dead when Wolf learns what you've done," Ryan warned, continuing to struggle against Iron Soldier's grip, refusing to make her rape easy for him. She was no match for his strength—he would be able to do whatever he wanted to her—but she knew that somehow she had to make him believe he had no power over her. If she had to prove she was *wakan* to anyone in the tribe, she had to prove it to Iron Soldier. She had to prove it now.

Her determination gave her fresh strength. Finally wrenching free, her feet landed on the ground and she whirled around to face him. With her knees quaking and her heart racing wildly, she was intent on keeping her fear hidden. She spit out her words. "It is you who will be shunned by your people. They won't look at you with their eyes—they'll turn away from you. It is *you* who will be called *dead*."

"The white whore tells *me* tribal law. I am a great man among the Lakota, I have taken many scalps. It is you who dishonors yourself with a *wanagi*, not I."

He reached beneath his breechclout and freed his sex. Holding it in his hand, he lifted it and stroked along its hard length, displaying himself proudly. "I will finally take for mine something that *Sunkmanitu Ceye a Pelo* wants." He pointed his penis at her. "I will leave a Lakota warrior's baby inside you and you will come and live in my tipi, fetch my wood, cook my food and bring me water. You and your gift from mighty Tunkasila will be mine."

"Go to hell, you sonofabitch!" Ryan cursed in English, her rage gobbling every fragment of fear and caution that remained.

The odd sound of her words startled Iron Soldier. Wide-eyed, he stepped back.

Sensing his uncertainty, a plan of escape, easy and workable, sped into Ryan's mind, and she seized what could well be her only chance to get away from the crazed Lakota. Perhaps the self-protection class she'd taken the past summer would finally pay off. She had to get Iron Soldier outside and away from the tipi.

Iron Soldier grabbed her arm with a painful twist. "You have nowhere to go but my tipi, white whore. I will catch you wherever you go. But first, I would see what kind of woman Tunkasila has sent to the Lakota." Gripping Ryan's shoulders, his fingers biting into her flesh, he tried to pull her against him.

Ryan allowed him to draw her into his arms. Just as she hoped, the man's conceit overshone his intelligence and he lowered his guard. He believed he had won.

Roughly holding her head between his hands, Iron Soldier tried to copy the kiss she had taught Wolf. Ryan allowed him only a moment's success to distract him as she seized his rawhide belt. Pitching herself backwards through the tipi door flap, she pulled Iron Soldier with her. Although the maneuver lacked finesse, it was effective.

They fell outside, landing heavily on the hard-packed ground, she on the bottom, Iron Soldier on top. He was heavy and Ryan was positive every bone in her body had been crushed. She tried to breathe, greedily gulping air to replace the wind he'd knocked out of her lungs, but his ponderous weight was suffocating her. She tried to roll out from underneath his smelly body and failed. He stayed with her, pinning her to the ground. If she could only gain enough easement to move again, but her muscles were beginning to tire and cramp. If she didn't get free soon, she would be lost. She prayed someone in camp had risen early and would discover her dilemma and help.

"Did you think you could be rid of me so easily?" Iron Soldier gloated with a mocking laugh, his breath falling hot and foul against her face. He thrust his hips forward and with short jabs, ground himself against her leg. "I could take you anytime I wish, even here—even now." His hand fumbled between them as he tried to raise her dress. With a little success, he lifted the skirt above her knees.

Placing both hands on his chest, Ryan tried again to push him away. It was useless. He was too heavy. Unwilling to give up, she eased a hand upward. She moved quickly, aiming for his eyes with her fingernails, but as quick as the strike of a rattlesnake, Iron Soldier grabbed her wrist and twisted her arm.

"You think it is that easy to fight this Lakota?"

"Go to hell!" Ryan spat, not ready to give up.

Grabbing her other hand, he forced her arms up over her head and pressed them against the ground. He leered at her and continued to thrust his hips, his hard shaft prodding her leg. She twisted, trying to rid herself of his foul touch.

"Are you so eager for me to fill you that you cannot lie still?" he taunted, moving against her again and again.

Caution vanished and rage, white-hot and complete, filled her. What did she have to lose? She would welcome death rather than submit to Iron Soldier. Waiting until just the right moment when he shifted against her and spread his legs, she drove her knee upward and landed a brutal blow.

Iron Soldier's eyes instantly widened and his mouth formed a wide, silent O. Tears filled his eyes and he choked out a strangled whimper that grew until it became a hoarse gasp. Rolling off Ryan, he brayed in agony, reaching between his legs and cradling his testicles. His voice dwindled, becoming little more than pitiful mewling as he drew his knees up against his stomach and rocked from side to side. His eyes glazed as he gagged and vomited in the dirt.

From its sleeping hole beside Eagle Deer's tipi, the small brown dog charged, its lips pulled back, showing a menacing breadth of white teeth. Growls rolled from its throat, and in less than twenty leaps, it was upon Iron Soldier. Biting and seizing whatever it could, the dog's teeth found a vulnerable target and gnashed into the flesh of the man's upper thigh. Its long incisors caught on the edge of Iron Soldier's breechclout and the dog tugged and pulled at the material until it ripped and pulled free. Shaking its head, the dog angrily whipped the fabric back and forth. Soon bored, it attacked again, snapping at the terrified Lakota's hands as he tried to push it away and keep it from biting into the most tender target of all.

Iron Soldier frantically scrambled backwards. Scuttling along the ground, he protected his shrinking manhood with one hand and tried to fend off the dog with the other. With each new attack, he feinted and flinched, hoping to shield himself. As Iron Soldier tried to get up, the dog lunged again. This time its teeth found two tender targets, first Iron Soldier's fingers and then the soft flesh of his testicles. The Lakota's agonized cry rose and the dog, encouraged by the fear it heard, renewed its charge with fervor.

Viciously kicking at the dog, Iron Soldier tried to save himself. Again and again he lashed out but the dog leapt to safety each time, keeping just out of reach of the Lakota's foot. The little brown dog renewed its attack. Charging again, it took another nip at Iron Soldier's crotch and hands. Finally Iron Soldier's foot found its target, landing a hard kick along the dog's ribs. With its tail tucked between its hind legs, the dog retreated, slinking down to the river to hide beneath a scrub of willows.

Iron Soldier pitched and stumbled and finally dragged himself to his feet. He stood swaying and bent over like an old man, with one bloody hand still protecting his crotch. His tattered breechclout hung between his legs like a deflated banner.

"We are not finished, *wasicu*," he hissed. "We are not finished." He staggered off to his own camp before anyone who might have been awakened by his yells could rush from their lodges.

Ryan fell back on the ground, closed her eyes and dragged breath after ragged breath of cool morning air into her lungs. She couldn't remember ever feeling so exhausted. Her body ached from head to toe. She shivered. The danger from Iron Soldier had been real. Until she escaped him by going forward to her own time, the peril would remain.

The false bundle would have to be made and buried as soon as possible. It couldn't wait any longer. *When it's done, then Charley can work his ol' red magic and I can go home.* In the next moment she realized what she would leave behind. *Wolf.* The notion quickly came to her and made sense. If Charley really was her travel agent, he wouldn't let her go home until the artifact was buried, and the longer she put off making it, the more time she could share with Wolf.

"My friend," a soft voice accompanied by a gentle touch interrupted her thoughts. "What has happened? Are you hurt?"

Opening her eyes, Ryan found Pretty Feather kneeling beside her, the shy woman's face filled with concern. "Kechuwa, who did this thing?"

"Iron Soldier."

Fleeting, but present nonetheless, a look of fear crossed Pretty Feather's face before she looked down to tug the hem of the dress over Ryan's knees.

"Did he . . . are you . . . wounded?"

Ryan shook her head. "No. He didn't hurt me. I'm just angrier than—than hell." Half Lakota and half English, her answer sounded absurd and the two women began to laugh, relief for Ryan's deliverance from Iron Soldier flooding over them both.

"Can you not see, *kola*? When you leave her alone at night, she is in great danger," Eagle Deer admonished his friend, stopping his horse by the river. "Even when you allow her to walk alone through the camp, she is in danger. If you have good regard for this woman, then she must be protected." He gave Wolf a sidelong glance. "Where were you when she needed your protection this time?"

"I was with my horses," Wolf answered, barely louder than a whisper.

"You must stay with her and keep her safe, brother." Eagle Deer's look was condemning. "Only a fool would leave her to the danger of Iron Soldier." Eagle Deer turned his horse toward a shady knoll.

Wolf followed, bringing his pinto to a stop beside Eagle Deer's dark buckskin. He angled a look at his friend and then turned away, shamed by Eagle Deer's censure. "And who will protect her from me, *kola*? Will it be you?"

"Your words are filled with strangeness. Why does she need protection from her husband?"

Wolf didn't answer. The silence between them grew lengthened and then Eagle Deer's eyes widened with surprise. Wolf knew his secret had been discovered.

"Why?" Eagle Deer asked, astounded. "Why do you keep yourself from her? Would you prefer Iron Soldier to lie with your wife, to hurt her and make you a fool?"

"No," Wolf answered strongly. "You know I do not want that." Wolf turned his pinto back toward the camp. "I promise you, I will make him suffer for what he has done."

Eagle Deer leaned from the back of his own horse and grabbed the pinto's rein, stopping Wolf from leaving. "Your punishment is not needed. Leave him. He has already been given more punishment than you could offer.

Your Dear One has left him crippled with one strike of her bravery and some help from a small warrior dog."

"If the filthy one touches her again, he will die. I will skin him as a rabbit and stretch his hide to dry in the sun."

Eagle Deer glanced at his friend, and his mouth lifted in a teasing grin. "And what will you do with your woman?"

Chapter 20

RYAN WATCHED WOLF return to camp and picket his horse beside the tipi. The morning sun had warmed the valley and he wore nothing but his breechclout and moccasins. He had tied his long hair back from his face and two eagle feathers fluttered gracefully from his scalplock braid. A light film of sweat coated his skin, highlighting the muscles on his chest, his shoulders and the washboard plane of his stomach. She knew from the tightened muscle along his jaw that Eagle Deer had told him about Iron Soldier's attack. Her glance slid away from his and she nervously plucked at the fringed sleeve of her dress.

Wolf stepped in front of her and stood quietly for a moment before he spoke. "I am greatly shamed. I do not deserve the special gift Tunkasila has given." His fingers lightly traced the fall of her hair down the side of her head and then his hand dropped back to his side. "I have promised I would help prepare a false medicine bundle to capture the evil *wasicu*. Today we begin. I do not wish to delay what you have been sent to do. I do not wish to anger Tunkasila anymore."

"Wolf . . ." Ryan reached out and touched his arm, but he brushed by and entered the lodge. Following, she dropped the door flap behind her. No one would disturb them.

Crouching at the foot of his bed, Wolf methodically searched through the parfleches and possible bags stacked against the tipi wall. On the ground, a pile of assorted objects grew with each selection he made from his cache. He glanced up at her, then returned to his task.

Kneeling beside him, she lightly touched the wound on his arm. "This can wait until your arm is better."

"My wound is nearly healed. There is no pain . . . in my arm." He moved his arm, proving his words, then pointed to the items on the ground. "We will take these things away from the camp where no one can see what we do." Wrapping everything in a large piece of red calico, he dropped the bundle inside a larger hide pouch and stood. "Come," he said, holding his hand out to her. "This will be a good day."

Ryan followed outside. Handing her the bag, Wolf nimbly leapt onto the pinto's back. She passed the bundle up to him and after placing it across the horse's back, he motioned to her with a crook of his finger.

"What do you want?"

"I want you to ride with me," he answered. The first smile he'd given her since returning to camp curved his full mouth, softening the hard expression on his face.

"I can't," she nervously whispered. "I can't ride."

"Then you will learn."

Wolf slid back on the Pinto, then leaned down, and using his left arm, grasped Ryan around her ribs. Before she could voice a protest, he lifted her, setting her on the horse in front of him.

"See how easy it is? You are now riding," Wolf teased.

"No, I'm sitting sideways," she laughed. "If the horse doesn't move, I'm fine. If it moves, I'm in trouble."

"We will see."

Wolf held the single rein in his left hand. Bracing Ryan with his right arm, he lightly touched the pinto's flanks with his heels. The animal pranced beneath the added weight on its back and moved forward.

"Oh!" Ryan cried, frantically wrapping her arms around Wolf's neck to steady herself. Shutting her eyes, she rested her head on his shoulder. If she fell, he'd certainly go down with her.

"I think I like how you ride," Wolf whispered in her ear.

A feathering of delight filled her but she quickly sobered, remembering how he had sent her away the last time they had been this close. She didn't want that to happen again.

Wolf felt her pull away. Positioning her more securely, he drew her against his chest again. He hated himself for leaving her vulnerable to Iron Soldier's attack. He would do anything he could to make it up to her. He had made the decision while Eagle Deer scolded him. Today he would begin to court his wife, this beautiful *wasicu* woman who smelled of wildflowers. He would court Kechuwa as if he were asking for a marriage. In a way, he realized, that was exactly what he was doing. He wanted her to tell him she wished to be his wife—soon.

"Where are we going?"

"You will see."

"Are we going to the river?"

"Be patient," he admonished lightly. "You will see."

Relaxing to the rhythm of the horse's gait, Ryan lowered her arms from around his neck, and instantly he longed for her embrace to return.

"Now that I haven't fallen off, don't you think it would be better if I had my own horse to ride?"

"I don't think that is a good idea. You still have much to learn." Wolf touched his heels to the pinto again and the horse plunged into a gallop.

Ryan shrieked. Slipping, she clutched at Wolf again.

Laughing, he eased the pinto down to a slow jogging gait. "It is best that you hold tightly to me."

"You made him do that," she accused.

Wolf feigned his innocence. "Sometimes even a great warhorse is frightened by an enemy."

"What enemies does a horse have?"

"I think he saw a rabbit."

"A rabbit?" Ryan rebutted skeptically. "He saw *a* rabbit?"

"You are right. One rabbit is not enough to frighten this horse. Maybe he saw two."

They continued north along the well-worn path between the circles of tipis and beyond the elbow of the Greasy Grass where the Medicine Tail Coulee joined the valley. They rode through the camps of the Sans-Arc, the Miniconjou, the Blackfoot Sioux and the Santee. They had ridden for almost a mile when the largest tipi Ryan had ever seen came into view. The tall poles soared high overhead and neatly placed stitches held the many carefully tanned white hides of the outer skin together.

"It's so large," she said.

"It is the council lodge," Wolf offered. "The leaders of the tribes meet here to talk." He reined the horse closer to the tipi. "I have heard that the *wasicu* have such a council place of this color."

Amazed, Ryan glanced up at him. Could he actually be talking about the Capitol building in Washington? Had this too been part of his odd visions? No, he must have heard of it from some of the chiefs in council. Chiefs of many tribes had been taken to Washington to meet with the "Great White Father."

They continued north, passing the Yankton camp. With so much to see, Ryan kept asking Wolf to stop so she could try to memorize everything in sight. No other anthropologist in the field of Lakota ethnography could ever glean as much information from years of studying as she could in a leisurely afternoon ride around the Little Big Horn encampment.

They neared the Oglala camp circle and Wolf pulled the pinto to a halt, waiting as a slightly built man approached them. Though small in stature and somewhat unimposing in appearance, the man carried himself with the presence of a giant.

"Crazy Horse," Ryan whispered in awe. *I am really going to meet the elusive champion of the Lakota.*

"*Hau, kola,*" Wolf called to his friend.

"Hau, mitakola," Crazy Horse greeted Wolf in return. "I am pleased you have come to visit the Oglala. We have not seen you for many days. All is well with my brother?"

"Much has happened since our return from Rosebud Creek," Wolf answered quietly.

Neither man acknowledged Ryan's presence as they continued to speak.

"You fought well," Crazy Horse stated. "I have not listened to the bad words of another. None of those who know your heart and your skill in battle have listened. I know my friend, *Sunkmanitu Ceye a Pelo*, well. His words are always true."

"Thank you, *kola*."

"Is this your reward?" Crazy Horse shifted his taciturn gaze to Ryan.

"She came to me in a special way," Wolf answered, resting his hand possessively on Ryan's thigh.

The cruel scar along Crazy Horse's jaw softened as his face moved into a warm smile. "The ones we love usually do," he responded and turned his dark eyes to Ryan. "Welcome."

"Lila pilayama. Thank you," she answered, recognizing how prophetic his words were. Crazy Horse's livid scar was the result of a jealous husband's revenge.

"Ah, then it is true. She does speak Lakota words," Crazy Horse said, with a trace of surprise in his voice.

"She knows many things about the Lakota. Things only one who has lived among us for a lifetime could know."

"Is it possible," Crazy Horse asked, "that she was taken from her own people many seasons ago and raised in our camps?"

"Would we not have known of her before this time if that were so?" Wolf rebutted.

"You are right, *kola*." Crazy Horse posed another question and closely watched for Ryan's reaction. "What does she know of the one called Yellow Hair, the bluecoat chief that our brothers, the Cheyenne, have welcomed to their camps many times?"

Crazy Horse was asking about Custer. Ryan tried to keep

her expression indifferent, but she shuddered. What should she do? What could she say? Should she tell Crazy Horse and Wolf that as they spoke, George Armstrong Custer, his brother Tom, Major Reno, Captain Benteen and the Seventh Cavalry were riding toward the Little Big Horn?

By revealing a few simple facts, she could make sure that the Battle of the Little Big Horn would never take place. But she knew that wasn't the answer. If it didn't happen here for the Lakota, it would happen somewhere else. At least here they would win. It would be a fight they would be proud of in the years to come.

"I don't know much," she answered, hoping her words gave some information that would be useful to Crazy Horse within the week. "I know only that he doesn't listen to his elders and that he makes foolish mistakes."

"Our brothers, the Cheyenne, say he has great wisdom," Crazy Horse replied, his keen eyes still watching her.

"The day will soon come when they know they were wrong," Ryan replied. As incredulous as it was to speak with this great warrior, she wished their conversation would end. She didn't want to face any more of his questions; besides, the temptation to tell everything she knew was much too great.

"Go, *kola*," Crazy Horse said, with a wan smile. "The day is beautiful and should be spent with a beautiful woman."

He bowed gallantly, reminding Ryan of a titled gentleman in a formal parlor. *What an odd man you are—the fiercest of warriors and yet sensitive, compassionate and humble. No wonder your warriors follow you without question.*

Wolf and Ryan continued on through the camps of the Brulé and Cheyenne. On the northern fringes of the Cheyenne camp, Wolf turned the pinto toward the river. With no guidance, the horse carefully picked its way through the belly-deep water, avoiding rocks and washes until it climbed the angular bank on the other side. Knee-high grass bristling with sage weed carpeted the hills and gulches.

Looking up at the rising hill to the northeast, Ryan felt

a cold shiver of foreboding. *That is where it will happen.* Her eyes scanned the rise, a hill void of trees. It hadn't changed at all. A few years after the battle, the government had scattered grave markers across the swell, marking where the soldiers had fallen, and a small fenced area outlined the place where Custer had died. But the hill was the same. *In three days it will be a place of death.*

Three days. She looked at Wolf. Was that all the time that remained? If Charley yanked her back before the battle, what would happen to Wolf? How could she leave without knowing what would happen to him? She rested her head against his chest. The truth filled her with wonder and misgivings. She loved him.

Wolf stopped his horse in a sheltered crook of the Greasy Grass. Cottonwoods on three sides completely closed in the clearing, creating a wonderful small and intimate glade. Knee-deep grass provided a thick emerald carpet and the pinto tugged impatiently on the jaw rein, trying to lower its head to nibble. Its lips made hollow popping noises as it reached to seize mouthfuls of the taller blades.

Wolf slid from the horse's back, then reached up to help Ryan to the ground. The thought of deliberately placing herself in his arms made her smile. Firmly setting her hands on his shoulders she slipped to the ground, hoping he couldn't hear the wild beating of her heart.

"This is beautiful," she exclaimed, looking around.

Frothy blooms of Queen Anne's lace and cream-colored daisies dotted the lush green, and sprinklings of tiny purple wild violets grew in the shorter grass and near-bare earth at the base of the trees.

"It is a good place to make the bundle. No one will come and see what we do." Wolf moved away. "We will be alone."

He sat under one of the cottonwoods and Ryan joined him. Sitting quietly for a while, neither seemed willing to break the tranquil mood. Ryan eased a glance at Wolf. He seemed deep in thought. Not wanting to intrude, she passed the time by, idly tracing different shapes in the dirt at the base of the tree with a small twig. First the shape of a circle disturbed the earth and then she wrote her initials through the middle. Erasing these with her fingers, she wrote her name in a flamboyant scroll, adding a few curlicues before smoothing the ground out again. Next she drew a heart, a slightly elongated one.

Wolf had been watching her make the pictures with interest. This woman puzzled him at times. She did many things he didn't understand, but each intrigued him. His gaze followed the twig as it moved. He frowned. The shape was familiar. As soon as Ryan had completed her drawing, Wolf remembered where he had seen it before. Amazed, he watched as she drew another and another and another. This was the shape of Kechuwa's female hair.

"What does this mean?" Wolf asked, the recollection of Kechuwa standing naked in the river very clear to his mind and to his body.

Ryan gave a shy smile. "It is a heart. It means love," she answered.

"Love?" A slight frown creased his bronzed brow.

"It is the *wasicu* sign for love."

Wolf shook his head with disbelief. *These white men are pitiful. Now it is clear why we see them so often without their women. They need a special sign to help them find the love place of their wives. Is it possible that many do not know the sign?*

His thoughts had caused his body to stir with need and he reluctantly pushed his mind to the calico bundle. Working quietly, he untied the long piece of sinew that held it closed. With studied deliberation, he unwrapped the red calico and spread it on the grass, placing a small rock in each corner to keep the breeze from lifting and blowing it away. Next, he placed everything he had brought on top of it.

He handled each object gently and with reverence, lightly smoothing the feathers of a dried yellow flicker bird and stroking the dark fur on a lustrous martin hide. He placed these beside a collection of six small smooth rocks, and half a dozen brass buttons from a cavalry officer's uniform. He added a pair of broken reading glasses. Breaking off a piece of sinew, he strung them all together and placed them beside four small, round hide bags decorated with colorful quillwork.

He set out an eclectic collection of herbs and roots, and then withdrew the last object from the bag—the dried body of a large black crow. Red glass beads replaced its eyes and the belly of the bird lay open. Sweetgrass and sage filled the cavity and a strip of red calico tied the feet together. A string of small brass hawk bells hung from the bird's legs. Another strip of calico bound the bird's beak and four snowy-white eagle plumes floated on the ends of the red cloth strips.

"I have chosen medicines that will protect us as we do this thing," Wolf said. "These small brothers," he added, lightly touching the birds and animals, "have given us their spirits that we may use the gifts Tunkasila gave to them." He touched the crow. "My brother crow has a voice that can be heard for a long distance when he warns his family of intruders." His fingers grazed over the four small sealed bags. "These hold the gifts of my brother wolf. He walks on silent feet and can see many things about him, even in the dark." Wolf picked up the string of buttons and the eyeglasses. "These are possessions of the bluecoats. It is wise to weaken your enemies by using their own medicine against them."

"I have chosen these things because they will be good together to stop the evil *wasicu* from stealing more medicine from the Lakota." Wolf glanced up at Ryan. "It is known that women should not be present when a bundle is made, but you must stay. I think Tunkasila would not have sent you to do this unless you would give special power to the bundle." He thoughtfully reviewed the objects, then turned his attention back to Ryan. "Something that belongs to you must also be put in this bundle. Only then will it have the power to do as *you* ask. Only then will these *wasicu* who would steal from the Lakota be stopped."

"I have the perfect thing," she replied, removing her left earring and handing the gold daisy to Wolf.

He turned it over in the palm of his hand. It sparkled in the sunlight. "*Wasté*. This will be good."

He tore a corner from the calico and wrapped it around the earring, then bound the packet with sinew, tying it with four knots. Picking up the crow, he pushed the little packet high up into the bird's hollowed neck.

"It is right that prayers to Tunkasila are spoken with each object that becomes part of the bundle," Wolf explained. "This one we make has only one purpose. My words will only be said for what you have given."

Standing, Wolf held the crow over his head and began to pray. He moved to face each of the four directions as he spoke. Sitting once again, he added the buttons, the eyeglasses and the thimbles. He added a few more things to the bundle along with the small packets of herbs and two of the egg-shaped stones, and filled the empty hollows with sweetgrass, flat cedar and sage.

Ryan watched with interest. "Perfect," she breathed. The bundle would fool any expert, at least until they removed the gold earring and read the inscription on the back.

Breaking off another piece of sinew, he picked up the four quilled pouches and tied them around the crow's body, securing her earring and everything else inside. His hands hesitated a moment or two, then putting the bird down, he looked at Ryan. A puzzled frown replaced the look of concentration his face had worn while he worked on the bundle.

"I would know something about this?" he asked.

She nodded.

"I do not understand. Why is it that you do this? Why do you go against your own people and seek the help of the Lakota to do this thing? Do you not have good feelings for your people? Do you hate the *wasicu* as we, the Lakota, hate them?"

She hadn't expected his question. Caught off guard, it was difficult to find the words to give him an answer. She looked across the clearing and watched his horse graze, all the while sorting out her response in her mind. "There are good and bad in all people," she began. "It is the bad that

I am ashamed of in my people, in the Lakota—in any tribe." She raised her eyes to meet Wolf's steady gaze. "It is wrong to steal from anybody, and the men who do this must be caught and punished."

"Would you do this if the thieves were Pawnee or maybe Crow?" Wolf asked, closely watching her.

"I don't know. I'm here because it's some of my people who are bad." She paused, remembering the hate that had existed for years between the Lakota and the Pawnee and Crows. It would remain strong far into the future. "Not all people are bad. Not all Pawnee are bad, nor are all Crow people bad."

"They are enemies of the Lakota," Wolf replied, his voice heavy with loathing.

"I know, but can't you see that if the conflicts were gone, you could be friends?"

"That will never be," Wolf answered, stubbornly dismissing the idea. "The Crow and Pawnee ride with the bluecoats and show them where to find our people and kill them. The Crow and Pawnee are not honorable or wise like the Lakota."

"Is a Pawnee elder less wise than a man like Turtle Rib? Is a Crow baby not as sweet and beautiful as a Lakota child?"

Wolf's face remained closed and cold to the topic.

His narrow-minded convictions began to irritate her. Why couldn't he see beyond the black and white of the issue? "Do you not all breathe the air, and bleed when you are injured?" Her anger put a sharp edge to her voice. "Does a Crow or Pawnee warrior love his wife less than a Lakota loves his woman? Does a Pawnee mourn less than a Lakota when a loved one dies?"

Wolf didn't answer.

"You say all Lakota are honorable? Was Iron Soldier honorable when he attacked me, not once but twice?"

Wolf quickly glanced up at her, obviously assessing her reasoning.

Not willing to allow her success to slip away, she added

one more question. "Are all *wasicu* murderers, thieves and liars?"

"I know of one who is not," Wolf answered. "I know you."

Ryan's heart flip-flopped, her anger evaporating as she tried to swallow the large lump that had suddenly materialized in her throat. How did he do that? How did he infuriate her one moment and in the next, turn her into love-sick mush? Silence fell between them and only the trill of a meadowlark calling its mate, the crunch of the horse's teeth on the grass and the rush of the Greasy Grass filled the air.

Wolf looked at her and felt the need to touch her. "There should not be anger between us." He leaned closer and traced Ryan's eyebrows with the tips of his fingers. "This day should be for smiles and good things." His caress traveled across the rise of her cheek and along the edge of her jaw, settling at the corner of her mouth. He tugged lightly against her skin, pulling her lips into a small smile. Her skin felt soft and he allowed his finger to remain at the juncture of her lips for a moment longer. A light beading of perspiration lay across her upper lip and he delicately lifted the moisture and licked the salty elixir from his finger with the tip of his tongue. He heard the small surprised sound she made as she watched him and an answering sigh rose in Wolf's own throat.

His hunger for Kechuwa grew stronger and he craved to ride every crest and hollow of her body with his tongue, licking and tasting every delicious essence of this beautiful woman.

"Why does your breath come so quickly?" he murmured, placing his cheek against Ryan's, smelling the sweet fragrance of her hair. "Is your heart like mine? Does it run and jump like a herd of wild antelope?"

"Yes."

He smiled. Curving his hand around the back of her neck, he drew her closer. His tongue grazed the rim of her small ear and then following its curve, he savored the flavor and silken flesh of her neck, lingering at the tender corner where it met her shoulder. He gathered her in his arms and lay back on the grass, taking her with him. She went willingly, and he was glad.

Raising on his elbow, he looked down at the woman who had captured his heart. She was taller than most of the women in his tribe. When they stood together her head came only to his shoulder, but laying down they would fit together well.

He smoothed her hair away from her cheek. It was soft and was the color of the mink he trapped up north, a dark brown that also showed the color of a red horse and the yellow of flowers when the sun fell on it. Her hair was long. If it was the way of the *wasicu*, she had not mourned for anyone in many seasons. His fingers touched the corners of her eyes. They seemed to be more blue than he remembered, reminding him of the color of an evening sky, the color that shows when early evening gives way to the oncoming night.

Wolf studied each feature of her face, from the smooth plane of her forehead down the slight upward tilt of her nose to the soft fullness of her mouth. Her mouth . . . he began to lower his head. He would give Kechuwa the pleasure of the *wasicu* 'ki-iss,' but he knew, with a curling of heat that began in the pit of his stomach, that he would enjoy it, too.

As he leaned over her, his hair fell forward, curtaining their faces. Impatient, he tossed the long strands back over his shoulder.

"Don't," Ryan whispered, reaching up and gently combing her fingers through the lustrous ebony fall. "It's so beautiful." She twined his hair through her fingers and marveled at its silken texture. "You are so beautiful."

Bewitched, she watched as he slowly lowered his mouth closer and closer to her own. Her tongue flicked across her lips in anticipation, moistening them, and finally, unable to wait for the last inches that separated them to disappear, she rose up and met his kiss with an urgency of her own.

Still new to the skill, Wolf brushed his lips back and forth across hers. Then, as if remembering his lesson or discovering some unknown instinctive expertise, he touched lightly along her upper lip, teasing and tempting until his tongue dipped into her mouth, thrusting and rubbing against hers in a sensuous dance.

She pressed against him, hungrily seeking all that love promised. She touched her hands to his chest. The warmth of his skin felt delightful under her fingers and she caressed upwards until each hand covered the reddened, raised patches of fresh scar tissue over each flat nipple. She circled each sun dance wound with a slow, light caress.

Wolf lifted his mouth from hers and watched her fingers. Before he could renew his kisses or say a single word to her, Ryan bent to his chest and placed several worshipful kisses upon each scar. Her hands moved around him and she smoothed her palms upwards, caressing the hard corrugated ridges of his ribs.

"Kechuwa," he whispered.

She didn't respond.

"Kechuwa," he said more firmly. "You must hear me."

She laid her head against Wolf's shoulder and once more tasted his bronze flesh with her mouth and the tip of her tongue, but still she didn't respond.

Wolf stalled her kisses with a light touch on the side of her face. "We must go."

Ryan felt him pull away. "What?" she asked, groggy with arousal. "Please, not again, don't stop this again."

"We must leave this place and return to camp. We must go now." Responding to her baffled look, he pointed across the river with a quick lift of his chin. "Look at the sky."

Twisting in his embrace, Ryan looked over her shoulder. A dark smutty gray had replaced the bright blue and an odd yellowish tinge suffused the outer edges of the massive storm clouds that had rolled over the horizon. As she looked, a jagged bolt of lightning split the distance between the center of the clouds and the ground and a loud, shaking boom of thunder immediately followed.

"Come," Wolf firmly demanded. Taking Ryan's arm, he pulled her to her feet. "Hurry! We cannot stay here," he added, stuffing the calico bundle back into the hide bag.

Vaulting onto the pinto's back, he reached down and lifted her. "It is best you ride behind me."

"I . . . I don't know if I can," she replied with alarm as another slash of light breached the clouds.

"Hurry. Place your arms around me and hold tightly. Do not be afraid. I will not let you fall." His words were almost lost in the growl of thunder.

The first heavy raindrops arrived, leaving large, wet splotches where they landed, and in mere seconds the water poured from the sky and drenched everything. A disquieting sense of déjà vu settled over Ryan. The storm that had started her whole implausible odyssey into the past had begun exactly like this. Surely Charley wasn't going to zap her back now? No, not now! Not yet! They hadn't finished the bundle and she still needed to bury it and she still needed more time with Wolf.

Ryan clung to Wolf as the pinto forded the river and climbed up the bank on the west side of the Little Big Horn. He kicked the horse's ribs and the animal bolted forward, almost leaping out from under them. She gripped the animal with her knees and frantically wrapped her arms around Wolf's waist. Laying her head against his back, she closed her eyes tightly and immediately discovered it was more difficult to keep her balance on the galloping animal with her eyes shut. Relenting, she opened them to find the world flying by at breakneck speed. Wolf's hair whipped across her cheek and she tightened her grip, praying she could stay on the horse.

The pinto followed the pathway that led along the fringes of the tribal camps, stretching its muscles in a ground-covering clip that ate up the distance from one camp circle to another.

Throughout the huge encampment women were quickly closing the smoke flaps on their tipis, keeping the wind from lifting and tearing the hides and stopping the rain from dousing the fire inside. Shards of lightning stabbed the dark sky all around them as the storm drew closer and closer.

Holding its ears pinned flat against its head, the pinto charged ahead. Its coat was soaked and slippery, with a combination of sweat and rain and Ryan began to slip. She pressed tighter with her knees against the animal's ribs and tried to keep her balance.

The wind drove against them and the rain came down in drenching sheets, muddying and puddling in hollows on the ground where the soil could not soak it up fast enough. Jumping across a fallen tree, the pinto slid in the mud and lurched to the left. Losing her tenuous grip, Ryan began to fall. Reaching back, Wolf settled her back onto the horse. His arm remained to steady her, but he never slowed the speed of the horse beneath them.

The pinto skidded to a stop at Wolf's tipi and Ryan quickly jumped down, her feet slipping in the mud. Mindful of the lessons she'd learned from Pretty Feather, she ran behind the lodge and grabbed one of the long smoke flap poles. Breathless and weak from the frenzied ride, she struggled and finally lifted it free. Gritting her teeth against its weight and the drag of the wind against the hide, she pulled the pole around to the front of the lodge. She leaned it against the wall of the tipi and then dashed around to the other side of the tipi to repeat the task. Overlapping one smoke flap with the other, she closed off all but a small portion of the smoke hole, shutting out the downpour of rain.

Wolf held the door flap open and she ducked inside, finally safe from the wind and rain. The last storm had brought a great change to her life. What would this one bring?

Chapter 21

RAINWATER TRICKLED DOWN Ryan's back and her wet hair lay plastered against her head. Completely soaked, the hide dress clung to her body and water dripped from the ends of the fringes, wetting the furs at her feet. She looked at Wolf. He fared no better. His skin was slick and glistening and water dribbled from his hair. She tried to conceal a grin behind her hand but couldn't keep from laughing aloud.

"You find my misery amusing?"

"We look like two muskrats," she chuckled.

"I have seen fish in the river who are not this wet," Wolf joked in response before turning toward his side of the tipi to place the unfinished medicine bundle in a storage bag.

"Please, don't. It's not finished and we're running out of time." There were only two days left until Custer arrived.

"It will wait until we are dry." Wolf's gaze rose from Ryan's toes to her shoulders, his eyes lingering where the hide stretched tightly across her breasts. "I will make more fire to warm us."

"That's a woman's task," Ryan quietly responded.

"This warrior can make a fire without losing his manhood."

I'm well aware of your manhood. She quickly looked away. Even in the dim light of the tipi, her blush would be impossible to hide. The memory of Wolf's body, aroused and hard, urgently pressing against her, was very clear in her mind. Ryan glanced back and found him watching her. Flustered, she moved away.

The buckskin dress felt so heavy on her shoulders. Dismayed, she touched it. The hides had soaked up water like a sponge and the fringes hung limply from the sleeves. "It's ruined," she moaned. "It's going to be stiff when it dries. I won't be able to wear it."

Wolf hunkered beside the fire pit and laid stick after stick of kindling over the embers that remained from the morning fire. "You must take it off to allow it to dry. The hides are well prepared; they will not become stiff. Take it off."

"What? I can't." She had nothing else to wear. "There's got to be some other way."

"You must take it off your body," Wolf repeated. "It must dry slowly, very slowly. It cannot be near the fire."

"How slowly?" Ryan asked warily.

"For a long time . . . all night, perhaps most of the early day tomorrow as well."

Outside, the wind and rain battered the tipi and great claps of thunder shook the ground. Inside, no one spoke and no one moved for moments that seemed to stretch into hours. Finally the silence ended.

"Maybe Pretty Feather has something I could borrow." Ryan moved toward the door, pleased she had found a solution to her dilemma. "I'll just go and—"

"There is still much rain." Wolf sounded as though he were speaking to a child. "Would you have Pretty Feather's dress get wet? Then you would have two nothings to wear." He looked up.

"I can't take it off. What will I wear?"

"Why are you so troubled? I have seen your body." He watched her for a moment and when he spoke again, his voice was soft. "It is very pleasing to me."

"Among my people . . . we . . . uh, they . . . honorable women don't take their clothes off—" she stuttered.

"Never?" he interrupted, earning a look of frustration.

She fidgeted, folding and unfolding her arms across her breasts, looking everywhere in the tipi except into his dark eyes. "Well yes, of course we do, but not in front of—"

"Good, then I will help you." He dropped the last small piece of wood on the fire and began to rise.

"N-n-no!" She quickly stepped back. "I don't need your help."

Wolf moved toward her and with each step he took, Ryan retreated. Lifting the buffalo robe from her bed, he held it out to her. "Here, you may hide in this . . . again," he teased.

"Hide? That's not what I'm doing," she countered, provoked by his baiting.

Wolf pressed his mission. "Let me help you."

"No!" she replied, testily rebuffing his offer a second time. "I can do it myself."

Snatching the robe from Wolf's hands, she scurried away. Keeping her back to him, Ryan tried to lift the wet dress over her shoulders. It was heavy enough when dry, but wet it was three times its usual weight—cumbersome, slippery and maddeningly unmanageable. She raised the skirt to mid-thigh, and slipping her arms under the capped sleeves, tried to lift the garment. It dragged against her skin and her arms soon tired from the struggle. Trying again and again, she found she could not hold the dress up from her shoulders long enough to get out from under it. Breathless and nearly exhausted, she turned to Wolf, the dress pitifully bunched up around her legs and neck. "All right. Please help me."

"Are you sure you cannot do this by yourself?" he baited, folding his arms across his bare chest and not moving any closer.

"Good grief," she muttered in English. "Most men would jump at the chance to undress a woman." With a haughty lift to her head, she gave him a scathing look and turned her back to him once more. "Fine, don't help. I'll do it myself."

If he could play this ridiculous game, then so could she.

Ryan cast a quick look over her shoulder. "It's almost night and you haven't left yet," she taunted. "Aren't you going to leave me again?"

"I am staying. Why do you ask such a thing?"

"Ah," she said, continuing to harass him. "So, tonight it's more comfortable to sleep here. Too wet outside, is it?"

"I go wherever I want, and go whenever I want," Wolf parried. "I stay because this is *my* lodge. What do you know about where I sleep or why I do not sleep here."

Refusing to speculate, Ryan didn't answer. She wanted him to answer his own questions. Again she attempted to lift the dress but succeeded in raising it only an inch or two. "Every night you leave and don't come back until morning or until someone else is with me. Why?"

"I leave to give you freedom to come and go as you wish, nothing more."

"I already have that freedom," she answered. "I can go anywhere in this camp." A playful smile curved her mouth. "Do I snore too loudly when I sleep?"

Wolf answered with an exasperated grunt.

Ryan pressed further. "If you want me to sleep somewhere else, I'll leave." She peered over the top of the dress, allowing the silence to grow awkward before she spoke again. "I think there's another reason you stay away at night."

Continuing her efforts to loosen the clinging garment, she turned away, her hips wiggling as she fought to raise the dress. "Don't you enjoy my company?"

The pause before he answered was slight, but definite. "Oh, yes," Wolf replied with a chuckle, "I enjoy it very much."

Glancing over her shoulder, Ryan caught him staring at her backside and a hot blush burned her face. Quickly changing strategy, she finally succeeded in dragging the soaked buckskin up over her hips. Once there, it stuck. Feeling the slight waft of cool air against her skin, she knew without looking down that only the fringed hem of the dress covered her naked bottom. Embarrassed, she battled harder,

only to have the fringes on the right sleeve tangle in the
bunched hide. She was trapped.

*My God, I'm going to suffocate in this damned thing and
no one's going to know who I am because all they'll see is
my bare butt hanging out!* She choked down a big dose of
pride. "Wolf, please, help me."

He quickly moved to her side of the tipi and stood behind
her. "It is night, Kechuwa. I have stayed and we are alone."
He gently pushed aside a lock of her hair that had fallen
over her cheek, his fingertips grazing her skin. "Know
this—if I help you, I will stay . . . all night." Lifting her
hair, he leaned close and whispered in her ear. "Do you
still want my help?"

His words once again ignited the luscious heat deep in
her stomach and lower, between her legs, and Ryan knew
what she wanted. Her love for this warrior was too great
to deny. "Yes."

"Do you understand my words?" he asked again. "I will
stay and I will be your husband."

"Yes." Her voice was no more than a soft, drawn-out
murmur. "My answer is yes."

He placed his hands on either side of her hips, resting
them there for a moment before moving them up over her
skin. With a gentle tug he released the fringes at her waist,
then effortlessly lifted the dress up and over her head.

Freedom! She could finally breathe unhindered by the
caul of wet deerhide, but with the protection of the garment
gone, she was completely naked.

Neither spoke. The only sounds inside the tipi were the
periodic crackling of the fire and the rhythmic patter of rain
on the outer skin of the lodge. But somewhere in the encampment, the sound of a drum filled the air with its deep
cadence. As the singers joined in, the drum became louder
and louder, its beat pulsing, throbbing like a quickening
heartbeat.

Wolf's fingers brushed up her arm and Ryan lightly shivered, unsure whether a chill, his touch, or the delicious
anticipation of what lay ahead was to blame.

"Wear this," he breathed in her ear, placing a warm trade

blanket around her shoulders, lifting her damp hair out from under its folds. He turned her around to face him, and closed the blanket over her naked breasts.

Breathless, she couldn't move. How much longer could she be with him like this and not want him in her bed, in her arms, inside her? This was the man, the lover, she had dreamed of all her life. This was the man who would meet her as an equal, who would love her because she was worthy of his love. This was the man who could kindle a fire within her and stoke it until it blazed wildly out of control.

Wolf stepped away and her disappointment fell heavily. She watched him return to his bed. Didn't he feel the emotions that smoldered between them? Could he be as unaffected as he seemed?

Whatever else this escapade into the past had in store for her would pale in comparison to the love she felt for *Sunkmanitu Ceye a Pelo*. If there was a choice, Ryan knew she would gladly give up any chance to go back to her own time, her own life, to stay with him—live with him—love with him.

Perhaps he's the wise one to ignore what could be between us. She settled the wet dress to dry over one of the willow backrests and returned to her side of the tipi. "*Sunkmanitu Ceye a Pelo*, my beautiful Calls to the Wolf," she whispered, her English words stifled by the pounding rain.

Suddenly an uninvited memory intruded, coming strong and clear. It pierced her mind and cut cruelly into her heart, leaving her chilled and shaking. When Buddy first introduced her to Charley Crying Wolf, he had said Charley's real name was Calls to the Wolf. *Sunkmanitu Ceye a Pelo* meant Calls to the Wolf. Was Wolf a relative of Charley's? An ancestor? His father? His grandfather? It was an odd possibility, one that left her unsure. Could she set the prospect from her mind? Did it really matter? Closing her eyes, tears spilled onto her cheeks. How could she deal with the possibility?

Scrubbing her tears away with the heels of her hands, she tried to push the thought out of her mind and busily placed her damp moccasins and leggings closer to the fire.

Finished, she drew the rough blanket more closely around
her. It carried Wolf's scent. As it brushed against her
breasts, her nipples tightened, puckering as if touched by a
lover's caress. She trembled and tried to ignore the fiery
longing that persisted. *I don't care who you are*, Sunkmanitu Ceye a Pelo. *I love you. I love you.*

Before he spoke, before he touched her, she knew he
stood behind her. The scent of cedar and sunlight that was
his alone told her so. He placed his hands on her arms and
gently turned her around to face him and her breath escaped
in a hungry sigh.

"If I stay," he whispered, his voice heavy with emotion,
his gaze ardently searching her eyes for approval, "it must
be because you have said I am to stay." He reached up and
tenderly wiped the remnants of tears from her cheeks. "Say
the words, Kechuwa, say the words."

Every doubt she ever had fled quickly. Raising her arms,
she wrapped them around his neck and the trade blanket
slid from her shoulders, falling into a puddling of red wool
at her feet.

"Stay," she answered softly.

Shy, she no longer felt the bravado of a modern woman.
She no longer felt like the self-assured, educated scientist.
She felt only the unique emotions of a woman in love, a
woman filled with a yearning for the impassioned touch of
her lover. She lowered her eyes and buried her face against
his chest. "I believe it is time for this wife to know her
husband."

"And it is time for this *husband* to know his wife," Wolf
replied, his warm breath falling lightly upon her cheek, igniting her spirit with its touch, inflaming her soul with his
words.

She closed her eyes. Nothing in her rational mind could
stop the tide of desire rushing to every secret place within
her body. She loved this Lakota warrior and she would
joyfully give him that love with her words, her touch and
her body.

Somewhere in another tipi in the encampment, the throb-

bing beat of the drum continued, its cadence now harmonizing with the meter of Ryan's heart.

She moved fully into Wolf's embrace, delighting in the
feel of her naked body against his. Pale skin touched dark
and she gave herself to him completely.

He placed his hands lightly on her wrists and moved
them upwards over her arms. The flat of his palms tested
the texture and contour of her skin as they moved toward
her shoulders. His fingers grazed the column of her throat,
over the ridge of her collarbone and downward once again.
"You are softer than a young rabbit," he murmured. "You
are soft . . . everywhere."

She trembled as his hands continued downward and
cupped her breasts. He lifted them and with a light brush
of his thumbs teased her nipples until each roseate point
was engorged and taut. Ryan moaned.

"Does this please you?" he asked, gently rolling the hardened peaks between his fingers.

"Yes," she breathed. "Yes." A scalding brew raced
through her veins and pooled with delicious fervor deep in
her belly.

He bent his head and kissed her cheek, his mouth nib-
bling lightly on her skin. An apt pupil, he had learned this
delightful caress well. Then pulling away, he watched her
reaction and smiled as she swayed against him, pressing
her breasts deeper into his hands.

He licked the shell of her ear, then slowly moved his
mouth to hers. Tentative and weightless, his tongue flicked
across her lips, tasting her, tempting her; and then resolute,
plundered deep inside, giving and taking, erasing all logic
from her mind.

No longer satisfied to be only a recipient, Ryan lifted her
hand and touched the juncture of their kiss. She loved the
taste of him, the smell of him, the feel of him. The hard
bulge, evidence of his desire, pressed against her belly and
she pushed the center of her own need against his leg un-
ashamedly. He answered with a hungry moan that became
an audible caress.

Without lifting his mouth, Wolf drew her down to the

soft heap of furs covering her bed. She fell back, stretching her body, arcing up to meet him as he lay over her. Supporting his weight on one arm, his long hair fell around their heads like an ebony shade, blinding them to everything but each other. He captured another kiss on her willing mouth and she clung to him, afraid to let go.

His lips moved along the side of her face until he spoke softly in her ear. "This Lakota warrior is thirsty for the love of his wife."

When had she begun to cry? She felt the slow slide of tears over the sides of her cheeks and Wolf caught each one with the tip of his tongue.

"Do you not want this? Is this warrior not to be your husband?"

She raised her hand and gently cupped the side of his face, her fingers moving to trace the outline of his lips. "This wife loves her husband. She wants this."

"Then my wife will have *everything* she wants."

Wolf's lips traveled over her chin and down her throat, following the caress of his exploring fingers. His tongue tasted and licked each discovered hollow and nook, inciting her to gasp with delight. She arched her back, raising her breasts up to receive his homage and her fingers delved into his hair as she held his head to her. She closed her eyes and sighed with rising desire as his mouth closed around her hardened nipple. Suckling, he drew on her tender flesh with sweet tugs, and invoked an amazing response deep within her womb.

Wolf moved his hand between her thighs and with gentle fingers, he parted the lips of her sex and opened her. She was already wet. His fingers slid through her sweet moisture and grazed the taut sensitive nub of flesh, causing her to drive her hips upward against his hand. With each stroke he dipped inside then retreated from her, over and over again, gliding like silk on satin, until the delicious rhythm robbed her of her senses.

Shifting, seeking another position, Wolf took her hand and led her to his erection, drawing a sharp breath as her fingers gently fisted around him. His flesh felt like hot, silken steel as her hand rode his shaft in the age-old rhythms of the most intimate caress of all.

Reaching between them, he stilled her hand. "Wait. I would not have it happen this way for us," he murmured, moving up and over her.

She could see the play of firelight on his skin as he looked down at her and the glow of the flames reflected in his eyes. "Neither would I," she answered.

Gently nudging her thighs apart, he settled himself between her legs. His penis jutted forward, hot and hard and heavy. It grazed her inner thigh.

She curled her fingers over his shoulders, her nails digging into his flesh. Needing to feel more of him, she moved her hands down across the hard plane of his back until she cupped his buttocks and drew him closer. The smooth tip of him touched and teased at the moist folds of her sex, dispatching tides of delight throughout her body and she opened, inviting him inside. "Please," she breathed. "Love me now."

Wolf slowly moved forward, downward, separating her silken flesh, filling her, inch by inch sheathing himself fully inside her. He closely watched her face as they joined and what he saw delighted him more than any joy he had ever known.

"*Mitawicu*, my wife," he murmured, his lips grazing her ear. "*Kechuwa*, my dear one. *Sunkmanitu*, the wolf takes only one mate for life. You are that one. You are my life."

"*Wicahca*, my husband. *Sunkmanitu Ceye a Pelo, waste cilake*, I love Calls to the Wolf more than . . ."

Her words fell silent as he began to move within her. He slowly drove forward and then withdrew, almost leaving her before another seductively slow plunge buried him deep inside her again and again. Each wonderful filling gave more than the last and time after time she eagerly met his thrusts. She wrapped her legs around his hips as he pressed into her and stretched her, filling her completely with each stroke.

As the meter of the drum in the encampment increased, Ryan and Wolf answered each beat with a tempo of their own until their passion became the rhythm, became the song.

Her climax bloomed, grew high until it finally burst. She trembled as it carried her beyond all reality. She cried his name aloud as she felt his deep impalement, felt the wonderful pulsations of his own hot release, filling and fulfilling her. She clung to him as the maelstrom continued to spiral throughout their bodies, binding them together, fusing their souls. And then, with sweet release, the waves ebbed and waned into sighs and soft caresses.

Staying deep inside of her, Wolf rolled onto his side, taking her with him. The long strands of his hair wound around them, binding them together, and they were one, the wolf and his mate.

Chapter 22

RYAN WOKE SLOWLY, guessing the time to be that halfway hour between night and dawn when the promise of the new day faintly touches the eastern sky. The fire had burned down to ashen pink embers and a meager thread of smoke wound its way upward through the narrow opening at the top of the tipi. She drew a deep breath. Sometime during the night the storm had stopped and now the earth smelled fresh and new. Early birds were already awake and singing their cheerful reveille to the encampment. She stretched. It had been a wonder-filled night.

A slight stirring on the palette beside her drew her attention and she lovingly caressed the bronze-hued chest of the sleeping man at her side. A smile lifted the corners of her mouth. She had never felt so content. Leaning close, she rubbed her cheek like a possessive kitten against Wolf's skin, then placed a tender kiss on the point of his shoulder.

When had they moved to his bed? Remembering, her smile broadened. She snuggled deeper into the curve of his body. It was a perfect fit.

Settling her head on his chest, her hair fanned out, blending with his long, ebony strands and she listened to the strong beat of his heart. Wonderful vivid vignettes of their

night together filled her mind, rekindling and feeding the
hot flame of want in her body. Never had she imagined a
lover who could satisfy her every desire again and again,
only to leave her hungry for more, so much more.

She trailed her fingers across the broad expanse of his
chest, lightly touching the sun dance scars, his dark nipples
and the place over his heart. Her touch continued downward to the hard ridges of his ribs and across the flat plane
of his stomach. Draping her arm across his waist, she co-
zied tight against his side.

"Am I lying with a restless prairie dog?" Wolf teased,
his voice a sleepy whisper that sent a delightful yearning
throughout her body. He turned onto his side and placed a
light kiss on her forehead, then brushed his lips in a soft
caress across her cheek. "Are you not going to allow me
to sleep?"

Her answer was a light kiss on his mouth.

"A good Lakota wife knows that if her husband is to be
a great warrior and hunter, he must rest for a long time to
be strong," Wolf said, drawing her into his arms.

"I can feel your strength," she teased, tipping her hips
forward to meet his renewed and eager erection. "I think
my great warrior is *very* well-rested."

"Ah, Kechuwa." Wolf sucked in a ragged breath and sent
his hand to wander the curve of her hip. "As long as you
are beside me I care not if I ever sleep again. Your touch
brings more strength than this warrior ever imagined could
be his." He rolled onto his back and pulled her with him,
easily accommodating her body on top of his own.

Surprised, she began to protest and move away but he
held her captive, nestling his head into the hollow between
her neck and shoulder. He placed tender kisses along the
column of her throat and across her chin to her mouth
where his tongue nimbly dipped, swirled and teased until
she neared the brink of bliss, responding with kisses and
sweet tongue strokes of her own.

He toyed with her breasts, softly kneading their full
swells with his palms. Raising up, Ryan gave him complete
access and she closed her eyes as his fingers pulled lightly,

sculpting her nipples into tight, hard points. Shock wave after exquisite shock wave rushed to the hot, moist folds between her legs. Closing her eyes, she responded with a throaty moan. Wolf answered with a deep murmur and pressed his hips upward against her as she massaged his arousal with her body.

He stilled her rhythm with a light staying touch of his hand on her hip and his urgently whispered words in her ear set her afire.

"Kechuwa, show me how well you have learned to ride."

She tilted her mouth into a mischievous grin and rose to her knees. Straddling Wolf as though he were a powerful horse, she eagerly complied with his wishes. There was no coyness, no pretense—only the glorious desire they shared for one another. She wanted him as much as she knew he wanted her. It was as simple as that and yet it was as complicated as hell. There was no turning back. They could only go forward.

Holding herself mere inches above him, Ryan gazed down into his eyes while her hands smoothed over his hot skin, baiting him, denying him her intimate touch, keeping him taut with anticipation.

Impatient, Wolf growled and pushed his hips upward until the tip of his penis lightly grazed against her, urging her to open for him. The silken touch caused an urgency she couldn't ignore. Too eager to delay a moment longer, she sank down, barely able to allay her rush to prolong the delicious deed.

Fraction by fraction, she eased his hard length up into her. She tipped her head back and arched her spine, offering herself completely to his caress, reveling in the thick pressure that stretched and filled her and pushed deep into the moist secret place within.

With fingers splayed wide, Wolf stroked upward across her stomach until his hands covered her breasts. He molded them in each palm and teased each dark aureole, keeping them distended and hard. Leaning forward, Ryan offered her breasts to his mouth and he hungrily suckled one and then the other, nipping them lightly between his teeth and driving her mad.

"I want to see your face," he breathed, his voice hoarse with desire.

Surrendering to his request, she sat up, settling her weight on her knees. Wolf raised his hips upward and the delicious deep pressure inside returned and pulsed with an insistence that demanded her response.

His hands followed the slope of her breasts and retreated downward. Unhurried and painstakingly, he touched every inch of her skin until one hand remained to rest lightly at her waist and the other, still inquisitive, traveled lower. His fingers traced the tantalizing heart-shaped outline of crisp hair at the juncture of her thighs and then he cupped her mound, pressing ardently against it, driving her further onto him. Sliding his fingers between their bodies, he opened her. Finding the sensitive kernel of flesh, he stroked her softly, mimicking the motion with his hips. Moving slowly, deliberately, he thrust and parried, giving and taking and giving again.

"Look into my eyes, Kechuwa," Wolf whispered. I want to see the face of my wife, as she rides the wild wind."

The tipi filled with the heat of the day as they dressed and cast lovers' glances and contented smiles at one another. Ryan's dress had dried soft and pliable, as Wolf had promised. She slipped it over her head and tugged it down into place, then bent to tie her moccasins. Pretty Feather would be coming soon to go with her to the river.

"I would ask something of you before you go," Wolf petitioned, coming to stand beside her. He lightly touched her hair, combing his fingers through its length. "I wish to braid your hair. I would have the people know you belong to me and no other."

Hearing his possessive request, Ryan's heart quickened with joy. Giving a slight nod, she knelt on her bed. Never in her life had she ever felt so cherished. How could fate and Custer's cavalry cruelly dare to stand in their way?

A pall of melancholy immediately settled upon her and

tarnished her mood. No matter what happiness had entered her life, fate's clock kept ticking. Tick-tock, tick-tock. Nothing could hold back time and in little more than forty-eight hours the most infamous Indian battle in history would take place, with or without her permission. Tick-tock, tick-tock.

I could tell Wolf or Turtle Rib what is going to happen in two days and my warning will confirm Sitting Bull's vision. The Lakota already believe I'm wakan—they won't question what I tell them about Custer and the Seventh. The people could leave and there'd be no battle, no one would have to die and I could stay with Wolf.

It sounded so easy but Ryan knew in her heart, in her head and in that special someplace deep inside her soul, that anything she did that might change the course of history was forbidden. Hidden from Wolf's view, she wiped away the tears that soaked her cheeks and sealed her fate.

Wolf's fingers gently combed through her hair and she felt the pull of the porcupine-tail brush that he used daily on his own waist-length hair. He parted her hair from the middle of her head to the nape of her neck. Brushing the left side until it lay smooth, he plaited it, bringing the braid over her shoulder and down over her breast. He tied the end with a quick wrap of sinew and a couple of knots. Stepping back to admire his work, he nodded and completed the task on the right side.

"*Wasté.*" Wolf pulled Ryan to her feet. "My wife is beautiful." He bent to kiss her, instantly igniting the flame between them once again.

"Wolf," Ryan whispered, wrapping her arms about his neck, lightly rubbing her body against his.

A light, yet persistent scratching on the door flap of the tipi intruded.

"It is me, *Wiyaka Wasté Win*," Pretty Feather quietly spoke from outside. "Does Kechuwa go with me to the river?"

Wolf pulled away, clearly irked by Pretty Feather's poor timing. His deep, loud sigh and the slight pout on his lips drew a chuckle from Ryan. Standing on tiptoe, she kissed his petulant mouth. "I promise, I'll be back soon."

He tenderly caressed her cheek with his fingertips and nodded, offering her a doleful smile. "If you do not return soon, I will come and pull you back to our lodge and—"

"And then perhaps we can finish the bundle," she interrupted with a teasing grin, knowing full well that the medicine bundle wasn't what Wolf had on his mind.

"It will be done in good time," he murmured against her lips. "We will begin and finish—all of it."

Ryan slowly drew her fingers through a thick lock of his hair that fell over his shoulder, her eyes held captive by his dark gaze. Offering another kiss, she turned to leave. Wolf's touch on her wrist stopped her.

He held out his hand. A necklace of exquisite multicolored glass Venetian trade beads lay in his palm. Placing the necklace over her head, he gently laid the beads on her breasts.

A large silver crucifix hung from the center and Ryan tentatively touched it. Although loose beads were readily available from traders and many of the Indians bartered for them at the soldier forts, the ornate crucifix and intricate clasp told her these had been strung together by a professional jeweler. It reminded her of a rosary. The exquisite necklace was clearly not Lakota. With that thought came another. How had the necklace reached Wolf's possession? She shuddered at the cold possibility. No. She didn't want to know the answer.

Pushing the troubling thoughts aside, she kissed Wolf's cheek. "This is so beautiful, *lila pilamaya*. I'll cherish it always."

"I would make a promise," Wolf announced. "My wife will have many beautiful beads and fine possessions. I will select only the finest ponies for you to ride and you will have only the best hides to make our clothes. Our sons will be proud and strong warriors, good hunters and providers, and our daughters will be beautiful and bring joy to our camp. You will see. I will make this promise true."

Ryan pressed her head against his chest and clung to him.

Renewed despair fell like a shroud over her heart. *God, how I wish it could all come true.*

"I did not know if you would be coming with me today," Pretty Feather said, walking on the path beside Ryan. "Are you well?"

"Yes, I'm fine," Ryan answered. "And you?"

"Oh, I am well," Pretty Feather replied with a smile, lightly rubbing her rounded stomach. "My little one has been restless—like a herd of ponies." She hesitated and then posed another question. "You are rested and are not ill?"

"I'm fine," Ryan answered, puzzled by her friend's questions. "Why do you ask?"

Pretty Feather ducked her head bashfully, muffling her soft giggle. "You and Wolf slept very late this morning."

"How did—"

"It is noticed when one's lodge door is not opened for a long time after sunrise." She glanced at Ryan, and then hastily looking away, placed her hand over her mouth to hide her smile. "I thought perhaps you were ill but now I see the reason for your late morning." Another giggle escaped from behind her hand.

Unsure if she really wanted to hear Pretty Feather's theory, Ryan pressed for more. "And what do you think is the reason?"

"Ah, my dear friend, you have the special smile of a new wife upon your face this morning."

A hot blush burned Ryan's cheeks and the simplest response failed her.

Pretty Feather peeked again at her companion. "Is your hair not different today as well?"

Ryan glanced at Pretty Feather and noticing her braids, her hands flew up to touch her own hair. "I forgot," she murmured. Although the tradition wasn't followed much in the twentieth century, among the Lakota of the 1800s, single girls wore their braids down their backs, but a married woman wore her hair with the braids falling over her breasts. A smile curved her lips. *So that's what he meant.*

It was more than just wanting people to know I belong to him, he wanted them to know we have a true marriage— in every way.

"Did your husband prepare your hair?" Pretty Feather asked, her manner demure once again.

Ryan nodded with a silly grin. "Yes."

"Are you happy, my friend? It is what your face tells me."

"Yes," she replied, the answer rising up from her soul. It was true. In spite of the impending battle with Custer, in spite of the unnatural way she had come to the 1876 valley of the Little Big Horn, in spite of it all, she had never been so happy in her entire life. "Yes, yes, yes!" She laughed and grabbed both of Pretty Feather's hands, dragging her into a merry-go-round dance, around and around on the path.

Pretty Feather gaily joined in Ryan's romp until she pulled Ryan to a halt, out of breath and holding onto her stomach. "It is *wasté*, my friend. There is much feeling between you and Calls to the Wolf. Everyone who has seen you together knows that is so." She took a few deep breaths. "This marriage will be good for the Lakota; it has Tunkasila's blessing." She hugged Ryan affectionately. "Soon, my new sister, you will be shaped like this." She took Ryan's hand and pressed it to the pregnant swell of her belly. "Soon you too will have a baby inside, growing strong from the love between you and your husband."

Stunned, Ryan's eyes popped wide. The possibility hadn't occurred to her.

Chapter 23

THE SHADY SECLUDED crook in the Greasy Grass where the women bathed held the warmth of the June sun. Downriver from the Hunkpapa camp, the glade lay protected from the view of the village by a regiment of trees and high bushes that grew in a deep thicket along the riverbank. Many of the women were already bathing when Pretty Feather and Ryan arrived. Removing their clothes, they stepped into the cool water.

Ryan soon noticed the covert glances and the giggles politely shielded behind bronze-hued hands. It was obvious the topic of the morning chatter was to be *Sunkmanitu Ceye a Pelo's wasicu.*

"Everyone has noticed your hair," Pretty Feather whispered, wading to Ryan's side, her large belly making each step clumsy.

Ryan tried to keep her face impassive, allowing the cool water in her cupped hands to trickle over her breasts and stomach. Her eyes quickly scanned the other bathers. Yes, everyone had noticed. Everyone including Ground Plum.

The girl's hatred was clear and her spiteful expression chilled Ryan to the bone. She had made a formidable enemy. Sooner or later Ground Plum would try to avenge the humiliation she believed Ryan had caused her.

Buffeted by the waist-deep water, Ground Plum waded toward Ryan. Her dark-tipped breasts swayed with each step and her mouth curved in a taunting smirk. "Does the white cow think that opening her legs for Calls to the Wolf gives her the right to say she is his wife?" With a contemptuous lift of her hand, Ground Plum flipped one of Ryan's braids.

Standing her ground, Ryan met the Lakota woman's challenge.

"Does the *wasicu* whore have no shame? I think he was asleep when you put his man thing inside your body." Ground Plum laughed harshly at her own words. "You are too ugly for him to ride you willingly."

By all outward appearances Ryan remained unaffected by Ground Plum's insults, allowing none of her anger to show. With everyone watching, Ryan swore she wouldn't be the one to yield or show weakness.

"Lakota women, listen to me," Ground Plum said loudly. "We have heard this *wasicu* is *wakan*. What proof does she show us?" Ground Plum turned to the nearest woman. "Has she taken the coughing sickness from your daughter?" Noting a slight shake of the woman's head, Ground Plum continued. "Has she brought back the great herds of buffalo?" She waited again for an answer. None was heard. "I give you warning. Stay upriver from this *wasicu* so she does not make you sick with the poisons she leaves in the water." Ground Plum lifted her chin and with a thrust of her lips, pointed downstream. "Even snakes and weasels will die when they drink after this *wasicu* has washed her body."

I have had enough. Ryan erased any friendly mien from her face. "I have no quarrel with you. Why do you continue to shame yourself trying to claim a man who does not want you." *We must look absolutely ridiculous. Two grown, somewhat intelligent women standing butt naked and waist-deep in a river, arguing over a man.* "I'm sorry you're hurt because he didn't chose you, but that's not my fault."

"If you had not come and taken him from me," Ground

Plum hissed, "*Sunkmanitu Ceye a Pelo* would be my husband."

Ryan held her ground. "He's a strong warrior. Isn't he able to make up his own mind?"

"He is a brave and mighty warrior," Ground Plum answered indignantly. "He has killed many enemies, counted many coups and captured many horses."

"If this is so, then how can I, one insignificant, stupid white woman, make him do something he doesn't want to do?" She cringed inwardly, knowing Gloria Steinem would shoot her dead for saying anything so ignoble.

"You have stolen him with the tricks and lies that only white whores know," Ground Plum answered peevishly. "Hear my words, cow, you will not be with Calls to the Wolf for long."

Had Ground Plum's words not struck so close to the painful truth Ryan held secret in her heart, she might have been able to ignore the girl's threat. *Once Charley zaps me back, she'll have Wolf all to herself again.* She tried to shove the painful thought out of her mind. It didn't cooperate.

Tired of Ground Plum's harangue, and beginning to feel self-conscious arguing without a stitch of clothing covering her body, Ryan modestly folded her arms across her breasts and abruptly turned her back to the girl.

A collective gasp resounded from everyone present and the silence that followed rang almost as loudly.

Damn! Now I've really done it! Ryan immediately turned to face Ground Plum. "I'm sorry. I didn't mean to—"

"You would dare turn your back and shun me in front of others as if I am one without honor?" Ground Plum's voice rose, her words barely coherent in her rage. "I have warned you before, cow, it is you who will die. It is you who will have every back in this camp turned toward you. No one will acknowledge you. You will see, white soldier-whore, my words will be so."

Ground Plum's gaze dropped to the necklace around Ryan's neck and her eyes widened with recognition. "Was Calls to the Wolf also asleep when you stole those beads from him?" She plowed forward through the water. Reaching her fingers like talons, she tried to seize the pendant from Ryan's neck. "I understand now that you are a thief of *all* things." Awkward in her greedy haste, Ground Plum's foot slid on the slippery river bottom. Frantically flailing her arms, she fought to stay upright, but the strong current quickly stole her dignity. With a loud splash, she lost her balance and disappeared under the water. She resurfaced ten or twelve feet downriver, her hair plastered to her head. Humiliated, coughing and spitting water, she yanked river weeds from her hair. Her hatred had grown. Casting one last loathing glare over her shoulder at Ryan, Ground Plum climbed out of the river. Slipping into her clothes, she disappeared down the pathway to the encampment, each step a testament to her rage.

Filled with a sense of victory, he waited patiently, crouched on a high cottonwood limb. The argument between Calls to the Wolf's white woman and Ground Plum encouraged him. Perhaps now would be a good time to involve her in his scheme. He needed an ally for his plan to succeed and if he understood her mood correctly, Ground Plum was like a red spring berry, ripe and juicy for the picking. Excited, he felt the spreading heat and the stiffening proof of his arousal between his legs. Although he was still sore from the wounds the brown dog had given him, he rubbed his hand against himself and grinned. It was time to pick the berry.

Waiting a moment or two for his excitement to ease, he lowered himself from the high branches without a sound and landed softly on the leaf-littered ground below. He waited and listened for one moment and then another before silently making his way through the bushes to the footpath. Hiding behind a stand of willow scrubs, he heard the light footfalls on the path coming nearer and nearer. Biding his time, he stepped out and blocked the path.

"Iron Soldier!" Ground Plum stumbled with surprise and the look in her eyes grew wary. "What do you want?" she demanded, her temper still hot from her clash with the *was-icu*.

"I think we have much to talk about," Iron Soldier said with his best smile, trying his utmost to beguile Bear Heart's daughter. She had been his choice for wife and no matter what it took, he would have her yet.

"There is nothing for us to say," Ground Plum coldly replied, moving off the path to step around him.

Iron Soldier blocked her way again. "That is not so. There is much to speak of and it would be good for you to hear my words." He glanced down the path toward the river and then back over his shoulder toward the encampment. "Meet me downriver by the dead tree. No one will see us. We will talk then."

"Why should I want to talk with you?"

"I think you want to have Calls to the Wolf to yourself, and I seek the *wasicu*." He shrugged and offered a slight complacent smile. "I think we can be of great help to each other."

Ground Plum's eyes narrowed with distrust and then, as if finding Iron Soldier's comments too enticing to dismiss, she reached out and lightly pushed him aside. Brushing by, she whispered, "I will meet you."

Iron Soldier arrived under the cottonwood before Ground Plum and he leaned against the dried trunk, pondering Calls to the Wolf's downfall with delight. Hearing the light snap of a twig, he ducked behind the tree and quietly waited. "Ah, it is you," he whispered hoarsely, stepping into view. "You are alone?"

Ground Plum gave a nervous jump. "Why do you hide like a coward?" she charged. "Who else should I bring? Perhaps I should have told the ugly white cow to come with me and hear of your plan?"

"Perhaps you should learn to keep your anger hidden?" Iron Soldier admonished with a sharp bite to his voice. He settled himself on the ground under the dead tree.

"You would dare to give me counsel? Was your anger so well hidden the morning you grabbed the *wasicu* from Calls to the Wolf's hands? Was your anger hidden when a

camp dog counted coup on your man thing?" Ground Plum
taunted, standing impudently before him, her hands on her
hips.

"You are a foolish woman," Iron Soldier spat at her.
"Anger tells an enemy that you plan revenge, but an enemy
never expects harm from someone he believes is a friend."

"You say I should become a friend to this *wasicu*?
Never!"

"Do you not want Calls to the Wolf to take you for wife,
to take *you* to his bed and not the *wasicu*?" Iron Soldier
saw the indecision in Ground Plum's eyes and pressed on.
"If you were to be friends with this white woman and if
she were to go away and leave Calls to the Wolf's tipi,
would he not soon seek comfort with another . . . his wife's
friend?"

"Do not call the cow his wife!" Ground Plum hissed. "I
am to be his wife."

"You are sounding like one who has no teachings."

Ground Plum looked with disbelief at Iron Soldier and
her eyes narrowed. "You think I have no wisdom. You are
trying to trick me. If the *wasicu* should go away, Calls to
the Wolf would look a long time for her." She paced back
and forth in front of Iron Soldier, then stopped and turned
to face him. "You think you can take the *wasicu* from Calls
to the Wolf? Did you not see how she now wears her hair?
Do you still want her even though you know she has taken
Wolf inside her?"

"I want her more because Wolf has ridden her and *still*
wants her for himself." Realizing he had almost told too
much of his own purpose, Iron Soldier moved to cover his
words. "If you become friends and gain her trust, you can
tell me where she goes alone. I will follow her. I will take
her away until she learns to stay with *me* instead of wanting
to return to Wolf."

"What is it that I am to do after you have taken her?"
Ground Plum asked, puzzled, a frown creasing her brow.

"Are you not able to make your own plan to win Calls
to the Wolf to a marriage with you once she is gone? He
will be unhappy for a few days, but you will be there to

comfort him and lie down with him when he is sad no more. I will make all this possible but *you* must devise a plan of your own."

"Then hurry and take the white cow away," Ground Plum hissed impatiently. "My stomach will give up all my food if I have to be friends with her for too long. Tell me as soon as you have taken the *wasicu* from this camp so that I may go to Calls to the Wolf." Ground Plum set her head in a haughty tilt and shooting Iron Soldier a less than friendly look, turned to leave.

Quickly rising, Iron Soldier grabbed her arm and pressed her tightly against the tree. His fingers dug cruelly into her arms. His breath came rasped and heavy. He mashed his mouth over Ground Plum's and tried to imitate what he had seen Kechuwa teach Calls to the Wolf. Roughly rubbing his mouth back and forth, he sucked and nipped on Ground Plum's lips and tongue. It was not as pleasing to him as he had anticipated. Looking down into Ground Plum's upturned face, he grinned. He frightened her. He liked that. Tightening his grip on her arms, he pushed himself against her body. He liked this more than putting his mouth on hers. This felt good but naked, without her clothes, it would feel even better.

Iron Soldier had carefully devised his scheme. It would bring him the satisfaction of many rewards. He wanted the white woman not only because he coveted the power Tunkasila had given her, but also because she belonged to Calls to the Wolf. But most of all, Iron Soldier wanted Ground Plum. His body hungered for her. In his own way, he had feelings for her.

Holding Ground Plum securely in spite of her struggling, he gave a small sardonic laugh. "Do you think I would do this thing for you without expecting a payment of some kind?"

"Payment? What do I possess that Iron Soldier would want?"

He laughed. "You will gladly give me whatever I ask."

"So, you *are* the snake, as I have heard." Ground Plum tried to pull away. "The women in camp have been warned to stay away from you because you treat them with no honor." She jerked hard against his grip. "Let go of me. I will speak no more with you about this plan. I will win Wolf without your help."

"I do not think so," Iron Soldier whispered in Ground Plum's ear just before releasing his grip on her. Ground Plum warily stepped away and he smiled at her blatant display of distrust. "Without my help, you will have no chance to lie in Calls to the Wolf's bed. Until I take the *wasicu* away, his bed will be too crowded." He allowed her time to think and then pressed his scheme once more. "What I seek as my payment will also be of great reward to you." He reached out and the tip of his fingers trailed down over the curve of her breast.

"What is it you would have?" she asked, her body stiffening with his touch.

The answer she sought came quickly as Iron Soldier's finger flicked at her nipple through the soft buckskin dress. "You will lie with me."

"You are lower than dung on the ground," she spat, stepping further back out of his reach. "How will I gain great reward by allowing you to crawl on me and spill yourself inside me?"

Her tone rankled him but he pushed his anger aside and continued to explain as though he were speaking to a child. "Do you have any knowledge of what enjoyments a man seeks with a woman? Do you know the tricks the white whore uses to keep your man with her on the furs?" He closely watched Ground Plum and waited for the only answer he knew she could give.

Slowly she formed the word with her lips. "No."

He gestured with his hands, opening them in supplication. "Do you not wish to please Calls to the Wolf more than the *wasicu* when you go to his bed?"

She watched Iron Soldier carefully.

"Then you must know more than the *wasicu*. I can teach you these things. I can teach you what a warrior wants when his woman touches his body. I can teach you how to make him feel much pleasure. I can teach you how to keep him from seeking any woman but you."

Ground Plum nervously chewed at her bottom lip with little white teeth that Iron Soldier knew would bring much delight if they nipped at his own flesh.

"When . . . how soon . . . where," Ground Plum asked, dropping her gaze, unable to meet Iron Soldier's hungry eyes.

"Ah, you agree then to my . . . trade?"

"Yes," Ground Plum murmured, her embarrassment complete. "I see no other way to get back what is mine."

Iron Soldier caught the fringes on the sleeves of her dress and pulled her close. Ground Plum sagged against his body, closed her eyes and shuddered as his hands began to fondle roughly and violate her. "I think your plan cuts both ways, like a knife," she murmured, stating her last complaint.

"Soon you will learn to welcome what a woman must accept from her husband," Iron Soldier growled. Then as he pushed Ground Plum to the ground, he knew he would get everything he wanted.

Chapter 24

"I SEE OUR husbands have decided to amuse themselves."

Ryan followed Pretty Feather's gaze across the river to the group of men on horseback. In the afternoon heat, they wore only breechclouts and moccasins and their bodies gleamed like polished copper in the sunlight. She could hear their voices and laughter and a smile tugged at the corners of her mouth as she picked out Wolf's voice from all the others.

The riders jostled together in a tight group at the south end of the field, all staying behind a lance that had been driven into the ground. A hundred yards to the north, another lance stood upright, its pointed tip buried deeply in the dirt. A strip of red cloth tied to the top, fluttered in the breeze.

"What are they doing?" Ryan asked, raising her hand, shading her eyes against the bright sun.

"You will see," Pretty Feather answered, the excitement in her voice further piquing Ryan's curiosity.

The men maneuvered their horses into a tight bunch, and the animals nervously danced and bumped into each other. A few tried to break rank, fighting against their reins but

well-placed heels in their flanks soon returned them to the
pack. As Ryan watched, one rider broke from the bunch
and galloped out, stopping halfway between two upright
lances. Excitement charged the air like an explosive, un-
tamed promise.

"Watch the one who stands alone," Pretty Feather whispered, as though speaking aloud would agitate the horses
further.

Ryan followed Pretty Feather's suggestion, watching the
man raise his hand and then drop it quickly to his side.
Wheeling his horse around, he galloped off to the side of
the field.

The whoops and yells of the other men immediately stole
Ryan's attention and she turned in time to see a wild free-
for-all race to the north end of the field. Twenty or twenty-
five riders converged on the lance in a mass of jabbing
elbows, kicking legs and colliding and shoving horses, each
man trying to grab the colored streamer. Some leaned far
off the backs of their horses and others reached over the
heads and bodies of other riders to be the first to snatch up
the prize.

From the midst of the dusty melee a riderless horse broke
out, and then another and another. The last horse stumbled
and fell to its knees twice before finally finding solid footing and galloping off toward the river, its tail held high like
a banner. The three unhorsed warriors darted away from
the frenzied fracas, dodging thrashing hooves as they fled
for their lives.

Unable to contain her excitement, Ryan jumped up and
down and cheered loudly. None of the fallen men had been
Wolf.

From the middle of the pack, one hand rose high into
the air, proudly shaking the streamer. A warrior's victory
yell resounded loud and clear and as the riders moved back
from the lance, the spotted horse belonging to the winner
pranced and tossed its head as if personally accepting the
accolade as its own rightful due.

"Wolf!" Ryan exclaimed with pride.

"He is the best at this game," Pretty Feather offered.

"Others try to take his victory but only a few ever succeed."

For more than an hour they played at their rough game. From time to time new participants joined in, and others, tired or injured, left. Wolf and Eagle Deer rode in each race and those that Wolf didn't win, Eagle Deer, Rabbit or No Ear did.

"We have seen all there is," Pretty Feather said, turning away as the men dispersed.

Looking back over her shoulder, Ryan's gaze followed Wolf. Pretty Feather took hold of her arm and pulled her back up the path toward the camp.

"Aren't they coming back now?"

"Do not be so impatient to reward your husband," Pretty Feather teased, stooping to hug the two small boys who ran to her with a couple of the camp dogs at their heels. "They will bathe before returning to camp. But before that, they will ride out to the herds and the winners will claim their prizes."

"Do you mean every time Wolf took the red streamer, he won a horse?" Ryan's eyes brightened with excitement.

Pretty Feather laughed and sent her boys off to play. "No, my friend, whoever wins the race takes a horse from *each* man who rode against him."

Ryan performed a nimble bit of calculation and a freight train could have run right through her gaping mouth. "That's over a hundred horses Wolf has won this afternoon!"

Stacking firewood and starting the cooking fire with a glowing faggot from Pretty Feather's camp had been easy, but the water in the cooking paunch refused to boil. Ryan had heated the rocks in the heart of the fire for over an hour before she had started to drop them into the paunch. The broth still wasn't hot enough.

Her muttering and impatience had started on a mild note but now grew hotter than the stew she stirred. "I promise I'll never laugh at another TV cooking show again."

She wiped a trickle of sweat from her brow. "I miss carrots, I miss peas and green beans. I'd kill for a Caesar salad with garlic croutons and a side of sliced tomatoes and cucumbers smothered in salt and pepper," she said out loud, lifting another rock from the red-hot coals of the fire with a forked stick and dropping it into the paunch. "Chicken cordon-bleu, twice-baked potatoes and key lime pie." The rock sank to the bottom of the broth. "Broccoli and cheese sauce, and yes, even a parsnip or two would be divine." She tested the temperature of the stew with her finger. "I want my microwave," she groaned, adding two more rocks. "Supper's going to be little more than stone soup."

Slowly and soon picking up speed, the rolling bubbles of a boil broke on the surface.

"Yes," she breathed with victory and added an extra rock for good measure. Happy with her simple accomplishment, she tried to forget her craving for food she could recognize, and failed. "I want ice cream, chocolate ice cream . . . gobs of ice cold chocolate ice cream, and a pile of nachos with hot salsa and jalapeño cheese sauce. I want a cold glass of milk or a Coke; maybe even a frozen Margarita; or how about a tall, icy cold glass of sweet and tangy sangria?"

With one last stir of the crude wooden ladle, Ryan settled down on the buffalo hide she'd placed on the ground by the tipi. Relaxing, she stretched her legs out in front of her and looked toward the river. The men still hadn't returned. "So the little woman stays at home all day, dusting the tipi, mending the moccasins and creating epicurean delights while the big brave warrior husband ventures out to bring home the buffalo bacon," she grumbled. No, not too much had changed in 120-some years. Instead of tee-off time at the golf course, Monday night football or a Friday night poker game, it was horse races, shooting contests with their weapons and swapping hunting and battle stories. She chuckled. "I bet they tell jokes, talk about their prowess in bed and slap each other on the back, too." She shook her head. "It must be something universal that transcends time and has a lot to do with testosterone."

Glancing around the camp, she watched the families nearby begin to settle down to a quiet late afternoon. Cook fires burned at many lodges and the evening meals being prepared gave the air a mouth-watering fragrance. Families drew together along the valley and a sweet peace and contentment blanketed the camp. It felt wonderful to be a part of it. Ryan knew she had finally found her true home.

Nothing she had learned in her years of anthropological studies about the Northern Plains people had come halfway to the truth. Granted, many of the facts had been accurate—the descriptions of the ceremonies, the societies, tribal laws and traditions, but all that had been little more than cold, matter-of-fact dissection of the tribe. Nothing had described the real people. Nothing told about the intangible elements of their humanity, the love and affection within the families, the caring friendships, the pride and sense of honor, or the gentleness and heart and humor of the people themselves.

This is the best damned field trip imaginable, she mused, tucking an errant lock of hair behind her ear. She sighed with resignation. *And I can't use anything I've learned. How could I substantiate the data? Citing personal conversations with Sitting Bull or Crazy Horse in the bibliography would bring the men in the white coats with their straitjackets to my door.*

A little more than forty hours remained until it would begin. She felt the cold caress of disquiet. *I've got to stop counting every minute as it passes. If I don't, I'll go stark raving mad.* She closed her eyes. *I don't even know if Charley can yank me out of here. Who knows, I may still end up an oddity in the history books.*

"Forgive me if I am disturbing you."

Startled, Ryan looked up, finding the last person in camp she ever expected would seek her company.

Ground Plum awkwardly shuffled her feet, her discomfort clear as she stared at the ground, seemingly reluctant to meet Ryan's gaze. "I have come to . . . to say I have shamed myself and beg your forgiveness." Her voice stammered as she held out a wrapped bundle. "I have brought you a gift, a peace offering."

Ryan ignored the package and Ground Plum set it on the buffalo robe, meeting Ryan's cool scrutiny for a moment before looking away. "My words to you have been unkind and I am ashamed. Calls to the Wolf has made his choice. It is not my place to say he is wrong." Her eyes met Ryan's again and she continued, the quaver in her voice still present. "Perhaps in time we could become . . . friends?"

Ryan didn't move. She didn't invite the girl to join her, nor did she offer a response to Ground Plum's petition. The gift remained untouched.

"Calls to the Wolf has chosen you as his first wife and this cannot be changed." Ground Plum's voice became a near whisper, "Should he wish me to be a second wife, I would—"

"What do you hope to gain by this friendship?" Ryan interrupted, not wanting to think about Wolf ever taking another wife.

"You misunderstand," Ground Plum replied. "I have no reason but what I have told you. You are Lakota now. We should meet and speak as friends, not enemies. It is good for the people." Her eyes scanned the encampment. "It would please me as well."

Right, Ryan cynically mused. *I don't trust you as far as I could throw a herd of buffalo. You're up to something sneaky. If I don't keep my eyes open, I'm going to find out what it is the hard way, and I bet I won't like it one damned bit.*

Ground Plum nervously glanced from side to side. Instead of ducking her head when others were near, she made a grand show of being with Ryan in Wolf's camp. Whatever Ground Plum hoped to gain by befriending her, it was obvious the girl believed it was worth the humility of eating crow.

"I will leave you now and hope you give my request some thought. Perhaps tomorrow you will tell me what your heart tells you . . . if we can be friends." Without a backwards glance, Ground Plum turned and left.

As Ryan watched the young woman's hasty retreat, her apprehension increased when movement off to the opposite side of the camp caught her eye. A little over thirty yards away, Iron Soldier slid back behind the cover of an outcrop of trees. He had moved too slowly and Ryan had recognized his dark face.

"So, I was right," she murmured. "I do have good reason to worry."

Standing, Ryan moved to the cooking fire. She went through the motions of stirring the stew and stoking the fire, but her thoughts kept drifting back to Ground Plum and Iron Soldier. *It's bad enough to deal with them separately, but if they've joined forces in some outlandish scheme . . . the whole thing makes me very nervous.* She eyed the package Ground Plum had brought. She would ask Pretty Feather what to do about it.

The sun had begun to set when Wolf returned. He wasn't alone. Eagle Deer and three other men accompanied him and Ryan heard their laughter and cheerful voices long before they came into view. Placing a gentle caress along Ryan's cheek, and meeting her smile with one of his own, Wolf moved away to picket his spotted horse outside the tipi.

"There is enough food for my friends?" he asked, his gesture encompassing the men who had returned with him.

My first dinner party, Ryan mused. "There's plenty."

With a satisfied and pride-filled nod, Wolf lowered his tall frame and settled himself on the buffalo robe, quickly joining into the lively conversation his friends had begun.

"Your husband has won my best horses," Eagle Deer said to Ryan. His grin told her the loss didn't upset him.

"Kola," Wolf countered. "Sometimes I think you grow tired of caring for so many horses and allow me to win. You would see me work hard instead." He offered Ryan a boyish smile.

Passing wooden bowls filled with stew from the cooking paunch, Ryan glanced at Wolf's guests. She recognized them all. Two were Oglalas. Otter Skin and Makes No Bow had been with Crazy Horse many times when he'd ridden into the Hunkpapa camp. The third, the one called Rabbit, lived in the Hunkpapa circle. The three closely watched her.

"I have heard much of your *wasicu* woman," Rabbit said,

keeping his eyes on Ryan. "I have heard she is *wakan*." He lifted the bowl to his mouth, drank some broth and then wiped the back of his hand across his lips. Tipping his chin upward, he pointed at her. "She is pleasing to look upon . . . for a *wasicu*. If I were you, *kola*, I would enjoy her for a long time before taking a second wife." Rabbit laughed heartily and dipped his fingers into the bowl, pulling out a large piece of meat. He tipped his head back and dropped it into his mouth.

"She cooks well," Otter Skin remarked, rubbing his hefty belly and holding his empty bowl out to Ryan for a refill.

"Otter Skin speaks the truth," Makes No Bow added. "When you tire of her, send her to my camp. My wife cooks water until it is hard to chew." His joke brought another round of laughter as he too lifted his bowl for another portion of stew.

"Perhaps *Sunkmanitu Ceye a Pelo* would share his wife with us pitiful Lakota," Otter Skin quipped. "I would have her live in my tipi until the next full moon and then she would go to Rabbit to cook for him until the full moon comes again."

"I think you would have difficulty making *Sunkmanitu Ceye a Pelo* agree," Eagle Deer laughed. "He would not be happy with your idea and neither would I. If his woman is not here to cook his meals, he would be at my tipi every day begging for food."

Laughing heartily, Otter Skin clapped Eagle Deer on the back.

"*Kola*, do you not find the color of the woman's eyes strange to look upon?" Rabbit asked Wolf, peering closely at Ryan.

"*Winyan ki le coku tawa ki wahtewalosni*. It is the color of her *wasicu* skin I do not like," the hefty Oglala, Makes No Bow, coldly remarked.

They had forgotten she knew their language. She understood every word. Unused to people openly talking about her in her presence, Ryan found it difficult to keep her anger from rising. Taking a couple of deep breaths, she tried to compose herself. Wolf had never brought company to his tipi other than Eagle Deer and Pretty Feather, but these men were his friends, too. Ryan knew if she showed the slightest displeasure, it would bring him dishonor. Quickly glancing at Wolf, she found his dark eyes carefully watching her. He hadn't joined in this conversation. A slight grin moved his mouth and he'd raised his left brow in a teasing lift. *He knows I understand everything. The scoundrel is enjoying this.*

"She is a good woman." Wolf finally spoke, squaring his broad shoulders and sitting up straighter. His eyes still held Ryan's gaze. "She knows much of our people. Tunkasila has given her the gift of our language, but there is still much for her to learn of our ways."

"It is strange to see a *wasicu* in our camp," Rabbit said, offering Ryan a solemn nod of thanks as she handed him his refilled bowl. "These white eyes are our enemies."

"We should ride against them and kill every one," Otter Skin added. "These hills would be red with their blood before this Lakota is satisfied." He struck his bare chest with his closed fist, punctuating his remark.

The muscle along the edge of Ryan's jaw tightened. Glancing at Wolf again, she saw his expression had changed. The teasing twinkle in his eyes had disappeared. His smile had left as well. In its place a grim tightness had settled upon his mouth. He watched her, gauging her responses and her mood. What was he looking for? What did he expect to find? Did he think the words of his friends wouldn't bother her?

She bent to accept the empty bowl from Otter Skin and the crucifix necklace swung forward.

"Ah," Otter Skin remarked, reaching up and catching the silver cross in his fingers. "I remember this well. It was a good day for the Lakota." Otter Skin studied the necklace for a moment before dropping the crucifix. It fell heavily, like a dead weight, between Ryan's breasts, and she quickly moved away.

Rabbit laughed. "It was not a good day for the *wasicu* who wore that. I remember the white eyes wanted to keep it but Wolf's knife made him very generous."

Ryan shuddered. Unconsciously, her hand reached up and her fingers closed tightly around the cross. The sharp edges dug into her flesh but she didn't feel the pain. Turning quickly, she met Wolf's steady gaze but his expression was unreadable. Her worst fears had been confirmed. The necklace Wolf had placed around her neck as a token of love had been paid for by the blood and the life of some poor white settler. The man who held her heart had killed one of her own for a trinket. She felt betrayed.

"It was an honorable fight," Wolf said, his eyes still imprisoning hers. "It was a good day for that *wasicu* to die."

"It is true, he met his death well," Makes No Bow agreed.

"He was a white eyes," Otter Skin spat. "What honor is there in the death of a white eyes?"

"There were others who were not as strong," Wolf added. "This one did not cry like a woman. His heart was good. The *wasicu* had the courage of a Lakota."

Ryan couldn't breathe. *Why don't they stop talking about killing? Why won't Wolf stop them? Can't he see how difficult it is for me to hear this?*

Finally able to drag her gaze from Wolf's, she ducked into the tipi. Bitter tears burned her eyes. Grasping the necklace, she gave it an angry tug. The cord broke and beads scattered across the tipi floor until only the silver cross remained in her hand. She fell to her knees and sobs racked her body. Her fingers slowly loosened their grip and the cross slid to the ground. She didn't hear the door flap as it was lifted and dropped back into place.

"Kechuwa," Wolf whispered, placing his hand on her shoulder.

"Leave me alone," she answered, shrugging away from his touch.

"I cannot," he replied, caressing her cheek with the back of his fingers. "There must be understanding between us."

Ryan recoiled from him again. Lifting her head, she looked at him accusingly. "Understanding?" Her outrage grew. "All I understand is that you killed one of *my* people. You took the necklace as your prize and probably took his scalp, too. You gave the necklace to me knowing full well where it had come from." She shuddered. "How could you do such a horrible thing? How could you give me something that had blood on it?"

Wolf's face remained impassive. "Would your anger be as great if the blood was Lakota or Crow or Pawnee? Is your anger strong only because the blood belonged to a white eyes?"

"It is killing," Ryan rebutted through her tears. "You murdered someone for beads . . . for trinkets."

He gripped her arms, his fingers biting into her tender flesh. Lifting her to her feet, he shook her. "Look at this one," he commanded, his fingers continuing to bruise her arms until she looked up at him. "I am Lakota. I cannot change what Tunkasila has made me. You cannot change the white color of the skin that Tunkasila has given you." Wolf released Ryan's right arm and tried to wipe the tears from her cheeks. She twisted away, avoiding his touch once again.

"Leave me alone."

"I will stay and we will talk." Wolf drew her to his side of the lodge. She moved stiffly, forcing him to cajole each step from her. Sitting on the thick pile of soft furs and blankets, he pulled her down beside him.

"Hear me, Kechuwa, I will tell you of the Lakota." Wolf paused, carefully choosing his words, knowing they could either drive this woman away from his side or keep her content in his arms. "My people's needs are simple. We wish to live in peace, to hunt and race our horses, to raise our children along the banks of rivers such as the Greasy Grass and teach them the beauty of being Lakota."

"But you killed—"

"Shh." Wolf gently placed his finger against Ryan's lips. "Listen first to this Lakota's words and then he will listen to yours." He tenderly brushed her hair from her face, pleased she didn't pull away from him again. "When there were only a few whites, our people welcomed them and we shared what we had with these pale brothers. Soon more and more came and they were greedy, taking our food, our women, our lands. They brought us bad spirits that left many dead or marked with the *wicaranran* ... the pock sickness." His fingers lightly brushed the soft, smooth plane of her cheek again. "They killed because of yellow rocks in the ground and they brought the fire drink that made my people wild but left them craving more." He tipped Ryan's head up until she was forced to look into his eyes.

"Now the *wasicu* tell us we must leave these beautiful places and move to the soldier forts. If we do this, the white eyes tell us they will stop war against us. The Great Father of the whites sends papers for our chiefs to put their marks on. My people are promised food and a good life if they go to the forts.

"The Great Father of the whites tells us he will care for us like he tends all of his children." Wolf clenched his fist. "It is lies, all lies. I have seen those places. The women weep and try to cook with meat that is rotten and grain that is nothing but bugs and worms. The children get sick and die and the hearts of the warriors and the hunters are ashamed."

Wolf searched Ryan's eyes for some sense of her thoughts. "My people, the Lakota, do not wish to move to the soldier forts. Because of that we are hunted like dogs and our women and children are killed as they sleep. I will not let these things happen easily. I will fight hard and many will die in these battles." He paused and bowed his head. "It is not good that the Lakota make war against your people. For that, this warrior's heart is sad."

Wolf stood and looked down at her. "I will not say I am sorry for the killing I have done. The one who wore this came to this place to take what belongs to my people. A warrior must fight to save what is his." He held his open hand out to Ryan. The silver crucifix gleamed in his palm.

Closing her eyes, Ryan felt a sadness wash over her. He had told her nothing she didn't already know. She knew there were things he would do as a Lakota warrior that she might never be able to accept. But, was the love she had for this man strong enough to give her peace? Reaching up, Ryan grasped Wolf's hand, enclosing the cross in their grip. Yes, her love was that strong and more.

Pulling her to her feet, Wolf took her in his arms. "Ke-chuwa," he breathed, his lips grazing her cheek. "We cannot make war with each other because our people are enemies. Understanding and love must begin here, in our embrace. You are my wife . . . forever."

Ryan laid her head against his shoulder and closed her eyes. How long was forever?

Chapter 25

NED SLOAN LEANED against the door frame. Holding the patient's chart at his side, he stared thoughtfully at the comatose man. He'd never had a patient who was such an enigma.

He had just about reached the end of his rope. Even the top neurosurgeons he'd consulted were baffled. By every right, Dillon Wolf should be conscious, up and walking around. The laceration on his forehead and the longer one along the edge of his left jaw weren't cause enough for a deep coma. The CAT scans and the MRI didn't show any reason, either.

Sloan flipped through the chart for the third time. What clues had he missed? What clues had they all missed? Every test done in the last twenty-four hours had come back with normal readings. Frustrated, he shook his head.

Dillon Wolf had been unresponsive for seven days. Other signs of a comatose state sometimes showed themselves by now, but fortunately none had begun. His hands hadn't drawn up and his feet hadn't shown any inward shifting. The Lakota lawyer looked as though he was taking a nap and had just dozed off.

"So, how do you think our mystery case is doing to-night?"

Sloan greeted the evening duty nurse with a slight nod as she entered the room. Beth Thomas carried a new bag of fluids to hang on the IV pole beside Dillon's bed.

"He's just the same. No change."

"Do you suppose in my old age I might be losing my magic touch? Usually my patients are up and chasing me around the bed by now." She looked up at Ned Sloan. "I've never seen anything like this in all *my* years." She adjusted the intravenous tubing. "He looks like he's just moments away from opening his eyes and yet, I know if an atom bomb were to go off in here, it wouldn't even bother him. He wouldn't even flinch. Got any bright ideas?"

Sloan shook his head. Dillon Wolf's condition hadn't come out of any textbook he'd read. "Not a one. I don't think there's a damned thing we can do but sit and wait." He set the chart on the bed tray and sank down into the nearby chair. Leaning back, Sloan settled his elbows on the armrests, steepled his fingers and rested his chin on top. "I'm stumped," he whispered.

"Have you talked with his family lately?" Beth asked, sponging Dillon Wolf's face and arms with a damp cloth. "From what you've said, his grandfather sounds like something out of an old 'B' grade Western movie."

"Don't kid yourself for a minute," Sloan answered. "That old man is as sharp as a tack. He's being real cool about this, too. Maybe a little too cool for my liking. When I called him this afternoon, he suggested that I just sit back and 'use up some of my well-trained patience.' "

"That's what he said?"

"Yup. Then he said not to worry, and quote, 'don't do nothing silly,' end quote."

Beth stopped bathing Dillon's arm in mid-stroke. "Silly? What the hell is that supposed to mean?"

Ned Sloan dragged his hand over the top of his head, his fingers raking through his unruly crop of red hair. "Well, he told me that, too. Said he didn't want us thinking we were heroes. He didn't want us doing anything like exploratory surgery." He watched the nurse's response and gauged her reaction. "He said if we kept his grandson comfortable for a couple of days, everything would be fine and he'd wake up like he'd just been snoozing."

Beth corkscrewed her hand at the side of her head. "Sounds like the old man is the one who got hit on the noggin."

"Yeah, it does, doesn't it," Sloan agreed. He leaned forward and watched Dillon Wolf for a few minutes. "Tell me, Beth, didn't you think it was kind of unusual for our Mr. Wolf to come off the ventilator so easily?"

"What do you mean?"

"Well for one thing, we had no problems weaning him to room air and he hasn't come up with any fluid in his lungs, either. Doesn't this whole thing give you the damn willies?"

"The willies?" Beth questioned, humming a few bars of the *Twilight Zone* theme. "Brother! First you're talking about silly treatments and now you're talking about the willies. What are they teaching you guys in med school these days? Is this some new kind of medical terminology?" She shook her head. " 'We're sorry, Mrs. Jones, your husband gives us the willies so we're gonna to do something silly to him.' Help me out here, Dr. Sloan, you're giving *me* the willies."

"You know, sometimes you old nurses can be pretty annoying," Ned Sloan teased, hoping to ease the tension that kept growing with each new twist to Dillon Wolf's care.

"Ouch!" Beth recoiled in a false cringe. "You docs are pretty pitiful yourselves. You always speak in broad generalities when you don't know what you're talking about. Dr. Sloan, I think the willies is just about the broadest generality I've ever heard."

"I think you're right on all counts, Beth." Ned Sloan sighed, easing his tall frame out of the chair. He yawned. The long hours had finally caught up with him. With one last glance at Dillon Wolf, he headed for the door.

"I'll call you if 'Sleeping Beauty' decides to wake up," Beth called after him.

"And I'll bring the champagne," Sloan answered with a wave.

Chapter 26

"SURE IT'S A shame," Stanton Adams agreed. "It's a goddamn shame. I don't like to see anyone get hurt, especially someone who works as hard to set things to right as Dillon Wolf does. We were so damned close to getting this job done with his help."

"Come on, Stan. Yeah, it's a tough situation. I'm not sayin' he deserved it, but Dillon Wolf is a hard-nosed, militant bigot," Herb Delveccio rebutted bluntly, settling himself in a chair beside Adams's cluttered desk. "He's a burr on your ass and you know it."

"I never said he wasn't," Adams replied. "I'll be the first to admit he can really rub you the wrong way and get your temper up. But there's . . . I don't know . . . the man is . . . hell, there's an integrity about him. He's dedicated to his people and there's never any doubt where you stand with him." Stanton Adams tapped the desk top, accenting his point. "Yup, in this city you don't get to see a whole lot of that—integrity, I mean."

"I've come across some bad asses from time to time," Delveccio offered. "White supremacists with their swastikas, militia and weird religious cults. I've even waltzed around the jungle with a few Colombian drug dealers, but

I can deal a whole lot better with those boy scouts than I can with an angry long-haired redskin in a sports jacket that costs more'n my damned car!"

"You're jealous," Stanton Adams laughed.

"I'm what?"

"You're jealous 'cause he's prettier than you." Adams made an attempt to straighten the mess of papers on his desk. "Well anyway, the bottom line is—we're stuck. His office says he's out of commission for a while and there's no telling when he can get back to work with us." Adams slapped a stack of files back down on his desk, his action testimony to his frustration. "We need him to make this scam work."

"So, are we dumping the deal?" Delveccio asked, reaching into his pocket for a cigarette.

Stanton Adams looked for the No Smoking sign on his desk, moving aside two piles of files before Delveccio could see it. "We're not dumping anything. We're in too deep to pull the plug now. You've been out there and talked with Gaffney. Do you know how long it'd take you to win his trust again if we back off now? No, we go ahead. We just make damned sure the trap is set nice and tight."

"Well, we'd better get something going soon. I've got a feeling our friend Gaffney's getting nervous and might slip out on us. If he does, we won't be able to get flypaper to stick in court."

"I know, I know," Stanton answered, exasperated with the turn of events. "Have you talked to him again?"

"Not since I was out there a week and a half ago when I put that gorgeous white rental Lincoln on my expense account."

"Yeah, well I'm glad you enjoyed those flashy wheels. I doubt if the pencil pushers upstairs are going to think it was so gorgeous when I plunk your expense tab down in front of them for approval. A Chevy or some nice little compact would've gotten you there just as well."

"Hey, come on. You know if you're gonna play the part of a rich, big-shot collector, then you gotta look the part. Right?"

Adams shrugged in mute agreement.

Delveccio withdrew a cigarette from his pack, tapped the end of it on his thumbnail, popped it into his mouth and searched his pockets for a match.

Stanton Adams picked the No Smoking sign off his desk and tossed it into Delveccio's lap. "In case you're near-sighted, the sign says 'no smoking.' "

Delveccio blew out the match and held the sign upside-down in his hand. "You know Stan, you used to be a lot nicer guy when you smoked two packs a day. Now you're nothing but a damned nag." He tossed the sign back onto the desk, scattering the newly stacked folders. "Did I tell you I saw that knock-out anthropologist from the Smith-sonian when I was out there? What's her name? Burke? Yeah that's it, *Dr.* Ryan Burke." His moved his hands in the imaginary outline of a female figure. "What a looker!" He gave a cartoonish leer. "If it's fossils she's looking for, I'm one old fossil I'd like her to meet."

"Herb, you're such a romantic."

"And you Stan—you're a pal, a real pal." Delveccio shot his associate a resigned grin, accompanied by a Groucho Marx waggle of his fingers under his nose. "Anyway, when she saw me with Gaffney, I thought *he* was going to have a stroke. I've never seen anyone so damned nervous in all my life."

"See, that's exactly what I mean. If we don't keep on with this, and if you don't keep in close contact with him, Gaffney's going to run scared and we won't get anything."

"I gotta have a smoke," Delveccio gasped, hauling him-self out of the chair.

"This is a no-smoking building." Adams pointed to the No Smoking sign again. "Can't you read?" He picked it up from the desk where Delveccio had tossed it, gave it a quick glance and threw it into the trash can.

"I don't wanna read. I wanna smoke."

"Fine. Go stand in the stairwell and puff your head off. That's where everyone else lights up."

"Good. Are we through here or do you have something else for me?"

"Just hang on a minute." Stanton Adams riffled through a paper-clipped bunch of papers. "Have you seen this?" He passed the letter across the desk to Delveccio.

"Sure haven't. Chicago's Field Museum, eh? When did this arrive?"

"Yesterday. This makes two museums in the past week who've been contacted. I got a phone call from the Eiteljorg Museum in Indianapolis three days ago." Adams took the paper from Delveccio, shoved it back under the paper clip and dropped the letters back on his desk. "You know, I've been thinking. Our bad boy must be driving to Hardin to make these calls."

"How'd you come up with that?" Delveccio asked.

"You don't think he'd be bold enough to go up to the tourist center at the battleground to phone these people?"

"Why not? Everybody knows him there. Who's going to question him using the phone? Or, he could be using a cellular." Delveccio rolled the unlit cigarette between his fingers. "You know, that's something else that doesn't make sense. Why is he contacting museums now instead of keeping a low profile and dealing with the private collectors? Only an idiot would contact a museum."

"I've been trying to figure that out, too," Adams responded. "The only thing I can figure is that maybe he's getting antsy and that's making him sloppy."

Delveccio considered Adam's answer. "Who knows. Some folks get real stupid when there's a lot of money involved."

"Yeah, but museums don't pay as much as a private collector."

Delveccio nodded thoughtfully and rolled his unlit cigarette between his fingers.

Adams began to shuffle through the stacked papers on his desk again. "Where in the hell is my Rolodex?"

"Have you ever thought about cleaning up this mess?" Delveccio asked, picking up a couple of crumpled pieces of paper and dropping them back onto Adams's desk. "You can't ever find anything when you need it."

"I cleaned it last week. *That's* why I can't find anything *this* week!"

Herb Delveccio held his hand up to ward off any further tirades from Adams. "If we're going ahead with the plan, what do you suggest?"

"Well, I've been thinking—"

"Hurry up pal, I've gotta have a smoke."

"With Wolf out of commission for a while, I think we need to work with someone else who's familiar with the site." Stanton Adams finally retrieved his Rolodex from under a pile of papers and held it up like a newly won trophy.

"Who'd you have in mind? Who's in Wolf's Tribal Coalition office that you'd feel comfortable working with?"

"No one," Adams answered bluntly. "I don't know if anyone else in his office is even aware of this case." Adams gave Delveccio a quick, speculative look. "I had someone closer to the battleground in mind."

"Who?" Delveccio asked warily, keeping a fixed look on his boss. "And why do I have the feeling I'm not going to like your answer?"

"I think we need to contact Dillon's grandfather, Charles Crying Wolf."

"What!" Herb Delveccio jumped to his feet. "Are you nuts? That old man is at least two hundred years old. What in the hell can *he* do for us?"

"I just think with Wolf out of commission for a while, this old man is our best bet. He knows the area, he's familiar with everyone on the project site and he's close to all the Indian people out there." Adams flipped through the small index cards on the Rolodex, mumbling to himself. "Where'd I put that old coot's number?"

"You're really going to do it?" Delveccio paced in the small, cluttered office.

"Herb, we don't have a choice. You said yourself that the old guy's there almost every day. He's been keeping Dillon supplied with info about what's going on at the project; so now, with Dillon in the hospital, why can't he keep us informed instead?"

"And you really expect him to work with us?"

"If he thinks the disappearance of these artifacts is important enough to try to shut the project down, yeah, I think the old man will work with us. You bet."

"Aw hell, then, I guess you'd better give him a call." Delveccio threw up his arms, yielding to Adams's proposal. "Great. As if Dillon Wolf isn't enough, now I'm working with a geriatric Geronimo," he mumbled. Turning to leave Adams's office, he saluted with the cigarette in his hand. "Now I really do need a smoke."

"Fine, but hurry up. We've got some more work to do. If we can't count on Dillon Wolf being out of the hospital by the time we're ready to move in and snap the trap, we'll need to have a damned good and solid foolproof plan B. You might have to go back out there and meet with Mr. Crying Wolf yourself in the next day or two."

"You told me yesterday she's getting better." Gaffney glared at Charley. The old Lakota silently answered with a complacent shrug.

"You told me she'd be back to work soon." Gaffney paced under the canvas shade. "So," he asked, his hands held palm up in appeal, "where is she?" Agitated, Gaffney's breath came in puffs. He sank into a camp chair at the table and poured himself a cup of coffee. "Damn it! I've got a project to run. I need my full staff."

Charley Crying Wolf slowly lowered himself into the chair across from Edwin Gaffney and slid his own mug over for a refill. Lifting the cup to his lips, he took a long, noisy sip, then leaned back and folded his gnarled hands across his chest. "I told you, she's sick. She's getting better, but it's gonna be slow." He reached for his mug again. "The doc's been out at Edith's a couple of times. He was there again last night." Charley swallowed another mouthful of the dark, bitter brew. "He told Edith that Ryan—Dr. Burke—needs more rest. He told Edith to keep her in bed a couple of days longer." Charley leaned forward. "It's the flu, you know. She got too wet and cold in that bad storm—"

"The flu?" Gaffney interrupted. "Yesterday you said she

had pneumonia." His eyes narrowed with suspicion.

"Hey," Charley responded, lifting his hands up in defense. "Just 'cause I'm an *old* Indian, that don't make me some kinda know-it-all medicine man or somethin'. How am I supposed to know what she's got wrong with her? Flu—pneumonia—whoopin' cough—bronchy-itis—it's all the same to me. All I know is what aunty told me the doctor said, and he said she ain't supposed to come back here for a couple more days."

"Fine," Gaffney ground out. "That's just damned fine." He squinted his eyes against the sun. "I don't like it one bit. I should have sent her packing that first night."

Charley hid his rising temper beneath a well-practiced veneer of impassivity. "If you want, I could take her a message." He shrugged his stooped shoulders in a nonchalant fashion and slowly drained the last drop of coffee from his cup, unable to stop the grimace that wrinkled his face as the acrid dregs attacked his taste buds.

Gaffney slapped the tabletop with the flat of his hand. "You tell her that I want her back here—" He stopped, then raised his finger and pointed it at Charley. "No, better still, take me to her. I want to tell her myself."

Charley held his hands up and shook his head. "Sorry, no visitors—doctor's orders."

"I'm not a visitor," Gaffney hotly responded. "I'm the woman's boss."

"You gotta understand," Charley countered, "Dr. Burke's feeling real bad and she might be . . . uh, contagious. She's spending a lot of time holding her head over a bucket and leaving everything she eats in that bucket." Charley set a mournful expression on his face and slowly shook his head. "It ain't a pretty sight." He wrinkled up his nose.

"There's going to be a commemorative ceremony at the battleground tourist center in two days for the anniversary of the Custer battle. I suppose it's too much to ask that she be here for that." Gaffney's eyes met Charley's dark gaze.

"Yup, that's a little too soon," Charley answered, with a

slow shake of his head and a sly smile. "She won't be back by then."

"Humpf!" Gaffney sighed with displeasure. "Well, you tell her to hurry up. There's almost thirty interviews lined up and if that data isn't collected—and if it isn't collected by Dr. Burke, her whole part of the project will have to be scrubbed." Gaffney rose. "You tell her that and we'll see how soon she gets over being contagious and how soon she comes skedaddling back."

"Don't worry 'bout a thing. I promise Dr. Burke'll get the best information you could imagine." The smile widened. "It's gonna be so good, you'd swear she'd been at the battle herself." Charley rose from the camp chair as quickly as his arthritic joints would let him. "Don't worry none, Dr. Gaffney, you just have yourself a nice day."

Charley Crying Wolf's good-bye wave looked more like a curt dismissal as he slowly walked toward Buddy's old truck. "Take me home, grandson. Get my tired bones away from these crazy, thievin' *wasicu*."

Charley settled himself into the passenger seat of Buddy's truck and pulled his old hat down over his eyes. The lowered brim hid the mischievous grin that still bowed his full mouth. So far, so good, but the days were slipping by. Soon things were going to have to be put back the way they were supposed to be.

"You okay, Grandpa?" Buddy asked, shifting the bouncing truck into gear with a grind, steering it up the dirt road and out onto the highway.

"I'm tired," the old man finally answered. "Men like your Dr. Gaffney make this old Lakota real tired."

"Is it true?" Buddy cast a sidelong glance at his grandfather. "Is Ryan really that sick?" He didn't wait for an answer. "You know, I guess I kinda gotta blame myself if she is. If I hadn't loaned her this old pile of junk . . ." Buddy angrily slapped the dirty dashboard with the palm of his hand. "I keep thinkin' that if this damn piece of garbage hadn't broken down, maybe she wouldn't have gotten sick." A slight quiver remained in his voice when he spoke again. "I'm just grateful you and Aunty happened to drive by and found her. It's good she's at Aunt Edith's. She'll be okay soon, won't she, Grandpa?"

Charley hated one thing about the last nine days. He hated the lies he'd had to tell. He hated the way the lies piled up higher and higher, one on top of the other, and most of all, he hated having to lie to Buddy. Besides, it took a lot of work to keep the lies all straight in his old brain. "Well, she's just kinda . . . out of it right now, Buddy, but I promise you, ain't nothing bad going to happen. In a couple of days she'll be back at the project, good as new and twice as ornery. You'll see." Charley angled a look at his grandson. The boy's face mirrored his worried thoughts. Charley patted Buddy's knee. "I know it seems like everything's falling apart what with Dillon in the hospital and Ryan out of sorts, but you'll see, they'll both be fine—better than fine." His hand rested on Buddy's knee. "Dillon's gonna snap right back and so's your pretty friend. You'll see." His hand gave Buddy one last reassuring pat. "I promise, boy, I promise." The old man tipped his head back on the padded headrest and closed his eyes. "Wake me up when you get me home."

Buddy glanced at his grandfather. A niggling feeling stuck like a piece of old frybread in his craw and he couldn't quite swallow it. Charley was acting as cool as a cucumber—too cool—and that's what bothered Buddy most of all. His grandfather was never this laid back unless the old codger was up to something. *You're drivin' me nuts, old man. There's something going on and I can't figure out what it is.*

As the old truck rattled down the road, the afternoon shadows lengthened along the valley of the Little Big Horn and the days and hours to the anniversary of the great Custer battle shortened in number.

Few houses on the reservation had telephones, but Dillon had had the phone company install them in both Charley Crying Wolf's and Edith's houses. If they were used for nothing else than calling each other to bicker, Dillon had told Charley he'd gladly pay the monthly bills.

With a long sigh, Charley eased himself into the old overstuffed recliner and settled his aching body back into the deep cushions. He cradled the phone in his hand.

"Damned irritating contraption," he grouched. He'd discovered early on in his relationship with Alexander Graham Bell's invention that only bad news and trouble seemed to follow the shrill ring of the telephone at his house. He punched in a series of numbers with a curt stab of his arthritic finger and then tapped the same finger impatiently on the arm of the chair. He waited for the ring to kick in and then waited longer for Buddy's Aunt Edith to pick up the phone at her house. He heard the click and her greeting.

"It's 'bout time you answered. Where you been?"

"Listen here you old *tatanka*, I answered to one man for thirty years and now that he's gone, I don't have to tell you nothin.' " Edith cackled gleefully at the long stretch of silence on Charley's end of the line. "What you want?"

"I'm just checkin' up on ya, and makin' sure you're still with me," Charley said. The line between his house and Edith's fell quiet again. Her reply seemed to take forever to come.

"I don't know what you're up to, old man, and maybe I don't want to know, but I'm still foolish enough to help you," she answered.

"Has anyone been nosing around asking about Dr. Burke?" Charley's nerves tightened as he waited for her answer.

"Just your grandson."

"Buddy?" he asked, surprised.

"You got another grandson living out here now? Yes, of course, Buddy. He asks about her every day when he comes to pick up my cookin' for the camp. I don't think he's gonna believe me much longer. He's got an idea you and me ain't tellin' him the whole truth."

"So, what'd you say to him, Edith?" Charley's fingers tightened around the phone. "You know I'm countin' on you."

"I tell him what you told me to say. I tell him Dr. Burke's

too sick to see anyone, or she's sleeping or she's in the bathroom. How much longer you goin' to keep askin' me to lie?"

"It's gonna to be over soon, old lady, so quit grouching," Charley grumbled. Quickly remembering that if it wasn't for Edith, his whole fantastic scheme would be in peril, Charley softened, contrite. "Look, sister, I appreciate all your help."

"What's this about, Charley? I'm too old to wait to see what happens. I need to know what kinda danger you've got me into."

"There's nothing like that for you. Trust me, something real good is gonna come of all this, you'll see. I know you don't understand or believe me now, but it's gonna make a lot of people happy. This is the only way things could be done."

The line between them fell quiet again, with only the occasional chatter of static breaking the silence.

"I don't question what you say," Edith finally added. "Ain't many of our people got the *wakan* given to 'em anymore. Yours has come from the old ones, your ancestors and your daddy, and it's real strong. I seen things all my life that no *wasicu* would believe and I'm too old not to believe what is so. I respect what you got." The tone of her voice signaled her resignation. "I'll keep helpin' as long as you need it."

Charley nodded, then remembered Edith couldn't see his silent response. "Thank you, sister."

The line crackled and carried silence for another long, expectant moment.

"*Wincincola ki tukte e he?* Where is the girl?" Edith quietly asked.

Charley had known that sooner or later she'd get around to this question. He wished it would have been later. "*Ioka kiye sni yo,*" he answered slowly. "Don't worry, she is well and will return, in good time."

"I must believe you, but—"

"Thank you," he said, wanting to get off the line before she pressed her question again. "Gotta go. Got things to do." Before Edith could speak again, he replaced the receiver in the cradle and rested his head against the back of the chair. His hat tilted forward. *So much has to be done before I can slow down . . . but damn, I'm tired.*

"Tunkasila, Grandfather." Charley closed his eyes and prayed. "Help me. Keep me strong. Keep my loved ones safe and keep Ryan Burke from harm. Tunkasila, thank you for the power you have given this pitiful old man. Tunkasila, send me the strength and good spirits I need to help me finish this—"

The telephone jangled loudly, jolting Charley's frayed nerves. He jumped, nearly knocking the phone off his lap.

"Damn," he spat, grabbing the receiver. "Hello."

"Mr. Crying Wolf? Charley Crying Wolf?"

"Yes," Charley answered warily. He didn't recognize the clipped accent of the white man's voice. What *wasicu* did he know who would be calling him?

"Mr. Crying Wolf, you don't know me but I've been doing some work in Washington with your grandson, Dillon Wolf. My name's Stanton Adams and I'm with the National Parks Service."

"You say you know my grandson?"

"Mr. Crying Wolf, I'm real sorry about Dillon's accident and I hope he gets better soon. In the meantime I . . . uh . . . I'm sorry to bother you, but we could sure use your help on the case at the Little Big Horn project that Dillon's been working on. How about it, Mr. Crying Wolf? Can we count on your help?"

Chapter 27

RYAN LEANED BACK into the crook of a branch high up in the oak. A pale line of wispy clouds hung in the darkening sky and she looked up through the leaves, picking out the glitter of the first evening stars. Wolf had ridden out of camp earlier and hadn't returned. Feeling lonely, she closed her eyes and tried to find solace in the evening chorus of crickets. The branch still held the warmth of the afternoon sun and she snuggled against the rough bark. The embrace of the tree offered little contentment compared to the embrace she craved.

Across the river a night bird whistled. A feathered resident in a nearby tree answered. From the densely treed bank at the twist in the river to the south, an eerie call joined in, sending a foreboding chill through Ryan's heart.

"Hinhanska." The skin on her arms roughened with goose bumps. Many tribes believed owls were the harbingers of death and tonight the bird's ghostly call set her on edge. "Custer's coming."

"Who, who?" the owl questioned.

"Custer's coming," she answered, suffering another shudder.

The low nicker of a horse drew her attention and she

turned to watch the Lakota she loved ride toward her tree. On the end of a long, braided rope, a brightly colored Appaloosa horse pranced and cavorted, tossing its finely sculpted head, blowing excited snorts from its wide nostrils.

"Is my little bird in her nest?" Wolf asked, his voice soft, barely breaking the quiet veil of evening.

"And what does a strong warrior want with a little bird?" she replied, covering her smile behind her hand. The manners of the Lakota women were second nature to her now.

"Your husband has a gift for you." He offered the long rope to her. "This spotted mare is for you. She comes from the Nez Perce people to the northwest in the Paloose Valley. She is gentle and will carry you a long, long way at my side."

Can she carry me at your side forever? The thought quickly bruised her heart. It was the twenty-third of June and nothing could impede the onward march of the Seventh Cavalry.

The mare fidgeted and shied, pulling back on the rope as Ryan lowered herself from the tree. With ears pricked forward and nostrils blown wide to sniff her scent, the mare listened to Ryan's soft, reassuring voice. Ryan offered a clump of tender grass and the filly quickly moved to her side.

"She comes eagerly, Kechuwa. You have won her affection."

Ryan laughed. "I've won nothing but her stomach."

Wolf slid from his pinto and turned the big horse loose to graze. Placing his hand lightly over Ryan's as she scratched the mare's neck, he leaned forward and touched his lips to Ryan's cheek. "Kechuwa, you have won *my* affection," he whispered. "Is that not enough?"

They walked slowly back to the village and darkness fell before they reached the tipi. The camp was quiet, reminding Ryan of evening family times in any neighborhood, in any century. Even the dogs that ran and gamboled throughout the campsite during the day had settled into their dug-out dirt beds and now lazily watched the couple walk by.

Wolf picketed the horses beside the tipi and tucked the end of the long ropes under the edge of the tipi. No one would steal the pinto without first waking the warrior who owned it.

"You must be hungry," Ryan said, filling a bowl from the cooking paunch. "You missed your supper."

With a nod, Wolf took his meal and settled himself on the buffalo hide in front of the lodge. He looked skeptically from the stewed buffalo and wild onions in the dish to Ryan and then back to the stew. "Did Pretty Feather help you cook this food?"

Ryan looked up, quickly taking note of the dubious expression on his face. "No, she cooks for her own family." She looked away, hiding the smile on her mouth. She had learned a great deal from Pretty Feather's cooking lessons and her skills had grown in just a few days. Covertly watching him as she pretended to pay great attention to her own meal, the smile on her lips broadened.

Wolf poked his finger into the bowl, tested the tenderness of a hunk of the meat and carefully chose his words. "She has cooked for a long time and—"

"And you think I need help," Ryan interrupted softly. "Wasn't the meal I gave your friends good?"

"It was, but you are still learning." He continued to look skeptically at the bowl.

"Have you even tried it yet?"

Shaking his head, Wolf tentatively lifted a piece of meat to his mouth and took a bite.

"Well?"

There was an astonished look on his face. The buffalo and onions had stewed long enough to be tender, but the rock salt that Pretty Feather had shared from her cache was what had made the difference in the stew.

"You are learning well," Wolf grinned, quickly finishing every morsel. "I am pleased," he added softly, dark eyes meeting blue, holding Ryan a breathless prisoner. "I am well pleased with my wife."

His tender words were like a caress. She had never known love could fill the human body as much as it filled hers, causing an ache, a delicious ache that only loving more could appease. Her fingers touched Wolf's shoulder and lingered. The sweet pang increased. She knew she would spend the rest of the night in her husband's arms.

"Kechuwa," Wolf whispered, his voice husky with desire.

She knew the same hunger had touched him, too.

"Sunkmanitu Ceye a Pelo," Eagle Deer called as he jogged across the camp to Wolf's tipi. *"Sunkmanitu!"*

Reluctantly, Wolf dragged his gaze away from Ryan. *"Hau kola,* what is it?"

"Rabbit and Tells No Lies have returned to camp. They have seen buffalo less than half a day's ride from here. We will hunt for fresh meat at first light. Do you join us?"

Ryan stiffened, quickly glanced at Wolf and held her breath. *No!* Her heart cried. *No, please, don't go. Tomorrow will be our last day together before . . . before Custer.*

"I will ride with you," Wolf answered, his enthusiasm obvious. "It will be a good hunt."

Ryan turned away. She could hear the hoofbeats of the Seventh Cavalry echo in her mind, coming closer and closer. Could she stop time? No. Only Charley Crying Wolf seemed to have a talent with clocks.

"Tonight you are very quiet," Wolf whispered against her cheek, carefully removing the rawhide thongs, releasing her braids and gently combing through her hair with his fingers. "I think you are tired from too much climbing in trees."

Ryan sat on his bed, her back to him, and leaned against his hard chest. She deeply breathed in his scent. She would never get enough of this man to ease the need that had grown steadily since he had first touched her. His long, black hair fell over her shoulder and mingled with her own dark brown strands and she slowly traced the coupled length with the tips of her fingers.

"What has this Lakota done to please Tunkasila so much that he has given me such a wonderful gift?" Wolf asked, tasting the flesh along the edge of Ryan's ear with his tongue. His warm breath touched her skin as he trailed a light row of kisses down her chin to the tender juncture where her shoulder met her neck. He suckled lightly on her skin where her pulse throbbed just beneath the surface and she shivered as a delightful tingle skittered throughout her body. Twisting in his embrace, she drew her arms up around his neck and buried her head against his shoulder. There was no other place in the world, his world or hers, where she had ever felt more safe or more happy. Cupping his face in her hand, she drew his head down and lightly flicked her tongue along the edges of his lips, teasing him, coaxing a kiss from him. He responded to her invitation, his mouth eagerly moving over hers. As his breath mingled with hers, she clung to him, afraid to let go.

"Ah, Kechuwa," Wolf murmured. "You make this warrior burn with a fire such as I have never known."

She slid from his arms and knelt before him, slowly lifting her dress. Raising the garment free of her body, she shook her hair back over her naked shoulders and gazed into Wolf's eyes, inviting him to meet her passion.

Wolf's gaze never wavered from hers as he lifted the bone breastplate from his neck. Rising to his knees, he untied the strings around his waist that held his breechclout. Laying his garments aside, he pulled her into his arms, driving his fingers into her hair and setting his mouth hungrily over hers. His tongue delved inside, meeting hers in an intimate caress. The soft touch of her skin against his own awakened passions he had never known with any other woman. His beautiful *wasicu* could ignite his desire with just a look, just a touch. Gently lowering her onto his bed, he stretched out beside her.

Breathing in the sweet scent that was hers alone, he closed his eyes. If he lost his sight in battle, he could easily find his wife among all the other women in camp. She smelled of wildflowers and morning air, of crisp and sunny winter days and of the sweetgrass from the prairies. He smoothed his hand down across her shoulders and her back, and dipped into the hollow at her waist. Moving lower, he pressed against the curve of her buttocks, pushing her closer to him until he nudged her with his desire-hardened shaft.

He wanted to bury himself deep inside her, move into her until their bodies fit together perfectly, until their spirits whirled and danced as one.

Exasperated, his breath left his body in a low-pitched, disheartened sigh. Tonight that would not happen. Tribal law forbade it. Tomorrow, at first light, he would hunt for buffalo. It was known that if a hunter bedded a woman before a hunt, the buffalo would leave and the people would go hungry. Wolf slowly eased his body away, reluctantly distancing himself from Ryan's touch.

Feeling his withdrawal, a moan of despair slipped through Ryan's lips. She had expected his retreat but still felt the disappointment. Wolf lived by tenets as old as the tribe. As an anthropologist she knew of the law and understood it, but as a woman in love, it touched her in another way, bringing her misery. For the first time since she'd truly become his wife, she'd never felt so close yet so far away from the man she loved.

She placed her hand on his chest and her fingers lightly stroked his smooth bronze skin. "I understand, my husband," she whispered. "I know why you keep yourself from me."

"Ah . . . Kechuwa." Wolf drew a ragged breath and then, allowing it to escape in a deep sigh, placed his lips against her cheek. "That is how it must be. It is not my wish."

She snuggled closer to his body, moving against him with a sinuous stretch, caressing his body with her own. "That does not mean I must keep myself from you."

"No. It is not allowed." His tone was firm and unbending. "If a hunter does this thing, the buffalo will leave and the people will be hungry. I cannot."

Withdrawing her hand from his chest, her soft caress migrated across his stomach, moving lower, touching the cluster of dark hairs at his groin and still moving lower until she closed her fingers around him. She lightly stroked the hard column of flesh, drawing her fingers across the sensitive tip.

Wolf groaned and quickly placed his hand over hers, stilling her gentle massage. "I cannot."

"Darling," she whispered, taking Wolf's hand and placing it between her legs against her soft curls. "*Tatanka*, the great buffalo, says you can't be inside of your woman, here, before you hunt. *Tatanka* does not forbid a wife from loving her husband in other ways."

She reached up and smoothed away the puzzled frown on his brow with her fingertips. "I will love my husband tonight."

With every movement slow and tenderly deliberate, she traced the line of his eyebrow, then down across the hard ridge of his cheek. Drawing her caress across his lips, she placed her mouth where her hand had just been before moving on to the next tender touch. She licked along the point of his shoulder and across the hard rise of his collarbone before following her fingers down over the rise of solid muscle on his chest to suck and tease his flat nipples into stiffened buds. The praise she received for her skill came in a hungry groan that escaped Wolf's throat and the increasing pressure of his own caress along her back.

His touch slid across her ribs and he filled his hands with her breasts, stroking and teasing her nipples until they, too, stiffened. Drawing her arms up over her head, causing her body to arch toward him, Wolf bent down to her, laving his tongue over one taut nipple and then the other, tugging her flesh with his lips and finally suckling her deep into his mouth.

A wild rush of heat erupted in Ryan's breast and rippled throughout her body, creating a delicious ache in the deep, moist place between her legs. Hungry, yearning sounds fled her throat and were met by a responding deep murmur from her Lakota lover. She pressed her legs together. Tonight would be for Wolf. Slowly pulling away, she took her breast from the caress of his mouth. Her touch descended along the taut furrowed plane of his ribs and her fingers splayed wide as she drew her hands together to meet in the middle of his stomach.

She rejoiced as he sucked in his breath and shivered under her touch. Bending over him, her hair fell forward and hid her intent. In a moment Wolf discovered her plan. Her

tongue caressed and tasted the taut skin across his belly,
swirled with a teasing dip into his naval and moved downward to suck lightly on the ridge of his hip. She moved
further downward to his thigh, purposefully avoiding the
very part of him that stood upright and demanded the touch
of her lips most of all.

Wolf moved beneath her hands, his breath ragged and
his pulse wildly pushing his hot blood throughout his body.
He eagerly sought her caress on his hardened shaft, but she
continued to avoid him, teasing him, making him dizzy
with need. With a craving that demanded her attention, he
roughly pulled her body up against his full length and captured her lips under his kiss, plundering the depths of her
mouth, meeting the stroke of her tongue in return. Each
motion mimicked the act of love they wanted most of all.
Tugging fitfully at her bottom lip with the edges of his
teeth, his breath left his lungs in a single gasp as she tilted
her hips forward to meet his rigid shaft. He groaned with
resignation and no longer cared what the elders taught. He
no longer cared if it meant hunger for the camp. Nothing
mattered but the pale-skinned woman in his arms. It did
not matter if he ever breathed again. As long as he could
feel this woman he loved hold him deep within her body
and exhilarate him with her moist intimate caress, nothing
mattered.

Wolf's hand moved between them and his fingers gently
opened her and stroked the wet, swollen flesh that was for
him alone. Gently moving her onto her back, he settled
himself over her. Pushing her thighs apart, his hard flesh
brushed against her, eager to fill her.

Ryan felt his surrender. He had abdicated completely to
his passion and she knew the jeopardy. *I can't let it happen.
If something happens tomorrow on the hunt, he would
never forgive himself.* She pulled away, leaving his embrace.

"Kechuwa?" Wolf reached out for her, trying to draw
her back beneath him, his hunger mirrored in his dark eyes.

"No," she whispered, gently placing her hand on his
chest.

With a deep sigh of resignation, Wolf fell back on the bed. He closed his eyes and Ryan watched him fight to calm the wild, demanding hunger, steady his uneven breathing and slow the rush of hot lava through his veins.

"There are other ways to pleasure my hunter." She placed a trail of light kisses across his chest.

"How is it that you are able to keep yourself from me and I am unable to be as strong?"

Couldn't he see how it was killing her, too? Didn't he know how much she wanted him? "Maybe it's because I want some fresh meat to cook, now that I know how," she teased. Wolf's laughter helped a little to ease the desire that still imprisoned them both but the ache filling her body refused to leave.

He lay on his back, breathed deeply, and closing his eyes, rested his arm across his forehead. Finally, he looked at Ryan and rolling to his side, touched her cheek. "I would gamble my life for you," he whispered.

"And I for you," she answered. "There's nothing I wouldn't give to keep you safe within my heart." Her lips moved to meet his and she reached between them. Her hand caressed his erection and her fingers lightly played along its generous length, moving from where it sprung between his legs to the silken head where she found a slick drop of moisture on the tip. Gently spreading the droplet as though it was a precious anointing, she slid her hand over him.

"Kechuwa," Wolf groaned, moving to still her hand.

"Let me love you, *mihingna*, my husband," she whispered. "I will love you in a way that won't displease the spirit of *Tatanka*."

Lowering herself down his body, she kissed and licked his flesh until her mouth replaced her fingers. "Be still, my love. Let your wife bring you pleasure until the sun rises in the morning."

Chapter 28

WOLF'S PLACE BESIDE her on the bed was empty. Ryan pressed her hand where he had been. It still felt warm. He hadn't been gone long. Why hadn't he awakened her?

Rolling onto her back, she stretched, dislodging the complacency of sleep and listened to the excited voices of the men and women gathering in the camp for the hunt. Even the dogs had picked up the sense of adventure and were barking with excitement. The sounds of the horses nervously stomping, eager to be on their way, added to the morning clatter. A keen edge of anticipation echoed in every sound.

Bundling the blanket around her body, Ryan stepped from the tipi into the cool morning. A ground fog, thick and heavy, rose from the riverbank and swirled around the outer edges of the camp. Its eerie shroud sent a shiver down her spine.

How far away is Custer? She tried to ignore the burn of adrenaline that touched every nerve. *It's a spooky morning fog, nothing more.* She shuddered. *Charley won't let anything bad happen—to Wolf or Eagle Deer or Pretty Feather—or me.*

Searching through the now-familiar faces, she quickly found the one of the warrior she loved. Already mounted on their horses, Wolf and Eagle Deer waited by the edge of camp for the rest of the hunting party to gather. Making her way through the maze of horses and riders, Ryan stood beside Wolf's pinto and placed her hand lightly on her husband's knee.

"You left me sleeping," she said, her voice hushed but carrying the slight ring of disappointment. "Were you going to leave me while other husbands took their wives?" She detested petulance in women and regretted the hint of it in her own voice. "Did you think because I am a *wasicu* I wouldn't be able to help on the hunt like the other women?"

A slow smile curved Wolf's lips and leaning down from his horse, he lightly touched her cheek. "Do you still not know that I want you with me always?"

Eagle Deer crowded his horse closer to Ryan. "I asked my brother if he would let his wife stay with Pretty Feather while we hunt," he interrupted. "The baby she carries made her sick again last night. I do not want her to be alone."

Wolf cupped his hand against her face and she wistfully looked into his dark gaze, pressing her head against the gentle curve of his palm. He gave a slight nod of encouragement. Stepping away from Wolf's caress, she met Eagle Deer's hesitant smile. "Of course I'll stay," she said, "I promise, I'll take good care of her. You're right, she shouldn't be left alone."

"*Wasté,*" Eagle Deer responded, his relief apparent.

From the edge of the camp a voice rang out strong and clear. "Lakota, we go!"

From the Oglala circle to the north, a warrior rode into the camp and Ryan immediately recognized the oddly colored pinto horse and its brown-haired rider, Crazy Horse.

"*Mita kola*, my friend," Crazy Horse invited Wolf. "I have come to ask you and Eagle Deer to ride with me this morning. We have much to talk of."

Wolf whispered only for Ryan's ears. "Know that this warrior's heart will be lonely while he is gone. I have asked my bullets to fly straight. I have promised the hides and tongues to Little Horse's wife if she and her daughters will butcher my kill before any others. I have promised my horse new grass if he brings me back to you as fast as he can run. What more can this warrior do to please his wife?"

"Be safe, my husband." Beneath her breast, she could feel the quickening beat of her heart. How could this Lakota make her feel more cherished with his simple words than any man she had ever known in her own lifetime? At the very brink of the battle of the Little Big Horn and at the end of freedom for the Indian people she had grown to love as family, the knowledge returned, strong and true. She would rather be with this Lakota warrior in his time than with anyone else, any time or any place.

She felt Wolf's caress trail once more along the back of her head, stroking the fall of her hair and then leaving her. In its wake the heavy weight of sadness filled her heart. It would be a long, lonely day.

The hunters moved out of camp, some riding single file, others riding three and four abreast.

"Bring us good meat," one mother called out to her son.

"I will bring enough to feed the *entire* camp," the young Hunkpapa bragged, immediately finding himself the target of laughter from the older, more seasoned hunters.

Wolf turned and looked back at Ryan once more. She made an effort to send him off with a bright smile but it felt like a lie, stiff and wooden upon her lips.

"Go with him," the quiet, nagging voice from within prodded. "If you hurry, you can catch up."

"No, I can't," she answered.

The voice returned. "Why should you stay? Pretty Feather will be fine. Lakota women were having babies long before you showed up." It goaded her mercilessly. "Go. Hurry. Tomorrow is coming and so is Custer. Tick-tock, tick-tock, tick-tock."

"Stop it," she upbraided herself aloud, balling her hands into fists, her nails digging painfully into her palms. "I've *got* to trust Charley. This is how it's supposed to be."

The hunting party rode westward out of camp, carrying their rifles and bows across their shoulders. The women, riding horses that would later carry the meat and hides back to camp, followed behind. One by one the riders disappeared, swallowed up in the eerie morning mist.

Standing alone and clutching the blanket around her body, she watched the last of the riders move off and the aching in her chest became unbearable. Her eyes burned with tears and her sight blurred. She was being childish. She scrubbed the tears from her eyes.

"You are unhappy to stay with me?" Pretty Feather asked, quietly moving to Ryan's side.

"Oh, no," she sniffled. "I'll just miss my husband."

"Ah," Pretty Feather sighed with a small laugh. She drew Ryan into a sympathetic embrace, offering her slight shoulder for comfort. "Our men will be back before nightfall and then there will be great feasting and dancing to celebrate the good hunt." Her hand gently patted and stroked Ryan's arm. "Come, we will enjoy a restful day together. Your husband is a very good hunter and tomorrow there will be much work for his wife." Turning back toward camp, Pretty Feather kept her arm around Ryan's waist. "Today we will sit and gossip together, watch the children play and watch this one's belly grow." Pretty Feather stroked her distended stomach and giggled.

With a subtle lift of her chin, Pretty Feather pointed to her two little boys who were playing with some of the other children in the encampment. They were chasing after the camp dogs, herding them together and pretending the dogs were buffalo. All of the little boys carried toy bows and arrows made of blunt sticks. One after another, each sent a volley of sticks in the dogs' direction. A sharp yowl accented every direct hit but instead of running away, the dogs stayed and put up with the rough play. When each animal yelped, the little girls cheered the boys on, encouraging them to hunt bravely.

"I have killed three *tatanka*," Little Hawk shouted. "I am *Cetan Cik'ala*, I am a great hunter!"

"I have killed too many for my horse to carry," another boy answered.

The herd of dogs and their little hunters ran, winding

their way between the tipis until they were soon out of sight.

"The day will go quickly. You will see." With the tip of her finger, Pretty Feather wiped a tear away from Ryan's cheek. "There is no need for these today, my sister. Later, after we bathe and sweeten our bodies, I will help you get ready for your husband's return." Pretty Feather stroked Ryan's hair, dividing it, testing its length. "I have a dress I will give you that is now much too small for my belly. The dress is made with the finest of white hides and will be soft to your skin and to your husband's hands. My mother made it to be worn by one, not two." Pretty Feather fondly stroked her stomach again. "It will look very good on you, my dear friend."

Had it been any other time, any other place, Ryan knew she would have enjoyed the idyllic morning with Pretty Feather, but the ominous tick-tock sound of passing time had grown louder. It soon became the steady, oncoming beat of horses' hooves, Custer's cavalry, pounding across the Montana hills drawing closer and closer to the valley she had come to think of as her home.

A small headache nagged at her as she tried to shove away all thoughts of what the next day would bring, but shoving it away became hard and so did the headache.

The daily routine of the camp had become as comfortable to Ryan as breathing and she looked forward to her daily bath in the river. Judging from the height of the sun in the sky, it was near ten o'clock by the time Ryan and Pretty Feather joined the other women who had stayed in camp. The June sun beat down on the valley, sending shimmering heat waves up from the ground and the women chattered and laughed, luxuriating in the cool water. The sound of pleasant conversation joined with the babbling sound of the river.

Ryan dunked beneath the water time and again, rinsing her hair. When she stood, rivulets of cool water trickled down over her shoulders, across her breasts and over her stomach. A dip in a chlorine-doused pool paled in comparison.

Dragonflies the size of hummingbirds flitted about and shafts of sunlight filtered through the leaves of the overhanging trees. Where the sun touched the river, it left the water glittering like the most precious of diamonds, twinkling and shimmering with each undulating ripple. She breathed deeply. The fragrance of sweetgrass and flowers, warm earth and fresh water combined to make the most marvelous perfume. Sweet and pure, the land was untouched, just as God's hand had created it.

"Look who is here," Pretty Feather whispered, tentatively touching Ryan's arm.

Ryan followed her friend's gaze toward the riverbank. "Ground Plum."

"I thought she would hide with shame after the other day."

"She's talked with me since and wants to be friends."

"Ground Plum has come to you with the offer of friendship?" Pretty Feather's eyes were wide with surprise.

Ryan met her friend's astonished gaze. "Yes, two evenings ago." She gave a slight shrug.

"You have given her what she asks?"

"If I found another woman living with the man I was going to marry, I'd be angry, too."

Pretty Feather shook her head. "My husband tells me I am too meek to cause anyone harm, but I think if Ground Plum attacked me as she did you, my husband would have to call me a she-bear."

Ryan chuckled and gave her friend a quick hug. "Remind me not to get you angry."

"I will make the growl of the bear to warn you," Pretty Feather teased, splashing some water in Ryan's face.

A scream shattered the peaceful morning and everyone quickly turned to gape at Ground Plum. She stood motionless on the riverbank and stared at the ground. Something moved at her feet and she shrieked again. Blood trickled from the calf of her right leg.

"Snake!" a woman near the edge of the river shrieked.

"She has been bitten by the snake that shakes its tail."

"Rattler," Ryan breathed, pushing her way through the water toward the riverbank. "Yellow Wing, come quickly. Help me." She grabbed the woman's hand and led her to the riverbank.

"No! I am afraid," Yellow Wing cried, pulling back. "It will bite me, too."

"Get a stick and beat at the grass to chase it away. If you find it, kill it. I've got to help Ground Plum."

"She is beyond help," Yellow Wing argued. "Now only *Ho K'a To*, Blue Heron, can help her with his medicine."

"He is not here. She needs help now!" Pretty Feather said, pushing the woman aside and awkwardly climbing up on the riverbank, her bulky figure making each step ungainly. "Let *Aupahu Zi*, Yellow Wing, cower like a baby fish in the water." Pretty Feather grabbed a long broken limb and began beating the ground. "Where did the snake go?" She watched for Ground Plum's answer but received only a terrified, blank-eyed stare.

"Sit here," Ryan firmly ordered Ground Plum, pointing to the rim of the riverbank. "Hang your legs over the edge."

Ground Plum backed away and fearfully glanced around. "I must go to my father's tipi. He will send for *Ho K'a To*." Without waiting for Ryan's response, she turned to flee.

Anticipating the girl's intent and ignoring the warnings of the other women, Ryan chased after her, oblivious to her own nakedness. She firmly grasped Ground Plum's wrist and hauled the girl back to the river, forcing her to sit on the bank with her legs dangling down over the edge.

"Don't move until I say you can. Do you understand me?" Ryan glared at Ground Plum, hoping her face appeared grim enough to make the girl obey. Ground Plum's eyes filled with terror and Ryan knew in a moment she would go into shock. "You," she pointed to Yellow Wing. "Get me some clothes. We've got to cover her and keep her warm. Give me a belt, too."

Finally gathering her nerve, Yellow Wing scrambled up on the bank. Picking up a leather belt, she held it up for

Ryan's inspection. Nodding her approval, Ryan slipped the
small knife from the rawhide case tied to the side. Holding
the knife in her mouth, she quickly wrapped the belt around
Ground Plum's thigh and drew it tight. Satisfied with the
makeshift tourniquet, she took the knife from her mouth
and tested the keenness of the blade against the pad of her
thumb. Hearing a whimper, she looked up at Ground Plum.

"*Iye-e-e-e,*" Ground Plum screamed. "*Niakte kte, kuseya
unpe!* She is going to kill me, *niakte kte kuseya unpe!*"

Undaunted, Ryan quickly motioned to two women who
stood watching, their eyes wide with misgivings. "Hold her
still, don't let her move."

Without hesitating, Blue Whirlwind and One Star quickly
seized Ground Plum's arms and legs, then looked to Ryan
for more instructions.

Grasping the girl's chin with her left hand, Ryan demanded her attention. "Look at me." Her fingers bit into
the girl's cheeks. "Look at me."

When she finally obeyed, Ryan spoke slowly and firmly.
Ground Plum had to understand each word if she wanted
to live. "I'm not going to kill you. We're friends, remember? You asked for a friendship and I gave it."

Feeling a slight slackening in Ground Plum's rigid body,
Ryan removed her hand and eased the girl back on the
ground, her legs dangling over the embankment and her
feet in the cool water. "I'm going to try to take out as much
of the snake's poison as I can, but you have to be still."

Ground Plum squirmed and fought, trying to escape the
strong hands that held her.

"Stop it," Ryan forcefully commanded. "If you fight you
will die. Do you understand?"

Ground Plum became limp, her eyes glazed and each
breath became a moan. Examining her leg, Ryan found two
puncture wounds in the calf. The snake had struck only
once. Looking at the women holding Ground Plum's arms
and legs, she gave a slight nod. Replying in kind, they
immediately tightened their hold. With a steady hand that
disguised her apprehension, Ryan deftly cut an inch-long
vertical slit through each hole. With the first slash of the

blade, a few of the women screeched and wailed.

"Be still, you silly cows!" Pretty Feather firmly demanded. "Stop your yelling. You do not make these noises when Blue Heron makes his medicine. Why should you doubt this one who has come to us from Tunkasila?"

Ryan quickly looked up, unable to mask her surprise. Pretty Feather smiled broadly, obviously proud of her firm stand.

The tight belt around Ground Plum's thigh had slowed the progress of the venom. Lowering her legs had helped, too, but Ryan knew that grave danger still threatened unless she could suck enough of the rattler's venom out of the girl's body. Not waiting another precious moment, Ryan placed her mouth over the fresh cuts. Ignoring the metallic taste of blood, she sucked time after time on the wound, drawing out as much of the poison as she could before spitting it onto the riverbank. After ten minutes, her mouth and jaws ached and the muscles along the side of her face began to cramp.

Someone placed a blanket over her shoulders. She had forgotten she was naked. As she glanced up, her gratitude increased. A number of people from the village had gathered to watch her. Blue Heron stood among them.

Standing close, the medicine man studied every move she made. Suspicion and hostility filled his eyes but she met his gaze without a falter. She knew if she seemed unsure of herself, and if she wasn't able to save Ground Plum's life, he would blame her, not the rattlesnake.

"Ground Plum is indebted to you now," Pretty Feather quietly said. "Saving another's life is nothing that can be forgotten until it has been paid for."

"I don't want anything from her," Ryan replied. "I hope she gets well soon, that's all."

"There is an obligation. It is the way."

Ryan sighed. "I wish it could be forgotten."

Pretty Feather shook her head and moved away. "To do so, or to ask it to be done, would be an insult."

"I know."

"Is it true?" Pretty Feather asked hesitantly.

"What?"

"Is it true she will live if her mother does what you have told her?"

"She won't feel good for a couple of days, but she'll live."

"*Wasté*, that is very good," Pretty Feather answered. She placed her hand on the small of her back and shifted her posture to accommodate the weight of the baby she carried. "Blue Heron watched you closely. He had anger because he was not called. He told many that your medicine was bad and would not work." She rubbed her back. "It was Turtle Rib who spoke out on your behalf," Pretty Feather said. "I believe Blue Heron is jealous."

"He's afraid, nothing more," Ryan replied, nodding when Pretty Feather disagreed. "Yes. He's afraid my medicine will be stronger than his and he'll lose face." She stood and began to leave the tipi.

"Where do you go?"

"Perhaps Blue Heron will be happier if I ask for his help."

"My *wasicu* sister is very wise," Pretty Feather agreed, "but must you go now? Soon your husband will return. I have brought the dress I spoke of. Do you wish to see it?"

Pretty Feather slowly moved to the bundle she had placed on Ryan's bed. Awkwardly easing herself down on the pallet, she unrolled the soft buckskin packet. The first items uncovered were a pair of moccasins and leggings. Ryan had never seen such wonderful pieces. The craftsmanship was exquisite. Traditional geometric patterns worked in yed porcupine quills of deep red, two shades of blue, yellows and greens had been worked with onto the white hide. Ryan hadn't seen anything finer in any of the museum or private collections she had ever studied.

Next, Pretty Feather lifted the dress and showed Ryan the magnificent quill-encrusted bodice. The patterns matched those on the leggings. The hides used to make the dress were the purest white possible, brained tanned and worked until they were supple and mole-skin soft. The fringes that fell from the sleeves were long and finely cut.

"This is . . . ," Ryan fumbled for the Lakota word that would fully describe magnificent dress. It eluded her. Giving up, she found an English word instead. "Fabulous." The frown on Pretty Feather's face made her laugh. *"Wasté,"* she added, knowing that although inadequate, Pretty Feather would understand.

"Hurry," Pretty Feather urged. "Your husband will be returning soon. It is time for you put this on."

"I'd like to go see Ground Plum first and make sure her mother is taking care of her properly," Ryan said. "Would you come with me?"

"No," Pretty Feather declared. "I will fix some food for my sons. Spotted Pony and Little Hawk have been playing all day and their bellies will be empty. I will wait for you to come back. But hurry."

Ryan lightly scratched on the side of the tipi to announce her presence, not wanting to intrude on Ground Plum's family without their permission.

"Ah, it is you," Ground Plum's mother said, warmly greeting Ryan. "My daughter sleeps like a new baby and she has little pain." The woman bowed her head. "Her family is very grateful to the wife of *Sunkmanitu Ceye a Pelo*. You will always be honored and welcome in this tipi."

Chapter 29

TIRED, YET SATISFIED with a good hunt, the buffalo hunters returned to the village in the late afternoon. The horses the women had ridden out of camp in the morning came back burdened with heavy carcasses. The travois poles bowed under the weight of butchered hindquarters and shoulders and dug into the dirt, leaving deep furrows marking the trail. Walking beside the travois, the women brandished severed tails and swished the hairy-tasseled tips over the meat to shoo away the flies and gnats. Camp dogs, dodging attempts to chase them away, darted close from time to time to nip off mouthfuls of fresh meat.

Fatigue etched the women's faces and dried blood stained their clothes and arms. They had worked hard in the hot sun dressing out the carcasses, but they greeted everyone in camp with broad smiles and excitedly told stories of the long day.

"My husband killed two young bulls and a cow," one woman called to her old mother waiting in camp. "Our bellies will be full."

"Were the buffalo many?" a bent old man questioned.

"There were many more *before* we found them," his son

bragged, pointing to the heavy loads his three horses carried.

The old man lifted his walking stick in salute, cackling with delight. "*Sunkmanitu Ceye a Pelo's* woman has brought us the buffalo." The Lakotas who heard him agreed heartily.

Pretty Feather peered out the tipi door. "I do not see Eagle Deer or Wolf. Perhaps they have stopped at the river to wash their bodies." She glanced back over her shoulder at Ryan. "You must hurry. You must be ready when he returns."

The finest dentallium shell earrings Ryan had ever seen decorated her ears. She tested their unfamiliar weight, turning her head first one way and then the other. Pretty Feather lifted a heavy breastplate of bone hairpipe and French brass beads from the bundle and settled it over Ryan's head and onto her shoulders. It covered the front of the exquisite buckskin dress, ending just above her knees with a row of shiny hawk bells that jingled each time she moved. The white man's trade goods had added many things to the Lakota's lives.

All that remained in the bundle was a wide belt, and Pretty Feather helped Ryan fasten it around her waist. Made from commercially tanned leather and decorated with evenly spaced pocket-watch backs, Ryan guessed the items had been taken from a white settler or acquired in trade at the fort. A knife and an awl set in colorfully painted cases hung from the belt.

Pretty Feather lifted Ryan's hair from under the heavy breastplate and after parting it down the middle, she plaited it into two, thick lustrous braids and securely tied the ends with pieces of red trade cloth. Using wide strips of otter fur, she wrapped each braid, securing the fur by tying it at the top of the braids. A large round shell disk covered the rawhide thong and knot on each side.

Stepping back, Pretty Feather carefully inspected her handiwork and offered a silent nod of approval. "You are very beautiful in the clothes of the Lakota—even though you are a pitiful, pale *wasicu*," she teased, adjusting the heavy breastplate. "Tonight will be your marriage night," she added with a shy hint of laughter in her voice. "You came to live in Wolf's lodge without ceremony, but tonight when he returns you will meet him as a new wife, dressed in fine buckskins with your hair braided and with a gift for your husband. It is how it should be done." Pretty Feather stooped and retrieved the colorful trade blanket in which the dress had been wrapped. Her pregnancy made her movement difficult. Folding the blanket in lengthwise quarters, she laid it over Ryan's arm. "Give this to Calls to the Wolf and call him *wicahca*, your 'husband.'" She lightly touched Ryan's cheek. "Enjoy your marriage to this good man. Have many children. This life you share together will be long; it will be *wasté*."

Ryan smoothed her hands over the white dress. It fit perfectly, skimming over her body as though it had been custom made for her. She had never seen a more beautiful wedding dress. It made the voluminous gowns in the bridal magazines with the yards of chiffon and satin, seed pearls and sequins seem tasteless and gaudy by comparison.

Will Wolf think I'm beautiful, or do I really look like a pitiful wasicu *dressing up in Indian clothes?*

She was eager for his return, but a deep sadness intruded. It was the twenty-fourth of June. In the morning, just hours away, Reno and Benteen would lead their men in a strike against the southern tip of the camp and the Battle of the Little Big Horn would begin.

Please, Charley, let me have one last night with Wolf. Tomorrow before it begins, I'll bury the bundle and you can take me back, but please, not tonight. Sadness constricted her heart. She could barely breathe. By this time tomorrow the fate of the mighty Sioux nation and the destiny of George Armstrong Custer would be sealed forever in the annals of history.

"They are here!" Pretty Feather exclaimed after taking another quick peek out the tipi door. "Your husband has returned." She gleefully clapped her hands and grabbing Ryan's arm, tugged her outside.

• • •

"Do Crazy Horse's words speak the truth?" Eagle Deer asked Wolf as they rode back to camp. "He says many bluecoats now look for the Lakota. He says the bluecoats will make war on us when they find us." Eagle Deer glanced at Wolf and then continued, his concern apparent. "They talk of the one called Yellow Hair. It is said he leads these long knives."

Wolf was silent for a moment or two. He had heard the words of Gall and Sitting Bull and of Two Moons from the Cheyenne camp. They had talked about Sitting Bull's vision of a battle, of soldiers falling like grasshoppers into the camp from the sky. He didn't want to believe the words of these wise men, but he knew they were true. Finally he answered. "They will come."

"But when?" Eagle Deer pressed.

"That is only for Tunkasila to know."

"Look, my brother," Eagle Deer said, pointing to Ryan with a lift of his chin. His words were unnecessary. Wolf had already seen her.

"Kechuwa," Wolf breathed. How was it possible that this pale-skinned woman could capture his heart so completely? In a reckoning as clear as any vision, he knew he loved her more than he had ever believed it was possible to love a woman. She would be the only one ever to hold his heart. It would be hers forever.

He slid from the pinto's back. Handing his Winchester to Eagle Deer, he walked toward Ryan, the cadence of his heart increasing with each step. His gaze took in every minute detail of his bride. He saw how the dark sweep of her eyelashes lay against her cheeks. He saw how she held her hands lightly clasped in front of her and how the soft hides of the dress lay over the swell of her breasts. Her shy demeanor surprised him. Moving closer, his smile broadened as he noticed the blush on her cheeks. He had already bedded this woman, he had already joined his body with hers, had left his seed inside her and yet her face still reddened like an innocent girl's.

He stopped a short distance from her. "Kechuwa," he

called softly and held out his hand. In an instant she came to him. Closing his fingers gently around hers, he lifted her hand to his mouth, pressing the palm against his lips. "Ke-chuwa, Ryan," he breathed, the English falling awkwardly from his lips. "Come, ride with me through this camp so my people will know my wife."

Leading her back to where Eagle Deer waited with his warhorse, Wolf vaulted up onto the animal's back. Taking the trade blanket Ryan held up to him, he placed it across the withers of his horse. With quick and gentle ease, Eagle Deer lifted her onto the animal, setting her down on the blanket in front of Wolf as though she were riding sidesaddle.

Wrapping his arm around her waist, Wolf pulled her back against him. No words came to his mind that could tell anyone how wonderful she felt in his arms. He breathed in her sweet fragrance, felt a contentment wash over him and vowed it would stay with him all of his life. This woman had brought him the gift of happiness. She had eased the bad dreams and frightening visions that plagued him; she had made them bearable with her love.

Keeping to a slow, easy gait, the pinto carried them throughout the camp circles, pausing often and patiently swishing its tail against the bites of pesky flies, waiting for well wishers to greet and talk with its riders. Without guidance the horse moved along the river's brim, gingerly placing each footfall. At the far end of the encampment, the pinto turned west and wandered through the great herd of horses. Following the worn path that led back to the southern-most camp, it skirted the tipis and doubled back. Having completed the circle, the horse stopped in front of Wolf's lodge.

With campfires lit, families gathered to enjoy the abundance of buffalo meat. Across the encampment, sounds of a drum and singers filled the night as many danced in celebration. The June evening was warm, a soft breeze stirred the air and peace and harmony enveloped the camp as night embraced the valley of the Greasy Grass.

• • •

Stretching her body, Ryan felt Wolf's hand on the crest of her hip. In the ember light of the tipi fire, she could see the rhythmic rise and fall of his chest and the slight smile that curved his full mouth as he slept.

He had led her into the tipi and slowly undone all of Pretty Feather's handiwork, satisfied only when the last piece of adornment fell from her body. Holding her hand, he had taken her to his bed. He had touched and caressed her, coaxing the most exquisite sensations from her body and twice her spirit had soared beyond all boundaries. She had shuddered, crying his name aloud as he touched her. He had used his fingers and his mouth to love her to completion and finally, after he had moved over her and buried himself deep inside of her, he began moving with long, slow, sensuous strokes. Over and over he gave and took and as his pace quickened, Ryan had joined his rhythm. Together they both rode the exquisite rising tides, until completely spent, they fell asleep wrapped in each other's arms.

She woke with a start. What had disturbed her?

She listened. Everything was quiet. But something had startled her. The fast pace and trip of her heart told her so. The shallow draught of her breath told her so. As if seeking assurance, she brushed Wolf's cheek with the back of her fingers. What had awakened her but left Wolf sleeping soundly?

With a subtle whisper deep in her mind, the answer came. It began as an elusive sound, and second by second became louder and louder until she could no longer pretend it didn't exist. Tick-tock, tick-tock, tick-tock. She shuddered. Company was coming. In just a few more hours the camp would have visitors. Custer was coming.

It felt so odd to be thinking about the events of the past when they were actually unfolding at that very moment. She remembered that around eight P.M. on June 24, 1876, Custer set up camp for the night about eighteen miles north of the site of the Rosebud battle. Then he posted an order that would later leave strategists scratching their heads. Instead of complying with his orders from General Terry and giving his men and horses a deserved rest until the next day, Custer ordered a night march.

Around two A.M., Custer had stopped his men and sent Lieutenant Charles Varnum, a man named Mitch Bouyer and his Crow Indian scouts out to locate the enemy. They would succeed. After an hour or two, at first light, from a high bluff that would later become known as Crow's Nest, Ryan knew the Indian scouts looked down into the valley of the Little Big Horn. There they discovered the great encampment that stretched for three miles up the west bank of the river. On the flats beyond the tipi encampment, they had seen the largest pony herd any of them had ever seen. Bloody Knife, Custer's Crow scout, would advise Custer to use extreme caution. Bouyer would tell Custer there were more Sioux than the amount of bullets they had brought with them. Together they would advise Custer there were enough Indians to keep the Seventh Cavalry busy fighting for two or three days. Laughing, Custer would foolishly brush the warning aside and say he could do the job in a day.

Ryan continued to recall what historians knew. Custer would ride throughout the bivouac, giving orders to break camp and head for the Little Big Horn. He would order a full one hundred rounds of ammunition for each man and then deliver the command that still dumbfounded historians. He would divide his strength. In an order that would be the beginning of the end, he would send six troops with Captain Frederick Benteen and Major Marcus Reno. One troop would remain with the ammunition train and Custer himself would keep five.

Between the commands of Reno and Benteen, 266 soldiers would cross the river and attack the encampment from the southeast. It was this assault that would begin the infamous battle.

Ryan knew the outcome.

She clutched the trade blanket against her breasts and tightly shut her eyes, trying to block out the sound of the phantom clock in her mind. All she succeeded in doing was making the tick-tock beat change in tone and cadence until it bloomed and swelled, becoming the ominous sounds of hoofbeats. Horses and riders by the tens of dozens, over six hundred in all, were headed toward the Little Big Horn. At their lead, the bright pennant of the Seventh Cavalry fluttered and waved in the breeze.

She heard the forlorn strains of a fife, teasing at the corners of her mind, playing the lilting notes of Garry Owen, the campaign melody Custer preferred over any other. Nothing could stop the Seventh. Nothing could stop the inevitable. Forward they came, moving through the shadows, slipping through the dark.

Shivering, she gazed into the sleeping face of her lover—her husband. Should she warn him? If she was going to, it should be soon. But what would happen if she did? Could she risk the possibility that history would be changed? Should she tell him what lay ahead so he could raise a warning? A doubtful sigh fled her lips as she weighed each possibility.

"What was that law of physics?" she whispered. "Something strange about 'ripples on a pond'?" She tried to remember and when she did, she almost laughed aloud. "It wasn't physics at all. Star Trek, that's where it's from . . . reruns." She shuddered again. "What did Captain James Tiberius Kirk call it?" She heard the dialogue in her mind. "Prime directive . . . don't interfere, don't make any changes, don't make waves. Don't make any ripples on the pond."

What difference would an hour or two make? Surely the outcome wouldn't change that much. Besides, there had already been some talk in camp about a troop of soldiers that a couple of the Lakota had seen while they had been out hunting. What would it matter? Custer would still be defeated—wouldn't he?

"Do it now," the small voice in her head urged. "Do it now before it's too late."

"Wolf." She nudged his shoulder. "Wake up. There's something I need to tell you."

Chapter 30

SUNLIGHT SPARKLED ON the Little Big Horn River, warming its clear, rushing water. In the crook of the river, boys and girls played. They spent the early morning swimming and splashing, the water glistening on their sun-browned bodies. Further downriver, two old men using grasshoppers for bait took advantage of the fish driven downstream by the children's games. Overhead, clouds of swallows darted through the cottonwoods, swooping over the river to pluck insects out of the air and carry them back to their hungry nestlings. June 25, 1876 was a beautiful warm and sunny summer day.

The knot in the pit of Ryan's stomach tightened with an ominous yank as she watched Wolf speak to the warriors gathering around him. Word about Yellow Hair and his long knives had quickly spread throughout the camp. Twenty or thirty warriors had gathered and now pushed close to Wolf, none wanting to miss a single word he had to say.

What had she done? Ryan felt the weight of doubt. She should never have played with fate. But there was no turning back now that Wolf knew about Reno and Benteen's attack. She had told him where they would strike, riding across the river from the east, but she'd told him nothing else. She hadn't told him of the other battle that would take place further north along the line of hills and gullies an hour or so later. She had only mentioned that Custer would be among the bluecoats. It was out of her hands now. Whatever was done, was done.

The crowd around Wolf steadily grew in number and their excitement rose higher and higher. Some of the warriors were already brandishing rifles and bows, hollering ear-piercing war cries and shouting out descriptions of the brave deeds they would accomplish in battle. The women and children held back in small, nervous bunches, their attention riveted on Wolf as well.

"Hear me Lakota. *Ecani u pi kte.* The bluecoats will come from where the river turns toward the evening sun, below the place of the tree without leaves," Wolf announced, pointing southward at the bonelike branches of the tall, dead cottonwood that housed the owl. "They will come soon. Kechuwa has said it will be so." He closely surveyed the faces of crowd as if gauging their strength. "My brothers, get your weapons. Be ready. My wife speaks of victory for our people this day."

The bustle in camp increased to a fevered pitch. As women gathered their children and clustered safely near their tipis, many charged their oldest daughters to keep the little ones together and safe. Boys, old enough to handle weapons, yet too young to ride with the men, joined in the excitement, fetching their lances and bows from their lodges. Each hoped to perform some brave deed in camp that would earn him the right to ride to battle.

Disquiet rose up like a threatening storm until the horses caught its scent and began to fidget nervously, rearing and fighting against the rawhide ropes that held them. Even the dogs felt the turmoil. They darted through the village, their hindquarters tucked close to the ground guarding their flanks, snarling at anyone who ventured too close.

"We must be ready," Wolf continued. "The one called Yellow Hair is among these bluecoats. Even the Cheyenne who once took him inside their tipis no longer call him brother."

"He will feel my bullets," Rabbit yelled, lifting his rifle into the air. "Sitting Bull asks for his scalp to hang on the council lodge. It will be done this day for the holy man."

Ryan suddenly trembled. Icy fingers, harbingers of dread, scraped down her spine. This was no longer an idyllic romp through time, this was real. This was the beginning of the most infamous Indian war in history. People she had grown to love would be put in harm's way throughout the entire day. An aching had begun to burn in her heart and her eyes never left her Lakota lover. "My God, what have I done?"

"Lakota, listen to me."

Ryan gasped. She should have realized *he* would have words to say.

Iron Soldier roughly shouldered his way through the throng, his face twisted into a fierce mien. Again his harsh voice rose above the excited din. "Listen to my words."

He stood apart from the people, forcing them to take their eyes away from Calls to the Wolf. "Why should we believe this *wanagi*?" Iron Soldier shouted, lifting his chin in Wolf's direction. "Why should we believe the lies of a *wasicu* cow?" He turned and glared at Ryan. "Can it be that she sends the Lakota to be killed like rabbits in the mouths of hungry wolves?"

"That is not so," Eagle Deer loudly countered. "*Sunk-manitu Ceye a Pelo's* woman is *wakan*." He glanced around, his eyes meeting with those men he knew well. "Lakota, did she not save Ground Plum from the snake death? Did we not see the buffalo return after she came to us? Is there any one of you who has not felt her friendship?" He stepped in closer to Wolf's side, showing support for his friend. He glared at Iron Soldier. "Did she not defeat the great warrior, Iron Soldier, with a touch of her knee and the help of one small brown dog?"

The laughter in the camp rose, then quickly faded as Eagle Deer continued to speak. "Calls to the Wolf's words are true. If he tells you that Yellow Hair comes, then it is so."

"Where are the bluecoats now? I see no one who resembles the *wasicu* . . . only *that* woman." Disregarding all Lakota manners and fired by humiliation, Iron Soldier turned and raising his hand, pointed his finger directly at Ryan.

"Lakota," Wolf shouted, trying to regain the warriors' attention. "Iron Soldier's words are false. Kechuwa's words are true. Did not Turtle Rib say she brought a message?" His dark eyes surveyed the crowd before him. "This is the message she has carried from Tunkasila to the Lakota, and to all our brothers in the valley of the Greasy Grass. Her words are for all."

"The vision of victory belongs to Sitting Bull, not the woman who sleeps with a *wanagi*. She has stolen Sitting Bull's words, nothing more." Iron Soldier raised his fist, striking himself on the chest. "This warrior does not ride to battle with those who are *dead* and lie with our enemy." Without a backwards glance, he stalked away, pushing aside anyone who dared to cross his path.

"We must be ready," Wolf called out. "The white eyes will be here soon."

Ryan's hopes rose. Ignoring Iron Soldier's remarks, all the warriors had stayed with Wolf. He truly was a leader. But, it was such a sad time to be a leader among the Lakota.

"Lakota, we must be ready to kill the bluecoats who come," Wolf shouted. "Go, prepare yourselves."

The warriors eagerly scattered, rushing for their weapons. Rifles, used only the day before to hunt buffalo, were reloaded to hunt a new quarry.

Wolf ran back to the lodge where Ryan stood. The gentle look that had moved upon his face the night before had disappeared. The hard-edged look of a warrior facing battle, facing death had taken its place.

He took the pinto's rein from her hand, then paused, his gaze holding her captive. Not a word passed between them but she could feel the heartache well up until it filled her chest and caught in her throat. He drew her into his arms, enveloping her, fitting himself tightly against her body.

"Kechuwa," he breathed against her hair, his lips moving to graze across her forehead.

Falling against him, Ryan wrapped her arms around him and rested her head against his chest. His breastplate pressed cold and unyielding against her face and she closed her eyes as another shudder seized her body. Wolf's arms tightened and his lips touched her cheek.

"Do not fear, my wife. Tunkasila will keep this Lakota and his people safe." Cupping her head in his hand, he tipped her face up until his lips captured hers with a kiss filled with tenderness and understanding. Steeped in passion yet tempered by the love he had learned to give freely, his kiss deepened.

One shot, then another and another rang out with the quick staccato of firecrackers. The pounding of iron-shod hooves and the distinct clanking of military saddlery joined the menacing din. Reno and Benteen had arrived.

Quickly ousting Ryan from the sanctuary of his embrace, Wolf placed one last tender kiss upon her mouth, and then turning away, vaulted onto the pinto's back. He looked down at her and the love she saw in the depths of his dark eyes took her breath away.

"Wolf, please . . ." Her voice faltered. No. She couldn't say the words that were in her heart. She couldn't ask him to leave the valley before the fighting began, to go away with her to some safe place, wherever that place might be. She would have to wait out the day, moment by agonizing moment, until he returned. She tentatively placed her hand on his knee and looked up through her tears. "Wolf, be safe. I love you."

A quick smile flashed on his bronze face. Then, wheeling his horse around, he left her, charging off through the breach in the line of tipis at the southeastern edge of the village.

All over camp, warriors leapt onto their horses, and following Wolf's lead, raced to meet the enemy. They drove their horses at breakneck speed until only the thick cloud of dust stirred up by their departure remained.

In the distance, over the war cries of the Lakota, over

the pounding sound of horses' hooves, and over the sharp retorts of rifle fire, for the first time in many, many days, Ryan heard the sound of English words. The frightened voices of the soldiers carried over the din on the back of a sweet June breeze. The Battle of the Little Big Horn had begun.

Standing alone in front of the lodge, she crossed her arms over her breasts, hoping to quell her shaking. She knew she should go into the tipi where Charley had told her she would be safe, but she couldn't tear herself away from catching even a small glimpse of a day that history would record in so many different versions. She wanted to see the truth for herself, even if she would never be able to report a single word of it.

A bay horse, dressed out in the brass and leather tack of the United States cavalry, broke through the ring of tipis and dashed into camp. The young blond-haired soldier on its back was wide-eyed with fear and riding as though hell was close on his heels. It was. Two Hunkpapas followed and before the soldier reached the middle of the clearing, he tumbled from his saddle. Two arrows, one driven into the base of his skull and the other protruding from his back, had taken his life. As he fell, his foot caught in the stirrup. His horse, never slowing its frantic pace, dragged the soldier's lifeless body through the village.

For close to an hour the sound of gunfire echoed and reechoed until finally it grew fainter and dwindled. Closing her eyes, Ryan could see the scene at the river playing in her mind like a Hollywood movie. The script called for Reno and Benteen to retreat back across the river where they would hide in the woods. Later, Reno would take his men to a high bluff where they would dig in for the rest of the day. Ryan paced in front of the tipi. Although this battle was over, the main feature was about to begin.

The sound of wild whoops and gunfire heralded the return of the warriors to camp. Trying to ignore the fresh bloodied scalps that decorated the ends of their lances, Ryan searched the crowd for Wolf. Finding him, she rushed to his side, maneuvering cautiously among the melee of horses. The smell of gunpowder, horse sweat and blood that polluted the air nearly made her gag.

Reining his winded horse to a halt, Wolf glanced in her direction and the wild look in his eyes softened. He slid from the lathered pinto and Ryan ran into his arms. Crushing her to his chest, Wolf lifted her off the ground and held her tight.

"Thank God, you're safe," she breathed against his neck.

"My woman should greet *me* like that," Rabbit laughed and heartily clapped Wolf on the shoulder.

"Eiyeeee!!!" Eagle Deer hollered, the fevered pitch of the battle in his voice. His horse charged through the crowd and he reined it to a halt beside Wolf's pinto. "It will be a long time before the *wasicu* will return."

"It isn't over," Ryan began, her voice a mere whisper. "There is more to come." When had she decided to tell them where Custer could be found? "Wolf, there are other bluecoats and Yellow—"

"Look," Rabbit called out with a laugh. "The mighty Oglala comes now that the fighting is done, but they only send the boy, *Kangi Takuni*, instead of a warrior."

The lone rider from the Oglala camp galloped toward them.

"Gall and Crazy Horse ride to meet the long knives and the one called Yellow Hair," the boy shouted. "They ask the Hunkpapa to ride with them. They ask *Sunkmanitu Ceye a Pelo* and his warriors to make war with the bluecoats. *Mahpiya Luta*, the one called Red Cloud, will also ride to battle today."

Eagle Deer grabbed the jawline on the boy's horse. "We saw no one like Yellow Hair." He pointed downriver where Reno and Benteen's men had last been seen. "We have already made war with the bluecoats today. The one you speak of was not among them."

The Oglala boy's horse lunged and tried to break away from the restraint on it's mouth, nearly tossing the boy from its back. "The bluecoats are many across the river, there!" The youth turned and pointed excitedly to the northeast. "Will you fight with us?"

Ryan felt Wolf's touch leave her and she grabbed at his hand, raising it to her lips. Kissing his palm, she folded his fingers over her kiss. She knew he would go. He would ride with Crazy Horse.

"Kechuwa," Wolf breathed, bending his head down to brush his lips across her mouth. "Wait for me."

"Always," she whispered. "Forever."

His hand lightly caressed her hair. "*Toksha ake wacin-yanktin ktelo*, I will see you again."

He sprang onto the pinto's back and although the horse had appeared tired and winded only moments before, it now danced and cavorted, eager to be gone. Responding to the touch of Wolf's heels, the pinto dashed forward, kicking up a spray of dust and dirt as its hooves dug into the ground. Every warrior who had followed Wolf to dispatch Reno and Benteen joined him again and the war party, over a hundred strong, rode northeast to the last great Indian war the Sioux would ever know.

Ryan turned away and closed her eyes, fighting a rising tide of tears. Had she stayed watchful, she would have seen the lone rider at the edge of the camp.

Moving furtively along the outer perimeter of the circle of Hunkpapa tipis, Iron Soldier guided his horse north to the battlefield.

Chapter 31

RYAN RACED DOWN the path to the riverbank. From the river's edge, she could hear the sharp reports of gunfire. So many shots fired at once, she couldn't begin to count their number. Nimbly climbing up into the large oak, she sought the highest branch that would support her weight. Four limbs above the kestrel nest, she found she could see over the first low hills on the other side of the river. A dense cloud of dust rose high and dirtied the blue summer sky over the battlefield. From time to time, horses and riders broke out on to the hills, only to be swallowed by the cloud. From this distance Ryan couldn't tell if the Indians she saw were Lakota or Cheyenne. Custer's men were easy to identify by their dark uniforms.

Every once in a while the breeze carried the sound of voices to her. Some were full of victory, others were full of terror.

"Tell me, what do you see?"

Ryan glanced down through the branches. Pretty Feather stood below with her two sons. She rested a hand protectively on each child. Her uplifted face mirrored her concern.

"I can't see much," Ryan answered before glancing back

across the river to the north. "I can't see anything more than a lot of dust and a few riders."

"Kechuwa." Pretty Feather spoke softly. "May I . . . may I ask something of my new sister?"

Ryan dropped her gaze to Pretty Feather again, puzzled by friend's hesitant manner. "What is it?"

"Does your heart seek victory for . . . for the white eyes this day?"

The question surprised Ryan, but the answer that immediately came from her own heart surprised her even more. "I seek a great victory for my husband and his people." Although she already knew the outcome of the battle, Ryan realized she *had* made a choice. She had chosen the Lakota way. Without a moment's indecision, she had chosen Wolf . . . forever.

"*Wasté*, my sister," Pretty Feather said, a warm smile lighting up her face. "You have truly become one with us. It pleases me. It pleases many others as well."

Movement on the path caught Ryan's eye. "Would you look at this. . . ."

Still weak and walking with a pronounced limp, Ground Plum moved toward the river's edge, each hobbling step punctuated with a slight grimace.

"Kechuwa, I would speak with you." An urgency lay in Ground Plum's voice. "There is something I must tell you."

"Do you wish to speak with this untrustworthy one?" Pretty Feather asked Ryan, disdainfully lifting her chin in Ground Plum's direction. Before hearing Ryan's response, she moved between Ground Plum and the oak, her pregnant belly offering an effective barrier.

"I'll talk with her," Ryan answered, crouching on the tree limb so she could see Ground Plum's face more clearly. "We've made peace between us. Isn't that right, Ground Plum?" She received a mute nod in agreement. "What do you want to tell me?"

"I cannot keep this terrible secret," Ground Plum began, her fingers nervously twisting the sleeve of her dress. "You have saved this pitiful one's life and now I must pay for what you have given back to me." Her eyes met Ryan's for only a moment before she humbly glanced down.

There was something about Ground Plum's sudden appearance and her behavior that set Ryan's nerves on edge. A flood of adrenaline swept through her body.

"It is about Iron Soldier and Calls to the Wolf," Ground Plum began. "I am ashamed of my actions against you. I wish to prove my friendship. You will see that I speak the truth when I tell you what I know."

The icy hand of fear slid its fingers into Ryan's chest and clutched at her heart. Its cold squeeze tightened. Not waiting a moment longer, Ryan climbed down from the tree. Letting go of the last branch, she dropped the last few feet to the ground and found herself face to face with Ground Plum. Eager to hear what she had to say, Ryan grabbed the girl's arm. "Tell me. What are you talking about?"

"It is Iron Soldier," Ground Plum replied. "He has gone over there to kill your husband." With a thrust of her lips, she pointed toward the battlefield. "Iron Soldier will kill Calls to the Wolf and take all that belongs to him. He will call himself a war chief and he will take you, the *wasicu wakan*, as his wife."

"That son of a bitch!" Ryan spat, unaware that her angry words were English. "No, I won't let him." She wheeled around and grasped Pretty Feather's hand. "Help me. I've got to get to Wolf. I've got to warn him!" The force of her grip increased. "I need my horse . . . and a gun! Where's my horse?" She cried, looking from woman to woman. "Where the hell is my horse?"

"Kechuwa," Pretty Feather quietly uttered. "You cannot go to the battle. You must stay here."

Frustrated, Ryan swiped her hand across her eyes, trying to eliminate the burn of threatening tears. "My God! Is that all I can do? Stay here and worry and blubber like a helpless idiot?" She paced a few steps away and then looked back again at Pretty Feather. "How can I think of anything but going to Wolf to warn him. Why won't you help me?"

"You cannot go," Pretty Feather reasoned. "It is no place

for a woman. You must wait until the battle with the blue-coats is done."

"But Wolf—I've got to stop Iron Soldier!"

"You cannot," Ground Plum interrupted, lightly placing her hand on Ryan's shoulder. "Your husband is very wise. He will not be fooled by Iron Soldier's tricks. His eyes are open to that one."

"How can you expect me to just wait here and do nothing?" She turned her anger on Ground Plum. "Why didn't you come before this? Did you purposefully wait to tell me until I could do nothing to stop Iron Soldier?"

"Would my words have stopped Wolf from going to fight Yellow Hair?" Ground Plum replied.

Pretty Feather pulled Ryan into her arms and placed a comforting hand on Ryan's head. "We all must wait."

Wolf felt as though he was on fire. Excitement, burning red hot and potent, coursed through his veins and sent his heart pounding in his chest. The hard muscles of the pinto driving at a full gallop between his legs and the sights and sounds and smells of the battle on the hill up ahead heightened his exhilaration and spurred him on. Holding his rifle over his head, he drove the pinto into the river. The horse crashed through the water, sending great splashes high into the air before scrambling up the embankment on the other side.

Rabbit and Eagle Deer rode beside Wolf and their horses jostled with his for the best footing as they climbed out of the riverbed and headed up the hill. At the crown of the grade, they pulled their horses to a halt. The battle stretched out across the hills. Everywhere they looked, clusters of bluecoated soldiers dotted the field. Some were kneeling in the open to fire their rifles, defending themselves as best they could. Others, using the carcasses of their dead horses for protection, lived a little longer. The loud reports of rifles, wild yells of the Lakota and Cheyenne and the frightened screams of the soldiers assaulted their ears. The biting, metallic stench of gunpowder and blood and death filled each breath.

A flash of recognition crossed Wolf's mind. He knew

this place. He remembered this hill. It was here that he had heard the sounds of the ghost horses and had felt the chill in his bones. He had felt the touch of the old ones, the ancient spirits, in this place and he had run to Kechuwa from this place as though all things evil were at his heels. Now he understood what he had felt that day. He had felt the touch of death.

Wolf scanned the field. Already many soldiers lay dead and the Lakota had added to their number of trophy scalps. Bodies dressed in the blue soldier coats of the Great White Father's warriors lay in bunches all over the hills. There were places where the grass was red and slippery with their blood. On the rise above him, a number of white eyes were putting up a strong fight, but their cause was useless. Completely surrounded, there was no place for them to go.

A bullet zinged close by his horse's nose and loudly whined as it ricocheted off a rock. The pinto pinned its ears tightly back against its head and squealed. It tried to bolt out from under Wolf, but gripping tightly with his knees, he stayed with the horse. Pulling on the rein, he turned to face the charge of two young white eyes. The horse one rode already had a bleeding wound. An arrow buried in its shoulder waved obscenely with each stride the animal took. Raising his rifle, Wolf gave out a shrill war whoop and squeezed the trigger. He didn't hear the shot in the din of the battle, but the kick of the rifle stock against his shoulder told him the gun had fired.

His face twisting with wide-eyed astonishment, the soldier clutched at his stomach. Blood dripped off the ends of his fingers as a dark stain quickly spread on his blue jacket. His eyes glazed with pain and as death quickly enveloped him, he slid from the saddle and landed facedown in the dirt.

Wolf looked up. The second trooper was almost upon him. He pulled the lever to drive another round into the chamber but his rifle was empty. There was no time to reload. Without hesitating, Wolf pounded his heels against his pinto's ribs and drove his horse into the side of the soldier's mount. With a frightened squeal, the cavalry horse stumbled on the uneven ground and fell onto its side. The soldier lay trapped, pinned beneath his horse. His pistol had been knocked from his hand and lay yards out of reach. Defenseless, he whimpered pitifully as he struggled to free his entangled leg.

Wolf leapt from the pinto and scooped up the long knife's pistol. The weight of it felt odd in his hand. He had handled the one Rabbit had taken from a dead soldier at Rosebud Creek and although he preferred his rifle, he knew how to shoot the small fire stick. Raising the gun, he aimed it at the white eyes. The bluecoat was young, perhaps only a year or two from being a boy, but he was the enemy. A split moment before the bullet from his own army-issue pistol struck him in the forehead, the white man stared into Wolf's eyes and they both acknowledged the sadness of the day.

Turning away, not willing to admit his regret, Wolf tossed the gun aside. He wanted no part of the soldier's weapon. Taking only a few moments, he dipped his hand into the buckskin pouch at his waist. Withdrawing a fistful of bullets, he slipped six into the Winchester and pumped one up into the chamber.

His long, black hair whipped about his face in the wind and the two eagle feathers tied to the scalplock braid at the back of his head waved like proud banners in the June breeze. A sheen of sweat covered his arms and broad chest and a grim smile curved his lips. Today would be a great victory for his people—hadn't his beloved Kechuwa told him it would be so? He vaulted back onto the pinto and reined the horse away from the dead soldier. He sought another foe.

Otter Skin and Makes No Bow rode up beside Wolf. Their horses were panting and sweaty and lather lay thick and high on their forelegs and chests.

"There will be plenty coup to count today," Makes No Bow shouted over the loud blasts of gunfire. He raised his bloodied war club, shook it in the air and reined his horse in a tight circle around his two friends. "Ei-yaaa, Ei-yaaa, Ei-yaaa! This day belongs to the Lakota and our brothers, the Cheyenne. Two Moons and his warriors are taking many scalps."

"We have taken our share as well," Otter Skin added, lifting his lance to show off the three bloody trophies that swung from just below the tip. "This day we will kill all the white eyes. They will be no more."

A sadness swept over Wolf and touched deep into his spirit. "It is true, this day will be ours. The Lakota and Cheyenne will earn many coup." He held his pinto in check, as the horse tried to lunge forward. "These long knives will die." He made a sweeping gesture with his arm, encompassing the entire battlefield. "But know this, my brothers, over that hill and over the next and the next, the *wasicu* are many. Our Lakota way is done. We will win no more."

Wolf turned his pinto away from his two friends and giving the horse a sharp kick, charged into a nearby foray. He joined the melee with a loud shout, firing his Winchester at the bluecoats at point-blank range.

Crazy Horse rode at breakneck speed across the rim of the bluff and raised his rifle over his head. "*Ho-ka hey!* It is a good day to fight! It is a good day to die! Strong hearts, brave hearts, to the front! Weak hearts and cowards to the rear."

Off to Wolf's left, three soldiers ran on foot down into a gully and tried to find cover in the scrubby bushes that dotted the hillside water wash. They had time to fire only once or twice before Wooden Leg, from the northern Cheyenne camp, and four of Gall's warriors found them and chased them further down the hill. The warriors charged their horses at the frightened bluecoats, playing a cruel and macabre child's game of tag before they overran and killed them at the bottom of the arroyo.

Wolf turned away from the bloody slaughter and found Eagle Deer had joined him.

"Look! There he is," Eagle Deer shouted, pointing to the top of the hill with his rifle, excited finally to see their main quarry. "*Wanyanka! Hecela pehin zi eciyapelo!* There is Yellow Hair." He tried to check his frenzied horse. The animal, too excited to pay heed, snorted loudly through flared nostrils and continued to skitter from left to right, trying to rear and dash up the hill. "Look, his long hair is gone." Eagle Deer sounded disappointed. "Yellow Hair has cut his hair away."

"Maybe he knew of this day and started his mourning before it began." Wolf never took his eyes off the top of the hill. He felt an odd dissatisfaction. Yellow Hair didn't look like a war chief. Where was his coat with many shiny buttons? He wore a shirt the color of a winter sky, buckskin trousers and boots that covered his legs almost to his knees. Wolf didn't know how white men could walk with their legs and feet in those stiff moccasins. Yellow Hair did not look as though he was mighty enough to be an enemy of the Lakota. He was slender and pale. Where was the strength to the man?

Wolf's eyes narrowed as he looked at Yellow Hair. Killing him would surely give him the status of a war chief among his people, but too many other warriors had already crowded around. It would be impossible even to count coup on the hated long knife. Two Oglala rode by, their horses bumping into Wolf's pinto as they dashed up the hill. The fight had become a hand-to-hand battle and he watched as the Lakota and Cheyenne encircled the remaining cavalry and began to end the battle.

"Follow me," Eagle Deer called back over his shoulder as he kicked his horse and sent the animal lunging up the hill.

"Sunkmanitu Ceye a Pelo!"

About to follow, Wolf heard someone shout his name. Turning, he felt a cold odd sense of portent. "Iron Soldier!"

"I have not yet heard you make the call of a brave warrior." Iron Soldier's mouth lifted in a callous sneer. "Are there no war cries to pass your lips? Have you not earned any tales of bravery to tell in camp tonight?" He held his rifle in a casual fashion across the withers of his horse. "Is this not a good day to die?"

"I will fight the white eyes, but I am not ready to leave this life," Wolf replied, closely watching Iron Soldier's every move. "I am surprised to see *you* here."

"Am I not a Lakota warrior?" Iron Soldier answered with derision. "What other place would I be?"

Wolf's pinto refused to stand still. The horse jumped and fidgeted, tossing its head and kicking out with its hind legs. It was difficult for Wolf to keep his eyes on Iron Soldier as the horse pivoted, but he persevered and his gaze never left the warrior. "Join your Lakota brothers in battle," Wolf said, taunting Iron Soldier, lifting his chin to direct his attention up the hill.

"I will do battle from where I stand," Iron Soldier coldly replied, lifting his rifle and holding it against his side, pointing the long barrel at Wolf.

Every nerve in Wolf's body became alert. This confrontation had been a long time coming. He had never tried to avoid it, but he would have preferred a more honorable encounter.

"You will see, *Sunkmanitu Ceye a Pelo*. It *is* a good day to die." Iron Horse's laughter rang harsh.

"Do you wish me dead so much that you would dishonor yourself among your people? If you kill me you would have no place with the Lakota. You would be put outside the tribe." Wolf tried to maneuver his pinto around to the opposite side of Iron Soldier's horse. If Iron Soldier intended to shoot him, he would either have to move his own pony or shoot the rifle from an awkward angle.

"They will believe you were killed by Yellow Hair's long knives. No one will look to me. You will be dead and your *wakan* woman will be mine."

As they cautiously circled each other, Iron Soldier lifted his rifle over his horse's neck and aimed it at Wolf again. Wolf's pinto was on the upward side of the hill and although the footing was uneven, he tried to turn the animal around. Just as Iron Soldier pulled the trigger, Wolf's horse stumbled.

He felt the bullet. Searing like a red-hot brand, it grazed along the lower edge of his left jaw, leaving a bloodied crease. Had his horse not tripped and pitched him forward, he knew the bullet would surely have killed him. Regaining his balance, Wolf quickly raised his Winchester. Iron Sol-

dier had struck the first blow; there would be no dishonor
in killing this loathsome Lakota now. Again the pinto stumbled and threw Wolf off balance as he began to lift his rifle.

The moment seemed to stretch into hours before Wolf
heard the sharp report of the rifle and then it felt as though
a horse had kicked him in the chest. The impact hurled him
backwards. The pain in Wolf's jaw was nothing compared
to the horrendous fire that now burned in his chest and kept
the sweet breath of life from filling his lungs. With clarity,
dimmed only by sadness and regret, Wolf knew he had
been shot.

Wolf clutched his rifle in his hand and his finger still
rode the trigger as he fell. Everything seemed to be happening slowly, every movement was exaggerated, every
sound seemed to deepen, becoming oddly drawn out and
magnified. An eerie roaring noise filled his ears. More powerful than the surge of a swollen river, Wolf heard the
sound of his blood rushing through his veins. He hit the
ground, and the impact drove most of his remaining breath
from his body. As his arm fell downwards, the edge of the
rifle stock struck the ground, pushing the trigger upward
against his finger. He heard the shot and felt the kick of
the Winchester before it fell impotently at his side. The
acrid stench of gunpowder almost choked him and through
the darkening haze that had begun to obscure his vision,
Wolf watched Iron Soldier fall. Where Iron Soldier's left
eye had been, blood flowed like rainwater and his face held
a frozen look of surprise.

Iron Soldier dropped his rifle and it landed on the ground
under his horse's hooves. In a moment, he followed. The
horse sidestepped as Iron Soldier's body rolled down the
hill and stopped beside Wolf. His remaining eye stared at
Wolf, but gone was the bravado. Iron Soldier was dead.

Using the last of the strength he possessed, Wolf pushed
against Iron Soldier's body until it rolled over onto its face,
imprisoning Iron Soldier's spirit in his body. There would
be no honor in the spirit world for this Lakota.

Wolf turned away and tried to drag a breath into his
lungs. He only succeeded in causing his chest to rage with

a pain so bitter that it drove his senses to the brink.

"Kechuwa, Kechuwa." He whispered her name again and again, using up what little precious life he had left. The sweet sound soothed his misery. "Kechuwa." A tight band of agony coiled around his heart and he struggled desperately to stay conscious. "My wife, my love. *Mitawicu tewahila ki e*, my beloved wife."

Through the darkening veil that dimmed his vision, Wolf saw a Hunkpapa warrior standing a short distance away. The man's long hair blew about his face and the two eagle feathers tied to his scalplock braid fluttered in a phantom wind. The warrior seemed familiar to Wolf. The man moved closer. A shudder racked his body as a bitter cold began to fill his soul. Wolf remembered the vision. He remembered this spirit man who looked the same as him. He remembered and knew there would be no going back to the village. There would be no warm, welcoming embrace and no ki-iss from his beloved Kechuwa. He knew there would soon be nothing more of this life.

The phantom warrior knelt over Wolf and his body was curtained by the fall of the specter's long hair. The apparition reached out to touch his face with a hand made of shadows and as its fingers grazed Wolf's skin, darkness fell over him, warming him like a welcome blanket. And then there was nothing but peace—sweet, restful peace.

Chapter 32

RYAN HEARD IT immediately. Silence. It resounded louder than any barrage of gunfire that had echoed throughout the hills for the last couple of hours. Ominous. Silence.

In the midst of listening for the slightest sound, she heard the cadence of her own heart. It resounded louder and louder until the rhythm joined the pounding of running feet. All around her, the women and children rushed out to the edge of the camp. Excitement filled the encampment as they anxiously watched the northeast horizon.

"They are coming!" one woman called out. "I can see them. Look over there . . . and there!"

"I see nothing but a big cloud of dust," another added.

"I see," an older woman cried. "*Ka mihignake kin e!* There is my husband!"

"There is my son," another shouted.

As the warriors neared, they raised their lances to show off the war trophies they had taken and their loud victory whoops told everyone of their success across the river. The men fired their rifles and the loud reports made their horses jump and fidget as if they were still on the battlefield.

With a sound that defied description, the women chorused together in a succession of high-pitched trills to honor

their men. Their lulus crescendoed, rising to a deafening
height and then they ran forward, hands grasping and grabbing, taking the bloodied scalps from the tips of the warrior's lances. Brandishing the grisly prizes over their heads,
they continued to yell for a long time. The victory celebration had begun.

Ryan wove her way through the crowd, scanning each
group of riders for Wolf. He hadn't been in the first party
that had come in, and she moved on. She dodged galloping
ponies and ducked under the lances as the warriors passed
them to their wives.

Standing on tiptoe, she tried to see over the heads of the
people. "Wolf!" She hoped her voice could rise above the
women's trilling. "Wolf!" Would he hear her and answer?
"Wolf!"

There was no reply.

A second war party rode into camp and her search began
again. A painful thud resounded beneath her breast as she
frantically looked from one war-painted face to the next
without success. A third and then a fourth band passed and
still she hadn't found him. An ominous chill suddenly slithered around her heart. She hadn't seen Eagle Deer, either.
Pushing through the crowd, she looked across the camp
toward the river.

More riders approached from the north and now nearly
mad with worry, Ryan rushed out to meet them. Stepping
into their path, she anxiously looked for Wolf, searching
the faces of thirty or forty men as they reined their horses
around her. Yes! Here were warriors she knew. There was
Rabbit and Makes No Bow, Keeps His Horse and Bear
Heart. Near the back of the group she spied Otter Skin.
Thank God! There was Eagle Deer. Relief washed over her.
Wolf would be with this group. He was safely home.

Moving back to the edge of the path, she waited. The
men's voices were hoarse from hollering their victory yells
and their horses, though tired from battle, still had enough
energy to prance proudly and toss their heads.

As he rode by, Rabbit glanced at her, his expression
stoic. His face held no warmth, no greeting, and then he

looked away. Riding on into camp, he never looked back. How odd. She frowned and watched him for a moment, toying with the puzzle, but soon let it pass. It had been a hard day for everyone. Maybe he was as eager to be with his family as she was to feel Wolf's arms hold her close.

Turning back toward the battleground, she realized Eagle Deer was no longer with the other men. He had stopped his horse beside her, blocking her view. Why didn't he move aside? She wouldn't be able to see Wolf when he rode into camp.

"Please, let me pass. I'm looking for Wolf."

Lifting her gaze to meet Eagle Deer's dark eyes, an icy current rushed through her veins and left her shivering. Something was wrong. Eagle Deer's cheeks were wet with tears. What a curious sight. Lakota warriors didn't cry.

"Kechuwa." Eagle Deer's rasping whisper nearly became lost in the noise of the celebrating camp. "You need not look for him. He is not among us anymore."

A numbness spread throughout her body and she felt paralyzed. Stunned. A roar of silence came from within; cold and empty, heavy and filled with anguish. "No!" she wailed as an unbearable pain robbed her senses. Rushing forward, she beat her fists against Eagle Deer's thigh. "No, it's a lie!"

He turned away. To watch her grief was not polite.

"Tell me you're lying." Tears spilled unchecked. "You're lying! Liar! Liar!" She fisted her hands and held them tightly against her breasts as an agonized scream tore from her throat. "No-o-o-o." Falling in the dirt beside Eagle Deer's horse, she didn't feel the sharp bite of the rocks as they bruised and cut her knees. "Wolf!" Rocking back and forth, she buried her face in her hands and wailed. "Wolf, my Wolf . . ."

She blindly fumbled at her belt, reaching until her fingers closed around the bone handle of her knife. Not questioning what she must do, she withdrew the blade from the sheath. Wolf had been her husband and she had become a Lakota. She would mourn as a Lakota wife should. Her physical pain would match the torment in her heart. Closing her eyes and biting down on her bottom lip, she slowly began to draw the blade across her forearm.

"No, my sister," Pretty Feather said quietly, stepping forward and placing her hand on Ryan's, stopping the knife's progress. "Do not mourn for your husband in this way." Prying the knife way, Pretty Feather wrapped her arms around Ryan's shoulders and held her close. "That is not the *wasicu* way."

"But Wolf . . . ," Ryan wept. Breaking into deep sobs, she surrendered to Pretty Feather's comforting embrace. "My husband was Lakota . . . ," she choked through her tears. "His ways have become mine."

"No, Kechuwa," Pretty Feather said. "What once was is now done. It is over. Now you must return to your own kind."

"How can I go anywhere . . . without him?" Sobs punctuated her words and shook her body.

"You will learn. It will not be easy, but you will learn."

Pulling away from Pretty Feather's embrace, Ryan scrambled to her feet. She rushed to Eagle Deer and grasped his hand. "Please. Take me to him. Show me where he is."

"That place is not for you," he answered looking across the river at the battlefield. "That place is full of death."

"Please. Take me there." Ryan tilted her head and boldly lifted her trembling chin, but her small gesture of defiance was proven counterfeit by her tears. Squaring her shoulders, she challenged Eagle Deer again. "If you won't take me, I'll follow the women when they go to take what they want from the dead soldiers." She backed away and turned toward the river.

"Come," Eagle Deer sighed, yielding to her request. He held his hand out to her. "I will take you there."

The buckskin picked its way back across the river, steadying itself and its double cargo against the strong current. It balked at the embankment until Eagle Deer dug his heels into its sides and drove it up over the lip of the river. Overhead, a flock of buzzards had already begun to circle the field, waiting for just the right moment to swoop down and fill their bellies.

Ryan gasped as the buckskin crested the slope. Nothing she had studied in history could have prepared her for what she saw. It didn't matter where she looked—the carnage of the battle that had lasted little more than thirty minutes lay everywhere. Two hundred and twenty-six members of the United States Seventh Cavalry lay dead, their bodies scattered across the hills and gullies. Some looked as though they were merely sleeping, while others lay twisted in grotesque poses, their bloody wounds plain to see. She clamped her hand over her mouth and nose, hoping to lessen the roll of nausea that coiled in her stomach, hoping to ease the bite of smoke and dust that still hung in a thick cloud over the field.

Eagle Deer's horse plodded up the incline and when it paused at the top, Ryan saw a sight that no other white, man or woman, had ever beheld. In the center of a circle of bodies that included his brother Tom and his cousin Boston, George Armstrong Custer lay dead.

"Stop," she requested. "Please stop here."

"This is not where your husband is," Eagle Deer said.

"There's something I have to see."

For a moment she became the scientist again. Here was her chance, the opportunity of a lifetime . . . of *two* lifetimes. The women from camp hadn't arrived yet to collect their plunder and Custer's body hadn't been touched since the Cheyenne and Lakota had left the field. Here was the chance to prove or disprove all the rumors that had circulated since his death. Had Custer committed suicide? Was the single bullet hole in his body from his own gun? Or, had he truly died a victim of the battle? For a long moment Ryan stared at the scene and contemplated the possibilities of finally knowing the answer. All of the evidence was right before her, fresh and untouched.

She tapped Eagle Deer on the arm. "Please, go nearer."

Eagle Deer kicked his horse and the buckskin moved closer.

Custer had fallen facedown over another soldier's body

and the bullet hole in his head appeared to be his only wound.

No, this is useless. Whatever I learn here is useless. She glanced away. What good would it do if she did find the answer? She could never write anything about her findings. She would never be able to cite any information she gathered here in any of her work. So, what did it matter? It would only answer her own curiosity, and she no longer cared. There was only one thing that mattered.

She turned away from George Armstrong Custer and the Seventh Cavalry. "Take me to my husband, now."

Eagle Deer turned his horse away from the hilltop. Crossing a slight wash, they rode down the other side of the knoll to a flat grassy place. "There," he said, directing Ryan's attention down the grade. "He is there."

At first all she saw was Wolf's pinto. It stood off to the west of the gully, grazing calmly. Raising its head, the horse pricked its ears forward, nickered and watched their descent down the hillside.

Near the bottom of the slope, she saw him. "Wolf. Oh, my God. . . ." Her voice caught in her throat.

Sliding quickly from Eagle Deer's horse, she ran the rest of the distance down the hill. The soles of her moccasins slipped on the grass and a couple of times she almost fell. Near the bottom of the grade, she slid again and stumbled the last few steps to Wolf's side.

He lay on his back, his eyes closed as if he were asleep. But the bloodied stripe along the edge of his left jaw, the seeping wound on his chest and the widening bloody pool beneath him proved his sleep was forever. For a moment she stood over him, still unwilling to believe that any of this was possible; unwilling to believe he was dead. A little voice tucked in the corner of her heart told her if she waited long enough, Wolf would wake up and it would all have been a bad dream. She knew the voice was wrong. The leavings of the battle were not a dream and they would haunt her forever.

She looked at the body next to Wolf. Iron Soldier! She frowned. Why was Iron Soldier so close? They weren't

friends in life—why would they have died so close together? Glancing around, she searched the surrounding
field. There were no other bodies in the arroyo. And then
the answer quickly uncoiled in her mind and she knew.
Ground Plum's words had been true. Wolf hadn't died
fighting the Seventh. Iron Soldier had killed him.

Nausea rolled from the pit of her stomach, and turning
away, she retched into the tall grass. As her belly emptied,
the heat of her rage filled her. She wanted to kick and
pummel Iron Soldier's body. He was nothing more than a
vile animal and she wanted to make him suffer for the pain
he'd caused. She wanted to kill him all over again for what
he had taken from her.

"*Wicahca*, my husband, my love," she moaned, falling
to her knees beside Wolf. She tenderly brushed away the
strands of hair that covered his face and plucked away some
twigs and dried grass that had become entangled in its
length. Her fingers lightly brushed a smudge of dirt from
his forehead and traced the wound along the edge of his
jaw. Bending lower, she lovingly cupped his cheek in the
palm of her hand and placed her lips upon his mouth for
one last kiss. His skin was warm.

Her heart leapt with hope and she glanced up at Eagle
Deer. "He's alive! *Ni ye!* He's alive!" She placed her fingertips on Wolf's temple and then on his throat. She
couldn't feel a pulse in either place, but maybe he'd lost
so much blood that his pulse was weak. She searched again.
Nothing. Was she doing it wrong? "Come here, touch him,"
she called to Eagle Deer. "He's warm." She bent down
again and laid her he cheek against Wolf's. "Please, hurry!
He's alive! Help me take him back to camp."

She looked up at Eagle Deer. He hadn't moved.

"What's wrong with you!" she screamed. "He's your
friend. Why won't you help him? He's alive!"

"No, Kechuwa," Eagle Deer finally answered, looking at
her with eyes filled with compassion. "My brother is no
longer among us. It is the sun that keeps his body warm.
Nothing more."

"No!" she cried, gathering Wolf up in her arms and cradling his head against her breasts. She laid her cheek on his head and tears rolled from her eyes, wetting his hair. How could she survive without him? How could she think of life when all she wanted to do was join him in death?

"Come, my sister, it is time we go."

"No," she moaned. "I won't leave him here." She wrapped her arms more tightly around Wolf's body. "I won't leave him out here for the buzzards. I won't leave him beside . . . that," she spat, glaring at Iron Soldier's body.

"What would you have me do?" Eagle Deer moved closer.

"Help me bury him," she answered between tears. "Help me take him away from this horrible place. Please."

Eagle Deer slid from the buckskin, and placing a comforting hand on her shoulder, drew a deep breath. "Show me where you would take him."

With the final rock set in place on top of the shallow grave they had dug using little more than sticks and their hands, Ryan knelt beside it. Barely able to see through her tear-swollen eyes, she placed a handful of white daisies on Wolf's grave, one by one.

"I will love you always," she whispered, the words catching in her throat. "No one else will ever know my love. It will *never* belong to anyone but you."

She had led Eagle Deer to the beautiful secluded place near the river where Wolf had taken her to make the bundle. Wolf would rest quietly here. She would be able to remember this special place, with happiness and despair. Kissing the last delicate daisy, she placed the bright little flower beside the others. Her fingers lingered, moving lightly upon the rocks as though giving her lover one last caress.

"Come." Eagle Deer placed his hand under her arm and pulled her to her feet. "It is done."

They rode back to camp in silence. She knew Eagle Deer's grief was as deep as her own. The two men had known each other all their lives. They had grown up together, had been closer than brothers, and now the friendship, that special bond between them, was broken by death.

Resting her head against Eagle Deer's back, she kept her eyes closed all the way back to camp and her body swayed rhythmically with each step the horse took. She felt empty. The horse slowed its step and stopped. Looking up, Ryan blinked against the late afternoon sun. At one camp after another the women worked, taking down the lodges and packing their belongings. Circles on the ground, completely trampled flat or denuded of grass, showed where each tipi had once stood. It wouldn't be long before the whole camp was dismantled. Horses with travois poles secured in place stood patiently, their tails swishing at flies, waiting for the bundles of belongings to be loaded. Some of the tipis had been completely torn down; on others the outer covers had been removed, leaving the lodge poles standing like tall, conical skeletons. Even the children worked hard, toting parfleches and storage bags and piling them onto the travois or stacking them beside the packhorses.

Pretty Feather waited for them outside Wolf's tipi, her hand resting lightly on her swollen belly. As Ryan slid from the horse's back, Pretty Feather stepped forward and placed her arms around her, holding her, comforting her. "Come, I would talk with you."

She led Ryan into the tipi. It was stuffy in the lodge and Ryan lifted the sides of the cover, feeling the rush of cooling air. With only one side done, she stopped, unable to concentrate on the easiest of chores. This simple task had been the first thing Wolf had taught her.

"My sister," Pretty Feather said, gently placing her hand on Ryan's arm. "Leave what you are doing."

Ryan didn't protest when Pretty Feather led her to the sleeping pallet on the woman's side of the lodge and pulled her down to sit on the bed. Her eyes sought out Wolf's place at the back of the lodge. Another wave of misery fell over her as her gaze fell on his possessions. She knew each item by heart—the neat pile of furs, the stack of well-made parfleches, his bed, the beautifully decorated storage bags, and the wrapped package holding the unfinished medicine bundle. Each filled her with memories of Wolf, memories that magnified her despair.

"Soon we will leave this place," Pretty Feather said, interrupting Ryan's cheerless thoughts. "It is no longer safe here. I have given it thought while you were gone. If you wish to come with us, my sister, there is a place in my tipi . . . and my husband's bed for you." She looked shyly at Ryan. "You were Eagle Deer's brother's wife; it is what should be."

Ryan offered a small smile. Pretty Feather's proposal came as no surprise. Eagle Deer and Wolf had been as close as true brothers. It was only customary that Pretty Feather would make this offer for Wolf's woman to become Eagle Deer's second wife. Anthropologists had a name for the practice: levirate.

Taking Pretty Feather's hand in her own, she mutely shook her head. "I'm honored," she said, "but, do you remember what you told me before?" She met Pretty Feather's dark eyes. "You told me the Lakota ways were no longer mine. You were right."

"What will you do? Where will you go?"

Ryan shrugged. What *would* she do? She didn't know. Where *could* she go? She had no answer for this, either. Reno and Benteen and their men were still out in the hills. She had become trapped in time and there was only one reasonable solution. She would have to live out the rest of her life in the 1800s and pretend for the rest of her life that the Lakota had captured her. Was this how people completely disappeared without a trace? Somewhere down deep inside her heart, a little grain of hope still flourished. Maybe if she stayed with the tipi, Wolf's tipi, maybe somehow she could go home—back, or was it forward, into the future. But that all depended on Charley Crying Wolf and his magic, didn't it?

She spied the package near Wolf's bed that held the unfinished medicine bundle. *The least I can do is finish it and bury it as Charley wanted. Maybe I can still help Charley and his grandson, Dillon, stop the thievery . . . even if I never make it back.*

"I'll stay here," she finally answered, looking at Pretty Feather. "I'll wait for the bluecoats and ask them to take me to the soldier fort with them." She lightly touched Pretty Feather's arm. "You must leave, though. Other *wasicu* come tomorrow and there will be more fighting."

"That is your decision?" Pretty Feather asked softly.

"Yes."

"I will miss you always, my friend, my white sister."

"And I'll miss the Lakota so very much. Especially you and Eagle Deer and your boys. I'll often wonder about this little one," she added, tentatively touching Pretty Feather's belly. "I'll think of you all and wish that—" Tears suddenly filled her eyes and tumbled from them.

Pretty Feather drew Ryan into her arms. "There will always be talk and good thoughts among my people for the *wasicu wakan* and the gifts she brought to our hearts."

She was alone. Little over two hours had passed since the last of the Hunkpapa had left the Greasy Grass and headed westward, kicking up a great cloud of dust and leaving a wide swath of travois and horse tracks on the ground. The good-byes had been difficult. She had given all of Wolf's belongings away until there was nothing left. It was the Lakota way.

Eagle Deer had proudly held Wolf's Winchester rifle over his head in a final salute and she had given most of the trade blankets and storage bags to Pretty Feather. Sitting Bull had solemnly accepted a buffalo robe and wished her well before taking his leave. Gall had silently accepted a beautiful quilled pouch and Turtle Rib had graciously taken the silver crucifix and Wolf's medicines and tobaccos. She gave a large piece of red calico to Ground Plum. The last gift she gave was Wolf's pinto. She had placed the pinto's rein in Eagle Deer's eldest son's hands and had smiled when the boy's eyes filled with wonderment. The rest of Wolf's horses were divided among the tribe. She kept nothing for herself except the memories that would never tarnish or fade with time.

North along the river, some of the other Sioux still

camped. Most of the Cheyenne were still there, too. Within twenty-four hours they all would be gone, burning the prairie behind them and raising a high wall of smoke to help their escape. One small skirmish with the cavalry would take place the next day, but the Battle of the Little Big Horn was over.

The phony medicine bundle weighed heavily in her hands. She had finished wrapping it in strips of red calico and tied the fabric in a series of knots down the front. Using an oilcloth rain slicker that had been confiscated from the battlefield and brought to her by one of the Lakota, Ryan tightly wrapped it around the bundle. Tucking in the coattails and tying up the sleeves, the bundle would be nearly impervious to moisture, dirt and time. It was done.

Searching through the camp debris, she found an old metal cooking pot. It would do in place of a shovel. Walking along the outer edge of the camp, she looked for familiar landmarks that would help her locate the exact spot where Stockard, Kovacs and MacMillen had been digging when she left. The trees weren't as tall and a lot of the scrub brush and grasses were different, but she found the large flat rock near the spot where Gaffney had ordered the latest dig grids placed. The site was perfect.

It was long after dark by the time she'd finished her second burial for the day. Packing the soil down over the fresh scar in the ground, she scattered twigs and dried grass over the spot. She didn't want anyone coming across this before the right time, over 120 years away.

Standing, she looked at the ever-moving Greasy Grass and rubbed the small of her back. She was exhausted. It was odd being in camp without another soul around. Knowing that Custer and his men still lay across the river where they had died added a cold, eerie quality to the whole valley. Would their ghosts be restless tonight?

Shivering, she turned, and without a backward glance, headed back to the tipi. It stood alone in the moonlight, the only lodge left where there had been so many only hours before. Stepping inside, she felt the tight misery of grief wrap itself around her heart. "Wolf," she wept. "My love."

Removing the buckskin dress and moccasins, Ryan carefully folded them, setting them at the foot of her palette. Unable to bear being in Wolf's bed without him by her side, she stretched out on her own palette. She lay awake for hours, remembering every wonderful moment she had shared with her warrior. Sometime, an hour or two before dawn, she finally fell asleep.

He came to her in her dream and touched her. The blue flame rose all around them and enveloped them in its embrace. In the misty world of illusion he touched her, he loved her and as dawn intruded, he said farewell.

Chapter 33

"WELL, WELL," BETH Thomas exclaimed. "Would you look at you." She quickly moved to the bedside and looked down at Dillon Wolf. Not only were his eyes open, but he had followed her movement across the room. He was conscious. "Welcome back, Mr. Wolf." She smiled. Scanning the monitors at his bedside, she couldn't find an illicit beep or a blip. Pulse, respirations, temperature, blood pressure, reflexes—each was normal. Checking his eyes, there was no hint of the sluggish pupil response to light and dark that had been there only hours before, either. "You gave us all quite a scare, but I told 'em you'd come back like you were just waking up from a nap." She couldn't help grinning.

Picking up the bedside phone, she called the unit secretary's desk. "Sharon, page Dr. Sloan. Tell him I won't be doing any naked dancing after all." There was silence at the other end of the line. "Sharon," Beth Thomas giggled, "just tell Dr. Sloan that Dillon Wolf is awake."

The exam had taken a little over twenty minutes and both Ned Sloan and Beth walked away puzzled.

"I don't get it—not one bit." Sloan double-checked the entries he'd just made in Dillon's chart. "Earlier today we thought he was a goner, and now this." He flipped the cover on the clipboard back into place and slid it into the chart rack. "He's complaining about some vivid dreams and I'm going to keep him for a couple of days for observation, but unless he takes another nosedive, there's no reason why he can't be discharged then."

"It's a damn miracle," Beth Thomas whispered, looking back through the open ICU door at Dillon. "If I didn't know better, I'd swear to God he's been through nothing more than a light bump on the head." Leaning against the nursing station counter, she crossed her arms over her chest and continued to stare at Dillon.

"See you girls later," Ned Sloan said, turning to leave.

Beth caught his sleeve. "Hey, tell me something," she asked, a frown creasing her brow. "Just what was all that stuff he was mumbling about George Armstrong Custer?"

Chapter 34

RYAN BOLTED UPRIGHT. Her heart wildly ricocheted beneath her breasts and a clammy film of perspiration coated her skin. She had been dreaming that she was falling, tumbling through space. Even now that she was awake, disquieting tendrils of the feeling remained. She tried breathing deep, calming breaths, but it was long moments before the rapid pace of her pulse settled and the queasy feeling tormenting the pit of her stomach dissipated.

She glanced up through the smoke hole. The sun was already high in the sky, shining hot and bright.

How long had she slept? It must be close to ten o'clock. A wry smile curved her mouth. It was the first she had thought about the hourly measurement of time in many, many days.

Something else was different. She listened. Silence. The camp was unusually quiet. Where was everyone? Why hadn't Wolf wakened her? Where was he?

And then the answers came. Cruelly unfolding, they brought a terrible aching to her soul. Wolf was gone. Tears spilled onto her cheeks. She lay still. Breathing in ragged, shallow draughts of air, she fought the agonized wails that threatened to break through. Gone. Every moment of the previous day came back in minute detail. Gone. She would never feel his arms holding her again. She would never taste his kisses or hear his laughter again. She would never know sweet, fiery passion again. Gone.

Ryan knew there was only one course she could take. She had no choice but to try to cope with her sorrow and survive, and that meant meeting up with Reno and Benteen and the ragtag remnants of the Seventh. Throwing in her lot with the cavalry was her only hope, but coming up with a believable story would be another problem entirely. *They're going to be damned surprised to find a white woman in this Lakota camp. I have to put my heart on hold and live each day as though Wolf never existed anywhere but in my dreams.*

Ryan raised her hands to wipe the tears from her cheeks. As she lifted her arms, the soft pink blanket fell from her breasts and puddled at her waist.

"What the . . . oh, my God!" She looked down the length of her body. *A blanket—a fuzzy, pink blanket!*

Quickly propping herself up on her elbow, she glanced around the interior of the tipi. Everything looked a little out of whack. Why? In a moment it was clear. The perspective was different from what it had been for the last couple of weeks. Yes, that was it. She reached down. The floor of the tipi wasn't where she had expected it to be. She was about two feet higher than the sleeping pallet. Running her hands along under her body, she felt the quilt-stitching of a mattress, and slightly shifting her weight, she heard the metal squeak of bedsprings. She was lying in her camp cot.

Swinging her legs over the edge, she sat upright. The trip-hammer beat of her heart picked up as she gawked around the interior of the lodge. Everything was as it had been the night she had returned from the Laundromat. The two camp chairs sat near the fire pit. Her shirt and underwear hung from the back of one and her jeans lay over the other where she had left them to dry. Her shoes and socks were on the ground by one of the chairs and her notebooks, tape recorder, cassettes and laptop computer still sat on top of her suitcase.

"Good God," she whispered. Her hand shook as she raked her fingers through her hair. Her pulse kicked into overdrive and her breaths were little more than raspy pantings.

"Was it all a dream?" Standing, she took a few tentative steps, moving closer to the camp chair where her clothes were. Within a few seconds she knew the truth. Pulling her jeans up over her hips, she made the startling discovery. There was a looseness to the pants that hadn't been there before. Her body felt different, too. She was thinner, more toned. She ran her hand up over her flat stomach and across her breasts. There was definitely a tautness that was new. Her hand traveled higher. One of her earrings was missing. "The bundle," she breathed. Her left forearm was sore. Looking down, she found the wound where she had cut herself. She lightly ran her finger over the bloodied welt. It was very tender. No, none of it had been a dream.

"Wolf." The sound of his name on her lips painfully wrenched her heart and again tears blurred her vision. No, it had not been a dream—the misery she felt, the heartache—it was very real.

She glanced to the back of the tipi where Wolf's bed had been. The place was empty. Turning away, she looked back down at her cot. The pillow and bedding looked odd to her after soft furs and trade blankets. Yes, everything was just as she had remembered and yet everything had changed. She was back where she started. It was June 26, 1999.

Buttoning the shirt that now felt too big, she moved to the tipi door. Reaching out to raise the flap, she paused, her hand hesitating against the soft hide. *If I really have been gone all this time, how am I going to explain it to Gaffney and the others? Maybe Charley took care of that, too.* There was just one way to find out.

Steeling herself against what might greet her beyond the tipi door, she lifted the flap and stepped out into the hot morning sunlight.

"It's 'bout time you got up," Charley greeted her. "Been wonderin' if I was gonna have to start makin' a lot of noise to wake you."

Ryan glanced quickly about the camp.

"Don't worry, ain't nobody here 'cept you and me." Charley Crying Wolf leaned forward in the camp chair. His dark eyes scanned her from head to toe and then moved back to meet her gaze. His concern was obvious but he made no move toward her, nor did he say anything more. He just waited.

If there had been any doubt in her mind about who was responsible for her slide back through time, absolutely none remained now. She met his scrutiny, and the longer he remained silent, the higher her anger boiled up inside her. Charley Crying Wolf was responsible for every bit of the anguish and despair she felt. How could she ever forgive him?

Her voice shook. *"Hotanin ye . . ."* Without thought and with the ease of someone speaking their own language, she had begun to admonish him in Lakota. She shook her head as if trying to dispell all knowledge of the language. "How . . . how could you do that to me?" She blinked, fighting back the return of her tears. Angry, with her hands tightly fisted, she fought the urge to beat mercilessly against Charley's chest. "You had no right—to—to play God with my life!" Using the heels of her hands, Ryan angrily scrubbed at her wet cheeks. "Just who in the hell do you think you are?" she raged. "Didn't you think I might be hurt—not just physically, but emotionally, too?" She glared at him, outrage and despair hot and painful in her chest. "Or didn't you care?" Sobbing, her body shook and she struck her fist over her heart. "It hurts so much—here—it's killing me."

Trying desperately to control her emotions and save whatever scrap of strength and dignity she had left, she turned her back and looked out over the riverbank. She saw nothing; the wash of tears in her eyes was a heavy veil.

"I loved him," she finally breathed. "I loved him and you not only took him away from me, but you left me there to find his body." Accusingly, she turned and faced Charley. "You left me there to bury him . . . with my bare hands." She lifted her hands up and held them out in front Charley. "I scratched away rocks and dirt and dug his grave until my fingers bled." Her voice cracked and trembled. "Damn you, damn you! You had no right."

Unable to stem the flow of tears, she met Charley's gaze again. "Why didn't you leave me there? I could have happily spent the rest of my life with them. But no," she gasped, drawing a ragged breath, "*you* had a master plan. You had a selfish, meddlesome, inhuman plan to save dried grasses and herbs, and beads and feather trinkets. What's so damned important about old moccasins and bundles, Charley? What about the people? What about just saving the people?"

Charley didn't answer as she continued to stare into his dark, impassive face. Wearily, she closed her eyes and stroked the back of her hand across her forehead. Then, meeting Charley's eyes again, she continued. "If you've known for a long time that you had this miraculous talent, or knowledge, or power, or whatever it is, why couldn't you have used it to stop the whole thing two or three hundred years ago? You could have had the treaties rewritten and made sure they were honored. You could have seen that the right men led the people and that the right laws were written and enforced, that Indian lands weren't taken and people weren't killed."

Charley remained still.

"Why waste all that power on me?" She tore her gaze from Charley. With hopelessness filling her heart, she looked up at the blue sky. "Why me, Charley, why me?"

The weight of her despair pressed too heavily and she dropped to her knees beside the old Lakota. Leaning against him, she rested her head on his thigh. In a moment she felt Charley's touch as he lightly rested his hand on her head and then began to stroke her hair. A sigh, filled with the sound of her misery, left her lips.

"There is nothing I can say to you at this time that will ease the wounds I have put in your heart," Charley Crying Wolf said softly. "Sometimes we cannot choose what we must do, even if it brings pain to others."

Ryan sobbed. "I hurt so much."

"I know," Charley answered. "I know." With his index

finger under Ryan's chin, he made her lift her head until her eyes met his. "Remember, granddaughter, nothing *Tunkasila* asks of us is cruel or wicked. Sometimes he asks for things that seem to cost us a price too great to bear, but it is for these things that he gives us the greatest rewards in return." He brushed a lock of hair away from her cheek. "I do not know all that you experienced with the ancestors. I hope someday you would share these things with me. You were promised safety, but I see a great pain in your sky eyes. I do not have the power to take the hurt away." He lifted her into his lap and cradled her, rocking her in his arms as if she were a child. "You will see. Someday you will see that you have received a great blessing," he said, holding her face in the palm of his hand. "And, you have done a good thing for the Lakota and the Cheyenne." He laid his dark cheek against hers. "You had an experience beyond belief." He wiped her tears away. "Can you not be happy and find good in that?"

"Good?" she questioned, pulling away, sarcasm touching her voice. "You want me to find good and happiness in loving someone completely with all my heart and soul and then having to bury him?" Sobs racked her body. She held her hands up again and then fell back against him, pressing her face against his rough flannel shirt. The mixed scent of cedar, sage and tobacco was strong on the fabric. "How can I forget him? I loved Wolf. Did you know I would love him? Did you know that would happen?" She looked up into his face. "How can I go on without him? What is there for me here?"

"Granddaughter, listen carefully and remember my words well. Often what seems to have already gone from us is really coming toward us." He gently rubbed her back. "You will see. In time, soon, the wound in your heart will be gone. . . . I promise." He hugged her close then released her. "Tell me . . . you made something special for the archaeologist?"

"Yes," she replied, her voice still unsteady.

"Good, child." Charley patted her shoulder. "What was it you left in the ground?"

Ryan whispered against his shoulder, "A medicine bundle." She felt the silent nod of his head.

"And, what did you put in it to prove it is false?"

"You mean you don't know?" Ryan challenged sarcastically, leaving his lap and settling herself into one of the camp chairs. "I was positive you knew everything." She sniffed and wiped away her remaining tears. "The dried body of a crow was used as part of the bundle. One of my gold earrings is wrapped in a piece of red calico and stuffed high up into its neck."

Charley nodded. "You did well, my granddaughter. You did very well."

"Then why don't I feel good about any of it?"

Charley didn't respond. He slowly rose from the chair and pointed to the large plastic bag on the ground beside him. "Here are the clean clothes you left in Buddy's truck. Go put them in the tipi and then we will sit, have some coffee and talk. We have much to say to each other."

"Just like that?" she asked, dismayed. "You expect me to be able to walk away calmly from everything that has happened to me these past two weeks? You want me just to sit down and chitchat about it like it was nothing more than an ordinary trip to . . . Frontier Land?"

"No, my child," Charley replied, his dark eyes narrowing as a complaisant smile played across his face. "There is much news we will share. My grandson, Dillon, is doing well. He came out of the coma last evening and when I talked to the doc this morning, he said they're gonna be sending him in a couple of days. We will talk about that." He looked at her and nodded as if asking her approval. "Then, I will tell you what Gaffney and everyone was told while you were gone. And when I run out of things to say, you can tell me all about your journey."

She looked at Charley and silently shook her head. "I don't know how you did it and I don't know if I really want to know. She glanced away, her gaze following the path from the campsite down to the river, and suddenly she felt the burden of her sorrow return. "I'm not even sure if I believe any of it really happened."

"It happened," Charley softly replied. "Every bit of it happened."

She drew a deep, ragged breath. The pain would be difficult to bear but she would learn to live with it—somehow. No matter how lonely it was going to be, life would continue. She offered a small smile. "Charley, I'm glad to hear about your grandson, Dillon. I'm happy he's doing so well and is going to be home soon."

"I knew you would be," Charley replied, turning away to hide his grin and to whisper faintly one last word. "Kechuwa."

The morning had been a futile four hours of digging away at the hard-packed dirt, an inch at a time. The others had headed back to camp for lunch and to catch up on gossip, but he had remained to work the dig. His new customer was getting impatient. "This damned ground better cough up something soon," he muttered, picking up his trowel.

Now that Ryan was better and back to work, the project was moving along smoothly. In the two weeks since she had returned, she'd not only continued with her interviews, but the data she'd collected was some of the best work he had ever seen. Her expertise surprised him. Having her on the project had worked out very well, but sometimes the memory of the other woman was difficult for him.

Wiping the sweat from his brow with the sleeve of his shirt, he stretched, relieving his back of the kinks and stiffness that had set in after hours of bending over the grid. The July sun had been unmerciful for the past few days. "I'm getting too damned old for this," he muttered, using the small trowel to scrape away another inch of dirt. In the middle of a delicate sweep with the tool, the point caught on what first appeared to be a piece of root. Changing to a smaller tool, he continued to clear away the hard-packed soil. Slowly, he uncovered more and more of the artifact. What at first had looked like a root proved to be a piece of yellow oilcloth. Excited, he began to dig a little quicker, still taking care not to damage the find.

I just hope I can get this damn thing out of here and see

what it is before the others get back, he thought.

Within fifteen minutes he had completely freed the whole artifact from the ground. It was like nothing he had ever come across before, and his pulse raced with excitement. His trained eye quickly appraised what he held in his hand. It was fairly large, at least two feet in length and every bit of twelve or fourteen inches around. Whatever the actual item was inside, it was wrapped in an oilcloth rain slicker, army issue, circa 1875. The coat carefully swaddled the item and intuition told him when he untied the sleeves, whatever the package held would be in perfect condition. Now his only problem would be getting it back to his tent without anyone else seeing what he had found or suspecting he had found anything at all.

"My jacket," he murmured. "I'll carry it under my jacket." His fingers itched to open the package right away, but common sense kept his impulse under check. There would be enough time later to discover what the coat held. If it was worthwhile, he'd use the pay phone up at the tourist center to call his customer.

For the next twenty minutes he worked diligently, refilling the hole and pounding the dirt down as best he could with a rock. Using the flat of his hand, he smoothed out the grid. If he left even the slightest indentation in the ground, it might be suspect.

Wrapping the package in his jacket, a small smile played across his lips. "No artifact cabinet for this." Satisfied that everything at the dig appeared to be normal, he headed back to the project camp.

The telephone on the bedside table rang loudly. Startled from his sleep, Stanton Adams fumbled in the dark until his fingers closed around the receiver.

"H'lo," he mumbled, his word barely intelligible.

"Bingo!"

"What? Who's this?"

"What d'ya mean 'who's this'? Stan, it's me—Delveccio. For God's sake man, wake up. I think we're ready to cook our pigeon."

"You're kidding," Stanton Adams exclaimed, all foggy remnants of sleep gone from his head. "When have ya got the buy going down?"

"Tomorrow evening at seven. You gonna make it out here?"

"Wouldn't miss this party for anything. Did ya talk to Dillon Wolf?"

"Yeah, he's with me right now. So's his grandfather."

"What's the artifact?" Adams asked.

"Medicine bundle. He says it's in the original condition."

"Fantastic," Stanton Adams exclaimed. "Herb, put Dillon on the line, I wanna talk to him."

"Okay, here he is."

"Dillon?" Adams asked.

"Yeah, right here."

"Good to have you back among the living. You gave us quite a scare."

"I wasn't too pleased with it myself," Dillon responded.

"We are gonna need both you and your grandfather with us all the way on this one," Stanton Adams said. "Neither of you have any problem with that, do you?"

"I told you right from the beginning, Stan. We intend to see this thing through. No, there's no problem. In fact, I think my grandfather is just the man to help you identify this particular artifact. What Herb didn't tell you was that the guy is trying to pass this piece off as coming from someplace other than the Little Big Horn. My grandfather is an expert on these bundles. He'll be able to tell you exactly where it came from."

"Great," Adams said. "I'll get the next flight out and see you there. Lemme talk with Herb again. Oh, Dillon . . ."

"Yeah?"

"I'm damn glad we're working together on this one."

"Me too," Dillon Wolf replied. "Me too."

Adams heard the telephone being passed from Dillon Wolf's hand to Delveccio's.

"What d'ya need, Stan?"

"I want everything on video. Make sure you get it all set up. I want the buy on film."

"Already thought about that. Listen, Dillon's gonna stick with us on the buy, but Charley Crying Wolf will be waiting for us at the project site. We're still going with the same plan, right? I do the meet, and make the buy and then my boys take him down. That it?"

"That's it," Adams replied. "Sit tight at the motel until I get there. We'll work out the fine details when I get in. Tell Dillon to stay outta sight and away from the project camp, too. I don't want this case blown because he gets recognized. I'll get there as soon as I can."

Ryan had only one interview scheduled for the morning. Buddy had been late going to pick the old Lakota up at his home and then a flat tire had delayed them further. It was late afternoon before she was finally able to sit and chat with her guest.

"See that big oak tree down by the river," seventy-one-year-old Bernard Makes No Bow said, lifting his chin toward the Little Big Horn. "My grandfather used to say it was called *winyan wasicu ska*, the white woman tree." Barney laughed. "I always thought it was a pretty silly name until I saw you sitting up there in the branches when Buddy brought me here today."

Her lips moved in a little secret smile. If Barney only knew. Not only had the tree been named for her, but she had met his grandfather. "I've heard the tree called that by many others I've talked with. Did your grandfather ever tell you why it was given that name?"

"Nope. Can't say he ever did—well, not that I remember, anyway."

"You 'bout ready to go home, Barney?" Buddy had quietly approached and now stood waiting for the old man's answer. "Doc, Grandpa's gonna to stay and visit with you for a while. I'll be back for him later."

Ryan gathered up her notes and clicked off the cassette recorder. "Thank you, Mr. Makes No Bow. I've enjoyed meeting and talking with you."

"This tape you've made today of all these stories I remembered," Barney said, "can I have a copy for my grandchildren? They ain't too interested in these old yarns now, but who knows—maybe someday."

"I'd be happy to make a copy for you," Ryan said.

Nodding his thanks, Barney Makes No Bow waved good-bye and followed Buddy to his truck.

"Looks a lot like his grandfather, doesn't he?"

Startled, Ryan turned to find Charley standing behind her. "Are you determined to give me gray hair like yours," she admonished. "And to answer your question, yes, he looks just like his grandfather." Once more, pain and sadness tinged her voice.

"You still haven't forgiven me, have you?"

"Oh, Charley," Ryan replied sadly as she embraced the old Lakota. "It's just going to take time."

"Maybe tonight will shorten the time you need," he answered with a broad smile.

"What are you talking about?"

"I think our thief is about to discover that the long arm of the federal government has a pair of handcuffs and a forty- or fifty-year lease on nice cozy cell just for him."

"Do you mean the bundle's been found?"

"I thought you'd have kept your eye on that spot like a hawk. It's been dug up since yesterday sometime."

Ryan saw the twinkle in Charley's dark eyes. When he smiled, as he just had, he reminded her of someone, but she couldn't place who. Something else had been bothering her quite a bit as well. Maybe now would be the time to settle the question. "Charley, would you tell me something about—back then and about your tipi, please?"

"I will tell you anything I can. I was wondering when you were going to start asking questions." He motioned for her to sit down and then joined her at the camp table. "Now, what would you like to know."

"Who was *Sunkmanitu Ceye a Pelo* . . . Calls to the Wolf?"

Charley held his hands together and steepling his fingers, rested his chin upon their tips, his dark eyes closely watching Ryan. "What you really want to know is whether he was an ancestor of mine, is that not so?"

"Yes," she breathed, fearful of what he would tell her.

"He was not."

She knew Charley had heard the deep sigh of relief that had escaped her throat.

"*Sunkmanitu Ceye a Pelo* was my grandfather's best friend," Charley answered, his voice hushed and reverent.

"Your grandfather?"

Charley nodded. "My father was a boy in 1876—about twelve years old. When the great warrior Calls to the Wolf was killed across the river over there, his *wasicu* wife gave his spotted warhorse to my father. Do you remember his name?" Charley's eyes never left Ryan's.

"Yes," she whispered with astonishment. "*Sinte Sunka*, Spotted Pony, his father's name was *Tonca Wanbli*, Eagle Deer, and your father's mother was a wonderful woman named *Wiyaka Wasté Win*, Pretty Feather."

Charley smiled, and slightly nodded, "Very good, my granddaughter, very good." He nodded again. "Maybe someday I will ask you to tell me more of my grandparents and my father and uncle. You never did know my aunty. She was born a week or so after Custer died. The name she was given was Dear One, Kechuwa."

She felt numb. It was unfathomable that they were talking calmly about people who had lived over 120 years before, people she had been with only two weeks ago.

"About a year after the battle, my father, who was perhaps thirteen then, fought two bluecoats at the soldier fort who wanted to take his spotted horse away from him. He lost the fight but because he showed great bravery for one so young, he was given a new name, *Sunkmanitu Ceye a Pelo*, in honor of his father's friend. It is the name I now carry. The white man who wrote it in the fort ledgers didn't listen when he was told its meaning and so today my family is known as Crying Wolf."

"And the tipi," Ryan pressed. "How did you get it? I was the last one there."

"My grandfather, Eagle Deer, came back looking for you. When he couldn't find you, he took the tipi skin to give to his eldest son, my father. It is from him that I now have it." Charley paused and watched Ryan for a moment. "This life of ours is like a large circle, only yours took a very special loop. Do not be sad that you had that experience. Someday you will see that it was a great gift."

"Maybe someday," Ryan said, shaking her head and looking away. "It's just too soon now."

Charley placed his hand over Ryan's and gave it a little squeeze. "Granddaughter, I would ask that tonight you stay inside the tipi," Charley said. "Do not say a word to anyone of the bundle. It will all come to an end tonight." Another smile curved his broad mouth. "Sometimes endings also bring new beginnings."

Surprised, Ryan looked back at Charley. "You mean Dr. Gaffney will be arrested tonight?"

Charley simply shrugged his shoulders. "The federal agents are setting the trap as we speak. Stay in the tipi until I call you. You do have the other earring, don't you?"

"Yes, right here," Ryan answered, showing Charley her right ear.

"Good. Now, go change into something pretty. Something other than your work clothes. Tonight will be a very special night to celebrate."

Chapter 35

THE BROWN SEDAN pulled up in front of Room 136 at the Best Western motel.

"He's here," Herb Delveccio said, letting the curtain drop back into place. Opening the door, he moved aside and let Stanton Adams into the room.

"Hello boys, glad to see you," Adams said, greeting each of the FBI agents with a nod. "Where's Dillon Wolf?"

"Next door. I'll get him," one of the agents said, knocking on the door that connected Delveccio's room with the one next to it.

"Where do you stand with your man?" Adams asked Delveccio.

"He's supposed to call on the cellular in about half an hour." Delveccio pointed to the small telephone on the bedside table. "That's when we'll make the final plans for the exchange and get this thing rolling."

"So, he doesn't have any idea where you are?"

"Nope."

Adams nodded his approval, then turned and heartily shook hands with Dillon as he came into the room. "Glad to see you back on your feet."

"Thanks," Dillon replied. "Me too."

"I bet." Stanton nodded, then glanced around the room. "Okay, let's get to it." He settled himself into the motel-clone chair and accepted a cup of coffee one of the agents had taken from a McDonalds bag. "Dillon, you know this area—any ideas where the best place for the exchange would be?"

"You want him close enough to the project site so you can take the bundle back and have Charley authenticate it for you, right?" Dillon waited for Adams's nod before continuing. "Okay. I'd say you get him to meet Herb up on the battlefield. Any one of the sight-seeing roads would work. The park closes at seven-thirty. If you make your drop time about seven-fifteen, the park will almost be empty." He looked around the room to see if anyone's opinion differed. None did and he continued. "Gaffney's Jeep is a common sight up there. The rangers aren't going to take any notice of it. So if he tries to back out of making the switch at the battleground because he'll be recognized, he won't have a leg to stand on."

"That reminds me," Adams said. "We're gonna have to tell the park rangers what's going down. We don't want any screwups at this point." He turned to the tall agent sitting next to him. "Russ, you got a video unit in Herb's car?"

"It's all set," Agent Russell Scott replied. "We replaced the headlight, using one of ours with the camera head in it. The mike is in the grille and the tape unit's under the hood. We installed the switch on the dash. When Herb gets out to make the buy, all he has to do is flip the switch and the video cam starts recording. He'll have a body microphone on him, too. We'll be able to pick up everything."

"Sounds good. What's gonna be your signal for us to come in for the bust, Herb?" Adams asked.

"How about having Herb ask about Reno's Hill," Dillon offered. "It's close to the route you'll be taking and it'll be distinct enough for your guys to pick up. I don't think it's anything that would make him suspicious."

"Good idea," Adams agreed. "We'll use it." Standing, he downed a gulp of coffee, grimaced and put the cup on the table. "How many tourist roads in and out of the battle-ground?"

"Just the one," Dillon answered. "He can't get in or out without passing through the gate."

Adams nodded. "Once we're in, the rangers can close the gate." He turned and looked at Dillon. "I want Herb to make the pickup by himself. But you know this guy, right?"

Dillon nodded with a sarcastic lift to his left brow. "Yeah, I know him."

"We'll need a positive ID." Adams paused and raked his fingers through his gray hair. "Dillon, normally we wouldn't take a civilian into an arrest scene like this—it's too dangerous—but we want you with us to identify him. So if anything starts going wrong—if he pulls a weapon or tries to run—you're gonna have to keep your head down and your ass out of it. Understood?"

"No problem," Dillon answered. "I just want to see the son of a bitch taken down."

"Okay, I think that's it," Adams said, nodding his approval. "Dillon, you'll ride with Agents Scott and Stevens. Jessop and I will be in the second car. After he's cuffed, we'll take him and the bundle back to the project site." Adams tried another sip of coffee. It hadn't improved. "Anyone see problems with any of this, or is it a 'go'?"

Before anyone could answer, the cellular phone on the bedside table began to ring.

Dillon glanced around the tourist center parking lot and then out over the hills. He had always hated the commercialism that had taken over the battleground. At least there was one small consolation; the name had recently changed. It was no longer the Custer Battlefield. The plaques now read, "The Little Big Horn Battleground." He supposed small thanks were due for that.

Other things had changed, too. He had felt the changes in himself almost from the moment he'd resurfaced from his coma. The anger and the hatred didn't seem to goad him half as much, nor bite as deeply. It wasn't that he had softened about the issues he believed in—it just seemed as though his biases and resentments had lessened. He was willing now to work with anyone who could help, white or red. Something had touched him, had changed his heart, but he couldn't remember what.

He sat in the car with Agents Scott and Stevens on the left side of the parking lot. Adams and Jessop were in another bureau car to the far right and Delveccio waited in the white Lincoln rental in front of the museum. Everyone would be able to see the red Jeep when it came up the hill.

"So, you were raised near here, eh?" Special Agent Scott asked, attempting to make small talk to pass the time.

"Yeah, not too far away," Dillon answered, then turned to look out his window again, closing off any further conversation. He scanned the area. It felt strange to be back after so long. No, there was more to it than that. It felt odd for another reason, too. There was something different about the place this time. But what? He hadn't been up on the battlefield since before he had left for law school but couldn't shake the feeling he'd been here more recently. On the way up to the tourist center they had passed Gaffney's project site on the encampment side of the river. He had felt the same stirrings there, too.

An unwieldy sense of melancholy had rested heavily on his heart since his release from the hospital. It had steadily grown worse each day and now, being back on the Greasy Grass made it almost unbearable.

Dillon rubbed his face lightly with his fingers and recoiled slightly. The wound along the left side of his jaw still felt tender. He would have a scar for the rest of his life, but it wasn't too bad a price to pay considering death had been a possible alternative. He was lucky to be alive, but he couldn't shake the uneasiness that had stayed with him since his ordeal in the hospital. It seemed to all be tied to the crazy dreams or hallucinations.

Dr. Sloan had told him most patients didn't remember anything after coming out of their comas. But in his case, this wasn't true. Ever since he had come home to Montana, bits and pieces of the dreams kept playing back in his mind like disjointed snippets of videotape. He remembered the

Greasy Grass, a tipi encampment, a buffalo hunt, and he remembered the battle. There were other memories, too—blue eyes, silky dark hair, a caress that sent his heart racing—but they only teased him, remaining shadowed and just out of reach. He lightly rubbed his temples, trying to ease the slight headache that began each time he tried to remember. *Come on Wolf, what's the big deal. So you had your own version of* Dances with Wolves *playing in your head while you were out of it. So what?* But it had seemed so real. Even now, looking over the hills and gullies of the battlefield, he could feel the excitement of the fight and smell the sharp odor of gunpowder.

"There he is," Agent Scott said.

Dillon looked up and watched Gaffney's Jeep come up the road.

Scott lifted the microphone to his mouth. "Heads up, guys. He's on his way in."

"Got him," Delveccio answered.

"Ten four," Adams responded through a bit of static.

The red Jeep slowed at the gate, then sped up as the park ranger waved it on through. Waiting a few more minutes, Delveccio followed.

"We're taking the left fork around the west drive," Delveccio broadcast through his body mike. "Come on in."

Spacing the cars far enough apart so as not to look suspicious, the agents entered the park and the ranger closed the gate behind them.

"He's pulling over," Delveccio reported after about five minutes. "I'm stopping now. The video cam is on."

Through the car speaker, Dillon heard the entire transaction taking place. He tried to maintain a stoic expression but failed as a broad grin took hold. They were finally nailing this guy.

Delveccio's voice came loud and clear over the radio. "So, tell me, you're familiar with the area . . . are we anywhere near Reno's Hill?"

Stanton Adams's voice blared over the speaker. "That's us, boys. The switch has been made and now it's show time."

"Let's rock 'n roll!" Russell Scott unsnapped the safety strap on his holster, affording ready access to his Smith and Wesson.

Picking up speed, the two bureau cars approached Gaffney's Jeep. At first it appeared they were just going to pass the spot where Delveccio and the archeologist were standing on the roadside, but in a maneuver quick and sure, Scott and Jessop brought their cars to a stop. They parked, one on either side of Delveccio's rented Lincoln and the red Jeep.

"Look at Bambi in the headlights," Scott heartily laughed at the shocked expression on the archeologist's face. "Yes sir, that's one surprised S.O.B."

The agents jumped out of their cars, guns in their hands, and Delveccio had pulled his as well.

Stanton Adams slowly approached the scene and motioned for Dillon to join him. "Is this our man?"

"That's him," Dillon answered, a contemptuous lift to his brow.

Adams gave a slight nod to Delveccio. "Do it."

"Daniel Randolph Stockard," Herb spoke coldly, "FBI, you're under arrest for the theft of federal property."

Not waiting to hear Herb Delveccio read Stockard his rights, Dillon turned and walked back to the car. Hearing the sharp, satisfying metallic click as the handcuffs snapped shut on Stockard's wrists, he smiled.

Charley, Gaffney and Buddy watched the headlights on the four approaching vehicles. The cars bounced down the access road to the encampment site, sending the beams of light dancing against the night sky.

"Well, I guess it's over," Gaffney said with a tired sigh.

"It's not quite finished yet," Charley added.

Shoving his hands deep into his pockets, Gaffney glanced at the old Lakota. "You're right. I owe Ryan a pretty big apology over this whole thing, don't I?"

Charley nodded. "It's due."

"That first night when she arrived and I discovered she was a woman," Gaffney shook his head, "I didn't know what I was going to do. My associate at the university had handled her hiring. I had no idea Dr. Ryan Burke was a young lady. Adams had warned me anyone in camp might be in danger. I figured Kovacs, MacMillen and I could take care of ourselves, but I wasn't sure about Ryan. I felt for her safety that I had to try to get her to leave. The only thing I could come up with was that stupid chauvinistic act." Gaffney turned and headed back to his chair at the table. "I didn't know what Stockard was capable of. He might have tried to gain her sympathies and, well, who knows what could have happened."

Charley nodded in agreement.

"I treated her very poorly," Gaffney confessed. "That young lady's got a lot of gumption." He looked about the camp. "Where is she?"

"I told her to wait in the tipi. I didn't want nothin' to go wrong and have her caught in the middle." Charley glanced at the lodge, pleased to see the flap remained closed. "Buddy'll get her if we need her." He tapped Edwin Gaffney on the chest. "You did a good job. You had everybody fooled, even this old codger." His smile was sincere.

"Man," Buddy exclaimed, wide-eyed. "Why didn't anyone tell me about all this? The FBI, man, this is just too cool!"

The four cars pulled to a stop but the cloud of dust they had kicked up coming over the hill continued to roll on until it dissipated among the tall prairie grasses.

Dillon stepped out from behind the steering wheel of Gaffney's Jeep and after shutting the door, leaned back against the vehicle, crossing his arms over his chest. Disgusted, he watched the agents escort Daniel Stockard over to the table. It made him sick to think that people like Stockard had clear access to things that held such meaning to the Indian people.

Looking up at the full moon that illuminated the old Indian encampment site, the odd feeling of having been here in the old days quickly returned. He gave a cynical laugh. *Must be some newfangled kind of vision quest for city Indians.* Until he could figure out the puzzle, he knew it

would goad him like a sharp nettle. The problem was, he
didn't know quite where to begin to find the answer.

Agent Scott pushed Stockard down into one of the camp
chairs and Herb Delveccio placed a yellow oilcloth bundle
on the table in front of him.

"You're making a big mistake here," Stockard com-
plained, pulling against the handcuffs. "Gaffney's the one
who's been stealing artifacts, not me." Stockard glanced
from Adams to Delveccio. "Ask him about the doll. Ask
him what he did with it. Ask him, but I bet he'll deny it."

Stockard turned his attention to Kovacs and MacMillen,
who stood off to the left of the table. His voice rose, becoming shrill. "Ask them. They know about it. They'll tell
you about the missing doll." He singled out Kovacs. "Pete,
tell 'em!"

"Tell them what?" Kovacs asked. "I don't know anything
about the doll; I never saw it. I only know what you told
us, Dan. There weren't even photographs to prove it ever
existed."

Stockard tried to rise out of his chair but Agent Scott
pushed him back. "Are you saying I lied about the doll?
You're the liar, Pete." He turned and glared at the agents.
"You're all going to get slapped with false arrest suits." His
attention settled on Herb Delveccio. "I told you this medicine bundle didn't come from here. This piece was something I've had for years in my own collection." He slouched
in the chair. "Since when is it illegal to need extra cash to
pay off some bills? That's why I was selling it. If you go
through with this ridiculous charade, I'll have your badge."

Ignoring Stockard's tirade, Delveccio turned to Charley.
"Okay, Mr. Crying Wolf, let's take a look at what we've
got here." He set the bundle in front of Charley. "I think
we're gonna need a little more light. Russ, you got the
video camera? I want every bit of this on tape." With a
turn of the knob on the kerosene lantern, bright light
flooded the table.

Dillon Wolf pushed away from the Jeep and moved to
the table. He tossed the car keys in front of Gaffney. "Next
time, I'd suggest you be more particular about who borrows

your car." Without waiting for Gaffney's reply, Dillon began to walk away.

Charley looked up. "Where you going?"

"I've had enough of all this," Dillon replied coldly. "I'm not needed here for anything else. When you're ready to go home, I'll be down by the river. Just give a holler."

Charley sat at the table and watched his grandson move off into the darkness. He allowed a smile to take up residence on his lips. The smile grew then, broadening to a grin.

"Okay, Mr. Crying Wolf, let's have a look," Stanton Adams said.

Charley's fingers began to move against the knotted cord that held the oilcloth wrap in place.

"Would you describe what you're doing and what you find as you go along?" Stanton Adams requested. "If it's on video it'll help us identify stuff when we go to court."

Charley nodded. Opening up the old raincoat, he exposed the calico bundle inside and began describing everything he was doing and everything he saw. Again his fingers went to work and began undoing the series of four knots that spanned the front of the artifact. Once these were open, he slowly unwrapped the strips of fabric that completely encased the bundle. Charley knew Wolf would have said prayers while he made the bundle and he silently said his own. Even if the bundle was counterfeit, it had been made with true medicine.

As he removed each item from the belly of the dried crow, he catalogued them for the camera. Within fifteen minutes he had extracted everything except a little red calico packet that rested high up in the neck of the bird.

"Gentlemen," Charley said, turning to look at Adams and the four agents. "I think I may have a very pleasant surprise for you, a little something that will save your case a lot of time and trouble." He looked at Stockard. "But *you* ain't gonna like this one little bit." Charley glanced around until he found his grandson. "Buddy, get Ryan for me. She's in the tipi."

"What's she got to do with anything?" Stockard sneered.

"Let's just say that her testimony in this case is 'pure gold.' " Charley chuckled at his pun.

Waiting until Ryan was standing beside him, Charley passed the bundle across the table to Stanton Adams. "I'm gonna to prove that Stockard's story about this being something he's owned for years is a lie. I'm also gonna to prove where it came from, when it was buried and who buried it."

"Impossible," Stockard laughed. "Utterly impossible."

"Mr. Adams," Charley said, ignoring Stockard's outburst, "I'd like you to remove the last item and open it up. This dried up old crow is about to sing like a canary."

Reaching up inside the bird's neck, Stanton Adams dislodged the small calico packet. Pulling it out he placed it on the table and opened the wrapping. As he pulled back the last corner, something gold glinted in the lantern light.

"It's an earring!" Adams exclaimed and then frowned. "So, what's it supposed to mean?"

"Mr. Adams," Charley began. "This isn't just any earring. Who it belongs to, how it got in the bundle and why it was put there are what's important."

"This is ridiculous," Stockard scoffed. "You all saw him open the bundle. It hadn't been opened in years. What does the old man know about this earring? I demand to be released at once. You've got no proof of anything."

"Shut up, Stockard," Adams interrupted. "Go on, Mr. Crying Wolf."

Charley carefully picked up the small golden disk. "Does this look familiar to anyone?"

For a moment no one spoke and then Buddy stepped forward, his eyes wide with surprise. "Yeah, it sure does. It looks just like Ryan's earrings—you know, Grandpa? The ones she wears all the time." He glanced at Ryan's ears. "Hey, you've lost one."

"No she hasn't," Charley said with a deep chuckle. "It's right here."

"What?" Stockard tried to stand up but Agent Scott pushed him back into the chair. "That's impossible. You can't prove it's hers. There are lots of earrings that look like that."

"That's possibly true, Dr. Stockard," Charley replied, slowly twirling the earring by its backing. "I'm no smart archaeologist like you. I didn't go to any expensive fancy schools and I ain't got no pretty certificates on my wall, but I don't think this kinda earring was available over a hundred years ago. I bet if Mr. Adams looks real close at the back of this earring, he's gonna find some engraving on it."

Charley passed the earring to Stanton Adams, who immediately put on his glasses and moved the kerosene lantern closer.

"Yup, there's three initials, RBB, and the date 6–11–70."

"Those three letters are Ryan's initials, and the date is her birthdate," Charley offered. "Gentlemen, I think you'll find this earring is identical to the one in Dr. Burke's right ear." Charley pointed at Ryan. "What it proves is that the bundle came from the ground here at the encampment and never was in Stockard's private collection. Dr. Burke will tell you she buried the phony bundle herself on the evening of June 25. Isn't that right, Ryan?" Charley looked up at her and winked. "Although the bundle's a fake, Dr. Stockard took it from the project site and tried to sell it as the real thing." Charley shook his head with disgust. "Some big-time *wasicu* scientist. Couldn't even tell a real one from a phony."

"It's . . . it's a lie!" Stockard spluttered. "You just planted that earring! You're trying to frame me!"

"Well, that does it for me," Adams said, ignoring Stockard's outburst and collecting the pieces of the bundle off the table. "Dr. Burke, I'm afraid we'll have to keep your earring for a while for evidence, but I promise it'll be returned to you." Turning to Agents Scott and Stevens, he pointed at Stockard. "Get him outta here, boys."

Taking hold of Stockard's arm, Agent Scott lifted him to his feet. "Let's go. It's time for you to take a little ride."

"No!" Stockard shrieked, pulling against Agent Scott's grip. "They're lying! There's no way you can believe this.

It can't be her earring. I tell you, she couldn't have buried that bundle just a couple of weeks ago." He dug his heels into the dirt. Shrugging out of the agent's grasp, Stockard drew a deep, resigned breath. "Okay, yeah, I'll tell you the truth. I dug that bundle out of the ground here, but it was hard-packed dirt. It was natural hard-packed dirt that hadn't been disturbed for years, a hundred years, over a hundred years." As the agents pushed him toward one of the bureau's cars, Stockard continued to rant. "Listen to me! There's no way, not even using a ten-ton roller to pack the ground down. . . . She couldn't have put the bundle there on the twenty-fifth!" Even after Agent Scott closed the car door, Stockard continued to rage. "I'm an archaeologist. Listen to me. I know about these things. That ground hadn't been dug up in years. It was hard-packed, damn it! I had to use a pick."

Stanton Adams offered his hand first to Gaffney, to Charley and then to Ryan. "We've really appreciated your help with this case. You'll be hearing from us." Stepping beside Ryan, he raised his hand and lightly touched the earring that remained in her right her ear, then shook his head. "Mr. Crying Wolf, have you ever thought about replacing one of those detectives on television? It'd be a helluva show." With a quick smile, he left.

"And this," Gaffney added, raking his fingers through his hair, "has been one hell of a summer."

"Will someone please fill me in on what happened here," Ryan asked, frowning. "I'm so sorry, Dr. Gaffney, but I was positive it was you who was taking everything."

"That's exactly what Stockard wanted everyone to believe," Edwin Gaffney replied.

"But I saw you the day of the storm when the man in the Lincoln—"

"You saw me meeting with Special Agent Delveccio when he brought me the information they had already put together on Stockard."

"I think Stockard saw him, too," Ryan said. "Weren't you afraid that would blow Agent Delveccio's cover?"

"No," Gaffney replied. "Stockard believed me when I

told him that Delveccio was a private collector who tried to push me to sell him something from the site. I even showed him the phone number where he could reach Delveccio. He contacted Delveccio the next day with his own offer."

"But why?" Ryan asked. "I don't understand."

"His motive was revenge, pure and simple." Gaffney sat down at the table and Charley and Ryan joined him. "His sister used to work with me. I had some personal problems with both her and her fiancé, another brilliant young man on my team. I discovered they'd brought drugs onto the project, marijuana and cocaine. I refused to tolerate their habits and, of course, I wouldn't jeopardize the project. I was forced to dismiss them both." Gaffney lowered the brilliance of the kerosene lamp until it offered just a warm glow. "Shortly after they left I heard they married." He shook his head. "It was a pity, but they were unable to control or quit their drug habit and both had trouble holding jobs. About a year or so later, I heard she had died—an overdose." Gaffney paused and offered a wan smile to Ryan. "I never knew she was Stockard's sister, not until Herb Delveccio told me. Apparently Stockard believed I was the one who ruined her career and, in some way, was responsible for her death. He never would admit his sister was an addict. He wanted revenge and his way was to discredit me."

"But what about the doll?" Ryan asked.

"There never was a doll, that's why there was no record of it in the ledgers. Stockard told Kovacs and MacMillen he'd found it, then made the phone calls to the museums to implicate me. There were a few other small items he did sell to 'salt' his plot, and those have since been recovered by the FBI." Gaffney looked at Ryan, his face warming with a broad smile. "And, as for my disapproval of you being on the site, I owe you an apology. The night you arrived, I didn't know what to do. I was concerned for your safety. I thought if I acted like a narrow-minded chauvanist you'd leave. I didn't want you to be put in a position where you might either be used as a pawn by Stockard or get hurt." He reached across the table and patted her hand. "My

dear, you are one of the best young scientists I've ever had
the privilege of working with. That compliment's been a
long time coming and you've earned every word of it . . .
and more."

Shyly smiling her acknowledgment, Ryan grasped Gaffney's offered hand. "Thank you. Apology accepted, Dr.
Gaffney. I must confess, I was very confused. Dr. Schueller
has such enthusiasm for you and your work and, well, Dan
Stockard's viewpoint just didn't agree." Ryan paused and
carefully gauged her next words. "I hope we can continue
to work together."

"Of course, my dear," Gaffney replied. "You've become
far too important to this project for me to let you go . . .
well, at least until Barton Schueller demands your return to
Washington. Your input has been invaluable. You have a
marvelous rapport with the Indian people. You seem to possess an uncanny sixth sense about this place, too. It's almost
as though you were here when it all happened."

Ryan shot a quick look at Charley, finding a Cheshire
grin that made use of every crease and wrinkle in his face.
Suddenly she felt very weary. Being a conspirator in two
centuries was very tiring. "If you gentlemen will excuse
me, I'm going for a little walk. This has been a very inter-
esting evening, to say the least."

"It's kind of a . . . magical evening, wouldn't you say?"
Charley asked with a sly glance at Ryan as she rose from
the table.

"I don't know how magical it is," Ryan responded softly.
Her melancholy had returned. "But it is beautiful."

Charley watched her walk toward the Greasy Grass. He
knew she would seek out the big old oak tree. *Wasté.* It
was good. In fact, it was just as he had planned.

"Hey, Doc," Buddy called, quickly rising to his feet.
"Wait for me, I'll go with you."

"No you won't!" Charley grabbed Buddy's wrist in a
viselike grip. "You're gonna sit right here and be quiet. I'm
too damned old and I've worked too damned hard puttin'
things in place for this evening. You aren't gonna mess it
up for me now."

Buddy's eyes widened with surprise but he sank back into his chair, too astounded by his grandfather's blunt edict to argue.

"Okay, Charley," Edwin Gaffney interrupted, "how about telling me just how you and Dr. Burke were able to bury that bundle and fool Stockard."

Chapter 36

STILL REELING FROM the surprise of Stockard's arrest, Ryan took the footpath leading to the old oak before realizing where her feet were taking her. She hadn't visited the tree since returning. The oak and the river still held too many sad memories, but tonight it seemed easier to surrender than resist.

Like floating pieces of a shattered mirror, the moon's reflection shimmered and bobbled on the rippling surface of the water, silhouetting the trees and bushes. It all looked the same as it did then. A razor-sharp pang of grief sliced into her, bringing with it images of her nights in Wolf's arms. A ragged sigh left her soul and tears brimmed her eyes and glazed her cheeks. With a determined swipe of her hand, she firmly scrubbed them away. "I have to let go—I have to."

Moving closer to the Little Big Horn, Ryan could hear the gurgle of the river as it poured over the rocks and lapped against the bank. But tonight another sound joined the river's voice. It was an odd noise. Puzzled, she stopped to listen.

Plunk. Plunk. Plunk.

What was it? She moved closer.

Plunk. Plunk.

With a slight catch, her breath caught in her throat. Someone was standing beside the old oak and tossing rocks into the water. Who could it be? Who would be at the river this time of night? "Buddy?" No, he was still in camp when she left.

Plunk. Plunk. Plunk.

It was a man, a tall man. But who? Adams and the agents had already left, taking Stockard with them, and she hadn't seen anyone else in camp after Buddy had called her from the tipi. She rubbed her fingers across the frown on her brow. There was something familiar about the height and breadth of the man, something that tugged at her memory.

He bent to pick up a few more rocks and his hair fell over his shoulders, long and braided. Straightening up, he pitched another stone into the water.

As he began to toss another, his hand halted in midair. The rock never left his fingers. Had he sensed her presence? Ryan's pulse quickened. He turned. In the soft glow of the moonlight, she saw his face.

"Wolf!"

No, it wasn't possible. It had to be her imagination. Adrenaline raced through her body in a wild, burning rush. Her breath came in shallow, raspy draughts and her knees threatened to buckle. Surely it was a cruel illusion. Had Charley performed more feats of magic? Had he flipped the days and weeks and years again? "Wolf?" She took an unsteady step.

Dillon heard a slight noise. Straightening up, he looked back toward the camp and saw her. The sound of the woman's voice saying his name came to him over the splash of the river as clearly as if she had offered a whispered caress in his ear.

How odd—she had used just his last name, yet it sounded so complete. Her voice was soft and familiar, like the sweet taste of spring rain on the tongue. He took a few hesitant steps toward her. He felt a quickening as something deep inside him responded with need and hunger. Before the

conscious thought struck him, his lips had already spoken.
"Kechuwa."

Bathed in silvery moonlight, they gazed at one another.

Ryan's pulse accelerated in a blitz of nerve-tingling
chaos. She felt dizzy. Had she correctly heard what he had
said? She stepped closer. Except for the blue jeans and
tailored shirt, he looked exactly like *Sunkmanitu Ceye a
Pelo*. No. That wasn't possible. It was decidedly impossible. Wolf was dead.

Dillon stared at the woman on the path. She was identical
in every way to the exquisite vision from his hallucinations.
That was crazy—totally impossible. *A bump on the head
wouldn't make me insane, but how else could I know her?*

Memories and images that held all the answers continued
to remain maddenly just out of his grasp. He watched her
mouth gently curve into a smile. He knew how her lips
tasted, how they pressed and moved when he kissed her.
He knew the gentle thrusts of her tongue as it fluttered
against his own. He knew . . . but how?

And then, as if someone had opened the floodgates, all
the memories and images came tumbling through his mind.
There were crystal-clear recollections of this woman in a
soft buckskin dress, memories of the sound of her laughter
and the taste of her tears. There were memories of her lying
in his arms, her body rhythmically moving beneath his, her
words and her sighs filled with passion, with love.

Daring to look away from her for an instant, Dillon
glanced around. In that moment he remembered it all. He
remembered how it had been along the river. He remembered the tipis, the sun and breeze and starry nights, and
the people. He remembered Crazy Horse and Gall, Red
Cloud and Sitting Bull. There were the clear memories of
the endless herd of horses, his friends, the battle, that
damned fool Custer. And, he remembered her.

Reality hit him with the force of a ten-pound sledge.
There had been no hallucinations. It had all been real. As
fantastic as it seemed, as impossible as it was, he had somehow shared a very special moment in time with this woman,

an odyssey that, defying reason, had come full circle to bring them together again.

Ryan knew all she had to do was reach out her hand and touch him. They were that close to each other. She looked up into his dark eyes and whispered, "Wolf." Raising her hand, she touched his warm skin, lightly tracing the fresh scar that edged the left side of his jaw. It was identical to the wound left by Iron Soldier's bullet.

She sighed. "It *is* you." Placing her arms around him, she pressed her body against his and rested her cheek on his chest. Closing her eyes, she breathed the sweet smell of sage and cedar. "Yes, yes . . . it is you."

Dillon stiffened in her embrace. Threads of apprehension and confusion still clung tenaciously to his reasoning. What had happened to him? What was going on? The pieces to the puzzle were still moving too slowly for him to grasp all the answers. Who was this woman who was both stranger and lover? He felt her hand lightly caress his cheek and then she drew his head down to hers. Her mouth lightly kissed along the length of the scar on his jaw and the sweet, familiar memory of her touch wrapped around his heart and a contented sigh escaped his lips.

Hungrily closing his arms about her slender body, he drew her into his embrace. Nothing had ever felt so perfect to him in all his life. Deeply breathing the wildflower fragrance of her hair, he began to leave a trail of soft kisses across the top of her head. And then he murmured one word: "Kechuwa."

Leaving her hands resting against his broad chest, Ryan pulled back from his embrace. Looking up, she searched his face for an answer to this fantastic riddle. "You . . . you're Dillon Wolf! You're Charley's grandson, aren't you?"

"Yes . . . I am," he answered, puzzled by the emotions that raced through him in a wild barrage. "And you're—"

"Ryan, Ryan Burke."

"Ryan." He breathed her name and it was like a tender caress. "I don't understand any of this . . . did it all really happen?"

Ryan nodded. "Yes."

He stroked the soft fall of her hair. "Do you remember everything—everything that happened between us?" He closely watched her face.

"Yes, I do." She reached up. Allowing her fingers to trace the fullness of his mouth, she looked into his eyes. "I was aware of the slide through time all along."

"The what?"

"The slide." She gave a little shrug. "I don't know what else to call it. Somehow it happened, although I'm not as sure about *how* as I am about *who* made it possible," Ryan replied. "Didn't you know?"

"No, I didn't, not until now. I thought it was a dream or fantastic hallucination brought on by my accident," Dillon said, still amazed at the inconceivable idea of the whole thing. He lightly stroked her cheek and gazed into her blue eyes, appeasing the hunger in his soul. "I saw your photo just before I was hit. I thought that was how you'd become a part of my dream." He frowned. "But how was the rest . . . the slide . . . possible?"

"I think you should ask that wonderful man over there," Ryan answered, lifting her chin to point up the hill.

Dillon looked up.

Charley Crying Wolf stood atop a slight rise on the footpath. A shaft of moonlight shone through the trees on the old Lakota and a gentle swirl of evening fog covered the ground and encircled his legs. Raising his arm, Charley waved. A moment later, he turned away and disappeared into the mist.

"Making the bundle and burying it . . . that whole scheme was my grandfather's idea?"

"Yes."

"But why me? Why you?"

"Maybe because we were the only two he could trust. Maybe because we were the only two who could make it all work or maybe because there were lessons we each had to learn for ourselves." Ryan gave another slight shrug. "I really don't know." Remembering Buddy's words about

Dillon's biases, she tried to read his expression. "Are you sorry it was me and not someone else, a—"

"No, Kechuwa, never," Dillon murmured, pulling Ryan back into his arms. "Never." Placing his fingers under her chin, he tilted her head upwards. "It's true we're not from the same people, you and I . . . I had closed myself off and allowed anger and hatred to fill me. I was wrong."

"Shh," she whispered, placing her finger against his lips. "We've left that behind in another time and place."

As though a heavy weight had lifted from his heart, Dillon released a deep moan. "Kechuwa, Ryan." His hand cupped the side of her face. "My God, I want to kiss you."

"Then why don't you?" She laughed as her arms curled up around his neck. "It seems as though it was only yesterday when you last kissed me."

Dillon lowered his head until his lips grazed her mouth. Moments before his kiss captured her heart and her soul forever, he softly replied, "But yesterday was over a hundred and twenty years ago."

The lone tipi stood on the bank of the Greasy Grass. Illuminated by the small fire inside, the old lodge softly glowed in the dark. A wispy trail of smoke drifted up through the smoke hole, twined around the lodge poles and then floated off into the October night, leaving a shadowy smudge across the full moon. A soft breeze coaxed the red streamers on the ends of the poles to flutter and the sweet smell of sage and cedar perfumed the night.

Dillon lifted the long, rich fall of Ryan's hair and placed his mouth at the soft hollow where her neck joined her shoulder. His tongue laved the satin surface. He loved the taste and texture of her skin. Reveling in the slight shudder she made and the catch in her breath as her body responded to his caresses, he continued to trail kisses along her shoulder. Removing her remaining clothes, his fingers trembled as they stroked each inch of silken skin he uncovered. Eager to feel her fill his arms, he drew her tightly against him.

Ryan wrapped her arms around his neck and he delighted in the heat that raced through his body beneath her touch.

She pressed her head against his shoulder and he felt the evidence of his desire, urgent and hard, pressing against her belly. Without hesitation, he scooped her up in his arms. "Come, lie down with me." His voice was husky with the heat of his desire.

Softly laughing, Ryan buried her face against Dillon's neck and kissed the column of his throat.

He loved the feel of her in his arms. He loved the touch of her lips on the side of his face and he remembered another place, another time when the man he had once been had felt her kiss for the first time. He carried her to the bed of soft furs and blankets at the back of the lodge. Gently, laying her on the palette, stood over her and stepped out of his own clothes. His eyes slowly swept her body. Captivated, he watched the accelerated rise and fall of her beautiful breasts as her breath quickened with anticipation.

Falling to his knees beside her, he traced a caress from the fullness of her bottom lip, down over her neck. His fingers trailed across the swell of her breast to her dusky nipple that tightened and excitedly crowned under his touch. Hearing the sharp intake of her breath, Dillon smiled. It thrilled him to know his touch could send wonderful sensations racing throughout her body to ignite every secret place within.

Ryan arched her back, pushing her hips up to him. Without hesitation, he moved his hand lower to cup her mound and press the heel of his hand against her. Again, another small breathless moan in her throat made a smile tilt the corners of his mouth.

Dillon felt her touch. Her fingers rode upward over his thigh, lightly stroking him from knee to hip to knee and back again. Her caress left him craving so much more. Impatient, he lifted her hand and pressed it against his turgid shaft. Sharply sucking in his breath, he closed his eyes as a wave of intense pleasure swept over him. Her touch was exquisite.

He was hard and hot. Ryan closed her fingers around him. He felt like silken steel beneath her touch. Moving her hand with subtle pressures, she began to imitate the delicious rhythms of love she craved. A moan, replete and resonant with the fervor of Wolf's desire escaped his throat and she sighed her response. Stretching out on the furs next to her, he drove his fingers into her hair and he drew her head to him. She eagerly settled her body against his.

Dillon kissed along the soft edge of Ryan's ear, moving downward until he covered her lips and drank the sweetness of her mouth. His hand moved downward across the hardened tips of her breasts, across the soft skin of her stomach to the cleft between her legs. Once again she impatiently pressed herself against his touch until he answered her silent request. His fingers slid gently amid the curls and along the delicate furrow. As a sigh filled with pleading escaped her lips he slipped his fingers into her creamy core. He caressed and teased, enticing her hunger with long, light strokes until she cried aloud for him to fill her body.

He moved between her thighs. Easing her legs apart, he hesitated, holding himself from her. "Ryan, look at me," he demanded, his voice an urgent whisper. "Let me see your eyes as I make us one." She looked up, her eyes shadowed, darkened by desire. Leaning forward, he coiled a strand of her hair around his fingers and lightly kissed her mouth. "*Wasté cilake lo.* I love you."

He pressed gently and passed through the tender portals slick with her desire. Slowly, inch by inch, he pushed himself deep inside, filling her completely. Tightly sheathed, he remained still, holding her, delighting in their union, savoring the gift of their love.

Gently brushing aside a lock of hair from her cheek, the firelight glimmered off the wide gold band that encircled the ring finger of his left hand. Taking hold of his hand, Ryan drew it to her mouth and placed little kisses all around the ring. "*Wicahca*, my husband," she breathed. "My Wolf."

"*Mitawicu tewahila ki e,*" Dillon responded. "My wife." Lifting her left hand to his mouth, he mimicked her kisses around the gold band he had placed on her finger during their wedding that afternoon. "*Kechuwa, wasté cilake*, this warrior loves you."

A soft smile played on her mouth and she tightened herself around him. The smile broadened as he responded with a throb that pulsated deep inside her, and then, together they began to stoke the white-hot fires of their desire. Long, slow strokes quickly left them both breathless. Increasing the tempo, each matched the rhythm and the hunger in the other until their passion erupted, melding in the crucible of their desire, bonding them together and blessing them with a love that would last beyond time.

On a hill at the north edge of the valley of the Little Big Horn, a lone gray wolf trotted up the embankment. The young male moved with a strong open gait, his hard muscles never tiring as he climbed the steep grade. After sniffing the cool night breeze, he shook out his shaggy coat and sat on the lip of the ridge overlooking the broad plain. Lifting his head and his voice to the full moon, he sang a song—a lonely, mournful song. Eee-ou-ooooo, yip-yip eee-ou-ooooo, eee-ou-ooooo.

She came from the arroyo below, a dainty-limbed female, answering the plaintive call that stirred her heart. Without hesitation she moved up the southern slope to the crest of the promontory and joined the large gray male. As he rose to greet her, she offered a contented murmur from deep within her throat. Nuzzling his neck, she closed her eyes and pressed her body against his, choosing him to be the only mate she would ever know.

Together, they sat at the rim of the hillock and their voices rose, one blending perfectly with the other. The sound of their duet filled the valley and was heard in the tipi by the Greasy Grass.

Eee-ou-ooooo, eee-ou-ooooo, eee-ou-ooooo.